LIFE OF HER

A NOVEL

ELIZABETH CONTE

This is a work of fiction. Names, characters, places, and incidents are the product of the author's imagination or used fictitiously, and any resemblance to actual persons living or dead, business establishments, events, or locales is entirely coincidental.

Published by Jane Writes Press

To the women who feel unseen
The the sisters, friends, and kindred spirits who have been made to
feel their worth is tied to youth and utility,
To those who have quietly held the world together, often without
recognition,
This is for you.

For every woman who has felt invisible,
Know that you are a masterpiece—rich with wisdom, beauty, and
depth. Your story matters. Your voice matters. You matter.
This book is a testament to your strength, your resilience, and your
undeniable worth.
You are not invisible.
You are not finished yet.
This is your time.
Don't be afraid. Explore. Keep soaring.

LIFE OF HER

LIFE OF HER, A NOVEL

by Elizabeth Conte

1

JUMPING

After Abby packed her bags, she set them by the door. Glancing at her watch, she realized she had just enough time for a glass of wine. Maybe it would calm her nerves, or at least soften the pounding inside her chest.

"You're really doing this?" Jossi's voice cut through the tense moment as she followed Abby into the kitchen, watching her pull a wineglass from a shelf and fill it, emptying the bottle.

Abby sipped her wine, allowing the red liquid to linger in her mouth as she purposely ignored her best friend's concern.

"You aren't answering me," Jossi pressed.

Abby's gaze drifted to the window where darkness had descended on the neighborhood outside. The streetlights had come on, casting a dim glow onto the pavement below. After another long sip from her glass, she finally met Jossi's gaze. "I don't know if I'm crazy or sane. But if I don't do this now, I'll drown."

"Jumping is frightening," Jossi warned.

"How would you know?" Abby narrowed her eyes. "You've never had to jump."

The two women locked eyes in a momentary stare until interrupted by the sound of Abby's son's voice. Abby turned away, giving Jossi a chance to slip out of the room without a goodbye, leaving her to deal with the inevitable confrontation. It was a family matter—Abby's family matter.

"Hey Mom, there's a taxi outside," Drew said as he came into the house, threw his gym bag at the base of the stairs, and beelined to the kitchen. "What's for dinner?"

Abby looked at her boy, seeing the man he was becoming. With broad shoulders and a lean, muscular frame, he was so much like his father. He had reached well beyond her husband's height of six feet. The way he was eating, she feared he would gain at least two more inches before he reached adulthood. His jaw was becoming strong and angular, with hints of stubble. But his cheeks were still round with boyish charm, and his eyes were bright and curious, reflecting a sense of innocence and boundless energy. There were no lines or wrinkles, just a vibrant complexion of youth.

Abby worried he would be lost without her.

Her gut wrenched. *Mothers don't leave their children!*

But he wasn't a child anymore. He had proclaimed that to her a dozen times. He was letting go—going out with friends versus hanging at home, ignoring texts, answering questions with as few words as possible—as he should. It was what teenagers did, no matter how much it may hurt their parents, or hurt her. She had been through this stage before with Emma. She just never thought it would be this hard the second time around.

"Mom," her son said, lifting his big unguarded eyes to hers. "Did you hear me?"

She nodded. "Yes, Drew, I heard you."

The door from the garage opened with a creak. Abby didn't turn at the sound, making a mental note to oil the hinges when she returned.

Of course, I'll return ...

Her husband Marcus sauntered in, set his coat over the stair railing, and pushed his briefcase under the entryway table. He glanced at the packed bags near the front door, then at Abby. "What's this all about?"

"Yeah, Mom, where are you going?" Drew interjected as he crunched through an apple he had found in a bowl on the counter. "And seriously, I'm starved. What's for dinner?"

Abby gave her son a big kiss on the forehead before answering. "I didn't make dinner tonight. There are pizzas in the freezer. Throw them in the oven ... and learn how to cook. Otherwise, you might starve." She gave him a partial smile and pushed him toward the freezer. "I love you, you know," she said before turning away.

Abby slipped into her coat and opened the front door, where a chilly blast slapped her face. The driver was waiting for her.

Marcus grasped her arm and asked again, "Babe, what's going on?"

"I'm leaving, Marcus," she replied, her voice calm but clipped. Anything else would have betrayed her fear.

"What do you mean, *you're leaving*?" Marcus's voice grew harsher. "Where are you going?"

Abby avoided his eyes. "I don't know yet," she murmured, hoping it would do, knowing it wouldn't. The weight of her words settled in the pit of her stomach.

"You don't know?" His voice rose. "You just pack your bags and what? Walk out without a plan? That's not good enough,

Abby!" Marcus stood motionless, his eyes searching hers, calculating, processing.

Abby would laugh if she wasn't so distraught. *Such a male defense*, she thought. He wasn't feeling anything. He was thinking. Maybe she was doing all the feeling and not enough thinking. Too late. She had already stepped off the cliff with one foot when she packed her bags. She just needed to get out the door with the other.

Am I strong enough? she asked herself, staring into Marcus's blue eyes. They were saying, "Don't go!" Those eyes always weakened her. But he didn't say the words. His hands retreated, and he stepped back.

Stop me! she screamed in her head.

The taxi honked, the sharp blast piercing the tension. Abby flinched, her breath catching in her throat. She swallowed hard, reminding herself to take a deep breath. Her heart pounded as her gaze drifted to the corner where Jossi had stood, hoping—desperately—that her friend's presence might somehow return and ground her trembling nerves. But she had snuck out before the hard part. As always!

Abby's gaze flickered back to Marcus. His stare was now cold.

"Abby, where the hell are you going?" he demanded.

Abby's shoulders tightened, forcing her spine to straighten. "I'll let you know when I get there," she said with resolve.

She buttoned up her coat, the long one she used for very cold weather, and swirled a cashmere scarf around her neck. She took out the gloves stored in the pockets but decided against them, placing them back before grabbing the handle of her luggage.

"I love you," she whispered, her voice unsteady. She leaned in, kissed Marcus on the cheek, and, turning on her heels, stepped out into the night, rolling her bags down the walkway to the street where the taxi driver awaited her.

"Abby …" Marcus's strained voice called out, but she didn't look back.

She had jumped and couldn't get back up if she tried. She was falling.

PART I: BEFORE

2

FAMILY RELATIONS

The long, lazy days of summer had petered out, and fall swept over the Midwest like a painter's swift brushstrokes across a canvas, turning the green landscape into shades of yellow, gold, and orange. Leaves piled beneath trees. Lawns browned. Summer flowers withered, their color lingering only in sunlit planters and on sheltered porches. The sun hung dimly in the sky, offering little warmth, as gray clouds gathered on the horizon, warning that winter was approaching. Abby liked to say it was the quiet before the storm. Soon, the temperature would plummet, and snow would pelt the landscape, sending nature into hibernation.

Abby grabbed her heavier coat from the back of the closet and stepped out to run errands. The crisp air met her with a shiver. Her breath crystallized in front of her, and she cursed the cold. Getting into the car, she immediately turned on the heater, along with the radio, praying for warmer days in the weeks ahead. She wasn't ready to retreat for the winter.

As Abby pulled out of the garage, she saw Jossi at the end

of the driveway, her hands tucked deep in her pockets. She rolled down her window.

"I saw you leaving. Want company?" Jossi asked, a mischievous smirk tugging at her lips.

"Do I have a choice?" Abby shot her a look, already thumbing the unlock button. "Get in."

Jossi slipped into the passenger seat and leaned over to turn up the radio, her hand hovering instinctively over the dial, just like she had done so many times driving to school or on the way to the mall.

Depeche Mode was playing, and Abby began to hum softly the familiar tune. Jossi, however, belted out the words, her voice strong and clear filling the car. Abby didn't mind being overshadowed by her friend's beautiful voice. There was no jealousy between them. They had been best friends since kindergarten and were as close as sisters. Nothing was a secret, and nothing got past either of them. They shared everything.

Everything.

"Gosh, that song was great. Remember?" Jossi rolled her shoulders and thrust her arms forward in a wave of gyration. "That's when music was actually danceable."

"Stop!" Abby laughed, casting a quick, self-conscious glance toward the cars speeding by. "You look ridiculous."

"So what?" She gyrated again.

Abby shook her head, knowing it was no use. Jossi was Jossi. Untamed. Uncontrollable. Undeterred.

As the song faded, Jossi gestured for Abby to lower the music. "You know what was ridiculous? Shoulder pads!" she declared, then mock-gagged as she rolled her eyes. "Where were the fashion police then?"

Abby smirked, remembering how stylish she felt when she borrowed one of her dad's jackets, rolled up the sleeves to display the satin lining, and layered it over a ruffled skirt. "They made me look like a football player." She grimaced at the memory of her younger self trying too hard. "And that hair! I should never have gotten a perm."

"Oh, it was a good look on you. At least you were tall. I wore those long jackets and just looked like a kid swallowed by her grandpa's coat."

Abby couldn't disagree. The boxy, oversized look was never suited for Jossi's petite frame.

The memories seemed so long ago. And they were—more than thirty years had passed. It wasn't possible that life had gone by so quickly. When Abby and Jossi were together, it seemed like they were still young girls. That's because Jossi never aged. Abby did. Gone were the big hair, flat tummy, and seamless forehead. Abby had traded in the wavy long hair for a timeless, shoulder-length cut with curtain bangs to the sides. Or at least it had been timeless for the last few years. The flat tummy left her after she had her children, no matter how many sit-ups or diets she tried. And wrinkles? She thanked her father's gene pool that there were few. There was just a wavy row of well-earned lines across her forehead. She worried. She worried about her kids' futures, her husband's happiness, saving the whales, Middle East peace, and the melting ice caps.

Jossi watched Abby's forehead crinkle. "You don't worry enough about yourself," she said, attempting to read her thoughts. "Remember when we thought we'd conquer the world together? What happened to that fire in you?"

"Huh?" Abby said, her inner chain of thoughts broken. "I guess life happened. No time. No room."

"Make time ... you'll need it."

Abby glanced at her friend. *Did Jossi know something she didn't?*

The phone rang, and Abby punched the control on her steering wheel.

"Hey Mom," a voice called out.

"Hi, honey. How's my baby girl?"

"Mom, I'm not a little girl anymore," her daughter reminded her. "Plus, I'm not your baby, Drew is." She was probably still mad that her little brother had dethroned her upon his birth. "How is the little rat?"

"I wouldn't know. He's too busy for his mother," Abby replied, the truth tugging at her heart.

"Oh, Mom, he's a bratty teen right now. Ease up. He loves you."

Abby sighed, not sure these days, recalling when Drew wasn't so distant. She couldn't forget the years when her easygoing son suddenly turned rebellious, coming home late, stoned, and defiant.

She recalled the day the school had called, informing her that Drew hadn't shown up. Furious, she jumped in the car and drove around town until she found him. He was smoking behind the grocery store. When she tried to get him into the car, she realized his six-foot, one-hundred-sixty-pound frame was too much for her. He was no longer a boy, but he was not a man either, leaving her no choice. She called the police and watched from a distance as they gathered him and the other boys in their squad car. When it was over, she drove home and cried. That cycle went on for almost a year—until he got a girlfriend.

Drew discovered being the bad boy was not as rewarding as being in love. Armed with condoms, Abby tried again to break the ice that had thickened into an iceberg between them. He didn't take kindly to her speech about behaving responsibly, but he accepted the tiny wrapped packages anyway, hugged her, and said he loved her.

Abby cried again but for different reasons.

After summer, the romance faded, and so did his defiance. His football talent caught his coach's eye, and he surrounded himself with good friends, healthy eating habits, and daily exercise routines. There was little time for rebellion, girls, or his mother. That was two years ago. Now, with graduation approaching, and college on the horizon, it felt like Abby had blinked, and suddenly he was all grown up. Their relationship was shifting, but neither of them had yet found their footing with the other.

"Mom?" Emma interrupted, pleading for Abby's attention.

"I'm here."

"Hey, I'm calling because ..." She hesitated.

Her tone gave it away—*she had disappointing news.* Abby swallowed hard, her throat suddenly dry.

"You know I've been seeing Teddy for a while ..."

"You mean Theodore?"

"Teddy!" Emma insisted.

Yes, Teddy, Abby repeated in her head.

His real name was Theodore Cameron Wilkes the Third. How Emma ever got mixed up with such an elite family was beyond her comprehension. They'd been dating for months, but Abby had yet to meet him. She'd hoped the holiday might change that.

Emma continued, "Anyway, his family has invited me to their house in the Caribbean for Thanksgiving."

She wasn't coming home for the holiday. Abby's heart tightened.

When Emma left for school at the end of August, the prospect of her return for the fall break kept Abby from sheer loneliness. They'd been close, really close, until Theodore.

"Their whole family is going. It's kind of tradition," Emma explained. "I'm hoping you and Dad won't mind."

Abby swallowed hard, stung by Emma's blithe disregard for the bomb she'd dropped. "That sounds ... wonderful. Meeting his family is a big deal," she said, with the kind of diplomacy she had perfected.

"I know, right?" Emma gushed. "Teddy wants me to meet the whole family. And Colette insisted—"

"Who's Colette?" she questioned.

"Oh, she's Teddy's mom. Really nice—you'd love her. She was a doctor but doesn't practice anymore. Now, she teaches."

"Of course she does. Beautiful and thin too, I assume?" Abby quipped, casting a sidelong glance at Jossi, who watched her with perceptive eyes.

"Mom!" Emma screeched.

"Well, is she?"

"Yeah, kind of ... but older than you, if that helps," Emma offered.

Not really.

"So, I was hoping you and Dad wouldn't mind if I spent the holiday with Teddy."

Abby felt a wave of pressure building in her chest. "I think your mind is already made up."

"Yeah, I guess so," she admitted. "You understand, right?"

"You're in love, and that's what new love does," Abby replied, her voice unnaturally upbeat.

"I do love him, Mom," Emma declared. "And I can't imagine this love ever going away. He's so wonderful."

Abby laughed. Not because she thought it was funny, just naïve.

"Come on, Mom, not everyone feels like you do."

Abby scoffed. "What kind of comment is that for your mother?"

"Let's face it. You and Dad aren't starry-eyed lovers. I mean, I know you love each other, but not like Teddy and I do."

Didn't everyone feel that way about new love—brilliant and consuming? But how about love after years of living, when real life takes its toll? Abby fell silent.

"Well, I gotta run. Teddy will be here any minute. He is taking me shopping to pick out a new bathing suit for the trip," Emma said. "I'll call you later."

"Okay. Say hello to Theodore for me."

"Teddy!"

"Love you," Abby got out of her throat before Emma hung up.

The remnants of "Like a Virgin" filled the car and Abby snapped off the radio.

"It's not selfish to want her home," Jossi said softly, breaking the silence. "You should have told her how you feel."

Abby forced a smile. "I'm fine."

"There's that *F* word." Jossi narrowed her eyes, challenging the nonchalant response.

"Stop that!" Abby protested, quickly turning her attention back to the road, avoiding Jossi's stare. "It's not just about Emma," she continued. "Drew and Marcus will be gone, too. They were invited to the coach's house for a football gathering. A kind of guy's day. Marcus thought it was a great idea." She paused. "None of them seem to realize that it matters to me."

Jossi studied her friend. "Maybe not right now."

Abby's gaze drifted to the window, the world outside feeling distant, like it was moving forward without her. The cold air and the falling leaves all seemed so separate from her. Yet she was always there, holding everyone else together.

"So, when will they?" Abby's voice cracked. She didn't really want Jossi to answer. It wasn't about Thanksgiving, and they both knew it. Abby blinked back tears. "But don't they see? Don't they realize I may not always be there?"

"Aren't you, though? Always there?" Jossi caught her teary eyes. "You're allowed to want more, Abby."

For a moment, Abby let herself linger on that thought. Jossi was right, she was always there. *But where else would she be?*

3

INVISIBLE

Marcus tugged at his tie, his eyes focused on his reflection. Abby leaned against the dresser, arms crossed, watching him as she always did. He tugged at the knot, straightening it, and she thought how handsome and how infuriatingly scrupulous he was. *Meticulous*, she said to herself. The word suited him.

She felt distant from him lately, and watching him now, so intent on aligning his tie perfectly with his belt buckle, didn't help. Something was missing, an unnameable void that gnawed at her that she couldn't quite articulate.

She sank back onto the bed, where earlier she had lain next to Marcus's naked body, and slipped under the comforter, hoping to stay warm in a room that suddenly felt so cold.

"Bye," he said, leaning in to kiss her forehead.

"What time will you be home tonight?"

"Late. I'm playing basketball with the guys. We'll grab a bite afterward," he replied. Seeing Abby's surprise, he added,

"Didn't I tell you?" He glanced at his phone and started to punch at his screen.

"No ... no, you didn't," Abby remarked as he walked away.

Her sarcasm was lost on him. She heard him halfway down the stairs, the sound of his napa leather loafers echoing against the wood. The clunking often made her rethink her decision to expose the eighty-year-old mahogany that lay hidden underneath the carpet, but every time she heard her son's sneakers squeaking up the stairs late at night, the reassurance that he was safely home outweighed the irritation of Marcus's pounding footsteps.

Abby propped herself up against the headboard, adjusting her pillow, and reached for the bottle of hand lotion resting on the bedside table. She squeezed a dollop of cream into her palms and dragged the lotion across her dry skin, gliding it to the tips of her fingers and down, one at a time. "He never told me his plans," she muttered to the empty room.

"You're upset," a familiar voice came from the door.

Abby looked up to see Jossi leaning against the doorframe. Her jeans and an oversized gray sweatshirt, the sleeves rolled to her elbows, were a welcome sight. "Hey Jossi, what are you doing here so early?"

"I saw Marcus leaving and thought I'd invite myself in. I knew you'd be up," Jossi said, walking in without waiting for an invitation. She pointed at Abby's knitted brow. "So, what's going on?"

"Sit," Abby said, motioning her friend to join her on the bed. "I'm glad you popped in. A fight with Marcus wouldn't be the same without you."

"You were fighting? He didn't seem angry when I saw him."

"He's not angry. I am!"

"About what?"

"Nothing. It's stupid." Abby waved her hand dismissively.

"It's me, Abby—your best friend," Jossi insisted, raising an eyebrow.

"I'm fine."

"Fine? You just used the *F* word again."

"*Fine* is not an *F* word," Abby shot back, then sighed. "It's Marcus and me. We're off—way off."

"What does that mean?" Jossi asked, her eyes narrowing.

As much as Abby valued Jossi's insight—she always had a way of helping her put her emotions into perspective—this time was different. Did she dare tell Jossi the truth—that her marriage was failing?

"Hmm, where do I start?" Abby tucked her legs to her chest, wrapping her arms around them. She stared blankly at the bookshelves, housing the dozens of unread books she had promised herself she would read. "We barely talk anymore. He mumbles things on his way out. 'I won't be home until later,' or 'I'm playing golf this weekend.' Like I'm his secretary, tracking his schedule. He seems to always have plans, keeping himself busy. We don't do things together or hang out anymore. He does his things, and I do mine. I feel like my only value to him is to fill up the empty spaces when he's not busy."

"Abby, you know his work is demanding. He's just finding ways to relax, or maybe keep himself interesting."

"Don't do that! You're defending him, *as usual,* Jossi," Abby snapped, shoving her sheets aside. She grabbed her robe and wrestled her arms into the chenille.

"Come on, Abby," Jossi said, her voice a mix of empathy and challenge. "That's not what I'm saying, and you know it. Your schedule has been just as hectic. Drew's game schedule, the town fundraising project last month, volunteering at the elderly home, not to mention taking care of your mom before she died last year."

"And your point?" Abby's expression tightened.

"You both have *things* outside of your relationship. It's life. It's marriage. It can't always be picture-perfect."

"I'm not looking for perfection," Abby muttered, then let out a sigh.

"So, have you talked to him about it?"

"Of course. But it only causes arguments. He says I'm being silly, which is code for him thinking I'm self-absorbed."

"Well, are you?"

"Jossi!" Abby's jaw tightened. She feared her emotions were getting out of control, eating her up. Tearing her down. Both. "It just feels like everything between Marcus and me has become routine."

Jossi leaned in. "What do you mean, routine?"

"I don't know ... it's like we're on autopilot." Abby sighed. "We run the household and handle everything, but the connection is gone."

Jossi tilted her head. "But you're still intimate, right?"

Abby gave a faint, rueful smile. "Barely. It's not even a desire anymore, just a part of the equation. No warmth. No passion. It's predictable, if that. Mechanical. No more lingering kisses, holding hands, or cuddling on the couch. *God, I miss that!* It's just ..." Abby's voice wavered. "It wasn't always like this."

Her mind wandered. *When had her marriage become a series of motions?* She and Marcus ran their life like clockwork. Efficient, yes, but the intimacy had blurred to familiarity. Sex had become an unspoken part of their routine, stripped of the warmth and passion it once had. The thought made her stomach sink.

She looked at Jossi. "We're just playing roles—mom, dad,

husband, wife—without any passion behind them." Her eyes lowered. "Marcus doesn't see *me* anymore."

She blinked twice to prevent the tears that threatened to reveal themselves, easing herself back onto the bed. "With Emma at college, and Drew soon to be off, too, I just thought our lives would come together, not move further apart. We aren't sharing a life. We just seem to be living together. Marcus does his things, and I feel shut out."

"I don't think that's what Marcus intends." Jossi's focus narrowed. "Have you ever considered that maybe Marcus is trying to keep things in control? Maybe the routine feels safe to him. He's not a talker, Abby ... we both know that. But that doesn't mean he's not feeling the distance, too."

Abby let out a heavy sigh, taking in Jossi's added perspective. "But the more I try to bring us closer, the more he pulls away. Like he's comfortable where we're at, fine with the distance between us. I don't know what else to do, Jossi. I'm trying to fix something he doesn't even think is broken."

Jossi shook her head. "I think you're overthinking it."

"You're not listening, Jossi. I ... I ..." Abby fumbled for the words. *Was there a word?* The emptiness inside her felt like a sinkhole, slowly collapsing the ground beneath her feet. It was a quiet heaviness, dragging her deeper into herself, hollowing out any sense of joy or connection. She couldn't pinpoint when the sinkhole had first appeared, but now it threatened to swallow her whole. "I feel as small as a breath in the wind."

Jossi let out a soft chuckle, shaking her head. "Abby, you're not that insignificant."

"Tell that to the man yesterday who held the door open at the mall for a group of twiggy, crop-topped teenagers, but let the door shut in front of me. Seriously? It was like I wasn't even there."

"Maybe he didn't see you?"

"It's not just with him. Everywhere I go, I don't exist. No one sees me anymore." Crossing her arms, she continued. "I go into the same coffee house at least three times a week. I order a tall black coffee every time. Plain. Black. Coffee," Abby reiterated. "Do you think the people behind the counter remember? They remember Hannah, the model-like blond in yoga pants who wants a grande-soy-decaf-light-foam latte. Or Bob, a retired guy who runs every day, and orders a double-shot almond milk cappuccino. But do they remember me, or my difficult order of black coffee?"

"Does it matter?" Jossi asked with a sage-like demeanor.

"Doesn't it?" Abby scoffed, her voice tinged with frustration. "I'm still here, still me, but no one sees that. Everywhere I go, I feel passed by, ignored, overlooked. The only time anyone cares is when I'm filling up some gap in their lives. When did it get this way? I'm still a vital woman. I'm not dead!"

Your life is vital until you're dead. The words echoed in Abby's memory of her mother's philosophy about life, being a woman, and aging. Her mother had three rules: (1) Never, ever go out of the house looking like you aren't going somewhere important. (2) Get your hair done, especially when it's turning gray. Gray is only for the old—the very old. And (3) always wear lipstick, preferably red. *No one disregards a woman with ruby lips*, she'd declare. One of her last requests before she died was to be buried with her favorite red lipstick on. Even upon her death, her mother would not be overlooked.

Abby wondered if her mother would be proud of how she was aging. She didn't consider herself vain, but she kept her style contemporary and updated and always wore a fresh shade of red lipstick. But lately, her mother's words of wisdom felt more like a warning. As the years progressed, Abby was more aware of becoming insignificant, fading into the background. No one seemed to notice her at all. Not her kids. Not her husband. Not the people at the coffee shop. She had become invisible.

"Funny thing is," Abby continued, "when Marcus left this morning, he was perfectly happy. He has no qualms about our life. He goes to work, does his things, never once questioning the state of our union. Our marriage works, is in harmony, for him. So, why am I questioning it?"

Jossi rose from the bed, pausing at the door. "Maybe because you're starting to notice what's been missing," she said softly. "And maybe you're starting to question what it is you want." She turned to leave but halted. "Only you can answer that."

Abby didn't move, staring at the space where her friend had stood. The silence was heavy, pressing in on her. *Was it really about Marcus?* For the first time, she had started to question her life. What was missing wasn't Marcus's attention, it was her own. She had become invisible to herself.

Abby lifted herself out of bed and drew the curtains aside. The weather was turning—the last of the leaves shivered on the trees and the rosebushes had been pruned back to empty twigs. A distant honk of the geese from a nearby pond caught her attention, offering a small comfort that it wasn't winter yet. For a moment, she watched them, envious of their inevitable escape to a warmer place. They were still here, holding on, for now. But they, too, would eventually leave.

4

REMINDER

Abby needed a cup of coffee, but none would be waiting for her if she braved the cold morning to get out of bed. She should've set the timer. But she hadn't.

Damn! she cursed her laziness.

Her phone buzzed. It was a text from Marcus.

Just landed. Headed to a meeting. Did you call the doctor?

She hadn't. She made up a hundred excuses. The bed was too warm. The office was closed. She needed coffee first. But the truth was she didn't want to think back to what Marcus had said before he left that morning, though the memory lingered, edging its way forward.

"Hey," he had called out from the bathroom. "I felt something."

She remembered all too well his cold hands fondling her breast at the ungodly hour of four a.m. She had finally fallen back to sleep when he rose to take a shower.

"Abby, did you hear me?" He tried again for her attention.

Abby lifted her head from the pillow and asked, "What?"

"Your left breast," he said, grabbing his watch from his nightstand. "I felt something."

Abby moved her hand to her chest. "Felt something?"

"Here, let me show you." He sat next to her and put his hand under her left breast. His cold hand smoothed over her skin, pressing against her flesh. "There ... do you feel it?"

Abby followed his fingers. She found it—a hard pea-sized ball. She gulped.

"How long has it been since you've seen the doctor?" he asked, his voice fading as he retreated into the bathroom.

Abby thought about it. It had been longer than she wanted to admit. She had meant to schedule an appointment but got so busy with Emma's college searches, graduation, and sending her off. And then it was Drew's football, physical therapy for his knee, raising money for the sports teams, or the other thousand daunting priorities in her life. She forgot to put herself on the list, and three years had flown by.

"Get it checked," Marcus said firmly, as he rolled his suitcase behind him. He kissed his wife on the cheek and headed out the door. "See you at the end of the week. I'll call you when I land."

It was the last thing he said before heading out the door.

An incoming text buzzed on her phone.

Going into the next meeting. Won't be able to reach me, it read. *Don't forget, call the doctor!* Marcus ordered, following up on their morning conversation.

Marcus was diligent about going to the doctors—annual physical with his primary, twice yearly for dental cleaning, a skin check with the dermatologist before Memorial Day. It was because his father had died of a heart attack too young. Regular checkups might have meant his father could have lived to see Marcus married, meet his grandchildren, and see what a success his son had become. It's a sadness Marcus had never let go of, and a fate he was determined to avoid.

Okay. Will do it now, Abby typed.

DON'T FORGET! he responded in caps, seemingly knowing she would forget.

"Mom?" Drew called, distracting Abby from her thoughts. "Where are my shorts? I threw them in the laundry last night."

Abby pushed out of bed, grabbed her robe, and headed to the laundry room.

"How should I know you need them today if you don't tell me?" she chided, making her way to the boy standing by the washing machine.

"Found them," he said with a grin, holding his dirty shorts.

Abby snatched them out of his hands. "Go get breakfast. They'll be ready by the time you leave."

His phone buzzed, and he pushed past her to read the incoming message.

"You're welcome," Abby yelled into the empty hallway.

By the time she had dressed, the dryer buzzed. She grabbed the shorts and headed downstairs to make a much-needed coffee. As the pot gurgled, she packed up two sandwiches, a banana, an apple, a yogurt, and a pack of almonds for her son. With football practice, his appetite was insatiable. Plus, he was on a strict diet of high protein and healthy snacks; another one of his coach's orders. When Drew finally headed out the door, shorts and snacks in hand, Abby couldn't shake the sense she had forgotten something—something more pressing than laundry or lunch, but as always, she pushed it aside, too distracted to face it.

5

DEATH

Weeks later, Abby was staring at the medical degrees on the wall. Stared at, not read. She was sure they were impressive, but she was too nervous to read the details. A stack of files labeled with her name on them sat on the desk. She desperately wanted to reach over and open them, but instead, she waited, straining her ear to make out the muffled voices in the hallway.

Abby could only recall being invited into Dr. Cushner's office twice before. The first time was when the doctor introduced herself and the second time was five years ago when she informed Abby that she was in early menopause. Abby had wondered if that was good news or bad news. The doctor gave her no sign either way.

Today was altogether different. She sensed it in her soul. Something was wrong.

The doctor came through the door and extended her hand for a firm handshake. "Abby, it's good to see you."

"Hello, Dr. Cushner," Abby said, her voice a thin, high-pitched squeak.

"I won't beat around the bush, Abby. Your scan showed a growth in your left breast. It's a small well-defined lump. Based on its characteristics, one possibility is medullary carcinoma, which tends to present this way. However, we can't be certain without further tests."

Abby swallowed hard. Her heart began to pound in short, heavy beats.

"I don't want you to worry just yet," the doctor continued. "We'll do a biopsy to remove some, or possibly all, of the lump. Once we have the results, we'll know more."

"Are you saying I have ..." her voice trailed off. "Cancer?"

"No, I'm saying that the mammogram confirmed what you felt in your breast. You have a lump, and there's a possibility it's cancerous. What type and how much it has spread are to be determined. But according to your mammogram, the growth is very small."

There it was. *Cancer.* The word no one wants to hear when it's about themselves.

Abby's instinct was to cry, but instead, her mouth dried and her vision blurred. The hallway voices faded into the background. The world seemed to stop.

When Abby looked up again, Dr. Cushner continued, "Abby, this is all preliminary. I've scheduled an appointment on Friday with one of the best oncologists. He'll take good care of you."

"So soon?" she questioned. "That can't be good."

"It's not bad, either. He had an opening, so I grabbed it. We might as well move on this as soon as we can."

"What do I do? What's next?" Abby asked, barely processing the information. Her brain was on autopilot, collecting data.

"They will send the biopsy to the lab and analyze the tissue. When we find out the extent of the abnormality ..."

"Am I going to die?" Abby blurted out.

"No, not today," the doctor assured. "I'm not saying that lightly, and I'm not making any promises. Cancer doesn't bargain. But you came here early, the growth was detected, and if it is cancer, there are varying treatments." She smiled, the kind of smile an older sister gives when she doesn't want to be authoritative but needs to be motherly all the same. "You will live another day, Abby. Breathe."

"I HAVE CANCER!"

"Abby," Marcus said. "Don't worry yet. Let's not rush to a conclusion until we get the test results."

Abby narrowed her eyes at him.

"Don't look at me like that," he said. "I'm trying to help. You always get worked up about things. We need to find out more, that's all I'm saying. Why worry beforehand?" He put his hands around her shoulders and gently shook her. "Come on, Abby, nothing is going to break you. You're a rock. You aren't going anywhere." He kissed her on the forehead, gave her a brief hug, and then retreated into the other room where news was streaming from the television.

Not worry? Abby's eyes rolled, and admittedly, her jaw clenched. She thought about the stack of medical journals and printouts scattered across her desk. Her fingers had scrolled through countless articles, the medical jargon now etched into her mind. She knew she was jamming too much into her head, but she wanted to find out if she would survive this.

Abby scuffed her feet across the kitchen floor, ripping the refrigerator open, only to slam it shut without purpose. She didn't know what she was looking for. Wine to numb her nerves? Ice cream to comfort her soul? Marcus to …

What did she need?

"Abby?"

Abby turned at the sound of her name.

"Are you all right?" Jossi asked, pulling out a chair and sitting down at the table.

"No." Abby sighed, joining her friend in a chair next to her. "Not after today. Not after the news."

"I can't imagine." Jossi let the words settle in the air. Eyeing Marcus, sitting in his recliner in the other room, she added, "Marcus is right, you know. You'll be okay."

"You always say that about everything hard," Abby snapped back. "But I'm not okay. Not this time."

"Well, you're better off than me," Jossi said with a wry smile. "Being dead and all."

Abby fell silent, a rash of red flushing her cheeks. She hated it when Jossi threw that at her. Tears surfaced, but she brushed them away with a swipe of her hand.

Jossi quickly apologized. "Sorry, that was unfair. This one is tough, for sure. But nothing is random, Abby. There's got to be a reason for this, even if you can't see it now."

"And what's the reason this time?" Abby questioned. "To teach me that life is precious? Because I learned that lesson when I lost you." Tears swelled again, but this time she didn't swipe them away.

"You didn't lose me."

"Yes. But it's not the same." Abby's voice lowered. "I need you *here*."

"I'm here," Jossi insisted. "It's the best I can do."

No, it's not, Abby wanted to counter. But she didn't. Her eyes moved to a faded photo on the kitchen counter—two young girls, arms wrapped around each other, smiling widely.

Her heart tugged a little tighter in her chest. Thirty years later, and she still ached over the loss of her best friend.

"You'll be okay, Abby. I know it," Jossi's voice breathed. "Your life will go on as it always does. As it should."

Your life. The words echoed in her head.

Was Jossi mocking her again? She was alive, and Jossi wasn't. Abby had the advantage. She had survived—the accident, the convalescence, burying her best friend—and her life had gone on. Death never granted her options. She would have bartered. But Jossi died before she got the chance to ask. She didn't think it was possible to go on with so much emptiness. So much loss.

Abby had tried again—to barter with Death—when she was eight months pregnant with her first child. The baby stopped moving. At first, they thought the baby was sleeping. But when they didn't hear a heartbeat, there was nothing anyone could do. After she gave birth, Abby held the stillness of her baby for hours before Marcus eventually took her away. She couldn't bear living after that. She prayed for death —to be with her baby girl. But Death wasn't listening.

Abby remembered sitting by her mother's hospital bed, holding her frail hand. She watched the slow rise and fall of her mother's chest, each breath a painful reminder of the brain tumor stealing her away. Her rock, her support, was being taken from her ... slowly. The woman who'd helped navigate her through life's messy maze of mayhem and mischance didn't deserve to die. Not like that—the tumor taking away every ounce of dignity until the end. Abby whispered countless prayers, wishing for death to come to her instead. Death still wasn't listening.

She buried her mother and her father two weeks apart. His heart didn't hold out long after his wife of fifty-five years died.

Abby kept living. She always did.

"You can do this, Abby," Jossi insisted.

"Do what?"

"Live."

"Or die," Abby blurted out. She lifted her eyes to the ceiling, the flat, white-painted expanse staring back at her.

Death, are you listening now?

"It's your choice," Jossi said.

"Is it?" Abby challenged.

"You always have choices, Abby."

"Maybe it's my time," Abby said flippantly. But when she saw Jossi purse her lips, she sat up in her chair, bracing herself for a verbal beating. She needed it. She counted on Jossi to help her see things more clearly. Set her straight. Push her forward. Give her hope.

"Maybe," was all Jossi replied.

6

ASEXUAL

Marcus woke Abby at five. Her hospital check-in was at seven. He was good at that—being reliable. One of the many qualities that had made Abby fall in love with him.

He'd made love to her the evening before ... before she would be changed. He didn't express it, but she knew he needed to have one more time with the woman he'd known and say goodbye to the body he had grown accustomed to, to the breasts that had enticed his need for her. They were beautiful to him. They were beautiful to her. *They were her.*

Abby didn't begrudge him for the attention to her womanly form. The woman she was that evening, being felt and fondled, would not be the same woman who would come home from the hospital. So, she allowed the nibbling of her nipples, the tracing of his tongue, the greed of his groping. He needed to experience them one last time.

She needed to experience that one last time.

Abby wished she had slept. But it never came. She lay in

bed with her eyes closed. Thinking. Praying. Hoping. Her mind drifted back to when she was a little girl on a bike ride with her father. He'd held back, urging her to keep going. The breeze whipped her hair around her face and the afternoon sun made her squint, but she kept pumping her pint-sized legs to move forward, to keep going. She wanted to show him she had it in her. So, she pushed and pumped, pumped and pushed her little legs onward.

Those were her thoughts the night before surgery. About her father, encouraging her to take on life with everything she had.

Marcus shifted his elbow from one side of the chair to the other as they waited. Abby sat with her back straight against the cushioned seat, filling out the endless paperwork they handed to her at check-in. When she finished, she gripped the pen between her fingers, not wanting the time to go too fast. If possible, she would linger in the moments of pre-surgery forever. In the time and place of her life she was familiar with.

Abby scanned the beige-painted walls, noting the uncluttered modern simplicity. Black framed artwork hung sporadically, each canvas a riot of splashed paint meant to add color rather than evoke a sense of connection—like mind candy. The cherrywood tables, cluttered with outdated magazines and pharmaceutical ads, clashed with the black metal-framed chairs lining the room. Running her hand over the mint green and turquoise swirls of her upholstered chair, Abby detected the room's recent redecoration in the lingering scent of foam and adhesive, mingled with the faint chemical tang of newly installed blue carpet. *Was the design meant to evoke the beach?* No matter how soothing the colors or patterns, the room remained somber and quiet, its mood set by its inhabitants.

Too quiet.

There was a man sitting alone. He had not shaved for days, the dark growth thick and untamed. Deep lines covered his forehead. His knee bounced up and down in short, quick pulses. When Abby met his eyes, he explained that his wife was in surgery. A few minutes later, the doctor came out, still covered in his blue scrubs, and informed the overwrought man that his wife would be okay. The lines on the man's forehead lessened, but his body continued to shed its fears through the restless leg.

An older couple shuffled in, their crooked-knuckled fingers interlocked. The white-haired man held his wife's elbow as he guided her into a seat. Once settled, he walked up to the desk and checked her in. The petite and frail woman scanned the room as if capturing the experience. She locked eyes with Abby and smiled. Her fading blue eyes offered Abby a motherly comfort, but Abby could see the deeper secret they held. She'd seen the same in her own eyes that morning.

Marcus reached for the paperwork between Abby's hands. "Here, let me take those up for you."

Abby conceded, allowing the attentive gesture. Although he tried to hide it, Marcus was afraid. The doctor had assured him Abby would live, and the cancer would be gone, having nothing else to attack once they had removed her breasts. She wouldn't need chemotherapy or radiation. She was lucky.

"Lucky?" Jossi remarked when Abby told her about the

outcome. "You have cancer, you're losing both breasts, and they say you are *lucky*?"

"Aren't you always the one encouraging me to see the glass half full?" Abby replied. "They can get the cancer out. I should consider myself fortunate." Abby wasn't sure if she was trying to convince Jossi or herself.

"Do you have to remove both? Isn't it extreme?"

"Marcus said the same thing. Gosh, you guys are alike!" Abby rolled her eyes, exhausted from addressing everyone's concerns. "Ultimately, it's what's best. The doctor said there was a seventy-eight percent chance, or higher, that cancerous cells could appear in my other breast. Who wants to take the risk, of finding cancer the second time? Would you?"

Jossi folded her arms, staring at Abby. "That's not a fair question. I don't have my body anymore."

"Humph," Abby huffed. "Well, trust me. Having this fear isn't something you'd want to deal with. No, this is the right decision for all of us."

Jossi's gaze pinned Abby in place "For whom?"

Abby waved a hand. "The kids don't need to worry about me. Nor does Marcus."

"Why do you do that?" Jossi questioned. "Why can't you accept that what you think, and what you want, has value? Your decision was for *you* ... and nobody else. And that's okay."

In the weeks prior to the surgery, Jossi had constantly interrogated Abby, pushing her to the brink. Of what, she wasn't sure. She just wanted Jossi's lecturing to stop.

Jossi disappeared after that conversation. Abby hadn't seen her since.

"Abby?" Marcus called. "They said the doctor is running a little late. Do you mind if I grab some coffee?"

Abby nodded her permission, and he headed into the

corridor, sidestepping a large man who had to duck to get through the doorframe.

Dressed in a black robe with a white sash and a wooden bead rosary around his neck, the man had a youthful face framed by neatly trimmed, thinning white hair. Pushing up tortoise-shell glasses, he scanned the room through the thick lenses that magnified his dark eyes. With a warm smile, he greeted Abby, offering a ray of sunshine in the somber room. She reciprocated the gesture, affected by his kind demeanor. He nodded toward the frail older woman before sauntering over to Abby.

"May I have a seat?" he asked.

"Good morning, Father," Abby greeted cautiously, darting her eyes to the empty seat next to her.

He smiled again before he fit himself into the chair.

"Father Gilly." He shook Abby's hand. "A hard day ahead?"

"I'm afraid so." She couldn't lie to a priest.

Father Gilly didn't rush to say anything. His dark eyes studied her from head to toe. Abby wondered if he was assessing her soul. Since her churchgoing was limited to holidays and special occasions since her parents had died, she felt undeserving of the large man covered in symbolism. She squirmed further back into her seat.

"I'm having breast surgery today," she said, breaking the silence. "Cancer."

"Oh." He sighed. "I didn't think you were here for the food."

Her eyes widened, but when she saw a sly smile cross his face, she laughed.

"That's nice," he said. "A soul should always shine, even in the darkest hours. How else will you find your way out?"

"I never thought about it that way," Abby said. "I'll take that with me today. It will help me get through this."

"Well, I guess I've done my job here," Father Gilly said, and got up from his chair.

"Father Gilly?" Abby reached out and gripped his forearm. He stopped his retreat.

"I'm afraid," Abby admitted to the stranger. She hadn't even confessed this to Marcus.

Father Gilly sat back down. He leaned in and descended behind the darkness of the wide eyes that stared at him.

"I don't say this lightly. I come here every morning to bring comfort to those going through this journey. And it is a journey, not a destination," he said, qualifying his statement. "I see death in some, hope in others. It's something instinctual when you have done this long enough." He paused, moving his attention to the old woman, whose name was being called. He smiled in her direction, watching the nurse take her by the arm and guide her through the door.

Abby watched the woman disappear behind the door. "Do you think she will be all right?"

"I pray she will," he said, not committing to an answer. "I'm afraid it's not her first time here."

He paused and closed his eyes. Abby joined him in a silent prayer for her, too.

"Where was I? Oh yes," he said. Taking Abby's hands, he wrapped his large hands around hers and gave them a gentle squeeze. "I sense you'll be just fine. You have much to go through, but you will find your way. Remind yourself you have a purpose. Every life does. You are significant."

Abby's heart tightened, and she felt compelled to hug him.

That's how Marcus found her, coddled in the embrace of the man too large to fit through the door.

"Hello," Marcus said, interrupting their embrace.

Abby pushed away and gave Father Gilly a smile. She couldn't use her voice without succumbing to tears. The priest bowed his head with understanding and stood. He shook Marcus's hand with instructions to take good care of Abby and left the room.

"What was that all about?" Marcus asked.

"A message."

7

AFTER

Beep. Beep.

Abby lifted her eyelids, blinking three times before squishing them shut again. Finally, she opened them, adjusting to the brightness of the stark white walls. She wondered why they didn't paint hospital rooms a warmer color. Sandy tan would be more comforting. She noted the curtain around her bed. It was once a blue color but had faded to gray. If they were trying, it wasn't working.

Beep. Beep.

Machines surrounded her bed. The IV bag was half full. She wondered how long she had been sleeping. The shades were open, and a blue sky filled the view. It was daylight. She found comfort in that. Jossi was next to her bed, her head resting in one hand as her elbow balanced on the metal-framed arm.

"How long have you been sitting there?"

"Since you came out of surgery." A gentle smile softened Jossi's face. "It's good to see you. How do you feel?"

Abby winced as a sharp pain spread through her chest.

She closed her eyes and took slow, measured breaths to steady herself. "Like crap," she finally said. "I'm sore and groggy, like I've been in a heavy sleep for a hundred years. And I can't imagine what I even look like."

"Like you. Beautiful."

"See, this is why I keep you around." Abby attempted to laugh, but the bandages constricted her chest from moving. She just gave Jossi a smile instead. "I feel weird, not human. Like a body the doctors have been slicing up, digging into, and cutting away—a science project splayed on the bed."

"Well, they have," Jossi gave a sardonic grin. "To save your life."

"What life?" Abby lifted her arms to reveal the tubes dangling from her sides. "I'm Frankenstein."

"A life I don't have ..." Jossi reminded her.

The sound of shoes squeaking across the linoleum floor approached, and a hand pushed aside the curtain. A full-bosomed woman in blue nurses' scrubs greeted her. "Nice to see you awake, Mrs. Kent."

"Abby ... you can call me Abby."

"Abby, then." The nurse walked to the side of the bed and checked the plastic bags that were attached to Abby's body. "Your surgery went well. You are a model patient," she stated, seemingly pleased with the fluid measurements.

"Model patient?" Abby drawled, her speech still groggy from medication. "Is that your standard sales pitch?"

The nurse laughed. "Ha! I've had my fair share of not-so-delightful patients."

Abby smiled, shifting her gaze to the door. "Is my husband lingering about? I'd like to see him."

"Oh, he left a few hours ago ... after they settled you in the room. He said something about fitting in a few hours of work."

Abby's lips fell flat.

"Oh, men," the nurse quickly responded. "I see it more often than not. Weaklings around hospitals. Don't take it to heart. We women are the stronger sex."

"Stronger?" Abby's voice croaked as she tried to lift herself. "This cancer kicked my butt."

The nurse rushed to help Abby sit up. "It was supposed to. Cancer has that effect on everyone it touches."

Abby met her eyes. "You too?"

"Five years and still alive," she announced. "I will tell you a little secret." She looked around to see if anyone was listening. When she saw the coast was clear, she continued, "Getting cancer is horrible. Dying from cancer is tragic. Surviving cancer is damn hard. It isn't cheerful. Surviving this won't take away the moment when you saw your life flash in front of you. You will never wake up without thinking you are surviving one more day. It changes you ... redirecting your DNA. Your mind is reprogrammed, and you can never, ever go back to your old self."

Did she want to get back to her old self?

Abby's gut wrenched. There was a pit in her stomach. Something deep. It had been there for a while. A long while. Long before the cancer. She had hoped it would be gone after the surgery. And yet the cavernous space was still there. Only it felt deeper. Darker.

"Cancer is a push—no, a shove—to your soul. It's a way of letting you know the direction you were headed wasn't working." The nurse patted Abby's arm. "It's time for a new direction."

"But to where?" Abby questioned, a quiet uncertainty lacing her words. "I didn't ask for this ..."

With steely resolve, the nurse declared, "Abby, if it's a cliff —jump. A dark forest—forage through. A raging river—let the current take you. Life is funny ... when you aren't ready for what you need, it will push you where you need to go."

Chills ran down Abby's back. "What if ..."

The nurse shook her head, stopping Abby mid-sentence. "There will be a thousand 'what ifs' along the way. Don't be afraid because you don't know how to do it, or where it will take you. This isn't about anyone else but you. With cancer, you must be self-preserving. It will seem selfish, but don't let it stop you from figuring out the message. Find the life you're meant to journey, don't go back to the one that got you here, at death's door. You survived cancer ... go live."

The phone next to the bed rang, and the nurse reached for the receiver. Handing it over to Abby, she gestured she was leaving and pushed the curtain around the bed.

"Hey Mom," Emma's young voice greeted Abby. "How are you?"

"I ... I don't know yet," she replied honestly.

"You sound groggy. Is it as bad as you thought? I mean ... you'll be okay, right?"

"I will, honey. Don't worry."

"I'm sorry I couldn't fly home, but school and all. Is Daddy there?"

No. No, he wasn't.

"I'm tired. Let's talk tomorrow. Okay?" Abby said, avoiding the answer.

"Sure. Call you then," Emma agreed. "Love you."

"Love you, too, honey."

Abby hung up the phone, albeit with a large moan, her body cringing with pain as her arm reached over to the table beside her. She sat back and sighed as she sank into the pillow behind her back. For a moment, she had forgotten that her body was torn apart and stitched up. Her eyes darted around the empty room, shadows now creeping in as the daylight faded. The blue skies darkened, and gray clouds formed, signaling storms ahead. *Was it a sign?* she wondered.

When the nurse returned, she asked for more pain medication, not knowing which she was trying to numb more, her body or her head.

8

REALIZATIONS

Abby drew the curtains back. The night had crept back into its cave and morning was awakening. Streaks of yellow streamed across the dark sky, slowly filling her room with light. Not warmth, though. Marcus had cracked open the window earlier, and cold air circulated through the room. It had snowed a few days prior, veiling everything outside in white, and the temperature was still below freezing. The lawn was blanketed, as was Abby's prized flower garden, now entombed in the frozen ground. The bushes were mere branches of wood poking through the layers of snowdrifts, the trees naked and lifeless. A dog was barking in the distance, but few other signs of life were apparent. The birds that remained were too smart to leave the warmth of their nests. All other critters, the squirrels that ran up her trees and the rabbits that ate her leaves, luxuriated in hibernation.

Was that what she was doing?

Abby slammed the window shut, stopping winter's invasion, while cursing the freezing air. She cursed most things of late. She crept back into bed, with no immediate will to start her day.

When she'd come home from the hospital, she'd tried—attempting to get her life back to a sense of normalcy. She'd wake up, take a walk, water the plants, get the mail ... mundane chores she used to do without thinking. Now they were monumental tasks she'd check off her list before retreating to her bedroom, sinking into a chair, wrapping herself in a blanket, and allowing her thoughts to idle. Naps usually ensued.

Marcus had hired a housekeeper to do Abby's chores. "So you can heal," he explained. Drew made his lunch, and Marcus often picked up groceries on his way home. Daily interactions had become few among them. *It was all so efficient!* Marcus claimed he was giving Abby her space, but with Drew in and out, like most teenagers, Abby's husband was coming home later and later, having dinner with his friends at the office or picking up another game at the gym.

He was avoiding her.

The holidays had come. Emma had arrived home after finals—alone. No Teddy. Abby was grateful. Emma gave her the attention she needed. She read to Abby, made her tea, and they played Scrabble and Word Search on their phones until they fell asleep. Marcus volunteered to sleep in the guest room. "To give you girls some time together," he proclaimed. Only after Emma returned to school and the holiday decorations had been stored away did Marcus move back in. They were once again sharing a bed, but not each other.

That was over a month ago.

Last night, Abby tried to awaken Marcus, awaken them. Lying in bed, swaddled in blankets as cold air swirled around them, her body yearned for the warmth of Marcus. She reached over and brushed her fingers through his hair. He moaned from her touch, but fell back to sleep, undisturbed. Abby smiled to herself, watching him, peaceful and content. It reminded her of the first time they'd slept together. Not the first time they had sex, just the first time they'd fallen asleep in each other's arms. She had awoken to him lying on her pillow, his soft lips slightly parted, blowing out rhythmic puffs of air. The sound wasn't quite a snore, but she teased him about it anyway. His hair was longer back then, a moppy mess across his forehead, covering his eyes. His face was tanned from all the time spent in the sun, riding bikes and swimming at the nearby lake. His body was lean and muscular, and she relished being cradled in his bear-like grip.

Over the years, he had changed from a mere boy to a man. The proof was in the lines gathering in the creases of his eyes and the short strands of silver hair reflecting through the darkness. She moved in closer to steal his body heat. How she wanted him, her need growing carnal. She missed his touch. She missed being wanted. She missed him inside her.

Abby nudged next to him, wrapping herself around his half-curled form. Brushing her lips along his neck, she nibbled upward, placing wet kisses behind his ear. He swiped, pushing the sensation away. Undeterred, her hands slipped under his shirt, and she softly brushed her nails down his back, creating tiny bumps—a sensual touch that usually aroused him. She slid her touch down his muscular buttocks, lingering long enough for him to understand her intentions before she dragged her palm across his strong thigh to the sacred place between his legs.

His eyes opened, the blue gems fixing their gaze at her. Even in the darkness, they were mesmerizing.

"What are you doing?" he asked, his voice raspy and dry.

"What do you think I'm doing?" Abby purred, continuing her strokes across his skin.

"Now?" He turned to the clock beside the bed. "It's just past two in the morning!"

Abby's need was erupting, her urge growling. The object of her desire was merely inches away. Without prompt, without permission, she leaned in and brought her lips to his, hoping to entice him.

"Abby, seriously?" He pushed her away. "I have a big meeting tomorrow."

How many times had she succumbed to his untimely requests?

Undeterred by his mood, she wriggled out of her pajama bottoms, tossing them to the floor, and moved on top of him. "Yes," she whispered. "Very serious."

He grew harder.

Without any immediate objection, he allowed her to slide his bottoms down, intertwining her naked legs with his. Pelvis to pelvis, skin on skin, she brushed her lips against his, pelting them with kiss after kiss.

Finally, his lips succumbed to the pressure and opened to take in her heated breath.

Abby ran her hands down his chest and motioned for him to lift off his shirt. He complied, throwing it to the floor, but lay back down, watching her as if waiting for the next attack. When she went to take her shirt off, his hands moved to stop her.

Abby froze, her hands gripping the hem of her shirt. His eyes stared at her through the gray haze that filled the room. Something was missing as she fixated on them. Passion.

He didn't desire her.

Abby jolted out of bed, searching for her pajama bottoms. Finding Marcus's T-shirt first, she threw it at him.

"Where are you going?" Marcus called after her as she walked away.

But he didn't move to chase after her.

She had forgotten. Forgotten, for a moment in time, that she was broken.

9

MARRIAGE VOWS

"It's time to get up and out," Jossi said, startling Abby.

Abby was still wearing her flannel pajamas layered with an oversized sweatshirt, bulky socks adorning her feet as she curled up in a chair by the window. It was two in the afternoon on Saturday. Marcus had darted out early to run errands while Drew went to the gym. She heard the neighbor blowing snow from their driveway. The mailman had already delivered the mail. People were coming and going, doing things, making the most of the day.

"I'm not ready," Abby replied, crossing her arms.

"I wasn't giving you a choice," Jossi countered. "And, by the way, you look like hell."

"Thanks," Abby snapped back before turning away from her friend's judging stare.

"Don't look away from me. Someone has to tell you." Jossi looked out the window, following Abby's gaze. She was watching a neighbor's dog dig into the snow, retrieve a toy, and run back to the owner, who was playing with him. "You must get back to living," she continued. "You have people who need you."

Abby heard Jossi, but kept her focus on the playful dog outside, ignoring her words. "I miss Abbot ... he was a good dog," she said absently, mindlessly, her voice trailing off into the void.

Jossi let out a heavy sigh. "You're feeling sorry for yourself. It doesn't become you."

"No, I'm not. I'm ..." Abby paused, searching for the right word. "Discombobulated."

"Okaaay. So how do you fix that?"

Abby blew out a heavy sigh. "I wish I knew."

Jossi sat down across from Abby, softening her tone. "You need to talk to someone, Abby. Release those pent-up feelings. Didn't the doctor recommend a counselor or therapist?"

Abby shifted in her seat, darting her eyes away from Jossi's. "I saw one," she confessed quietly. "But after a few private sessions, she said I might benefit from a support group."

"And?"

"I hated it," Abby admitted, her tone exceedingly harsh. "I mean it, Jossi, I really *hated* it! All the women were sitting around, acting like victims. Claiming they survived cancer. Hooray for them!" Abby threw her arms up in mock excitement. "Like that's some kind of badge of courage."

"You sound bitter."

"I'm not bitter," Abby protested, a little too quickly, a little too sure.

"Mmm-hmm ..." Jossi's left eyebrow jutted upward. "Abby, what's going on in your head?"

After a long silence, Abby finally answered, "I didn't have to go through losing my hair or being pumped up with chemicals. I walked away with just scars across my chest. I was *lucky*."

"So, it's guilt?"

"No. I'm a fraud," Abby clarified. "The women in the group had to fight. They had to stare death in the face. I'm not one of them. I don't deserve to be a part of the collective of survivors. I didn't survive death. It passed me by." Her voice dropped to a whipper. "*Again.*"

Jossi leaned forward. "You shouldn't regret surviving, Abby. It wasn't your time." She paused, her gaze steady, before adding, "This time ... or last time."

Last time ...

Abby was never told that Jossi had died on impact that fateful night. She was in a coma for twenty-four hours before regaining consciousness. It was another twenty-four hours before she realized that no one had mentioned Jossi. When she asked, her mother began to cry. She never said the words, "Jossi died." Her mom avoided answering her question altogether, cheering instead, "You survived!"

Her family huddled in support. The nurses and rehabilitation workers praised her progress, rejoicing in her achievements in healing. "You were the lucky one," they all said. But no one wanted to admit the sad truth. Abby survived, and Jossi didn't. Celebrating her life meant disregarding Jossi as equally important. It wasn't a badge of honor to have lived. It was a chance of fate. There was no victory in that.

"Abby, fate is a choice. You are too close to see it. But you will."

"When? Will I suddenly wake up and understand?"

"No, not straight away. It's a journey. But if you don't put your feet into motion, you will never get there."

Abby wrapped her arms around herself. "I'm drowning, Jossi. I'm so disconnected ... to Marcus, the kids, even you. I look at myself and I don't know who the woman is staring back. I'm half woman and ..." She smoothed her hands across her chest. "And half cadaver. I was invisible to the world before the cancer, and now I'm invisible to myself after. No wonder Marcus doesn't want me."

"I've had enough of that!" Jossi said. "Get up. Take a shower. Do your hair. Remember who you are, not who you think you have to be for everyone."

"And Marcus?"

"That is something you'll have to explore, but you can't if you don't at least start." Jossi pointed toward the bathroom with a firm hand.

Abby lifted herself from the chair and walked to the mirror, aware of Jossi's glare pressing her forward. She tucked her hair behind her ears and leaned closer. *She did look like hell.* But before she could admit it aloud, Jossi was gone.

"You can do this," Abby said to the woman staring back.

Lifting the sweatshirt over her head, she gasped. It was hard to see her naked chest after it had been cut up and put back together again. It amazed her what plastic surgery had accomplished thus far. The new pink skin was working its magic, sealing the cuts across her breasts, but it wasn't pretty. Not yet. Maybe never. She had breasts again ... mounds on her chest to replace the ones that had been there before, only smaller. Perfectly round. Perfectly unnatural. But they didn't look the same. Feel the same. Reconstructive surgery was still a few months away. Until then, she had to adjust to the disfigured woman standing before her.

Too bad they couldn't surgically put back her disassembled spirit.

She slid off her pajama bottoms and threw them in the hamper. It was empty, thanks to the efficiency of the housekeeper. *She definitely would keep her longer.*

"Abby?" Marcus's voice called out.

"In the bathroom."

Marcus cleared the corner. "Oh God, Abby, I didn't mean to ..." he apologized before darting out.

Abby grabbed a towel, wrapped it around her naked body, and followed him.

"Marcus, why are you running away?"

"I'm not. I thought ... you'd want privacy or something," he answered, flustering his words.

"You're my husband. You've seen me naked a million times. What privacy could I need from you?"

"Abby, you were looking at your ..." he broke off and pointed to her chest.

Abby looked down. "My what?" she asked, demanding he say it.

"Come on, Abby, don't do that to me. You have scars across your chest. Of course, it's shocking. Don't act like it should be easy for me."

"No, Marcus. It isn't easy. None of this is easy, for you or me." Abby bit down on her lip to stop her from saying more, from crying. She turned away and escaped back into the bathroom.

Marcus huffed and followed her. "What do you want from me?"

"I wanted you to make love to me that night!" she shouted, saying what had been eating away at her heart.

He looked at her with a blank stare.

"Do you realize you haven't really touched me?" she said. "Since we came back from the hospital, you haven't put your arms around me. Your body hasn't crossed over to my side of the bed. You kiss me on the top of my head like a child when you leave for work. You barely make eye contact when you come home. You're avoiding me."

"What are you talking about?" he questioned. "I didn't want to bother you."

"Bother me? Seriously, that's your defense?" she mocked. "I have hands you can hold. I have lips to kiss. I have other body parts you can touch besides my breasts!" She raged. "I'm still here."

Marcus said nothing.

Abby fell silent, too. She was angry with him. She was angry with herself. It wasn't fair to put all her discontent on him. She didn't have all the answers, and neither did he. This was about more than her scarred body. But the cancer was the excuse. It allowed Marcus to retreat further, and she let him do it by hiding away in self-pity. Neither one of them knew how to navigate this part of their life—*for better, for worse, in sickness, and in health.*

"Look Abby ..." He broke the silence. "Things have been weird. I dislike arguing as much as you. So, how about we start over, okay? I'll make reservations at your favorite place. Café Luna? Go buy something new. Heck, buy me something new. We'll make a fresh start." His blue eyes caught hers and it transported her to the time when he first kissed her.

God, those eyes were her weakness!

A smile spread across her face.

"Then it's a date?" he asked.

"Yeah, it's a date," Abby said, her voice soft, the fight drained out of her. She was too tired of the distance between them to argue anymore.

"Great!" he said, a smile crossing his face. "I love you."

"I love you, too," she called after him as he walked away.

He still hadn't touched her.

10

DATE NIGHT

"You look stunning," Jossi said, walking into the bathroom and settling herself on the edge of the bathtub.

Abby leaned closer to the mirror, carefully applying a layer of red lipstick. She pressed her lips together, smoothing the color evenly, before adding a second coat with precision.

Abby stepped back and assessed herself in the full-length mirror. Hair colored, eyebrows shaped, nails painted, she was a fresh version of her former self. She'd even treated herself to a bikini waxing. *And it wasn't even summer*, she thought, smiling to herself.

She flashed her shoes in front of Jossi. "What do you think? These heels are higher than I would usually wear, but aren't they fabulous? Especially against the blue silk of my dress." Brushing her hand down the fabric, feeling the silkiness against her hand, she felt sexy. "Gosh, I hope Marcus likes the dress." Her eyes widened, but then a slow smile came across her face. "My stomach is in knots, but in a good way, though."

"You're giddy," Jossi said, a smile crossing her face. "Just like on your wedding day. Remember? You spun around in your dress, giggling like a little girl, saying you never felt prettier."

"I feel pretty now," she confessed, butterflies fluttering inside her. "I saw Marcus leave for work in the shirt and sweater I bought him. I even noticed he got a haircut. Just for me! Do you know how long it has been since he has asked me out?"

"You went out to the sports bar that one night." Jossi touched her chin, tapping at it lightly. "Last September."

"Umm, that was because our power went out and Marcus wanted to see the highlights of a game," Abby replied, shooting down Jossi's recollection. "I drank two glasses of wine, staring at Marcus's profile. I don't even think he knew I was sitting next to him."

"You also consumed a whole plate of nachos, if I recall," Jossi teased her.

"What else was I going to do? My husband was to the left, ignoring me, and two young professionals were to my right, who turned away when they realized how old I was. It's like they would turn into stone if they looked at a woman past the age of forty."

"Well, not tonight." Jossi swept her gaze over Abby, taking her in from head to toe. "Marcus will have to look at you in that dress, if the other men don't steal you away. Now turn around so I can see all of you."

Abby twirled around for her. "I even bought a pair of very expensive lacy panties." She lifted her dress to reveal the French lace.

"Niiiiice," Jossi purred.

"Mom," Drew's voice yelled out. "Your phone is ringing. It's Dad."

"Answer it, please," Abby shouted back.

Clicking her way through the hall and down the stairs, she found Drew writing her a note.

"What did your dad say?"

"Oh, hey Mom." Drew looked up and handed her the note. "I gotta run," he said, grabbing his gym bag and heading to the front door.

"You couldn't come and tell me?"

"I'm in a hurry—the guys are waiting for me," he answered, rushing out.

A cold blast of air swept through the door as he pulled it open. Abby shivered in her sleeveless dress.

"Hey," she called out to him. "How do I look?"

Drew stopped and turned around. "Oh wow, I hadn't noticed. You look great. Bye, Mom."

Abby shut the door quickly, sealing out the gust of cold air that had rushed inside. She read the note in her hand.

Dad is still in a meeting. Running late. He'll meet you at the restaurant.

Abby's excitement dimmed slightly. But she pushed her feelings aside. Tonight wasn't going to be ruined that easily.

ABBY CHECKED HER PHONE. Marcus was fifteen minutes late.

The hostess smiled at her. Not a friendly smile with sincerity. It was one of *those* polite smiles—contorted lips stretching across the face without showing teeth, mixed with a deadpan gaze. Abby wondered if the young twenty-something, with her mini dress and strappy stilettos, was feeling sorry for her or hoping she would give up a much-sought-after table.

As the lobby filled with people, Abby scanned the

crowded bar, hoping to find refuge and a glass of wine while she waited for Marcus. She maneuvered into a spot at the counter, murmuring apologies as she nudged the shoulders of the two people flanking her. The woman on her right glanced briefly at her before turning away, uninterested. Abby wasn't an attractive or rich man. Either would have probably sufficed for her, both being probably preferable.

The man on her left didn't budge. He was too absorbed in trying to charm two women half his age sitting beside him, his metallic wedding band not stopping him—*or them!*

Abby set her handbag firmly on the bar, staking her claim. She smiled at the bartender—a younger version of Brad Pitt, she thought—hoping to catch his eye. He nodded in her direction but veered toward the woman beside her, whose empty martini glass seemed to radiate urgency. The woman, impossibly young and flawless, batted her lashes and tapped her empty martini glass. Apparently, a smile was no longer considered attention-grabbing.

Young Brad Pitt soon returned with a sugar-rimmed martini, placing it down in front of the young woman. Before Abby could say a word, he threw up his hands, barely glancing at her, abruptly saying, "I'll be right back." He scurried away to the other end of the bar.

Abby's phone buzzed repeatedly, rattling against the lining of her purse. She hesitated before opening the flap, then reached for her phone, a sinking feeling coming over her.

Crazy day. Just wrapping up at the office now.

Traffic is brutal, and it's starting to snow.

GPS says it's at least fifty minutes to get there, maybe more.

Thinking best to pivot ... How about I grab your favorite from Marco's, and we do dinner at home instead? I've had a heck of a day.

Be careful out there ... see you soon.

Abby stared at the screen, her finger tightening around the edges of her phone. It wasn't just the texts, it was the casualness of them, as if cancelling the evening meant nothing more to him than a minor inconvenience. Her heart sank and a wash of nausea swept over her.

"Can I get you a drink?" Young Brad Pitt finally asked.

"Huh?" Abby looked up, the sound of clinking glasses and the low murmur of conversation amplifying the emptiness she felt.

"A drink?" he repeated.

Abby shook her head, and he moved on.

She glanced down at her blue dress and her suede pumps in resignation. "I guess I'll have to impress him another day," she said, holding back tears. Sending Marcus a reply, she pushed away from the bar, walked past the hostess without making eye contact, and slipped out the door.

Abby tipped the clerk at the coat check and dragged her arms through the sleeves, waiting for the valet to bring her car around. Her feet were freezing by the time she shut the door. She peeled her pumps off her feet, threw them onto the seat next to her, and turned up the heat, directing the warmth from the vents to her toes. She waited for the numbness to fade. A young valet knocked on her window. She rolled it down halfway, the heat instantly sucked away.

"Excuse me, lady, but could you pull out of the way? There is a line waiting." The valet pointed to the waiting cars and stepped aside, gesturing for Abby to move.

As she drove onto the highway, the lines of the road became blurred in front of her—she needed windshield wipers for her eyes. Knowing better, she veered to the side and turned off the car. Searching through the glove compartment, she found napkins and blotted her eyes. When she looked in the mirror, her mascara had bled down her face. She wetted the napkins and tried to wipe up the mess, but it only made it worse.

Her mother would not be proud.

Maybe she was being unreasonable. Maybe this was just work, traffic, and snow. But deep down, she knew it wasn't about the snow or the traffic. It was about priorities. And she wasn't one.

11

THREESOME

Abby remembers the first time she met Marcus. It was the early nineties and taverns throughout the city of Chicago were hosting bands on every third corner. Jossi had managed to sneak them out of the house—she was clever that way—and they hitched a ride downtown with her older brother and his friends.

The band was forgettable, but meeting Marcus was not. Blue eyes like his were never unforgettable. He had bumped Jossi's arm in the crowded room, spilling her soda. He apologized and bought them both a beer. Since they were underage, the gesture was thrilling. He made them laugh and danced with them all night long, but his eyes never rested on Abby for too long. Jossi got all his attention.

She always did with men. Jossi's allure was captivating, yet it was her smile that magnetized everyone's attention. Her lips were a perfect blend of fullness and softness, curving gracefully into a natural pout. Their deep rosy hue against radiant white teeth, sculpted by two torturous years of braces, caught the attention of anyone who had the privilege to witness her smile. Her warm olive skin and her luscious dark hair only accentuated the sparkle in her golden eyes. She was undeniably exotic, if not stunning.

Most people never noticed Abby when she was next to Jossi. Not that Abby was unattractive. Abby was cute, with hair caught somewhere between mousy brown and dark blonde—a quiet forgettable shade—usually pulled back in a clip with bangs. Her hazel eyes—shy to commit to either green or brown—were muddy against her pale skin. Although she was grateful for her fair complexion, which never seemed to blemish, any slight embarrassment inflamed her cheeks, her face an open book for most of her emotions. Against Jossi, who was electric, inside and out, Abby had no chance of capturing Marcus that night. Not then, anyway.

Jossi and Marcus exchanged numbers that evening, and they were soon dating. Abby hung out with them often enough to know that Marcus was a nice guy. Many Saturday nights, the three hung out at Jossi's house, watching movies, listening to music, or playing pool. They had fun. A cama-raderie was born.

Marcus was always kind and polite to Abby. They both seemed to get what they needed from Jossi, with little conflict. A respectful friendship emerged. Marcus didn't complain that Abby was a third wheel, as long as he got private time with Jossi. And even then, Abby was privy to the times when she wasn't there. Jossi shared everything. *Everything!*

She didn't think much about Marcus then. Not in the way of being attracted to him. He was Jossi's and thus off-limits. They seemed to belong together. Almost soulmates, if she were to put a name to what they had. Abby and Marcus had been dating for three months after Jossi was gone before she even realized that they had become a couple.

A few weeks after Abby had come home from the hospital, he had called. "Did you want to meet for ice cream?"

Still battered and bruised, limping when she walked, she agreed.

Abby was the closest thing to Jossi that Marcus had. She felt the same about him. Their loss was mutual. Ice cream turned into lunch, lunch turned into a movie, and a movie turned into hanging at the lake. She would read while he swam, he would nap while she swam, and they played Frisbee and paddleball in between. They'd walk late at night when the bugs were gone, eat popsicles in the park, and search the night sky for shooting stars. They talked. They shared. They healed. It was only when Abby was leaving for college that they both realized they would miss each other. On the day she was loading her car, Marcus came to say goodbye. When he hugged her, it seemed only natural to place her lips on his.

When she stepped back, he looked at her with his big blue eyes and said, "I'll be waiting for you."

And he did.

They wrote to each other from college and spent the holidays and breaks together. When the summers came, they returned to their usual things—swimming at the lake, eating ice cream, making wishes upon the stars. In the summer before Abby's final year, they finally made love for the first time. Abby hadn't planned on waiting so long, but Marcus suggested that they wait until he finished college. He was finishing his master's program and claimed he wanted to stay focused on his grades. Abby thought he was too scared to open his heart again. Either way, Abby wasn't in a hurry. Living up to a first love was already unsettling. But living up to Jossi wasn't something she was sure she could do.

Marcus's parents were gone for the weekend, and he

invited Abby for dinner under the stars in his backyard. Abby felt suspicious about the evening, not because she knew they were going to have sex, but because she wasn't sure that Marcus could cook. If he prepared dinner, they never ended up eating it. When she walked out the screen door, a pathway of lighted candles led to a blanket sprawled out on the lawn under an oak tree.

"You like?" Marcus asked.

"It's perfect," Abby cooed, unable to peel off the grin from her face.

Marcus brought his lips to hers and cradled her in his embrace. His lips lingered on her neck before he reached for the hem of her top. Abby raised her arms, helping him lift it over her head, and he tossed his own shirt on the lawn. His mouth came to hers again, and she succumbed to his rapturous kisses. Without apprehension, she unhooked her bra, letting it drop to the ground. He stroked his fingers across her breast, awakening her very perky, very responsive nipples. Cupping one breast with his right hand, he leaned over and placed his mouth around the other. A warmth spread through her. She broke out in goosebumps, which only encouraged Marcus to continue the titillating sensations.

Abby never knew a touch could send a thousand electric ripples along her skin, or in between her legs. An erotic rage roared inside her. Her brain was too distracted for her to notice how he unbuttoned her shorts or slid off her panties, but when his warm hands caressed her backside, it wasn't important. One hand slid between her legs, and she moaned, surprising and scaring herself at the same time. Embarrassed, she shifted away slightly.

"Do you need me to stop?" he asked.

"Sorry," she said, her cheeks flushing pink. "I ... I'm not sure what that sound was."

Marcus laughed. "Abby, if I make you moan, that's a good thing."

"Oh." Her cheeks flushed a deeper shade. "I just never imagined I would be so ..."

"Sexy?"

"No!" Abby giggled and rolled her eyes. "I just never imagined I would like it so much."

Marcus smiled. A big smile. "It's you and me, babe. We're good together." He placed a gentle kiss on her lips and motioned for her to lie on the blanket. "God, you're pretty," he said, standing over her. "And I'm not just saying that because you're naked."

Abby purred inside. She reached out, inviting him next to her. With eager hands, he stripped off his jeans and stood statuesque in his nakedness.

"God, *he's* pretty ..." a voice said.

That's when Abby heard Jossi for the first time.

"Isn't he dreamy?" Jossi added.

Abby shook her head, thinking she had imagined the familiar voice. But when Marcus moved down to the blanket, Jossi was standing before her, no longer hidden in his shadow.

Abby's body jerked, shrugging Marcus aside.

"What's wrong? Am I hurting you?" Marcus said, his voice soft with worry.

"No, I ... I just ..." Abby stuttered, darting her gaze between Marcus and Jossi. She blinked, hoping it was her mind playing tricks on her.

It wasn't. Jossi was still there, standing just beyond. Her golden eyes glinted, carrying their usual mischief.

"What are you doing here?" Abby demanded, her voice

trembling.

Marcus tilted his head. "Making love to you, Abby. What do you think I'm doing?"

Jossi laughed.

Abby grabbed Marcus's shirt, frantically yanking it over her head. "You don't see her?" she said, pointing into the distance.

Marcus looked over his shoulder. "Come on, Abby, no one can see us out here."

Abby squeezed her eyes shut. *Go away, go away, go away*, she repeated in quick succession. When she opened her eyes, all she saw were Marcus's crystal blue eyes on her.

He wrapped his arms around her, bringing her to him. "Come on, Abby." Brushing a strand of hair from her face, he asked, "What's going on?"

"Nothing." Abby shook her head, not wanting Marcus to think she was crazy or, worse, acknowledge Jossi's appearance was real. She glanced over his shoulder to assure herself that Jossi was gone, guilt and longing warring within her. She had spent so much time thinking that Marcus was Jossi's, not hers, so how could she love him without feeling like a thief? Even now, with Jossi gone, the ghost of her best friend lingered.

She shook off her uneasiness, returning to Marcus and his loving gaze. His blue eyes were now her only distraction. She melted into his embrace, her body yielding to his as he drew her irresistibly closer. A tremor of raw sensation swept through her, igniting her every nerve as their bodies intertwined. "I want you, Marcus," Abby whispered. "As close as two people can be."

Marcus locked eyes with hers. "Abby, I don't just want you; I love you, with all my heart."

He loves me! Her breath caught. The words felt like a

warming tonic coating the inside of her body. She wanted to repeat the same back to him, but she couldn't. Not when she saw that Jossi hadn't disappeared.

Abby shot up, meeting Jossi's stare. "What?" she shouted. "Do you want me to give him up?"

Jossi's voice was softer now, almost wistful. "God, Abby, no! Look at him. Just love him. He needs you. And you need him. I wanted to make sure you two would be okay. I can see that." She turned away but looked back and smiled. "Take care of him, Abby. He's got a good heart ... and it's all yours." She winked and walked into the trees, the darkness swallowing her mirage.

Abby blinked, and Jossi was gone.

Marcus's hand cupped her cheek, drawing her back to him. "Abby? Everything okay? Did I say too much? God, I'm an idiot," he murmured, his voice tender but shaky.

Abby exhaled and leaned into his touch. "No, no, no," she assured, letting his touch warm her. "I mean, yeah, I'm okay. I just had a weird moment." Seeing his confusion, she put her arms around him. "I love you, too," she said and brought her lips to his.

The tension in Marcus' shoulders eased as she kissed him, his touch gentle, but insistent. Abby surrendered to the moment, the doubts and ghosts fading as she allowed herself to feel—really feel—the tenderness between them.

Marcus proposed to her at the end of the summer. They were married the following year at the Fairmont. Abby wanted to get married in Hawaii in an intimate ceremony, but her parents, as well as Jossi, insisted it be *the event* of the year. It was.

Both Marcus and Abby landed corporate jobs in the city and settled into married life. But Jossi was never too far away from it all. She visited often. It was still a threesome.

12

DECISIONS

Abby stopped at the laundry room to grab a sweatshirt she had folded that morning. It was one of Marcus's, with the logo of his alma mater stitched on the front. The collar was stretched and the cuffs tattered. She threw it over her head, letting the brushed flannel lining warm her. Rolling up the cuffs, she wiped the tears from her cheeks with the soft, absorbent fabric. She didn't bother to turn on the lights as she made her way down the stairs, grasping the railings instead. She dragged her slippered feet off each step, feeling her way through the dark until she made it to the bottom, ignoring the mirror on the landing. She didn't need to see herself; she knew her eyes were puffy and red.

Switching on the light of the kitchen, she squinted. As she adjusted to the brightness, she found Jossi at the kitchen table, whose eyes were soft with concern. Abby ignored her, beelining to the coffee pot instead. She noted the green numbers illuminating the time on display—it was almost three. A car's headlights flashed through the window as it drove by, catching her attention. She recognized the Volvo. It was Anderson from down the street, an ob-gyn, likely heading out for another delivery. Memories of many sleepless nights with her kids flooded back, moments when Anderson's car was a familiar sight during feedings, vomit clean-ups, or midnight snuggles after a scary nightmare. It didn't seem possible that almost twenty years had passed since Emma or Drew were waking her so early.

The coffee machine stopped gurgling, and Abby grabbed a mug from the cupboard and filled it to the brim. She cupped the hot mug between her hands and glanced down instinctively for her dog at her feet. He wasn't there. He'd died a year ago. But it was still a habit she couldn't break.

"Do you want to talk about it?" Jossi's voice broke the silence.

"No."

"He loves you, Abby."

Abby grumbled, never able to decipher if Jossi was there to look after her or watch out for Marcus. She sat down, placing her mug on the table.

"He's rejecting me," she finally said. "Not just tonight ... for a long time. I just chose to ignore it, hoping it would correct itself or go away." She brought the mug to her lips, fighting tears. "He didn't show up for our date because he's not ready for me. Heck, I'm not ready for me!" She paused and looked up, at nothing in particular, her thoughts twisting in her head. She let out a sigh. "I just need ..."

Jossi leaned in. "Say it, Abby. What do *you* need?"

Meeting Jossi's eyes, Abby struggled to speak, her voice cracking. "I don't know. And if I don't know, how should anyone else? How should Marcus?" Memories of Marcus played through her mind. "Is this how couples grow old, one person stops desiring the other and you act like it doesn't matter? Should it matter? Do you just get used to it?" Abby's voice dropped to a whisper. "What happens when a marriage becomes fractured?"

Jossi leaned back in her chair. "You put it back together, Abby. What other choice do you have?" Her voice was low but certain.

"But the pieces are so fragmented, I don't recognize anything. I think that's how Marcus must feel, especially about me."

"Sure, things have changed. *You've* changed. Neither you nor Marcus are the same, and you shouldn't be. So, where do you go from here? You need to answer that question before you can move on. You're building walls, Abby, shutting yourself off to avoid conflict. But all you're creating is a fortress where no one comes in, and you can't get out. You're stuck."

"Why are you telling me this? I'm fully aware that *I* have changed ... I have the scars reminding me of it every day. But I can't do this alone. Marcus isn't just on the other side of the wall; he's left the city. Why isn't Marcus fighting for us?" she demanded, her voice breaking. "I'm not the one turning away from me."

Jossi met her eyes, unflinching. "Aren't you?"

Abby stiffened, falling silent. The tears came soon after. She searched for a tissue box, finding one next to the kitchen phone. One by one, she ripped out a handful and wiped her nose with the ball of tissue. "I'm such a mess."

"No, you're hurting."

Abby grabbed more tissues and blew her nose. "I'm running on empty, Jossi," she finally admitted.

Jossi fixed her with a deadpan stare. "I can see that."

Abby searched Jossi's face for answers, but all she could see was her beautiful friend, still young, untouched by life's hard choices. Even under the bright, unflattering kitchen lights, Jossi's skin was flawless, a stark contrast to Abby's, marred by time. "It should have been you," she whispered, her voice catching. "I was never meant to be the one to marry Marcus. It should've been you." The admission hung in the air, a truth that had been buried deep within her heart.

Jossi shook her head. "You still don't get it. This isn't about me. It never has been."

"Ha!" Abby barked out a laugh. "Then why are you always in the middle of my life, spewing wisdom but never offering solutions?"

Jossi chuckled, an indulgent laugh, as though humoring a child trying to act grown up. "It's what best friends do," she said, her smile lingering.

Abby's eyes narrowed, locking onto Jossi's. "This can't be where you belong." The thought of Jossi trapped here, forever lingering, twisted her gut. "There has to be more. Why haven't you moved on?"

"Why haven't you?" Jossi countered, throwing the question right back at her.

PART II: DURING

13

IN MIDAIR

A*m I leaving Marcus?* Abby wondered as the taxi drove away from the house.

"Are you?" Jossi asked.

Abby turned to her friend, now sitting beside her. She'd wondered where Jossi had gone, leaving her to face Marcus alone. "I don't know," she said, unsure if the answers lay where she was heading.

"What lady?" the taxi driver called out, glancing in the rearview mirror.

Abby met his gaze. "Nothing," she replied.

"Abby," Jossi continued, unfazed by the driver's backward glances. "You should've explained what you were doing. He didn't deserve the way you left."

Abby sighed. "Explain what, when I don't even know?" She closed her eyes and counted to ten, willing Jossi to disappear. But when she opened her eyes, Jossi was still by her side.

"I'm still here," she said, as if reading her mind.

Abby groaned, rolling her eyes. "Can't you leave me alone when I want you to?"

"Lady? Did you need something?" the taxi driver barked again.

Abby shook her head, more firmly this time. She slid the plexiglass closed with a sharp click and turned to Jossi. "What do you want from me?"

"Are you sure about this?" Jossi questioned.

"No." Abby's voice quivered as she took a breath to steady herself. "I'm not sure about anything. But pushing me isn't helping. If I can't even answer Marcus, how am I supposed to answer you? And weren't you the one pushing me to do something?"

"I didn't tell you to run away! Maybe make some different life choices, but ..."

A smirk tugged at the corner of Abby's mouth as a low chuckle slipped out. "Really Jossi? What do you know about life choices? You copped out."

"I didn't have a choice," Jossi shot back.

She didn't. Abby knew better. Neither one of them could have predicted how different their lives would become— Abby married to Marcus with two kids, and Jossi all alone.

"It wasn't supposed to be this way," Abby said, her voice trailing into a whisper. "We picked a college and found an apartment in the city. Remember? I was going to be the best wedding florist in Chicago, and you were going to be an amazing middle-school teacher." A smile crossed her face. "You and Marcus were going to get married ... a huge wedding at the Fairmont. And me? If I were to marry—and it was a big *if* since I wasn't dating anyone—I'd have a small wedding on an exotic island. Tahiti, maybe. Our kids would only be a few months apart so they could be best friends.

Mine would be twin girls, named Amanda and Lily, and you had a boy and a girl named—"

"Emma and Drew," Jossi interjected.

Abby scrunched her brow, hating when Jossi was making a point. "Don't do that."

"Do what?"

"Make me think I did something wrong."

"Abby, you honored me when you picked those names. But that's not the point, is it?"

Abby pursed her lips. "No."

"Abby." Jossi met her eyes. "This is *your* life, not mine."

Abby glanced behind her. Through the back window of the taxi, everything appeared blurry, covered in grime. "You mean, the one I just tossed out the window?"

Jossi's brow lifted. "Whose life did you toss out the window?"

"My life," Abby insisted.

"No, Abby." Jossi shook her head. "You tossed my life, not yours. You made my dreams come true. But what are yours?"

Abby's face fell vacant, as if Jossi had slapped her across the face. She turned away, holding back tears, unable to speak.

The taxi drove through the neighborhood, taking her farther away from home. She could have stopped him. It wasn't too late to change her mind. But she didn't. She watched house after house go by, their porch lights glowing in the thickening darkness. Mr. Adams, an elderly widower who lived alone, was sitting in a chair, flashes from the television lighting his face. Three houses farther down, a family Abby didn't know sat at a table eating dinner. As they turned the corner onto the highway, she saw a man getting out of his car, fumbling with his keys. His house was dark, and he took his time walking to the front door. She wondered what his story was, what all their stories were.

What would someone see if they passed by her house and looked through the windows?

It started to rain. Abby heard the slushing of water as the cars whizzed by, making a muddy mess. She smirked at the symbolism. Crossing her arms, she slumped back into the hard cushion behind her and closed her eyes. There was no need to look anymore. She'd let the driver get her where she needed to go.

BY THE TIME Abby reached the airport, the weight of her decision hadn't lifted. If anything, it pressed harder as she boarded the plane, leaving Marcus and everything she knew behind.

Abby grabbed the flight attendant's arm in desperation as soon as the food service began. She needed a drink. She needed lots of drinks. The two Bloody Marys she'd downed at the airport had worn off. The second glass of wine finally helped her relax enough to sink into her seat and close her eyes, but when the lights dimmed, she only managed to doze for an hour because her thoughts spiraled out of control.

When she shut her eyes, all she saw was Marcus's face—the deepening lines between his brows, the confusion and the pain etched on his face as he tried to understand what she was doing. She hadn't had the strength to turn back when he called her name as she walked toward the taxi. She hadn't wanted to give him hope.

Abby ordered another drink while the rest of the passengers slept, the errant sound of snoring echoing through the quieted cabin. When the flight attendant returned with two mini bottles, she winked, as if saying that she understood. Abby thanked her quietly and tucked them into the seat pocket. The man next to her stirred and shot her a glare. Abby muttered an apology, but he turned away, clearly unimpressed.

Tears pricked at the corner of her eyes. She grabbed a mini bottle and downed it in three burning gulps. With a sigh, she reached up, turning off the overhead light. She leaned back, her eyes slowly adjusting to the dark abyss outside. With no land below, there was no way of telling which way was up or down. The only direction Abby needed to go was away—far, far away—from everything she had left behind.

Would it be far enough? she wondered. *Or too far?*

Either way, it was too late to go back.

14

LANDED

Abby's eyes opened. She stared at the ceiling, trying to remember where she was. Rolling over, she drew the heavy comforter closer. She blinked a couple of times to gain her focus, and pale yellow floral wallpaper came into view.

Her hand reached over instinctively toward the nightstand, but her phone wasn't there. She remembered—it was still in her purse, buried in the large pouch she'd thrown into the armoire when she arrived.

Lifting her head slightly, she glanced toward the cabinet near the door. It was too damn cold to get out of bed and retrieve it. She curled into herself, sinking deeper into the cocoon of warmth. The heavy comforter smelled faintly of lavender and old wood, stirring memories of childhood sleepovers at her grandmother's. She drew the blankets closer. She didn't care what time it was or where she was. None of it mattered.

She squeezed her eyes shut and surrendered to the silence, letting sleep draw her back under.

15

THE INN

When Abby finally opened her eyes, the room was cloaked in shadows, her surroundings blurred in a heavy, quiet stillness. She glanced at the wall of windows. The shades were drawn, but a sliver of light from a streetlamp slipped through the shades, casting eerie shapes on the walls. She groaned, not wanting to be awake. But her bladder throbbed, pushing her out of bed. Groggy and disoriented, Abby threw her covers aside and found her footing on the hardwood floors. She reached for the lamp next to her bed, fumbling for the switch, but soon gave up and felt her way along the walls in the dark. *How had she not bothered to notice the details of the room earlier?*

Abby thought back to when she first arrived. Everything had been a blur as she rushed in, barely taking in the details. She rolled her suitcase into the room and placed her bags by a large armoire next to the door. Opening it, she contemplated unpacking, but hung her purse on a hook instead and closed the cavernous space to be dealt with later. She kicked off her boots and stripped off most of her clothes, leaving on leggings, a tank top, and a pair of thick socks. She crawled into the bed and had not left its shelter since her arrival.

The old woman who had greeted her at the inn seemed friendly enough. When Abby handed back the registration card, she noticed the woman's kind eyes—a faded blue— standing out against the silver-white hair loosely pinned in a sloppy chignon at the base of her neck. *Very WWII*, Abby thought. The woman's gaze lingered for a moment on Abby's face, but she offered no judgment, just a knowing glance before handing over the keys. Abby sighed with relief, grateful for her discretion. The woman pointed toward the dark, steep stairwell and directed her to her room.

Since she'd made a last-minute reservation, Abby didn't expect to be given the honeymoon suite. But the old woman, Mrs. Landry, said she wasn't expecting it to be needed for a few weeks and it would be silly not to offer it, especially since Abby was the only guest at the inn. Abby didn't care one way or the other. But when she found out it was the only room with a private bathroom, she was grateful for the upgrade. The room was located on the third floor and was the only one on the top floor. No neighbors to run into sounded good to Abby. With no elevator, the task of toting her luggage up the steep stairway was daunting, but the privacy factor kept her motivated as she climbed. When she opened the door, her only focus was on the bed. Four huge pillows and a fluffy, white down comforter beckoned her to sink into them. The color of the room, whether there was a chair or a dresser, or where the light switches were, hadn't seemed significant. Now, as she gripped the edges of the counter after stumbling over the bathroom rug, she regretted not paying more atten- tion when she first arrived.

Moonlight filtered through a small opaque-glass window, casting a faint glow onto the sink. Abby turned the faucet handle and splashed cold water on her face, hoping to wash away the remnants of her troubled dreams. Leaning into the mirror, she peered through the haze of darkness. A wave of disgust washed over her. A tangled mess of hair framed her face, and smudged mascara ringed her eyes like war paint.

This couldn't be the same woman who once organized team fundraisers or scheduled community events. Her eyes widened in disbelief at the wild-haired stranger looking back. Her shoulders slumped, and her face twisted with a tight, pained expression. Was she insane? The reflection didn't match the person she had been yesterday—before she left everything behind. Now, she was in a small town in Scotland, tucked away in an obscure old house, standing alone in the dark with no plan or purpose. A wave of loneliness crashed over her and a tightness pressed down on her chest.

When Abby was at the airport, she'd watched the purposeful crowds, all seemingly headed toward a clear destination. She, on the other hand, wasn't sure. Not exactly. She had decided quite spontaneously. Yesterday afternoon, as a matter of fact. She looked up flights, picked the most direct one, scanned the bank account her grandmother left her for such an occasion—to travel—and hit the button to purchase. She prayed her passport was still valid.

Abby had always been mesmerized by Scotland, her grandmother's homeland. The words in her thick Scottish accent would roll off her grandmother's tongue and into Abby's ears, hypnotizing her with tales from another place and time. Rich tales filled with magical beings, beautiful lands, and fantastical adventures.

One story, in particular, stayed closest to Abby's heart: *The Flowers of Muir*. It told the tale of a young girl fleeing from her abusive father, who had been cursed and turned into a bear-like creature, then enslaved by an evil queen to fight in her army. Lost and frightened, left to fend for herself, the girl stumbled upon a field of blooming flowers where fairies made their home. Each morning as the flowers opened, the fairies would burst forth like sparkling confetti. Their swirling skirts and jewel-studded slippers shimmered in the morning light. Upon meeting the girl, the fairies took her on daily adventures, teaching her virtues like courage, kindness, and wisdom. Once she acquired the wisdom of these virtues, they granted her one wish: for her father to be restored. With the curse lifted, the father and daughter were reunited, and they lived happily ever after together in the magical land of flowers.

Abby wanted to escape to that mystical place, to get lost. Maybe it would help her find solace. But she knew better. Fairy tales didn't really happen, and she wasn't an eight-year-old child who could indulge in such a fantasy.

But why not Scotland? As she stared at the computer screen, the cursor taunted her to decide. Her finger pressed down, and it was done. With one bold move came another. She booked a quaint inn just south of Perth, nearest where her grandmother was born. There were plenty of castles to visit and areas rich in garden tours to get lost in. More importantly, it was far, far away.

A chill crept up Abby's back, causing her to shiver. She wrapped her arms around herself and jumped back into bed, finding her way under the covers, curling the edges tightly under her chin. She perked her ears at the stillness of the inn, hoping something would sound familiar—the soft hum of the dishwasher or the faint whoosh of a car driving by. The only sound was the steady ticking of a clock from somewhere in the darkness, breaking the eerie silence that surrounded her.

What did I do?

16

GETTING COFFEE

Abby stared at herself in the mirror. This time, it was in the harsh light of day. She moved closer to fully assess the mess that stared back at her. Her bloodshot eyes stung with every blink. Dark patches loomed above her cheeks, evidence of her restless nights. Her hair, greasy at the roots and tangled at the ends, hadn't felt water in days—three, or was it four? She bared her teeth. They needed a morning brush. Grabbing her toothbrush, she vigorously brushed her teeth, spitting out the foamy residue that frothed over her lips. Noticing the deepening line between her brows, she cursed again. *Age!* She grabbed the sweatshirt from the floor, slipping it over her tank top, noting that the mornings weren't offering any relief from the cold nights. In less than a week, the temperature had plummeted, leaving her unprepared for the biting cold lingering in the house. She shoved her feet into her moccasins and headed out the door. She needed her morning coffee.

Downstairs, Mrs. Landry leaned over the sink, washing

the morning dishes. She did not turn around when Abby's footsteps came behind her. "Good mornin'," she said.

Abby grumbled her response, shuffling to the counter. She tapped the electric kettle to boil water and reached for the coffee canister sitting beside it. Lifting the lid, she peered inside. "No more coffee?"

"Oh, there was coffee this mornin'," Mrs. Landry replied, finally facing her. "You missed it two hours ago. I rather enjoyed a second cup, as to take the chill off me bones."

Abby checked the clock, an old cuckoo clock detailed with a stag's head at the top and oak leaves protruding from the side, carved in wood. The stag seemed to stare at her accusingly. "It is only eleven," she protested. "You've had coffee every morning."

"Well, my dear, if you want coffee, you'll have to get out of this house and go get yourself some," Mrs. Landry said in a no-nonsense tone.

Abby looked out the window. The sky was gray and heavy with clouds. She saw people walking the streets bundled in coats and scarves. Her brow pinched. "Who would want to go out there?"

"*There* ..." Mrs. Landry said, pointing out the window, "is where life is. *There* is where people interact and talk to one another. Out *there* is where ya need to be," she scolded.

Abby crossed her arms. "I don't want to go out *there*."

"Well, if you'll be wantin' coffee in the mornin', *there* is where you'll find it. My friend Hazel makes a fine cup of coffee, and some lovely scones to boot." Mrs. Landry gestured toward the window, indicating the streets below. "And that's where you'll find it from now on." She met Abby's narrowed stare, crossing her arms as well.

Abby opened her mouth to argue, but Mrs. Landry's beady eyes and pursed lips stopped her. She stood no chance against the stern old woman. Not that morning, anyway. She still needed coffee.

"Can I at least get some water?" Abby asked.

Mrs. Landry pointed to a cabinet. "The glasses are in there. Help yourself." She wiped her hands and then folded the towel, placing it on the counter before heading out of the room.

Abby leaned against the kitchen sink and peered out the window again. It still looked cold. She filled a glass of water and retreated upstairs.

Abby wasn't sure when she drifted off again, but her growling stomach woke her. Without morning coffee to fuel her, her energy was in short supply. Her stash of granola and almonds from her carry-on had run out long ago, leaving her grateful for the Snickers and Reese's Peanut Butter Cups she had picked up at the airport magazine stand. They had been her meals for two days. But now she was running on empty. Should she satiate her appetite or continue to escape from the world? The heavy fog outside the windows made it easy for her to decide. She pulled the covers up, looked up at the ceiling with empty thoughts, and waited for sleep to save her.

THE ROOM HAD GROWN dark when Abby decided to re-enter into the world of the awake. She glanced at the small ticking clock she'd found nestled against a stack of books atop the dresser. Half past six. It felt much later. She didn't want to get up, but her bladder was deciding for her, once again. When she threw the covers off, she shivered at the stark reality of moving out of the warmth of her comforter. She hurried to the bathroom, hugging herself to stay warm. Sitting on the toilet, she grabbed a towel and wrapped it around herself.

She wondered if Mrs. Landry was trying to freeze her out of the room.

The water offered relief as Abby placed her hands under the faucet, letting the warmth seep into her chilled body. A hot shower seemed like the perfect remedy for the bitter cold that had settled inside her. Turning on the shower, she waited for the water to heat while she stripped down. She stared at her naked body in the mirror. Pale and thin, her body bore the signs of neglect. The hair between her legs had grown thick and curly. Lifting her arm, she noticed dark patches of growth beginning to form underneath. Her fingers brushed against her legs, feeling the soft hairs lying flat, no longer poking outward.

"Who could make love to this?" she said aloud, grimacing at her reflection. "I'm gross and unlovable."

"You're beautiful ... and lost," Jossi said, her voice stirring the air behind her.

Abby startled, catching Jossi's piercing gaze in the mirror. "Why do you have to do that?"

"Because I can," Jossi giggled. "I'm glad you're up! I've been waiting."

"Why? So that you can scold me?" She quickly grabbed a towel and yanked it around herself.

"No," Jossi replied. "Well, yes, actually. I've seen enough, Abby. You're hiding, wasting away in this room. It's time to do something."

Abby looked through the mirror at Jossi. "I don't know what to do. Can't you see?" Her voice cracked.

"Get out. Go anywhere. Go!" Jossi said, pointing to the tiny window, mimicking Mrs. Landry's earlier instructions. "Just start somewhere."

"I'm not ready," Abby whispered. "And not without you."

"Where do you think I'm going? I'm always with you. *Always*." Jossi held her gaze, as if willing Abby to believe it.

"Always?" The room filled with steam, fogging the mirror. Abby quickly swiped away the condensation, not wanting to lose sight of Jossi. But it was too late—she was gone.

"I miss you." The words vanished into the thick mist, leaving her feeling more alone than before.

Abby stepped into the shower and let her head fall back, allowing the water to pour over her face. A guttural groan escaped from deep within as the water cascaded down her scarred body. She reached for the bar of soap that was neatly wrapped in wax paper and a ribbon and tucked in an alcove of the tiled wall, and then scrubbed her skin with urgency. The lavender scent of the soap filled the air and wrapped around her senses. Like a magic potion, it melted her muscles to mush and quieted her racing thoughts, momentarily masking the dread that consumed her. The creamy lather slid down her body and swirled around feet, disappearing into the black hole of the drain. How she wished it was that easy to banish the emptiness that dwelled within her, to free her soul from its tomb. Still, she knew it was a start.

Washed and shaved, her skin aglow, she slipped into the white robe hanging behind the door, submerging her body in the terry's softness, and wrapped her hair in a towel. Crossing the room, she pulled out her phone, which was still tucked away in the armoire. Turning it on, she saw a litany of texts from Marcus.

Where are you? Are you okay?
We need to talk.
When will I hear from you?
You're scaring me.
Please call me!
Abby?

Her son had sent some too:

Mom?

Talked to Emma.

Said you're ok.

We're fine here. Really.

Love you.

Emma was the first person she had called to say where she was. Although her daughter was close to her father, she knew Emma would keep her location a secret.

"Are you sure you're okay, Mom?" Emma's voice had been laced with concern.

"I'm good right now," Abby said, though she wasn't sure she believed it herself. "I just need some time away ... by myself."

"This isn't some midlife crisis, is it? I mean, couldn't you have taken a pottery class or gone on a spa retreat?"

"Emma, I'm fine," Abby reassured her, her tone firm but tinged with weariness. "Really, I just wanted a change of scenery. Scotland has always called to me—home of Muir and the flower fairies."

"You know that is a fantasy, right? A lovely, fantastical tale, but made-up. You're a grown woman with a family, not an eight-year-old girl running away from her abusive father under an evil spell." Emma gasped. "Wait, Dad isn't being abusive, is he?"

"No! Your father would never ..."

"Thank God!" Emma exhaled. "You had me worried there for a second."

"Enough of your imagination," Abby scoffed. "How is Theodore?"

"Wonderful, as usual."

"Of course he is," Abby replied, more sarcastically than she intended.

"Mom?" Emma's voice raised an octave.

"Yes?"

"I have faith in you ... whatever it is you're doing. Just be careful. And take the time you need. Oh," she said, before hanging up. "Send pictures!"

Abby suddenly recognized that Emma had grown up and that their relationship was transitioning into a new phase. Change was in the air.

Abby typed a message to Marcus and looked it over twice before hitting send. She turned off her phone and placed it back in the drawer.

I'm fine. Will be in touch later. Love, A.

17

KIND GESTURES

A bby heard a fire crackling. She followed the sound to the back of the house, where she found Mrs. Landry in a room bathed in yellow light, watching television. The old woman was sitting in a chair with her feet resting on an ottoman, her eyes half closed.

Abby poked her head in. "Am I allowed to come in?"

Mrs. Landry cast her eye toward Abby. "Oh my, dear, please do. Come," she said, patting the seat of the chair next to her, "make yourself comfortable."

Abby made her way to the wingback chair covered in green plaid with a bright red pillow tucked to the side. Sinking into the seat, she turned slightly and offered a smile. "Oh, this is cozy. I could easily fall asleep in it."

"That used to be my Willie's chair," Mrs. Landry said, tapping the arm of the chair. "Too many nights I'd find him fast asleep, snorin' like a bear." She paused and glanced toward the paned windows that looked onto the backyard. Eyes unfocused, she stared into the darkness, a heavy mist obscuring any shadows of what lay beyond. A faint smile touched her lips. "He was a big man—Willie, that is. Not only in stature but in heart as well. He'd scare ya if ya found yourself in a dark alley with him. Och, but it would be for not. He was a gentle giant. Could barely kill a spider. Left me to do all the dirty work." She rolled her eyes. "He'd help anyone, though. All ya had to do was ask. Even when ya didn't, Willie easily spotted a person in need, knowing just what to do. He would have liked ya, I think." She winked. "Wouldn't have been so hard on ya as I was this mornin'."

Abby dropped her head, looking away from the old woman's gaze.

"Now, now," Mrs. Landry cooed, patting Abby's knee. "We all have our bad days."

"I was terrible to you this morning. And yesterday morning ... and the day before. I'm not making a good first impression. I'm better than that. Or, at least, I used to be. Just not lately. Not for a long time." She sighed. "For that, I'm sorry. I hope you can forgive me."

"No need. I assure you. Managing an inn makes it necessary to understand people." Mrs. Landry reached over and lifted Abby's chin. "Sometimes we need to forgive ourselves before we ask it of others."

Abby simply nodded, not ready to share.

"And sometimes it may take the simplest things to push forward. Maybe a little nudge from a grumpy old woman?" Mrs. Landry lifted her brow. "Now tell me, why should one be hidin' from the world?"

"I'm not hiding," Abby quickly protested.

"Humph!" Mrs. Landry crossed her arms.

"I'm not ..." Abby tried to explain. "I'm just taking some time for myself."

"Aye, if you say so. I guess ya don't owe me an explanation," she said. "Just know, you're safe here ... whatever, or whoever, you're runnin' away from."

"I'm not running away," Abby insisted.

"Humph!" Mrs. Landry bellowed deeper and harder, watching Abby finger her wedding band, twisting it around and around.

"I ... I ..." Abby mumbled. Biting her lip, she didn't answer.

"Again," Mrs. Landry put up her hand, "none of my concern."

Abby sighed, her chest tightening as she fought to contain the swirling storm of frustration and fear. Her eyes met Mrs. Landry's fading blue ones, and for a moment the tension eased. The older woman's gaze, soft and unwavering, seemed to reach into Abby's soul, wrapping her in a warmth that felt familiar—safe. Abby's lips trembled, and she could almost smell roses and jasmine, which reminded her of her mother. As if Mrs. Landry was giving her permission, Abby allowed herself to cry.

Mrs. Landry rose from her chair, grabbed a box of tissues, and handed it to her. "Cry away, little one. No one is watchin' ya here."

Abby wiped her nose. "You're very kind," she sniffled. "I didn't mean for you to get involved in my emotional mess."

"Och! No need to apologize. I've enjoyed havin' your company ... grumpy or not." Her eyes twinkled with amusement. "Winters are lonely. This old place is very quiet most days. Hearin' you rattle around upstairs has been the best thing for me. Your company, even if it is just for a few moments in the mornin', has been a blessin'."

Abby gave the old woman's hand a gentle squeeze. "Thanks for understanding. I'm going through some ... stuff. And I just need some time to sort it out." She let out a sigh, the confession feeling heavier than expected. "For whatever it's worth, I appreciate your patience. And I promise to behave better."

"Understood," Mrs. Landry said, squeezing Abby's back before withdrawing it. "Now, don't tell me you're not hungry ... unless you've been sneakin' out at the wee hours for a bite."

Abby grimaced. "My last meal was a half of a candy bar."

"No!" Mrs. Landry's eyes widened. "Follow me, I have a pot of stew on the stove. Was just going to have a bowl before ya walked in. Join me?" Without waiting for a reply, she turned and disappeared into the kitchen.

Abby heard a cupboard door squeak and the clapping of a spoon against a pot. She hurried to the kitchen and found Mrs. Landry hovering over a wooden board, slicing bread.

"What can I do?" Abby asked, a mixture of gratitude and unease stirring at the rare sensation of someone fussing over her.

Mrs. Landry pointed to a cabinet to her left. "You'll find some whiskey there. But if you'd prefer some wine ..." She gestured to the counter. "Take your pick. Guests leave them behind—quite an assortment, French, Spanish, even some Californian. Not much for my taste, but you're welcome to it."

Abby poured Mrs. Landry a whisky and found a nice bottle of French wine for herself. By the time she seated herself at the table, a bowl was in front of her, steam curling from the stew within. The board with the bread and a bowl of whipped butter soon followed.

Abby took a bite, her stomach gnawing for real food. "This is delicious!" Abby spooned another bite. "You used lamb and turnips, just like my grandmother's recipe."

"Aye. A good stew is nourishment for the soul," Mrs. Landry said, eyeing Abby's voracious appetite.

Abby put the spoon down, letting the stew settle in her stomach. "More than you know. It's been a long time since I've had something comforting," she admitted, her fingers lightly tracing the edge of the bowl, lingering in the warmth of the moment—the way it made her feel *at home*.

Mrs. Landry gave her a knowing smile. "Good food does that—anchors us when we feel ... lost."

Abby looked up, her eyes meeting Mrs. Landry's. "I seem to be indebted to you ... but thank you. For this. For everything. I needed a safe place to land, and I think I have found it here."

Eyeing Abby's almost-empty bowl, Mrs. Landry lifted her old body, slowing and carefully, from the table. "Leave room for shortbread. I made a fresh batch yesterday," she said, shuffling her feet to a tin resting on the counter. Opening the lid, she put the container on the table and pushed it toward Abby.

Abby eyed the buttery treats. "I could smell them cooking yesterday. It was driving me mad." She narrowed her eyes at Mrs. Landry but then smiled. "You almost got me out of my room."

Mrs. Landry's eyes sparkled with satisfaction as she reached for the tea kettle. "A tassie of tea?" she offered, ignoring the confession.

"No!" Abby put her hands up. "You have done enough for me. Go, sit yourself down in the other room, and I'll make the tea." When she saw the old lady's hesitance, she added, "I used to make it for my grandmother, who taught me that the key to a good cup of Scottish tea is to let it steep."

"Aye, you've been taught well." Mrs. Landry smiled and, grabbing her aching back, shuffled out of the room. "I take a wee bit of sugar," she added, her craggy voice drifting back to Abby.

AFTER CLEANING the dirty dishes and tea brewed, Abby placed the sweetened-filled cup on the table next to Mrs. Landry and reclaimed the comfy seat of Willie's chair. She noticed a new log on the fire sending off a soft glow into the room.

"As you see"—Mrs. Landry pointed to her surroundings —"we don't get many guests this time of year. Aye, maybe in Edinburgh, and the main cities where there's much more to see and do. But here, people wait until it gets warmer to set out and explore. I'm sorry my little inn doesn't have much to offer in the way of company."

Abby glanced around the cozy room. It wasn't large, likely once a space for travelers to relax or hold private conversations. Dominating one wall was the fireplace they now sat in front of, and wood beams stretched across the ceiling. One wall still exposed the home's antiquity with stonework, while the others were covered in lime plaster. The earthy yellow paint lent the room a warm, welcoming feel. "I don't mind the empty inn or the cold. It's still winter at home."

"And where's home?"

Abby bit into a cookie. As she brushed away the crumbs that fell onto her shirt, a girlish giggle escaping from her lips. "Oh," she looked up. "I live in a small city outside of Chicago."

Mrs. Landry gave a small nod. "I've not been to the States. My Willie didn't like to travel. He liked *home*. Oh, I suppose he would have taken me had I wanted. The man would have taken me to the moon had I asked." Her eyes dimmed as she brought her cup to her lips and sipped a few times before she cradled it back on its saucer. "My son travels a lot. He lives in London now—an important banking position. My oh my, he travels all over the world. My, he's seen enough of the world for both me and Willie!"

"Is he your only child?"

"Aye," Mrs. Landry said with a soft nod. "We tried for more, but God wasn't on the same page. Lost a few along the way. It just wasn't meant to be."

"I'm sorry," Abby said, all too familiar with the ache of that loss.

"Thank you," Mrs. Landry said, her tone carrying a quiet melancholy. "He was married once, to a nice girl. But it didn't work out. He just hasn't found the right person to complete him. That's important, you know—to have someone who balances you."

Abby looked at her, the words hitting her harder than she expected. The pain of her broken relationship weighed on her.

"Willie balanced me," Mrs. Landry continued, her voice wistful. "Where I was weak, he was strong. He wasn't perfect, mind ya, but he made me feel safe. Whole. A good partner helps you grow into all you're meant to be. Not by fixin' ya— God does that—but by standin' by ya." She gave Abby a pointed look. "A partner doesn't take from you, Abby. They give you space to discover yourself as ya grow and change, to be yourself, with patience and acceptance."

Abby wondered if she and Marcus had all those elements. She thought they did. Did she complete Marcus? Was she failing him? She swallowed hard, blinking back tears. "And what if a person fails to complete the other?"

"Oh, that is a complicated question, shaped by the tragedies." Her brow lifted. "Being whole doesn't mean perfect. It means learning to hold space for each other through the best and worst times. Willie wasn't my savior; he uplifted me. Now that the dear Lord has taken him, I'm not lost without him—just lonely. He was the companion who made my life better. Ya have to be whole on your own; no one can do that for ya." She reached out, giving Abby's hand a gentle squeeze. "You're on a journey, Abby. Don't waste it hiding in your room. The answers aren't there."

Abby closed her eyes and took a deep breath, feeling the weight of Mrs. Landry's words. What she was saying seemed so far out of reach right now.

Mrs. Landry rose from her chair, her joints slowing with each movement. "I'll be off to bed. Hazel's café, Scran, is just down the road, and she makes the best eggs this side of Scotland. You might try it in the mornin'."

Abby watched as she shuffled to the fireplace and stoked the embers.

"Stay as long as you like. Have some more tea. Goodnight, dear." Mrs. Landry teetered down the hall to her bedroom.

Abby listened as the old hinges creaked, first when the door opened, and then again as it closed. Now alone, the house achingly still, she leaned back in her chair, picked up another cookie, and stared at the dwindling light of the fire.

"She's right, you know." Jossi's familiar voice broke the silence. Abby turned to see her friend perched in Mrs. Landry's chair, her feet dangling.

Abby let out a soft laugh, despite herself. "I know, I know," she said. "It's time to start living."

18

BREAKFAST

Until she saw a hint of light, Abby fought the urge to rise, ignoring the grumbling in her stomach. It had started its desperate plea for food an hour ago. As the minutes clicked by, she stared at the ceiling, waiting for a ray of light to break the dark barrier of the room. Lifting the shade, she peered out the window to catch the sun just lifting on the horizon. It was still too dark for most to begin their day; the streets below lay empty and quiet, the cold uninviting to all but the bravest of souls. Yet Abby was wide awake. After sleeping for five days, her mind had clicked into gear long before sunrise.

She threw on a pair of yoga pants, an oversized sweatshirt, and Ugg boots, then tiptoed down the stairs. She bundled up in a cashmere scarf, a long down coat, and a baseball cap before slowly prying the door ajar. Heavy and old, it creaked with every inch, echoing against the wood-paneled walls. Abby held her breath, eyeing Mrs. Landry's door, and prayed the old woman didn't awaken. Her door remained closed, and Abby sighed as she slipped out.

Standing on the landing, protected by a covered arched roof overhead, she surveyed the landscape below painted in shades of gold, green, and brown. The colors of Scotland differed from home—it was more vibrant and intense. It didn't hurt that a rainstorm that hit during the night coated everything in a glistening dew. Old and worn stone buildings with peaked roofs and chimney stacks dotted the landscape. A lime-washed building, with a turret in the front, stood out among the stone and rock, pointing her to the main street of town, where Mrs. Landry had informed her she would find all kinds of shops and pubs.

A sharp gust of wind lifted her coat, sending a shiver up her spine. Her breath hung in the frosty morning air, swirling in soft white wisps. The cold bit at her face and fingers, prompting her to zip her coat to her neck and reach for her gloves in the depths of her pockets. A lingering mist blurred the streets, making them feel distant, but the growing pangs of hunger urged her forward, her boots crunching against the frosty ground as she started down the hill.

Passing by windows of quaint shops displaying their wares—fine teas, stationery, books—all darkened with Closed signs, Abby continued to walk, mesmerized by the town's original medieval layouts, narrow and winding, mixed with Georgian stone–facade buildings. It was exactly as she pictured a Scottish town, described many times by her grandmother.

A white-haired couple adorned in wool coats, arms entwined, passed her. The man nodded, and his companion offered Abby a smile before looking away. She watched their steps fall in sync as the man wrapped his arm around the woman, drawing her closer when she leaned in. Abby smiled at the tender moment, but something deep within her tightened, a quiet reminder of why she was thousands of miles away from home.

She rubbed her wedding ring, twirling it around her finger. Closing her eyes, she shook her head. She wasn't ready to ask that question. Or maybe she didn't want to face the answer.

A door opened and Abby heard the jingle of a bell. A young woman walked out carrying two cups, the smell of bread and coffee trailing behind her. Abby saw the words *Scran Café* scrolled in black ink across the window.

Another waft of coffee grinds and yeast hit Abby's nose as a man exited the café, the bell jingling again. He moved aside and held the door open. "Are ye comin' in?"

Abby nodded and dashed in, thanking him in a quick breath before the door closed behind her.

The café exuded a rustic charm, with its stone walls, wooden plank floors, and antique tables with mismatched chairs. Industrial lights hung from the ceiling, contrasting the sleek, modern coffee makers behind the counter. A short line of twenty-somethings eyed their phones as they waited for their coffee orders, while a mix of regulars and a few tourists sat at tables eyeing the menu.

"Abby?" a woman's voice called to her.

Abby looked up, searching the room, wondering who would know her.

A large woman with frizzy red hair swept up in a clip walked toward her. "I'm Hazel," she said with a smile. "Agatha said you'd be visiting us today. I'm so pleased!"

Abby gave her a blank stare.

The woman touched her shoulder. "Now, why don't ya sit by the window, and I'll make ya a nice plate of my famous fluffy eggs and salmon, or do ya prefer sausage?"

"Sausage," Abby said, obediently following her to a table.

The woman walked away but turned back. "I've got fresh scones coming out of the oven that you'll not regret. Coffee?"

Abby nodded. "Americano, please." She peeled off her coat and scarf and placed them on the chair next to her.

She stared out the window, watching the town come alive. Every few minutes, the bell at the top of the door would ring, tracking the morning crowd coming and going. Most ordered their usuals, which was confirmed by the help behind the counter, who greeted the incoming patrons: "The usual today, Sean?" Or Rory. Or Mrs. Wallace.

A young couple, speaking German, sat down at a table next to Abby. They eyed her for a moment before greeting her with an American accent. "We got married this weekend," they said, not able to conceal their happiness with big smiles and bright eyes.

"Congratulations!" Abby said, wishing them many years of love before turning away.

Her heart squeezed a little tighter.

Two older men occupied another table nearby. One read a newspaper while the other sipped his coffee. They had similar wide noses, large foreheads, and matching thinning hairlines. Abby guessed they were brothers. When the server brought their plates of food, neither of them looked up. As if on cue, they both lifted their forks and began to eat.

Abby heard a dog bark, drawing her to the window. Across the street, she noticed a hotel and several closed businesses, except for one with the door slightly ajar, an old bike leaning against it. A German shepherd sat at the entrance, his tongue lolling from its mouth. The dog barked again and a man appeared, patting the dog before rolling the bike inside and shutting the shop's door. The dog watched its owner dart across the street, then lowered its head and closed its eyes.

Just as Abby was about to look away, she realized the man was in front of her, staring through the window. Startled, she quickly looked away.

"Good mornin', Thom," Hazel said when the man entered the café. She turned to the woman at the coffee bar. "Dark roast, Edna," she reminded her.

"Thank ye, Hazel," the man said in return.

A woman behind the counter poured hot water into a filter and let the coffee brew before pressing it. She transferred it into a large mug, handing it to the man. "Just as ye like it," she said.

"You're a kind lady, Edna. What would I do without ye?"

"You'd have to settle for McAllister's poison down the street," she teased.

"You'd not make a man suffer such a travesty, now would ye?" He leaned in and gave her a gentle kiss on the cheek.

"Ye kin, that gets ye perks every time." Edna laughed.

Hazel came out of the kitchen balancing a plate on one arm and nudged the man with the other. "Don't you go on flirtin' with all the ladies while they're on my time," she scolded, but then gave him a wink.

"Aye," the man said, giving Hazel a side-glance as she passed.

"Here ya go," Hazel said to Abby, placing the plate down, filled with eggs, sausage, black pudding, baked beans, and grilled tomato. "This should put some life back into those eyes."

Was it so obvious? Abby looked down at the full plate, wondering if she could eat it all, though she knew she'd give it a good try.

"Don't mind me, lass. I'm always buggin' into things I shouldn't." A corner of her mouth lifted. "Let me know if ya need anything else."

The bell at the door jingled again and a group of teenagers dressed in school uniforms entered, causing Hazel to scurry behind the counter.

The man grabbed a newspaper abandoned on the counter and sat himself across from Abby. Tall, he squirmed into the antique chair, finding a comfortable position and spreading his legs under the table. Then, with a quick flick, he opened the newspaper and held it up, shielding his face as he began to read. Every so often, he'd brush it aside, bring the mug to his lips for a sip, and steal a glance at Abby.

Abby pretended not to notice, scrolling on her phone. But she could feel his glances every time he took a sip, the clink of his mug as it settled back onto the table drawing her attention. Finally, with a soft rustle, he set the newspaper down.

"Hiya," he called to her, his voice breaking the quiet tension between them.

Abby glanced up, caught a little off guard.

"Are ye from the States?" His question hung in the air, casual yet curious.

A flicker of confusion crossed her face. "Yes, but how?"

He pointed to her cap, the stitching on the front revealing the Chicago Bears logo.

Abby felt a rush of embarrassment as the realization dawned on her. *But of course, that's why he was looking at her.*

"I went to university in Chicago," he added.

"But your accent ... you aren't from there." Abby noted his thick brogue.

"Aye, I moved here with my mum when I was a wee lad. My da remained in the States. When I was nearly sixteen, I gave my mum a bit of an attitude. She threw me off to my da. Good thing. He didn't put up with anything I was putting out," he recalled.

"You didn't want to stay in the States?" Abby asked.

"I stayed through university. But Scotland is my home. It's where I belong. A better man, though, or so my mother said, because of my da," he explained. "But if I may correct ye, it's not I who speaks with an accent."

Abby laughed at the realization.

The man's lips curved into a smile, dimples deepening on his cheeks. A flicker of mischievousness sparked in his stormy blue-gray eyes, hinting at the rebellious teenager hidden beneath the mature, polished facade.

"That's got to feel good," Hazel said, grabbing Abby's almost-empty plate. "A full belly and a smile on your face. Agatha will be pleased to learn of it."

Pink tinged Abby's face. "It was delicious. Thank you."

"Anythin' else for ya, then?" Hazel asked.

Abby thought about it. "I need some maps. Is there a tourist office nearby?"

"Where are ye staying? The hotel across the street?" The man pointed out the window. "They should have a good collection of maps and tourist information."

"She's staying at Agatha's," Hazel interjected.

"Then you're staying at Brynmoor," the man said matter-of-factly.

Although he seemed friendly enough, Abby wasn't sure she should confirm or deny the place she was staying. This was the first time in her life she was traveling alone— without Marcus at her side to guide or protect her, if need be.

"I'm here to tour gardens, mostly," she answered with no commitment. "Did you know there are over twenty-two garden tours in Perth and Kinross alone?"

"Aye, well, I might have a little knowledge of that." The man grinned. "You'll find twenty-four more in Stirlingshire, and another twelve in Fife. But check the openings before you visit. Some aren't open all year round, and they have special times they're open to visitors," he noted.

"I'll do that." Abby nodded.

"Not here for the castles then?" he continued, closing his paper and folding it. "There's one around every corner."

"I'm here for ..." She paused, her breath catching. She was there to do anything but face her life. "I'm here for it all," she finally said.

"Aye, ye might need to come back to accomplish that goal." He chuckled, his eyes meeting hers. "Scotland has a way of getting under your skin. Ye might fall in love and may never want to leave."

Abby scrutinized his gaze. There was something about his tone that made her feel his words were a prediction, or maybe a warning.

"Here's ya coffee," Hazel said, placing a paper cup in front of Abby. "It's rather cold out, and you'll be wantin' to walk around the town for a bit. Check out the chocolate store—no one makes truffles like Andrea. She's not born a Scot—married to a Fraser—but we don't hold that against her." Hazel smiled, revealing her laugh lines—stories of her life etched on her face. "Now, anythin' else?"

Abby shook her head. "Just the bill, please."

"Already taken care of," she said, putting up a hand. "Agatha insisted." Hazel winked. "Since she technically kicked you out."

Abby wondered what exactly Mrs. Landry had told Hazel. She had fled home seeking anonymity—a place to disappear and avoid life. Yet, here she was, already found out, at least between Mrs. Landry and Hazel. The thought of being looked after, or worse, pitied unsettled her. "It is quite unnecessary, but I'll be sure to thank her," Abby said, not sure if she was ready to be grateful for being cared for, or if it made her feel exposed.

She rose, put on her coat, and grabbed her scarf. When she turned back to bid the man farewell, he was gone. Looking through the window, she saw him already across the street, pulling open his shop door. That is when she noticed the name scrolled across the window: *Flowers of Muir.*

19

CURIOSITY

Mrs. *Landry was right*, Abby thought. Getting out was doing her some good. The sharp, fresh country air nipped at her cheeks and filled her lungs, drawing her out of the haze she had been in. She drew in a breath; the brisk cold urged her to quicken her pace. It lifted her spirits to walk among the living again and hear the fragments of conversations of strangers around her, the excited laughter of children exploring the store windows, and the steady rhythm of footsteps on the street. The buzz of energy tempted her to imagine the next few days—places to go, things to do—as if the world was waiting for her to wake up.

She stopped at the local tourist shop and gathered a stack of maps and brochures of the various sites and tours. A chocolate store next door enticed her to buy a bag of dark chocolate caramels, and she couldn't resist buying some lotion from an old-fashioned apothecary shop. Passing by a clothing store, she pressed against the window to peer inside. The wool sweaters of Scotland tempted her, but she decided to pass. There would be plenty of time to browse through stores—she was in no hurry. The time was all hers, and she was free to do with it as she willed. The thought both excited her and burdened her heart, a guilt she couldn't quite shake, even in moments like this.

As she turned away, her reflection in the glass caught her eye. She paused, her fingers brushing her lips, surprised to find a quiet smile she hadn't realized was there. It wasn't joy exactly, but something softer, a momentary peace amid the storm—a reprieve.

Heading back to the inn, she came upon the flower shop the man from breakfast had disappeared into. Looking inside, she saw that the man was talking to an older woman who was pointing to a bucket of ranunculus. He gathered two bunches and began wrapping them in paper when he caught Abby standing outside. He motioned for her to come in.

Abby balked, stepping away from his purview. But before she could turn away and run, he rushed to the door, opening it for her.

"I didn't mean to interrupt you," Abby said. "I was just looking to see what your shop looked like. It's a flower shop," she said, embarrassed about her earlier comments.

Of course he knew about the gardens in Scotland.

"I love flowers," she blurted out, trying to explain her lingering at his window.

"Aye, ye mentioned earlier," he said, releasing a smile. "Please, don't keep standing there like a stranger ..." He gestured for her to enter.

Abby tugged at her scarf, eyeing the hill to the inn. All she wanted was a glimpse inside. Flower shops were her sanctuary, her Disneyland. Back home, she'd lose hours wandering through flower shops, studying the arrangements, watching florists work with a kind of artistry that felt almost sacred.

Once, a store owner had even offered her a job because she visited so often. She laughed it off, too busy with her kids to take it seriously, but the idea lingered—a career filled with blooms and beauty. If only.

Abby reached for her phone to check the time, but halted, letting the device slip through her fingers and fall to the bottom of her purse. "If you really don't mind ..." she said, following him through the threshold.

The shop was no less than charming, almost magical. The building was ancient, eighteenth century, he mentioned as they entered. Thick walls made of stone and timber beams across the ceiling caused the space to be dark and cool. But a three-tiered crystal chandelier that hung from the highest pitch of the ceiling centered the room, and the two large windows at the front of the shop easily compensated for the tenebrosity of the aged building. Suspended from the other beams were flowers, bunched and dried, tied with ribbons of twine and satin, which created the impression of a field of wildflowers floating in the sky.

The air inside was heavy with mingling scents like musk, roses, and lilac, but it was a vase in the center of the shop that demanded Abby's attention. Walking up to it, she leaned in, lifted a lily to her nose, and inhaled the sweet scent, the colors and textures awakening something deep inside her.

To the left was a glass refrigerator showcasing fresh flowers in tin buckets, while on the right, an antique buffet displayed gift items from English linens, art books, and candles. Abby picked up a frame, turned it over, and noted the expensive price tag before gently putting it back down. Atop the buffet sat live topiaries in varying shapes and sizes. She brushed her fingers across the glossy leaves and sniffed the earthy fragrance, their oils clinging to her skin. Every corner of the shop felt alive with care and devotion, a place where the love of flowers and beauty thrived.

A bell jingled as an old woman walked in, cane in hand, disrupting Abby's dreamlike browsing.

"Mrs. Henry, fine day, isn't it?" the owner greeted. He rushed to her, taking her arm, leading her to his counter, making sure her feet held steady across the uneven floors.

"Good day, Mr. Emerson," the old woman replied in a scratchy voice. "Mr. Henry is in the mood for heather. He always loved the smell of heather."

"You'd be just in luck. I got a delivery early this morning. Let me take a peek in the back and grab ye a bunch." He winked and disappeared through a draped doorway.

Abby glanced at the old woman, who sat herself down in an overstuffed chair near the register. It had a high back and rolled arms, with a matching lumbar pillow, perfect for the comfort of an older lady who needed to rest her feet while waiting for an order. Abby wondered if someone had placed it there just for her. When the older woman looked up, Abby smiled at her.

"Mr. Henry was a horticulturist. He loved his flowers," she explained. "But who doesn't love flowers?" The woman closed her eyes and leaned her head back. "Who doesn't love flowers?"

The shop owner returned and laid the heather bunches on his counter to wrap. After putting a green ribbon at the end, he handed the bouquet to the elderly woman. Lending his hand, he helped her up from the cushioned seat and then walked her to the door.

"You'll put them on my tab, now, won't you?"

"Aye, Mrs. Henry, like I always do."

"You're a dear man, Mr. Emerson. If I was just a little younger ..." She winked at him.

He smiled at her, waving goodbye, before he turned his attention back to Abby.

"That was sweet," Abby said, eyeing the old woman as she wandered out of sight. "It was like watching a dance between you two."

A smile tugged at the corners of his mouth. "Aye, well, she's a good woman. We've known each other for a long time. You get to know how to step with someone, like a waltz."

"And Mr. Henry?"

"Passed a year ago. She comes in here every week for flowers to set upon his grave," he explained. "It keeps her connected to him."

"What a lovely tribute ... to love someone so dearly," Abby said, the thought drawing her back to her own memories. They seemed so far away now.

The owner tilted his head, and his eyes fell to hers, as if reading her thoughts. Did he sense it—the sadness she carried within?

Abby quickly turned away. "May I go in?" she asked, pointing to the glass refrigerator.

"By all means." He cued her to the door. "It's unlocked."

She tipped her head with gratitude and opened the door, quickly closing it behind her to seal the glass house that preserved the flowers. Cold air surrounded her, causing her to shiver. She twisted her scarf tighter around her neck, welcoming the frosty air filled with intoxicating scents. She glanced outward, through the glass barrier, only to find the owner's eyes hadn't left her. She shivered again.

The door of the store opened, and two ladies walked in, distracting him. They said something to him and he disappeared into the back, leaving Abby alone to drift from bucket to bucket, brushing her fingertips along the stems and cradling their leaves, or diving her nose into the centers of the blooms, inhaling the scents, as if they could fill her emptiness.

A gush of warm air breezed in, and Abby heard the door seal shut. She turned to find the owner standing next to her.

"Ye love flowers," he said plainly. "Ye greet them, as if friends. I know a fellow lover. It's the way ye touch them."

"Oh." Abby blushed. He had been watching her. Now he was standing next to her, the two of them tightly squeezed into the refrigerated space meant for one. Abby swallowed, a feeling of panic washing over her. She hadn't noticed when they met how tall he actually was, or the faint creases of time etched on his face. By years of laughter? Thoughts? Heartache? Did it matter? The effects were a kind of hand-someness that didn't fade but evolved, growing only richer with time. Silver flecked his well-groomed beard, and his eyes were framed in crow's feet, their warmth contrasting with the sharp angles of his jawline. The ridge of his nose was slightly crooked, a feature that should have detracted from his good looks, but somehow didn't. It suited him, although she couldn't explain how; she felt as if she had already known him for a very long time.

It suddenly dawned on her that she had been staring at him. How long, she didn't know, but the effects were the same. Embarrassment washed over her, sending a rush of red to her face. She eyed the door but knew she would have to press against him to get to it. That wasn't an option.

He didn't seem to notice, or if he did, he dismissed it, glancing over her, as if distracted by something. When he looked back, he seemed to have forgiven her for her indiscre-tion. "Are ye in the business, then … of flowers?"

Abby shook her head, amused by the notion. "No. But I'm an avid gardener when the weather allows. I've had a passion since I was a little girl. My mother gardened, and I'd help. I couldn't wait to get my fingers in the soil, bringing to life that which was once dead, watching life bloom before me. It's truly magical." She looked up and found him staring. "Well, you obviously get it. You have this beautiful store."

"Kindred spirits," he proclaimed with a gentle smile.

It was his smile, or maybe it was the warmth in his eyes. Had she not seen him use it on the women in the café and the customers in his store? As if he had a power, she felt the compelled to reveal more. "I always wanted to open a flower shop. Although I majored in business, I studied color theory and art history, with the hope of one day owning a floral business. It never happened, though." Snapshots of her life—college, jobs, marriage, kids—flashed in her head, and a sinking feeling of how quickly life had passed by settled in her chest. "Had it," she continued, gesturing to the store outside of the glass refrigerator, "it would be something exactly like this."

He followed her gaze around his store, then looked back at her. "Why didn't ye ... try for your dream?"

"Oh," Abby said, brushing off the depth of his question. "It was a childish fantasy. Like wanting to become a famous actor or a star athlete."

He lifted his brow. "Don't people become star athletes and famous actors where ye come from?"

Abby smirked. "You know what I mean. Besides, doesn't every little girl imagine a life of fairies and flowers?"

"No, but everyone does have dreams of some sort. My wife did, and we opened this shop. She was passionate about flowers. A passion she got me to believe in. And we made it happen."

His eyes lit up with the mention of his wife. It was obvious that she was his spark for life, for love, for inspiration, to open a beautiful business together. "Or maybe she was so intoxicating you couldn't resist?" Abby teased.

He chuckled, revealing the soft lines of his eyes. "Aye, well, that is possibly more true."

Abby couldn't help but bathe in his joy, unable to stop her face lighting up with a smile. "She must be very special. Will I meet her?"

The man's smile suddenly disappeared, as if a switch had been turned off. He cleared his throat. "My wife passed away several years ago."

Abby felt a pit in her stomach, her smile fading. "I ... I'm so sorry."

He shook his head. "No, don't. It has been many years; you'd think it wouldn't be so hard to explain." His lips curved gently as if the memories still lingered close. "We had a wonderful life together."

When he looked up, Abby caught his gaze. His blue eyes reflected gray in the dimmed light of the store, but their meaning was not lost; his loss was great, but his love was greater. Instinctually, she wanted to reach out ... share in something larger than herself.

She extended her hand. "I'm Abby, by the way. I heard Hazel call you Thom?"

"Aye, Thom Emerson."

His shake was firm, his hand enveloping hers in a mighty grip. Overwhelmed by the warmth of his touch, she quickly retreated and shoved her hands in her coat pockets.

He quirked a small smile. "It's cold in here, why don't we ..." He gestured to the glass door.

Abby followed him out, stopping short of leaving. She nodded in the direction of the shop's sign. "I know you're going to find this foolish, but I came to Scotland because of your shop. In a roundabout way."

Thom's eyes widened. "Really?"

"The Flowers of Muir," she said. "My grandmother told me the story. I'd imagine myself the little girl, running to the land where the Muir fairies lived to hide from all my woes ... well, woes of a little girl." Abby laughed. Remembering. "It was a place where all my dreams would magically come true."

"I'm not surprised about ye coming to Scotland with hopes of finding a magical fairyland. Those are ten-a-penny here." He brought his hand to his stubbled chin. "I'm just surprised an American woman would know of it. My wife used to tell the tale to my daughter when she was a little girl. It was a story handed down to her by her mother, and her mother before her. When it came to the naming of the store, it was only obvious we would name it after the fairy tale, the magic of flowers, and the power of love."

"I agree," Abby said, her voice lifting with an unanticipated octave of excitement. It was a sign—like the universe was telling her she was exactly where she needed to be. "It's a perfect name."

Thom smiled softly, his eyes expressive, quietly urging her to share more.

"My grandmother was Scottish," Abby began. "She grew up in a small village closer to Crieff. I don't know ... coming to her homeland seemed like the perfect place to run—" She stopped herself. "Anyway, I want to visit the beautiful gardens I've heard so much about," she added quickly, "and the castles, of course."

Thom nodded slightly, a soft chuckle escaping. "Of course."

For a moment, they held each other's gaze. Was there more to say? It felt as though they were old friends rather than strangers who had just met. The thought lingered—she could talk with him longer, but it was absurd. They didn't really know each other. She shrugged, brushing the notion aside. "Well, I should be going. You must have a lot of work to do."

"Aye," he murmured, glancing at the pile of papers sitting atop his counter.

Abby reached for the door.

"Abby," he said, stopping her. His eyes narrowed on her, his expression intent. "Ye know, your dream isn't foolish. My wife, Coira, had many of them. We tried very hard to achieve as many as possible before she died. She said, 'Life is not to be wasted on daydreaming, but doing.' Unfortunately, she ran out of time to see everything come to fruition. But she left damn well trying. As long as ye have breath, there's still time to make something beautiful. Don't let it pass ye by."

This was the second time Abby had the urge to reach out to him, but she held back, standing mute, staring at him.

"I've made you speechless," he mused, a glint in his eye. "Don't mind me. I'm just spewing out my bit of wisdom to anyone who will listen ... so my daughter says." He raised his hands, palms out, as Abby shifted. "Hold on—don't leave yet. What's your favorite flower?"

"Hmm." She scratched her head. "That's like asking who your favorite child is."

He laughed. "Alrighty then, your favorite color?"

"Yellow," she exclaimed. "It's such a happy color. A bouquet of daffodils, sunflowers, or daisies is like holding sunlight in your hands." Abby blushed. "I don't know why I just told you that. Kind of silly, really."

"Naw, you described it perfectly." He grabbed branches from a tin, water dripping from the ends. "These are called solidaster, a cross between an aster and solidago," he explained as he ran his fingers through the lacy leaf. "They make a great filler for arrangements, but on their own, in a vase, it's like sunshine bursting from the glass."

He scooped three more bunches from the bucket, walked out to his counter where he wrapped them up, and handed them to her. "Ye shall have a bit of sunshine to take with ye."

"I can't take those. At least let me pay you for them," Abby insisted, taking out her wallet.

He brushed away her outstretched hand. "They're a gift," he replied. "Your love of flowers honors me."

Abby couldn't remember the last time someone gave her flowers. "You're very kind," she said, cradling the bunch in one arm. "Thank you."

"It was my pleasure, really. Maybe they'll inspire ye to keep dreaming."

A wave of gratitude washed over Abby, but she was relieved when a young woman walked in with a child in tow, distracting Thom. The interruption gave her the perfect excuse to escape with nothing more than a quick wave good-bye. Had the woman not appeared, she might have done something foolish—flown in his arms for a hug or, worse, cried.

As the door shut behind her, she paused at the curb, glancing back at the shop. The flowers in her arms felt heavier now, their sentiment pressing against her like an unspoken question.

What was that all about?

20

NOT INVISIBLE

The wind was colder than Abby expected when she opened the front door. She pulled up the collar of her coat and braced herself for the walk to the tavern Mrs. Landry had suggested for dinner that evening.

"You can't miss it. Just keep heading down, and when you come upon a big sign with a pig on it, that's Dunbar's."

"I think I can see it from my bedroom window ... at the end of the main street, right?" Abby recalled seeing the sign blowing back and forth in the wind.

"Aye," Mrs. Landry confirmed. Eyeing Abby from head to toe, she noted, "You're lookin' mighty pretty with your hair done and color in your cheeks."

Abby ran her fingers through her hair. It had been some time since she'd styled it, curling it and brushing bangs into a sweeping curtain across her face. Before she left the room, she glanced in the mirror. The image stopped her. Dressed in a pink silk blouse, straight jeans, and a pair of short boots, she almost didn't recognize the thinner woman with her hair tucked behind one ear and an earring dangling from it.

While shopping that afternoon, she had found the earrings—crafted from heather and designed with a Celtic Tree of Life, or the *Crann Bethadh*. The salesperson explained that the symbol stood for strength and wisdom, particularly female strength. As if an invisible hand were pushing her, Abby bought them. Now, as they looped through her ears, she could almost feel an inexplicable energy stir within her.

"You were right," Abby admitted, her fingers brushing the heather earrings. "It was time. Time to get out again."

"Oh, I was doin' what I'd do to my own," Mrs. Landry said, handing Abby her scarf hanging by the door. "You'd have gotten there, eventually. I was just pushin' ya along. Now get out and put some food in ya. You'll have no energy to do it again tomorrow if you don't."

Abby looped her scarf around her neck. "Will you be up when I get back?"

"Naw. I'm an old woman. I'll be sleeping before you get to the end of the street. I'll leave the light on."

Abby nodded, and without apology, hugged Mrs. Landry. "Goodnight," she said. She shoved her hands in her pockets and began her descent down the hill to town.

Abby walked through the darkening streets, the adventures of the day lifting her spirits. The town was quiet compared to the afternoon when people had crowded the town center, browsing the shops. Now, in the dark, few people were trampling the pavement. An elderly man was sitting on a bench in a corner park, drinking from a coffee cup; his little dog huddled against him, stealing the old man's warmth. He smiled at Abby as she walked by, and she gave him a wave in return.

Further ahead, Abby came upon a mother who was bending over her daughter, securing her coat. The young girl was squirming as her mother wrestled her little arm into the sleeve. As she passed them, thoughts of Emma at the same age stirred a longing for the days when her kids were small, needing her constantly. She took a deep breath, and retrieving her phone, typed *Emma* and *Drew*. An old group chat came up.

Miss you both. Love you! she typed and hit send.

She stared at the screen, knowing a response was unlikely —they were both busy with their lives. A faint ache rose in her chest, realizing how far apart they had grown. Lost in thought, she almost scrolled by Marcus's name on her chat list. Her finger hovered over his name.

A tug on her coat startled her. Abby peered at the little girl now snug in her coat, buttoned crooked at the belly, who was looking up at her.

"Mummy told me to give this to you," the girl said, gripping her scarf in her tiny hand.

"Oh my, how did that fall off?" She took the scarf from the girl, thanking her with a smile, and waved to her mother, who nodded in reply. Scarf and phone in hand, Abby promptly dropped them into her purse and continued down the street.

Abby spotted the sign with the pig, lit from above. The door opened as a couple walked out, music spilling into the street. She grabbed the handle before it closed and stepped inside. A man behind the bar turned in her direction and told her to sit anywhere. Abby scanned the room for a cozy seat, away from the larger crowds. Most tables were occupied, but there was a table tucked in the back, against the wall, with room for her and her purse. She scooted past a couple at the table beside her, took off her coat, slung it over the chair across from her, and sat down, claiming her space. A server promptly dropped off a menu, and Abby ordered a glass of wine before she darted off.

From her table in the back, Abby had a good view of the

pub. It was an authentic pub, housed in a seventeenth-century building with paned windows, wood-paneled walls, and a low beamed ceiling. A long bar greeted patrons as they entered, while small round tables scattered around the wide-planked wooden floor. A large fireplace, surrounded by river rock, with a roaring fire in its bowels, was against the wall on one side, while bench-seat tables lined the other side. Three young men in the corner, their bodies balancing on stools, played instruments, while a woman sang, her rich, sultry voice filling the room with Scottish folk songs. Chatter and laughter wove through the space, mingling with the music.

Abby watched the server give the bartender her order as he simultaneously poured whiskey into a glass. A young girl, no more than twenty, walked up and flashed him a smile. She flipped her red curls to her back and leaned closer, whispering something in his ear. The bartender turned, filled a pint, and handed it to her, before leaving Abby's wineglass to the side for the server to pick up.

"First time here?" the lady next to Abby asked, drawing her away from the happenings at the bar.

Abby smirked, comparing her own silk blouse and sleek boots with the attire of the bearded men with cabled crew-necks and the women layered in long-sleeve knits and cardigans. They all wore boots made to tread wet and wobbly streets. "I stand out like a tourist, don't I?"

"Well, usually no, but during this time of year, it's more of a local pub," the woman explained. "We crawl out into the cold from our daily routines, don rugged boots and woolen sweaters, to grab a pint, a hot meal, and some local music."

"Mrs. Landry sent me—" Abby started to say.

"Ah, so you're at the Brynmoor Inn, then, with Agatha," the lady said. "A wee bit empty this time of year. Agatha usually has a full house from April 'til October. Cozy little place, though, all year round."

"Yes, very," Abby agreed. "I'm lucky to have the place to myself. I'm liking the quiet."

"I reckon it will get busier in a few more weeks. As soon as the weather warms." The woman eyed the empty seat across from Abby, her coat over the top. "Not travelin' with anyone?" the woman asked.

Abby hesitated, twisting her wedding ring around her finger. She shook her head. "No."

The woman winked. "Havin' a vacation just for you, then?"

Abby nodded. There was nothing more to explain.

"You've picked a mighty fine town. Although it's best known for our beautiful flowering spring and our temperate weather in the summer, my husband and I wouldn't trade the winters here for anything." She referenced to her husband sitting across from her, who was partially paying attention to his wife, but listening more to the band across the room. "The cold makes a nice reason to cozy up." She reached over and squeezed her husband's hand. He turned to her and brought her hand to his lips.

As the couple shared a moment of tenderness, it stirred a pang in Abby. It wasn't jealousy, per se … it was loss. When the waitress reappeared, she turned to them, breaking the moment. "Any suggestions?"

"Well, Dunbar's cook is a mighty good one. You'll have to come back a few times before you taste it all," the woman's husband said, meeting Abby's gaze. His rugged beard and faint crow's feet hinted at his age, but the brightness of his eyes gave away his youth. Abby guessed they were both at least ten years her junior. "You won't be disappointed with the steak and Guinness stew." A boyish grin crossed his face, solidifying her impression.

"Don't listen to my Brannan. It's the only thing he orders here," the woman said as she slapped his arm. "I wish he felt so enamored with my stew."

Her husband flashed a smile. "Aye, well, 'tis as good as yours," he boasted, giving her a wink.

They both laughed.

The waitress tapped her pen against her pad, an expression easily readable, a blend of patience and expectation.

The woman's hand shot up, her voice bubbling with enthusiasm. "Oh, please join us. We're practically havin' dinner together already, the way they have these tables so close." She gestured toward the narrow space between them. "We'll have three stews and another round of drinks," she said to the server, sending her off. "I'm Effemy and this here is my Brannan."

The man nodded at Abby.

"You're very kind, but I don't want to impose ..."

"Ah, not even a second thought. You'll make it a wee bit of fun. We've some friends comin' ..." The woman halted, her eyes lighting up. "Ah, there they are." She waved at the couple entering the pub. "Over here," she called.

Her friends responded with smiles and headed toward them.

Abby's heart skipped a beat, a mix of surprise and something else she couldn't quite name, when she saw Thom Emerson, his hand on the small of the woman's back. They halted at the table.

"It's ye?" Thom said.

Abby nodded.

"You know each other?" Effemy questioned.

"No," Abby insisted.

"Aye," Thom corrected her.

Effemy's brow shot up.

"We just met today ... at Scran," Abby explained.

"Technically, it was at my shop," Thom corrected her. He extended his hand to her. "It's nice to see ye again."

"Yes, of course." Abby found his warm hand wrapped around hers hauntingly familiar.

Stepping aside, he introduced the woman standing to his right. "This is Mairi." He quickly added, "She and Effemy are school mates."

"What Thom means is that we're both teachers at the same school," she explained, and shook Abby's hand. "May I scoot in?"

Abby bowed her head, and the woman seated herself next to her. As she moved closer, Abby inhaled the sweet scent of her perfume. She thought it matched her appearance. It was pretty, like her. The kind of beauty men notice across the room. Her green eyes dazzled against her creamy complexion, which was dusted with freckles that softened her beauty. Red ringlets framed her oval-shaped face, falling along her shoulders and stopping just above her breasts. She wasn't overtly sexy, the cream turtleneck sweater and fitted jeans she was wearing were modest, but nothing could conceal her fit and shapely figure.

For a fleeting moment, Abby envied her, so effortlessly lovely, as if life had been especially kind. But when their eyes met, Mairi's warm smile revealed a flicker of something familiar—a quiet ache of emptiness.

Thom dragged the chair from the table, the legs scuffing across the floor, turning her attention. "We seem to be crossing paths," he said with a smile.

"So, it seems," Abby replied, her words measured. She

wasn't sure if she was pleased to see him again or unsettled by how easily his presence seemed to draw her in.

"Aye, the town's small. No doubt we'll see each other again. That's if you're staying long enough. Are ye, then? Planning on staying long?"

Abby shook her head.

"Too bad," he replied.

"What would you like to drink?" The waitress said, interrupting Abby before she could read into his meaning.

Did he have a meaning?

Drinks arrived quickly, and with them, conversation flowed as easily as the laughter around the table. Effemy and Brannan shared stories of their two young boys, revealing that they were high school sweethearts still madly in love. Mairi spoke of her life as a widow with a son in university. She lived alone, not far from town or from the school where she taught—third grade for her, fifth for Effemy. Thom regaled them with humorous tales of his granddaughters, their recent shenanigans causing laughter among the group.

Abby couldn't help but smile. Their stories were simple, yet they held a way of making her feel included. The easy camaraderie among them reminded her of how much she'd been missing by hiding away.

"So, Abby," Mairi said, turning the table's attention to her. "What brings you here, to our little village?"

"Oh, I ..." Abby swallowed, searching for an answer—anything to steer them away from the truth.

I ran away ... from my family, my husband, my life!

As if she could sense Abby's unease, Effemy leaned in, her tone conspiratorial. "She escaped for a holiday! I think it's brilliant, gettin' away all on your own. Lord knows a woman needs that once in a while."

Abby's eyes softened, her heart slowing as she nodded to

Effemy. "My daughter is away at college, busy living her life ... being in love. And my son will graduate from high school soon. He spends his days out with friends and only comes home when he's hungry." They all laughed, each knowing a teenager's appetite. "Anyway, it just seemed like a good time to take a break. So, here I am."

Thom tilted his head, his gaze steady, as if piecing together a puzzle. *What is he looking at?* Abby forced a faint smile, brushing her hair behind her ear. The way he looked at her unsettled her, as if he could see straight into the secrets she was keeping.

He lifted his glass to the group, breaking the moment before it unraveled further. "To escapes, big and small," Thom cheered, his gaze lingering on Abby a moment longer.

"Aye," they all shouted, raising their glasses with enthusiasm. The toast lingered, filling the group with joy, before they flagged the server for another round of drinks.

21

FLIRTING AGAIN

Abby was drunk.

She remembered ordering two glasses of wine, but as the evening continued, more glasses appeared. *Did she have a shot of whisky, maybe two?* She wasn't sure why she'd behaved in such a carefree way. Maybe even a little reckless. She could count on one hand how many times she had ever been drunk, and tonight was one of them.

Her new friends were equally intoxicated, or at least they should have been, with the amount of alcohol they consumed. With each empty drink, Brannan's hand shot in the air for the server to bring another. She remembered a half-empty bottle of whiskey left on the table but wasn't sure if it was the first one or the second one ordered.

Thom wasn't drunk. There was no slurring of words or staggering out of the pub for him when they all said goodbye. He was sober as a judge on duty when he offered to walk Abby home. She had no choice but to accept his offer. She had a hard time knowing which direction to go. He pointed upward, and she followed his lead. He kept pace with her slow and mostly steady stride, inching her forward and keeping her moving.

The streets were damp from a mist that lingered in the night's air. She prayed she didn't slip, or worse, fall. She didn't want to look foolish in front of a man she hardly knew. *Was he still considered a stranger?*

An icy breeze blew across her face, and Abby inhaled, hoping the crisp air would soon sober her up. She lifted her collar and hunkered into her coat, quickening her pace with the sight of the Brynmoor Inn ahead. She was eager to get back to her room, relieve Thom of chaperoning, and free herself from the warm, steady hand against her back.

"Ye warm enough?" Thom asked.

Abby nodded, noting he seemed immune to the cold. His wool coat hung open, a cashmere scarf casually draping around his neck. Unlike her own reddened cheeks, his showed no sign of the biting air, and his hand radiated warmth against her back. In contrast, her hands were buried deep in her pockets, her fingers tingling from the chill. It was a sign her senses were sharpening—the alcohol buzz fading, making her more aware that she was walking in the dark with an unfamiliar man. The shadows of the night made him seem taller and broader, a forceful presence next to her.

A sudden shiver ran through her, unbidden and sharp.

"Feeling better?" Thom asked, watching Abby's breath puff in the cold.

Abby nodded again.

"Scotland's weather can do that to ye ... force ye to drink too much but it quickly sobers ye up once outside."

Abby's cheeks flushed with embarrassment. She was grateful for his graciousness—not shaming her drunkenness. "You didn't have to walk me back," she said when they reached the door of the inn. "But I appreciate it." Her eyes steadied on him, no longer blurred by an alcoholic haze. "I really do."

"It's an unspoken Scottish rule. If there's a lassie who's had a wee bit too much drink ..." He smiled. "It's only proper to get her home safely."

"That's not a *thing*," she said, arching her brow.

"Aye, well, it's my take, then. When someone asks for directions, a true Scot will walk them to their location. But I might have changed the rule for my benefit."

His benefit?

"And what about Mairi?" Abby asked, wondering why he wasn't standing at her doorstep.

A sly grin tugged at Thom's lips. "Effemy and Brannan pass her place," he quipped.

Abby noted he hadn't answered the question. "I enjoyed meeting her. She's smart, and pretty."

"Aye."

Abby laughed, all too familiar with the art of avoidance. She'd been practicing it herself all night. She tried again. "Do you two spend much together?"

Thom's lips moved upward, his facial hair disguising the full value of his smirk. "We keep busy enough when our schedules allow." He leaned against the frame of the door, moving closer to Abby. "Did ye find your maps, then? Plan out your stay?"

Abby let the change of subject pass. "I did. Thanks for your help. There seem to be treasures around every corner in Scotland. I don't know if I'll fit it all in." She looked out, the moonlight casting shadows obscuring the lochs and woodlands waiting to be explored, then turned back to him. "My husband and I planned to visit when the kids got older, but life got busy, things like braces and tutors taking priority. We spent most vacations touring local attractions or historic sites." She paused, remembering back to when she'd slather sunscreen on the kids, screaming in protest, as they traipsed through trails and hiked up hills. "My husband would announce, 'We're going on an adventure!' and we'd pretend to be out-of-towners with guidebooks and maps in hand. The kids would fight, and someone would end up crying—sometimes it would be me." She brought her hand to her lips to cover up the laugh escaping her. "In the end, the memories were worth it."

Thom fixed his gaze on her. "That's the first time you mentioned him ... your husband."

"What?" Abby asked, feigning surprise.

"Your husband," Thom repeated. "Ye talked about your kids—one graduating, the other busy with a lad at university —but ..."

"Didn't I?" Abby said, turning away, her eyes shifting to a distant tree, seeking anything to focus on other than him. "We've been married for years." Abby laughed nervously. "I guess it's old age settling in."

"Abby," Thom interrupted. "Yer a tidy lass. Ye may be forgetful, but it's not your aging to worry about."

A rush of heat spread through her, Thom's deep tone and slow cadence making the compliment feel too personal.

Was it?

He stroked his graying beard. "I'm a wee bit more familiar with aging than ye might be."

Abby eyed the silver flecks and laughed. "Well, it suits you." When a smile spread across his face, she immediately regretted her words. "It's late," she uttered. "I wouldn't want Mrs. Landry to worry." She reached for the handle of the door, but it wouldn't budge. She fought with it, wanting to move it by sheer will, and prayed Mrs. Landry hadn't lock her out.

Thom slipped his body between her and the door, and with one push from his shoulder, the door swung open. "It's an old door," he explained.

"Thank you," she muttered, crossing the threshold. "It was a fun evening," she said, sinking into the darkened entry.

"Aye, it was fate to have run into ye," Thom replied. "Maybe we'll be lucky again before you leave."

"That would be nice," Abby said, not sure why she agreed. *Did he think she was flirting? Was she?* She retreated further inside, her body slipping into the shadows.

He turned and began to walk away, his voice drifting toward her. "G'night, Abby," he said.

He put his hand in his pocket and whistled into the night's air, the tune echoing between the buildings. His silhouette grew smaller with each step as he drew farther away, never looking back. Abby didn't close the door until he disappeared from sight.

22

LIFE STORIES

"Mairi's waiting for you at the door, dear," Mrs. Landry's craggy voice called to Abby.

"I'll be right down," she shouted, putting on the last touches of makeup.

Three outfits lay discarded on the floor before she settled on jeans, a white long-sleeve T-shirt, treaded boots—essential for Scotland's muddy, wet terrain—and a plaid wool scarf she'd bought in Aberfeldy during a bit of retail therapy. *Why was she making such a fuss?* Truth be known, it was less about the outing and more about wanting to make a better impression on the women this time. She cringed, remembering how she had stumbled through the pub, ambling between tables in a rush to leave, only for Thom to steady her with a hand on her waist and whisper, "I've got ye."

She cringed again, accompanied by a flash of heat.

When she had parted with Thom that evening and heard Effemy slur, "I'll be callin' you ... we'll have a girls' day out," she assumed it was said out of drunkenness. After all, they were mere strangers who'd shared an evening of food and drinks. So, when Effemy called a few days later, she accepted the invite, admittedly eager to welcome their company again.

It was rare Abby was alone, by herself. Marcus and the kids were her constant companions. Then there was always Jossi, but she was nowhere to be seen. To say Abby was lonely wasn't quite the word. She wasn't. She had her thoughts keeping her company. She had all of Scotland to keep her preoccupied. However, as beautiful as the Scottish countryside was, wandering through echoing abbeys, hollowed castles, and hushed museums only highlighted her aloneness. Tours and sightseeing, especially among tourist groups made up of families and friends, only amplified her solitude and didn't fill the void she was feeling.

Habit, or maybe guilt, was pushing her to call Marcus, to say she was coming home. But she hesitated, never following through with the task. Deep down, she felt something wasn't quite healed. Not yet.

Abby lingered for a moment, staring at her reflection, as if it might hold the answers she sought. Instead, it only sent her spiraling into thoughts, wondering if she'd ever find them. With a shake of her head, she dabbed a tissue against her lips, spritzed perfume on her neck, and grabbed her coat. Slinging her purse over her shoulder, she headed downstairs.

"Oh, don't you look pretty," Mairi said, meeting her at the door. "Effemy is waiting for us in the car."

Abby peered out, seeing Effemy sitting at the wheel of a small SUV.

She stuck her head out the window. "Sit in the front, Abby. I want you to see the views as we drive."

Abby glanced at Mairi, who gave her a nod of encouragement, and then crawled into the passenger seat.

They hadn't made it down the street when Effemy slowed the car. Thom was ahead, balancing a stack of boxes as he made his way toward the shop door. Effemy gave a quick honk, catching his attention just before he disappeared inside.

Thom turned, gleamed a smile as he recognized them, and motioned for them to stop.

Effemy rolled down the side window. "Hiya, Thom."

Setting down his boxes, Thom leaned into the car. "Abby! We see each other again. I looked for ye at Scran, but ye haven't been all week."

"Oh," she said with surprise. "I've been busy." Which wasn't a lie—she had filled her days with tours and sightseeing. But if she was honest, she avoided Hazel's café, knowing he might be there. Why? She wasn't quite sure. It wasn't him. His behavior was nothing short of a gentleman. It was her. His presence unsettled her, drawing her in ways she wasn't ready to admit—should admit—even to herself.

"As it should be," he said with a wink, seemingly oblivious to the way his presence affected her. He turned to the others. "A bunch of lovely ladies in for mischief, are ye? Where are ye off to?"

"Innerpeffray Library, maybe a stop in Crieff," Effemy said. "Any suggestions?"

"Not Greyfriars Burial Ground?" Thom suggested.

Effemy eyes widened. "Who wants to see dead people?"

"Oh, no," Mairi warned, rolling her eyes. "Sit back, Abby, this could be a while. Like rivaling kin, they battle about who knows the best of Scotland better."

"We're not *that* bad, are we?" Effemy asked Thom with a mock pout.

Thom grinned, a sly twinkle in his eyes. "Aye."

The banter flowed easily between them, their laughter mingling in the car. Abby leaned back in her seat, momentarily lost in their camaraderie. Yet, despite herself, her focus shifted to Thom. His voice, low and measured, seemed to wrap around her, lulling her into a trance.

She hadn't meant to let her guard down. Hadn't she avoided places where she might see him? Yet, here she was, caught off balance by his controlled cadence, the soft rise and fall of his accent, the effects like a gentle tide washing over her. *Was it a superpower?* His muted-red lips moved against the short gray of his beard, each word carefully formed, deliberate, drawing her in. The faint scent of his leather and musk lifted around her, a fragrance she now associated solely with him. He had worn it that night he walked her home, and she had carried the memory with her since.

"Abby?" Thom broke through her thoughts, drawing her back.

"Huh?" she stammered, startled.

"Which shall it be?" Effemy asked. "An old library and shopping around a quaint town, or exploring roadside ceme-teries and hiking through trails?"

Abby blinked, scrambling for the answer. "I ... I ..." Her tongue felt paralyzed. "Don't we have time for it all?" she managed, her voice faint.

Thom's smile widened, and he crossed his arms. "And there ye go ... a diplomat among us."

They all laughed, except for Abby. She shrugged, hoping her expression didn't betray her inner thoughts.

"I should go." Thom slapped the car door before pushing away.

"Hey, Thom." Effemy stopped him. "Busy tonight? Meet Brannan later at the house. We'll have drinks when we get back, maybe play some games."

"Sounds good," Thom agreed. "I'll bring some spirits." He glanced at Mairi. "Whiskey for ye?"

She signaled her approval with a wink, releasing a wide smile.

"And wine for ye," he said, glancing at Abby. "Have fun, lassies," he added, waving them goodbye.

Once they had cleared town, Effemy eyed Mairi in the back seat. "Wouldn't hurt ye to give him more of a chance."

Mairi moaned. "You know it's not that way between us."

"But yet you can lay with him all the same?"

Abby's eyes widened.

"What?" Effemy laughed at Abby's reaction. "You haven't wanted a man for a little romp?"

Abby shook her head, not ready to discuss her sex life with strangers.

Mairi reached over, softly touching Abby on the arm. "It's not what you think."

"Oh aye," Effemy scoffed, "what's it then?"

"Effemy, I'm not some kind of loose woman," Mairi said, her eyes narrowing. "And Thom's not that kind of man, either."

Effemy rolled her eyes. "Every man is *that* kind of man."

Mairi scoffed and sank back into her seat.

Abby said nothing, letting the two friends bicker about it. Besides, it was none of her business. The news merely confirmed her suspicion that Thom and Mairi were involved, albeit casually. It also explained Thom's reluctance to answer her questions the other night.

"All I'm saying," Effemy continued, "if you're gonna sleep with a man, you shouldn't pretend it means nothin'."

"Sure, you can say that because you have a man. And a fine one at that. Brannan loves you, and you love him equally," Mairi refuted. "Not everyone is lucky to have forever with someone, Effemy."

"Thom and Brannan have the same gold running through

their veins," Effemy reminded her, as if stating a fact obvious to anyone who knew them. "They're both priceless."

"My Lyall has been gone for a long time now." Mairi quickly did the sign of the cross. "And there's no one who can have my heart the way he did. Thom and I are ... well, let's just say we're broken. We understand that about each other. That's how it is between us."

Effemy pursed her lips. "So, you two aren't datin'?"

Mairi shook her head. "We spend time together, that's all," she said, adding, "but just as friends."

"Friends with benefits," Effemy quipped.

"Well," Mairi hawed. "Not anymore. It's only when the loneliness gets the best of us."

"I'd be lonely at least three times a week," Effemy teased, her eyes sparkling with mischief.

Mairi hit her on the arm.

"Ouch!" Effemy feigned pain, dramatically rubbing her arm.

They both laughed, sharing a playful banter that allowed them to support each other without judgment.

Abby wondered where Jossi was. Her absence was palpable—no head popping out from doorways or voice startling her from behind. She cleared her throat, pushing down her concern, and her hurt.

"We're sorry, Abby. We don't mean to unearth all our dark secrets with ya," Effemy patted her knee. "Sometimes it's good to unburden yourself."

Abby smiled. "No worries. Your secrets are safe with me."

Effemy's voice softened. "And yours are safe with us."

Abby nodded, feeling a gentle nudge to open up ... in time. She hesitated, then spoke. "You all seem so close. It's clear you've been through a lot together."

"Aye," said Mairi, with a wistful smile. "We've had our share of trials. It binds you in ways you don't expect."

Abby's thoughts snagged on Mairi's words. Was she speaking generally, or hinting about her relationship with Thom? She wasn't sure, or why she cared.

Yet curiosity—about one of them in particular—gnawed at her. She glanced at Effemy, steering the conversation in a direction that felt safer. "And Thom? He mentioned his late wife. What's his story?"

Effemy's expression softened. "Coira," she began, "was beautiful, and full of life. I don't think I knew a more suited couple. Unfortunately, she didn't survive a year after the diagnosis, leaving them little time to cope or say goodbye. Gosh, it's been"—she paused, calculating—"seven years now."

Mairi confirmed with a nod.

"Marleigh, their daughter, had just welcomed her first baby when Coira discovered the cancer," Effemy continued, keeping her eyes on the road. "It brought a little joy to a tragic situation. Coira said it was God's way of balancing things— one life for one death." She paused, as if saying a silent prayer. "Jenny, the youngest of the two, is a spittin' image of Coira—dark red hair curling in every direction. She would've liked that. And Caroline, the older one, is just like Thom— gray-blue eyes and an old soul." A smile crossed her face. "I think Coira made a deal when she got to heaven—two beautiful lives for her one."

"With Thom's stories of them, I feel like I already know them," Abby said, recalling the way his face lit up when he spoke of his granddaughters. "They seem like a close family."

"They are," Effemy said. "He dedicates himself to those girls. They are such a consolation to him."

Mairi gazed out the window. "Only the lucky survive

cancer," she said softly, her words carrying the faint echo of sadness.

"Is it luck?" Abby uttered under her breath.

Effemy shot a glance at Abby but didn't probe her for more. "Marleigh almost lost Thom, too," she continued. "After Thom's heart attack ..."

Abby gasped. "When was that?"

"It was about a year later, I'd say," Effemy said, turning to Abby. "I think the loss was more than his heart could take. One day, he collapsed in his shop. If a customer hadn't been there, he might have died. He was fortunate. We like to say Coira was looking out for him."

Mairi crossed herself again. "Thank God for the angels that watch over us."

"Actually, it wasn't an angel," Jossi's voice cut through, startling Abby. She turned sharply to find her sitting beside Mairi.

Jossi tipped her head. "He didn't want to go. His will to live outweighed his sorrow."

Abby stiffened, her breath catching. *How did she know?*

Mairi blinked twice at the vacant seat, then turned back to Abby. "You don't believe the dead can come back and watch over us?"

Abby squeezed her lids shut. *Go away! Go away! Go away!* When she opened them, the seat was empty. Relief washed over her, but a feeling of unease lingered. She glanced at Mairi, who stared at her, eyes questioning, waiting for her response.

"Yes, maybe they do," Abby said at last, her voice steady despite the truth echoing in her mind.

23

AWARENESS

Abby walked out of Scran, a large cup in hand, hoping it would be enough to get her through the evening. She had tried to excuse herself from Effemy's invitation to join them for drinks and games, but the two women would have nothing of it.

"Please, Abby," Mairi begged.

"You're one of us now. It wouldn't be the same without you," Effemy insisted.

After a day of laughter, the three of them behaving like college girls on spring break, her head was just now clearing, but her feet and back ached. Despite wanting to refuse, she found herself agreeing.

Abby gulped a long sip of her double espresso latte, gripping the cup as if it was a tossed raft saving her from drowning in the depths of the dark sea. It still did not prevent her from yawning. Rubbing the sting from her eyes, she spotted Thom across the street turning off his store lights, his dog following his every step. The big German shepherd ambled behind him and waited as he fumbled for his keys in his pocket, closed the door, and locked it.

"Hiya?" Thom shouted, waving his arm when he saw her. He dodged a few passing cars and crossed the street. The dog stayed put, deciding to lie down by the locked door instead. "How was your day with Effemy and Mairi?" he asked when he reached her.

Abby hesitated, caught off guard by the ease in his manner, as if they were old friends sharing their day. *Did she dare share all they had said and done?*

"Fun," was all she said, certifying the girl code Effemy, Mairi, and she now shared. But glancing at Thom, she couldn't help herself. A giddy laugh seemed to escape her. She quickly covered her mouth. She wasn't sure if it was about discovering Thom's relationship with Mairi or him standing in front of her, armed with a reciprocal grin, his sparkling eyes drawing her in. Whatever the cause, a mischievous smile spread across her face.

"What?" he questioned.

"Nothing."

"Humph, I'll bet." He smirked. "Those two can be trouble. I should've warned ye."

Abby shook her head, laughing softly, trying to deny it, but she knew exactly what he meant—Effemy was the ringleader of the mischief. From sneaking on private property exploring remnants of a laird's house—explained as the "right to roam" and perfectly legal in Scotland—to whiskey tasting before noon.

"Effemy nearly got me two dates with some college boys who worked at the distillery," Abby said, as she told him about the day. "She made me speak with a Scottish accent. No one was falling for it, though." She laughed. "I can't get the roll off the tongue just right. Then we did karaoke in a pub."

She paused, remembering the moment. When Abby had felt the vibration of her own voice in her chest, the sensation was both terrifying and thrilling. For once she wasn't thinking about what anyone else expected. It was just her, the music, and the moment.

"Me! Singing in front of strangers. Well, not strangers, per se. It was more like an elderly British couple having tea, three men drinking pints, and the bartender wiping down the counter. But an audience all the same." Abby grinned, the memory vivid and warm. She wondered briefly what Marcus would think. "My cheeks hurt from so much laughing," she said, her eyes lifting to meet Thom's, his smile matching hers.

"That sounds just like her." He chuckled. "And did ye get that date?"

Abby rolled her eyes and smirked. "I'm married, with nearly two grown children, remember?" She glanced away, but something lingered inside her, a newfound zeal, a glimmer of the woman she could be if she let herself take up space, let herself matter. For the first time, she wasn't afraid to shine.

Thom nodded. "It was a good day, then?"

"It was a good day." Abby beamed. "The best."

He pointed to her smile. "Scotland has her spell on ye. Your face is like looking at the Harvest Moon—shining brightly, full of light. It's a spectacle to be cherished," he said, unabashed at the meaning.

He used his superpower again, and she had to catch her breath. His eyes held hers, tempting her to dive in. She should have looked away, but she didn't. At that moment, she understood Mairi's struggle. It wasn't hard to see what he could offer.

Be careful, she warned herself. Or was it Jossi's voice whispering? Either way, she heeded the warning and stepped back, breaking the trance.

"I shouldn't keep you." She lifted the large paper cup. "And probably drink two more of these so I can stay awake for tonight."

"Aye," he said, but made no attempt to leave.

"I'll see you later, then." Abby pivoted, making her escape.

"Wait!" he called after her.

Abby halted, as if he willed it.

"I've got a car. I'll pick ye up?"

Before she could stop herself, the words slipped out. "Great! See you soon, then."

"Aye. I'll come by in an hour if that works for ye." He didn't wait for her reply. Calling his dog, he crossed the street and disappeared up a flight of stairs.

A light turned on above the shop, and Thom appeared at the window. Abby glanced up and froze as he bowed his head in acknowledgment—they'd been watching each other. Her cheeks flushed. She turned abruptly, her heart racing. With long, quick strides, she headed home, hoping each pounding step would erase her embarrassment.

Jossi suddenly appeared, falling into step next to Abby. "Well, that was interesting," she said, ambling alongside her.

Abby glanced around quickly to confirm she was alone before speaking. "Don't do that, Jossi," she said, quickening her pace.

"What?" Jossi replied, struggling to keep up. "And why are you running?"

"I'm not." Abby insisted, her heels only pounding harder against the street.

"I was just pointing out—"

Abby stopped abruptly, cutting Jossi off. "I'm not attracted to him!"

"You said it, not me," Jossi replied with a smirk.

Abby growled, glaring at her, her thoughts a tangled mess. *Nothing is going on,* her mind screamed. *Nothing!*

"I'm married," she added sharply.

"Yes, I know, you've mentioned it twice tonight." Jossi quipped. "But you're still a woman."

Why was she defending herself? She shook her head, hoping to scatter her thoughts like puzzle pieces pushed off a table. Without a clear image, there was no possibility of piecing them together.

Abby's head lowered; her voice softened. "I didn't mean to say that. Or to sound angry," she said. "Can we not argue? Because I don't have the energy right now." Abby looked at the darkened streets below, the streetlights dimmed by the increasing mist enveloping them. "And ... and, well, I've missed you."

"Me too," Jossi cooed.

Abby wanted to tell Jossi where she had been, share her adventures, confide how much she missed the kids, and, yes, maybe even admit she was attracted to a stranger—all while feeling unable to reach out to Marcus. But as they neared the inn, Jossi disappeared into the night as if she had never been there at all.

Mrs. Landry peeked her head from the kitchen as the door creaked open. There was no missing the scowl on Abby's face. "Not the day you expected?"

"No. Yes. I mean ..." Abby's thoughts tumbled in her head. This was Jossi's fault. She hated when Jossi did that—forced her to come clean with herself. "It was a nice day. I'm just tired," she finally said.

"Aye, well, maybe you'd like a wee glass of whiskey?" Mrs. Landry eyed the large-sized coffee gripped in Abby's hands. "It might help ya relax better."

Abby offered a small grin. Wriggling her fingers free from the paper cup, she placed it on the entry table and slipped out of her coat, hanging it by the door. "Thank you, but I'll have to pass. We're heading to Effemy's in a bit, and I've got to get ready."

"We?" Mrs. Landry questioned.

"Oh, Thom is picking me up." When Mrs. Landry's eyes narrowed, Abby added quickly, "He's offered me a ride. It was only polite to accept."

"Well, it's a fine thing you're gettin' out," Mrs. Landry said, her tone not entirely dismissing the innuendo. "Why don't you go and get yourself gussied up?"

"No need to make a fuss, Mrs. Landry." She smirked, recalling her disastrous date night with Marcus, when her efforts to appeal to her husband had fallen flat. "Who's looking at me, anyway?"

"Hmm," Mrs. Landry mused. "You've caught the eye of Thom, haven't ya?"

Abby's eyes widened. "No!" she protested a little too hastily. "I mean"—she cleared her throat—"of course not."

Mrs. Landry waved her protest away. "Nothin' wrong with turnin' an eye of a handsome man. It's a nice compliment. Just this mornin', old Mr. Winslow who delivers my wood was askin' about ya. I said, 'What's an old geezer likely to do with a lassie like her?'" She shook her head. "Men! No matter how old they get, they still think they can keep up with ya. They can't even keep up with ya when they're spry."

Abby thought of the scrawny old man she often saw stacking wood on the side of the house. He'd only tipped his hat to her in passing, with a faint smile. It was a wonder he even noticed her. "I can't imagine old Mrs. Winslow approving of him eyeing your guests."

Mrs. Landry let out a laugh. "Ha! She'd say, 'Take 'em!'"

Abby joined her in the amusement, the humor softening the insinuations. *Was it all so bad to notice and be noticed?* With Mr. Winslow, it was harmless. But with Thom? That was a whole other matter, one she wasn't ready to untangle.

"Good! Your smile is back. We've worked hard to get it there; I'd hate to lose it again." Mrs. Landry gestured toward the stairs. "Run along and make a fuss over yourself. Might be just what you need to keep that pep in your spirit."

Was that what she needed—a lift in her spirit?

She wished it was that simple. Her soul had been adrift for a long time, abandoned somewhere she could not reach. Finding it again—that was the challenge. And after that? What would come next?

24

SUBTLE GESTURES

The doorbell rang. Mrs. Landry shuffled to the entry and turned on the light. "Thom, come in," she said, shooing him in. "You're lookin' mighty dapper this evening."

"Agatha, you're a flirt," he said, kissing her on the cheek. "Here, these are for ye." He handed her a bouquet. "I threw in those pink lilies you like."

"Now who's charming whom?" A childlike grin appeared. "And yellow tulips?" Mrs. Landry said, eyeing the other paper-wrapped bouquet. "She's a pretty lassie, Thom, but a forewarning, a taken one."

"And when did you scold a man for bringing flowers? Had I Hogarth's meat shop, you'd both be getting fine center cuts wrapped up in that brown paper, instead," he teased. "Don't begrudge me my living."

They both laughed.

Mrs. Landry had no reason to question Thom's intentions. She knew him to be an honorable man. But the strong scent of his cologne, the crisp collar peeking from his sweater, along with the flowers, hinted at more than just neighborly kindness. It wasn't her place, but she couldn't help her instincts. She knew Abby was married, but she had no clues as to the state of the relationship or why she was alone. She would find out in time, when Abby was ready to share. Until then, her maternal protection was on guard.

"Hand them over, and I'll find a vase," she offered. Filling her arms with the two bouquets, she scuttled to the kitchen.

THOM TURNED toward the sound of boots clacking down the stairs.

Abby appeared in a pair of jeans and a bright sweater, carrying her purse over one shoulder and swinging a scarf around the other when she startled. "Gosh, I'm sorry if I kept you waiting," she said, seeing Thom at the bottom of the stairs.

He opened his mouth to speak, but Mrs. Landry beat him to it.

"My, don't ya look pretty," Mrs. Landry said, eyeing Abby up and down.

"Thank you. I took your advice and gussied up."

Mrs. Landry gave her a nod of approval, then handed her the yellow tulips, neatly displays in a vase. "Shall I put these next to your bed?"

"For me?"

"Aye," Thom interjected. "A shipment of white tulips arrived with one bouquet of yellow. It was a sign that they were meant for ye," he explained.

Abby felt a rush of heat course through her. "That's so thoughtful," she said, her voice pitching higher than she intended.

If the lift in her voice didn't betray the flutter of her heart, the way her hand brushed her neck might have. She met his gaze briefly, only to find Thom's eyes glinting with a knowing. The damage was done.

"Shall we go?" Thom suggested, grabbing her coat and holding it open for her.

Abby slipped her arms through the sleeves, momentarily enveloped by his body. As she waved goodbye to Mrs. Landry, his hand settled gently against her back, and he escorted her to his car. With a swift motion, he opened the passenger door, grabbed a gym bag and a jacket off the seat, and tossed them in the back.

"Sorry," he said. "I don't have many guests in my car. Well, few bonnie ones, anyway." He winked.

Abby felt the corners of her mouth twitch as she forced a laugh, not sure *bonnie* was the right word, keeping her gaze on the car's interior rather than his smile.

He walked around the front and climbed in, fitting himself into the seat. He turned on the car and fiddled with the heat, directing a vent toward her, before he plugged in his phone and slid the seatbelt across his body. He looked to make sure her own belt was locked in place.

Abby watched, noting his routine. It felt strange being in a car with another man, each movement novel and unfamiliar. As he adjusted the mirrors and checked the dashboard, she observed his habits with quiet fascination, like watching an animal in the wild. She felt a mixture of awkwardness and fascination. There was something instinctual and untamed about it, leaving her feeling both awkward and intrigued.

He had changed since she'd seen him earlier, and it did not go unnoticed—the effort he put into pulling himself together was clear. Dark jeans paired with a navy cashmere sweater, with rolled cuffs revealing the blue-and-white patterned shirt beneath. His belt matched his brown boots, and an orange plaid scarf added a splash of color.

Was the fashionable influence from a wife, or a deliberate gesture for a woman?

Mairi—or her?

She glanced down at her outfit, knowing she had done the same. Her jeans were a little more fitted, the blouse more refined, and the sweater had just enough flair to stand out. She'd paid close attention to what she wore that evening.

For her new friends—or for him?

Thom maneuvered through traffic on the narrow streets with an ease that mirrored their conversation. He pointed out bits of history and quirky landmarks, inviting Abby's curiosity, while steering the discussion toward her likes. Abby confessed her obsession with The Weather Channel and heartwarming videos of dog rescues, which made him chuckle. He admitted to being a self-made historian, which guaranteed his unpopularity with girls when he was younger, and, to his dismay, with women now. When Abby balked at the notion, he sealed his reputation by revealing his hidden fascination with cryptids. She quirked a smile, not because she doubted the existence of things like Big Foot or the Loch Ness Monster, but because she realized how effortlessly she could share parts of herself with him.

"Ye listen to jazz?" he asked, reaching for the radio. "I'm kind of fond of the American greats."

Abby nodded.

He scanned his playlist, picking one, and the car soon filled with the sultry sounds of Miles Davis.

"So, Abby ..." Thom paused, rubbing his forehead, as if trying to jog his memory. "Come to think of it, I don't think ye told me your last name?"

"Didn't I?" she asked, feigning nonchalance. "It's Kent. Abby Kent."

"And your husband's name?" He caught her gaze. "I don't think ye mentioned that, either."

"Marcus," Abby said rather quickly, as if it were just another forgotten detail. She hadn't been forthcoming about herself, limiting the information for fear of saying too much ... or fearing there wasn't enough to say.

Thom let out a warm laugh.

"What?" Abby wondered if he was making fun of her.

He hesitated, a grin spreading across his face. "I dunno, it sounds very"—he paused, searching for the right words— "strong and all-American. 'Hello, I'm Marcus Kent,'" he mocked, trying on an exaggerated American accent.

Abby couldn't help but laugh, too. There was no disguising the roll of his native tongue.

He was right, though, Marcus did have an all-American name. It was one of Jossi's favorite things about Marcus, a contrast to her Armenian surname, Petrosyan. Abby remembered Jossi's spiral notebook filled with scribbles of *Jossi Kent*. She never imagined she'd be the one who was writing his name beside hers.

"You're laughing. It's good to hear," Thom said. "I heard it a wee bit the other night. Effemy has a way of coaxing happiness out of people. The melody of joy escaping your soul ... now that's a beautiful thing, even if it's at my expense."

"I *laugh*," Abby defended herself, catching the amused gleam in his eyes. "All right, maybe not all the time ... but I do," she insisted. Her voice softened. "I ... I just haven't felt like laughing for a long time," she admitted quietly.

Thom tilted his head, his voice lowering. "And why is that? What makes Abby Kent not laugh anymore?"

Abby shook her head. Where did she start? That she'd run away from her life, her family, her husband? That she was hiding in Scotland, avoiding explanation, trying to escape the sadness that felt like it was drowning her? Would he understand, or think she was a self-indulgent crazy woman having a breakdown? No, she couldn't reveal any of that.

"I came to Scotland to find out," she said, answering the best way she knew how.

"Fair enough," he said, not pushing the issue. "And how long are ye staying?"

Abby hesitated. "I'm not sure."

She had left over three weeks ago. It seemed like a lifetime, her old life—Marcus and the kids—put on hold. It wasn't fair to treat them like sweaters to be put in a drawer, waiting for the season to return to bring them back out.

She closed her eyes, resisting the urge to cry. She thought the solitude would help her to escape the scrutiny of others and her self-criticism. All she wanted to do was to break free from the emptiness and failure—to make it stop! But no matter how far she ran, she couldn't escape herself.

The first week, hiding under the covers in an unfamiliar room, drowning in her thoughts, solved nothing. She felt suspended between what she'd left behind and the uncertainty of what lay ahead.

Meeting new people, breaking free of routines and expectations, was helping. Each morning felt like a small awakening, living in the moment without motive. Something was emerging within her, a release, a breath she didn't want to stop. Did she need to travel so far to find this? It was too late to question now. She hadn't set a time frame and had only bought a one-way ticket.

"When it's time to go, I'll know," she finally answered.

"That sounds rather metaphysical," Thom said, his tone unexpectedly serious.

Thom's mood shifted, though his tone carried no pressure, only curiosity. She couldn't fault him for wanting to know more about her. His sincerity was disarming, and she appreciated his discretion. Reaching over, she placed her hand on his forearm—surprisingly solid and warm to the touch. "I'm on a journey. Can we leave it at that?" she said softly.

"Aye," he said with a nod, his eyes steady on the road. "But when you're ready, I'm here to listen, if ye need me."

Abby gave his arm a gentle squeeze, the warmth lingering on her fingertips even as she let go. Neither said more, letting Miles Davis fill the silence until they reached their destination.

THOM AND ABBY arrived at Effemy's door as it was opening. Two gangly boys, backpacks bouncing on their shoulders, ran past them without looking up, almost knocking the wine out of Thom's arms.

"Be careful, and text me in the morning," Effemy called after them. "Sorry about those little beasts," she apologized. "I've tried my best with manners, but they don't seem to catch on."

"Your boys?" Abby asked as they darted away.

"Aye. Only eleven months apart," Effemy said with a smirk. "Couldn't resist my Brannan then, or now." As if on cue, her husband appeared behind her, wrapping her in a hug, a silence testament to their enduring connection.

Though Brannan towered over her, Effemy's commanding presence defied her small stature. Her creamy complexion and full, pouty lips needed little makeup—her natural beauty shone effortlessly. Rich, chocolate curls 'owed to the best salon in town,' as she liked to say, framed a face brimming with life and laughter. Her big brown eyes sparkled with mischief, reflecting her playful nature. Yet, beneath her cheerful exterior lay a fierce, protective mother lioness whose warmth was impossible to resist.

Effemy nudged her husband aside and wrapped Abby in a warm embrace. The hug barely ended before Brannan stepped in with his own bearlike hug, his massive hands carrying the strength of his rugby days. His rough-hewn appearance—wavy dark hair, bushy beard—was softened by the easy warmth in his voice as he said, "Good to see you again, Abby. You're a nice addition to us."

Abby hugged him a little tighter before letting go.

Effemy reached for Abby's hand. "Let's get you a drink," she said, grabbing the bottles in Thom's hands and leading her to the kitchen, where a makeshift bar was set up.

The doorbell rang, and Mairi's voice echoed through the corridor, warm and familiar, drawing Abby's attention. She peeked around the wall just in time to see Thom embrace her. Mairi's face beamed with a wide smile, and her cheeks flushed as he stepped back from her. Abby followed as Mairi placed a quick, friendly kiss on Thom's lips, and she found herself holding her breath, waiting for his response. She couldn't see Thom's face, but she was sure he was smiling. How could he not? Mairi was stunning, with her hair swept back to reveal her sculpted jawline and high cheekbones. Her lips were glossed in red, as were her cheeks, and her green eyes were alluring, shadowed in smoky hues. It was a far contrast from the light mascara and clear lip gloss she'd worn earlier that day.

For a moment, Abby felt a confusing mix of admiration

and envy. She quickly dismissed it with a shake of her head. Thom and Mairi were just friends, which Mairi had admitted that afternoon. Still, she didn't miss the effortless way they connected, or the gleam in Mairi's eyes.

"Abby," Mairi waved, spotting her and rushing over. A hug ensued. "You're wearing the pretty sweater you bought today. It suits you."

"I think it was you who insisted I buy it," Abby reminded her. She wasn't sure of the feminine style, more fitted and shaped to her body than she was used to. Oversize and baggy had become her mainstay after the surgery. However, the girls insisted it was flattering on her.

"Aye, Abby," Effemy agreed. "It looks pretty on you."

Brannan nodded his approval.

"Come on." Abby blushed. "You're all being too nice."

Thom leaned in, his breath warm against her ear. "Maybe it's time you noticed what's obvious to everyone else—you're a beautiful woman," he whispered, before retreating just as quickly.

Heat surged to her cheeks as she struggled to compose herself, but his words lingered, impossible to ignore. There had been no flirtatious edge to his tone, just a quiet sincerity, but it made her pulse quicken all the same. Why had he said it? Perhaps it was his simple nature to notice, to speak truths that others might leave unsaid. Could it be more? She drained her glass, her gaze darting to Thom across the room, now deep in conversation with Brannan. Silently, she cursed him. Not for what he said, but for how it affected her.

She wasn't sure why she was reacting this way. Was it the way his voice carried a steady confidence? Or the intensity of his gaze that seemed to strip away pretense? It wasn't like her to feel this off balance, and she didn't want to dwell on it or give it credence. But the feeling lingered, simmering at the edge of her awareness.

Brannan's exuberant gestures broke her reverie. He spoke with his hands, waving them in the air, his brow dipping and rising as he animated his point. In contrast, Thom leaned against the bookcase, stroking his beard in calm deliberation, his lips steady, and his eyes intent. They were opposites in every way. If Brannan was an exuberant, solid bulk of reassuring strength, Thom exuded a more composed and measured power. Despite their differences in age and appearance, both men possessed a quiet magnetism that was impossible to ignore. Something was compelling about Thom's composed authority and Brannan's rugged warmth. Abby could see why they held the hearts of the women in the room.

Her thoughts drifted to Marcus. His athletic build, clean-shaven face, and quiet confidence came to mind—so different from the two men yet sharing a charm all his own. Memories of their life together rose unbidden; the chaos of family, shared laughter, and small intimate moments that had once tethered them. For the first time in weeks, she missed him.

But now, miles away, untethered and disconnected, the life she left behind felt distant. She wondered if the bond of those familiar moments could ever be recaptured, or if they were already lost. After his initial texts, she hadn't heard from Marcus. He wasn't asking her to come home. He was probably angry, hurt, or most likely both. Abby wasn't sure what she wanted him to do. Fight for her? Miss her, too? Let her go? They were both being stubborn. Or maybe they both needed time to figure things out. Time she could give him. She only hoped he was allowing her the same.

A sharp pain shot through her chest, snapping her back to the present, where she heard the easy laughter of Thom and Brannan filling the room.

"More wine?" Effemy asked, swinging a half-full bottle in front of her.

Abby held out her glass, inviting a refill.

"Those two are as different as night and day," Effemy said, noting Abby's distraction across the room. "Thom runs a flower shop, while Brannan works in computers—a left-brain, right-brain thing. But they can talk for hours. Thank God! Thom relieves me of listening to Brannan's incessant chatter about ancient wars and battle strategies." She rolled her eyes. "But they're molded from the same clay. All heart. Real softies." Effemy filled her own glass, placing the bottle on the table. "They would never admit this, but they like British sappy romance movies. And I swear, I've seen them cry at weddings."

The two giggled together like girls sharing a secret in a high school hallway.

Mairi walked over to the two women. "What are you two laughing about?"

Effemy nodded toward Brannan and Thom.

Mairi eyed the men, grabbed the bottle on the table, emptying the remaining contents into her glass, and then sauntered over to them. She inserted herself between the two men, leaning into Thom. He continued his conversation with Brannan, seemingly oblivious to her arrival, or the sensual waft of her perfume. Anyone with a nose would find its intoxicating power impossible to ignore.

Abby wondered if all men were clueless about the desires of a woman. Was it intentional, deliberate ignorance, or were they truly oblivious? She thought of Marcus and the times she had tried to capture his attention, only to feel unseen. How often had she misread signs or longed for acknowledgment that never came? Thom, for all his quiet confidence, seemed no different. Or perhaps he was choosing to ignore what was so obvious to everyone else.

Abby sighed, her thoughts tangling in the unspoken complexities of human connection. Effemy's voice cut through the room, jolting her back to the present.

"Right then, it's time for Pictionary," Effemy declared, setting her empty glass down. "Brannan, get everyone more to drink. We've a new player and I think she might be competition." She winked at Abby.

"The boys against the girls, then?" Brannan asked.

"Oh, that would be a slaughter," his wife teased. "But you called it."

Effemy placed a platter of bite-size food on the table while Brannan set up the easel, propping a large drawing pad upon it. He then brought various bottles onto the counter.

Abby pointed to the selection. "How many kinds of whisky can there be?"

Brannan laughed. "Well, lassie, you're about to find out."

"Oh no," Abby protested, remembering her reckless night at the pub. However, Brannan pushed a glass in front of her and told her to taste it. The slow warmth that spread through her body as the golden elixir glided over her tongue was convincing. "Oh my, that's good," she said.

"That's my girl ..." Brannan smiled, pouring more into her glass. "There's more to taste as the evening progresses," he offered, handing a tasting to everyone.

"Find your seats," Effemy ordered.

The room came alive as everyone fell into a familiar rhythm —Effemy organizing the cards, Brannan adjusting the easel, and Mairi scattering pens across the table. Thom, ever composed, retrieved his glasses and gestured for Abby to sit beside him.

"Best seat in the house," he said.

Abby surveyed the cozy room for an alternative. Seating was limited, if not intimate. She eyed the curled arm of Mairi's chair, but Thom's hand reached for her, saddling her beside him.

"Are ye afraid of sitting too close to the competition?" Thom teased, his eyes glinting with mischief.

"No ..." Her voice wobbled. "Of course not."

"Aye, then," he said. He leaned into her, the heat of his body radiating against her side. "I like to know what I'm up against before I make my move." He pointed to the others. "Them I know. You're unchartered territory. Ye know the saying, 'Keep your friends close, but your enemies closer?'" He flashed her a smile. "Let the best man, or woman, win."

"Don't let him get into your head, Abby," Effemy warned. "He hates to lose to anyone ... especially to someone pretty."

Mairi lifted her glass. "To girl power!"

Effemy and Abby raised their glasses to a cheerful clink, but as Abby glanced at Thom, she realized Effemy's advice had come too late. He was already in her head, occupying more space than she cared to admit.

25

UNVEILED

"**W**ake up, sleepy head."

Abby moaned as the sunlight forced its way through the curtains, blinding her when she reluctantly opened her eyes to Jossi's voice. The pounding in her temples matched the assault of the brightness, and she turned over, pulling the sheets over her head to shut it out again.

"Don't turn away. The day is promising, and you shouldn't waste it tucked away in bed," Jossi beckoned.

"My head is spinning," Abby moaned. "I overdid it with the whisky, or maybe it was the Drambuie. Oh, who cares, my head hurts."

"Well deserved after last night," Jossi reprimanded. "Remember how you got home?"

Abby shot up from her pillow, her heart pounding. "Thom!"

Jossi laughed, the sound echoing like a breeze through an empty house.

Abby looked at her, horrified. "What did I do? I didn't ... I mean ..." Her voice trailed off, fear creeping in.

Jossi shook her head, her expression both amused and compassionate. "You? I only wish you grabbed onto life with such abandon long ago." She raised a brow. "Don't worry, Thom couldn't read your mind." Jossi smirked. "But I could."

"Ohhh," Abby groaned, sinking back into her pillow. She tried to piece together the night's events, but her memory was blurred in an alcohol-induced haze. But as silence filled the room, memories returned in fractured pieces—the smell of Thom's musky cologne enveloping her, his arms wrapping around her like a blanket of warmth, and the coarse brush of his beard against her cheek. "Ohhh," she moaned again.

"Abby?" Jossi's voice broke through, jarring her back to the present.

Abby opened one eye reluctantly. "What?"

"You're awakening, Abby. No need for shame. You're discovering a part of yourself that you've hidden, buried under the weight of expectations, guilt, and the life you thought you *should* live. It's not a bad thing."

"Please, Jossi, not now," Abby begged, rubbing her head and avoiding Jossi's stare. "I'm in no shape for your deep revelations."

Jossi didn't let up. "This isn't about *handling* anything, Abby. It's about letting go. You've been wearing *my* life like a second skin, never allowing yourself to slip out of it, even when you were suffocating. Something is shifting. This trip, this time away, is giving you the chance to be exposed, step into the sunlight, and to explore feelings you've kept hidden. You're doing things without self-judgment, without the weight of who you think you *should* be, and it scares you."

Abby closed her eyes for a moment, allowing Jossi's words to settle into her thoughts. "Let's face it, I'm being reckless. I got drunk—*again*. So drunk I can't remember what I did last night." Her eyes widened. "Isn't that irresponsible for my life? To Marcus? God, I'm a grown woman with responsibilities, yet here I am acting like I don't care, betraying everything I'm supposed to be."

"And who are *you* supposed to be?" Jossi questioned. "Maybe sometimes being reckless is necessary, Abby, to break the bad habits. It isn't about abandoning your life, it's about waking yourself up."

Abby turned and curled into a ball. She placed her arm over her eyes to block the morning light, hoping to dispel the pounding in her head. She needed coffee.

On cue, a knock sounded at the door.

Abby looked at the door, then at Jossi, signaling her to leave.

"I'm going," Jossi insisted. "Try to remember what I said. And most of all, Abby, forgive yourself."

Abby crunched her brow. "I thought you said I did nothing to worry about?"

Jossi didn't answer, disappearing as a repeated series of knocks rapped against the door.

"No need to keep knocking, Mrs. Landry. I'm awake," Abby called. "Come in."

The door creaked open, revealing a hand holding a cup of coffee. It was unmistakably a man's hand, with a strong forearm following behind it. Thom peeked his head in, his boot making a soft thud against the wooden floor. "Can I come in?"

"Oh, it's you!" Abby exclaimed. She quickly sat upright, wiping sleep from her eyes and pushing loose strands of hair behind her ears. "Of course, come in. I wasn't expecting you at my door." She eyed the paper cup in his hand. "If I didn't need that coffee, I'd probably turn you away."

"Really? I come bearing gifts." He showed his other hand, which held a bottle of ibuprofen.

Abby tried to laugh but winced as her head throbbed. "Don't make me move," she pleaded. "It feels like my head is about to explode."

Thom handed the coffee to Abby before pouring out four capsules into his palm. "You need the Scottish dosage," he said, handing them to her.

Abby dutifully swallowed the pills.

"Ye make a good patient." Thom slipped a smile across face. "I'm sorry about last night, I should've warned ye, we can get a bit competitive ... and a wee bit drunk. Ye can blame the Scots. We'll fight 'til our death. Literally. Even if it's over a game of Pictionary."

"I remember Mairi warning me ... or was it Effemy? Does it matter? After Brannan's whiskey tasting, I'm not sure I was sober enough to agree to anything."

Thom's eyes lingered on her face before he lifted his chin slightly. "Ye don't seem any worse for the wear."

Abby's eyes narrowed. "Now you're just making fun of me."

Thom shook his head slowly, his tone softening. "You're almost prettier in the morning ..." His voice drifted off, leaving the compliment hanging between them.

The flattery wasn't lost on her, though she was sure he exaggerated. Flustered, she threw the covers aside and bolted to the bathroom to see for herself the disaster in the mirror.

After a night of drinking, Abby imagined the telltale signs on her face—pallid skin, smudged mascara, puffy bloodshot eyes. Her lips must be dry, cracked, with a hint of last night's lipstick still lingering. She pictured her hair tangled in the back like a bird's nest, and the stale scent of alcohol on her breath.

However, Thom hadn't lied. She was indeed "no worse for the wear." Her hair lay flat across her shoulders, her skin clean without a trace of makeup. Her eyes were bloodshot, as expected, but there was no smeared mascara or eyeliner. Abby grabbed her toothbrush, scrubbing away the remnants of dry mouth, then looked twice at the reflection in the mirror to be sure she was seeing clearly. She glanced down at her pajama top, her fingertips brushing the neatly buttoned placket, and a realization struck her.

She peeked around the corner of the bathroom to find Thom looking at her. "What exactly happened last night?"

Thom let out a bellowing laugh. "Abby, if ye recall, ye asked me to help ye into bed. And that I did."

Abby covered her face. *Think, you idiot!* Nothing immediately surfaced.

"What exactly does that mean?" She swallowed hard, waiting for him to explain.

He gestured for Abby to sit down, placing himself next to her. "It means I helped put toothpaste on your toothbrush, then made you rinse twice," he said with a smile. "I handed you a towel after you washed your face ... some night creams followed, I brushed your hair, and after making you drink a glass of water, I tucked you into bed."

Abby's face went pale, and she jolted away from him, crossing her arms around her chest. She knew he must have seen her, at least partially exposed, but she wasn't sure.

"Abby," he called after her, his voice smooth and low. "I helped my wife many times in her life, especially when she was too weak to even dress herself. Caring for someone is second nature to me. It was nothing more than that." He continued, "I would've let ye do it yourself, but ye stumbled, and I had to catch ye. I had no other choice."

Abby's expression tightened as the memories trickled in.

She rubbed her arm, the soreness of a bruise confirming what her mind had begun to piece together.

"You fell into the corner of the dresser," he explained. "I was quick enough to prevent more damage."

"And then what?" She knew there was more. She could still feel his arms around her, the touch of his hand on her skin. She gulped.

"We talked …"

26

TRUTHS

Jossi had assured Abby she hadn't done anything wrong, though she didn't deny her recklessness. *What had she done?* She tried to believe it was an innocent night, but the pit in her stomach said otherwise.

"We talked?" Abby asked. "About what, exactly?"

Thom moved closer, touching Abby on the shoulder. As his touch lingered, fragments of memory rushed back. Disjointed at first, then flooding in a vivid cascade.

She remembered stumbling, the alcohol buzzing in her veins and impairing her balance. She had fallen into the armoire, knocking against its sharp corner. Thom steadied her, his hands firm but careful.

"Come on," he said gently, guiding her to the bed. "That'll be enough of that. You'll be covered in bruises before morning, and I'll have some explaining to do."

Abby giggled. "I think I see two of you."

"Nae, lass, there's only one of me," he replied. "What do ye sleep in?" She pointed to a drawer, and he grabbed the flannel pajamas covered in Scotty dogs. "Cute, verrry cute," he teased.

"*Verrry cute*," she mimicked, attempting his accent with a laugh. Then, tugging at her sweater, she complained, "Is it me, or is it hot in here?"

"Easy there, you just bought that," Thom said, catching the sweater before it hit the floor. "Why don't you sit back and let me help ye."

"Are you trying to undress me?" Abby quipped, her grin playful.

"No," Thom replied in a steady tone. "I'm trying to help a very inebriated woman get into bed without breaking her neck. It seems ye have a habit of getting drunk around me."

Abby brought her hand to her hip. "I don't get drunk," she insisted, adding, "It would be out of character, you see ..."

"Aye, well, that's a relief."

"It's your fault, really. Well, all of you—Effemy, Brannan, Mairi—you're all a bad influence. Bad, bad, bad ..." She waved her finger at him. "God knows how I will explain this —the two of you in my room, undressing me." She smiled at the thought. "Of course, no one would really believe me. Should I take a picture to prove it?"

"Probably not." Thom chuckled, removing her boots with care. "Do ye want to keep your socks on? My wife always did. She couldn't sleep without socks—even stark naked."

Abby bit her lip, vivid images flashing of laying naked next to him. Shaking her head, she yanked off her socks and began removing her jeans. She stumbled again, falling into Thom's arms.

"Careful now," he said, steadying her. "You're going to have to trust me with your care tonight."

Abby nodded, straightening herself upright. "I'm not used to getting help," she murmured, allowing him to take over.

As he knelt before her, guiding her to step into the pajama bottoms, his fingers grazed her skin, gliding the fabric upward with a subtle reverence. A shiver ran through her as his hands paused at her waist, his fingers warm against her belly as he fumbled with the drawstrings. She pushed his hands away and tied them herself. When she looked up, their eyes met briefly, and she felt his breath blow against her face —a mixture of whiskey and mint—making her knees weaken.

"I can only see one of you now," she said, holding his gaze. She wondered if he wanted to kiss her. She wanted him to.

He tucked her hair behind her ear, his fingertips grazing her cheek. "Why are ye here, Abby ... alone?" he asked, his voice sending a tremble through her.

Abby's lids fell. "I don't know," she whispered.

He lifted her chin, forcing her to look at him. When her eyes filled with tears, he brushed the droplets away. "I suppose you'll tell me when you're ready." He grabbed her pajama top and held it open for her to slip into it.

Abby brought her fingers to the buttons of her blouse, then hesitated. She knew how this scenario would end for most women. But for Abby, it was different. She instructed him to close his eyes before letting her blouse drop to the floor. Sliding her arms into the sleeves, she tugged her top closed, her fingers grasping the fabric's edges.

"You can look now, I'm decent," she said, as if warning him. As if warning herself.

Thom opened his eyes to see Abby clutching her shirt across her chest, her eyes no longer playful but darkened and targeted on his.

"Give me your hand," she ordered.

Thom hesitated, but when she asked him again, he laid it before her.

She took his hand in hers, turned it over, and studied it. He had strong lifelines and thick, rugged fingers, calloused from work. She pressed her palm to his, matching the lines of their hands. A flush of warmth filled her. She wondered what it would be like to have him caress her skin. She closed her eyes and let herself savor the thought. But only for a moment.

His hand remained in her control as she slid her top aside, guiding his touch along her breasts. Thom didn't look down at her exposed nakedness but held her gaze as she guided his roughened fingers over the healed cuts along her chest. Had he looked, he would have seen red raised scars standing out against her pale skin. She wanted him to know the truth, stripping away any illusion of who she was beneath the facade. In case he had any illusion that she was desirable.

Thom withdrew his hand from hers, closed her top, and slowly buttoned it, letting the silence sit between them.

Tears filled her eyes again. "I had cancer ..."

"Ye don't need to explain yourself, Abby."

"I, um ..." she started. "It's part of the reason I'm here."

Her words lingered in the air. The alcohol that had dizzied her earlier now left her fragile, unsteady, and exposed —a truth serum.

She drifted away from him and placed her head against the glass of the window, leaning into the cool, solid surface. A partial moon hung in the night sky, its shards of light illuminating the rooftops below. The town was quiet; the shop doors were closed, and no lights were visible except for the streetlamps glowing softly in the dark. The air was still, almost expectant. With her thoughts settling, she turned to Thom, who was leaning against the wall, arms crossed, watching her quietly. His presence felt stable, waiting without judgment, as though giving her space to find her way back to herself.

"I've been struggling with my life," she began. "Not only because of the cancer, but it was the final blow. I've run away from my life. I just left." She looked for a reaction, but he gave her none that she could detect. "Don't ask me what it is I'm seeking. I don't know." She paused, thinking, scrambling for clarity. "I felt claustrophobic where I was. And if I didn't do something, anything, I was going to implode."

"I understand that," Thom said, conveying the quiet resonance of someone who had faced his own battles.

"Do you?" she questioned. "Because I don't. I can only imagine what Marcus must think," she whispered. "But I'm not ready to go home, to face what I left. Not yet. And I don't know where to go from here."

Thom studied her for a moment, his expression unreadable. Stepping to her, he wrapped his hand around hers. "Abby, it's really okay. Sometimes, stepping away is the only way to see things clearly."

Abby locked eyes with him. He was calm and composed. "I thought you might judge me. You've all been so kind, but I feared that if you all knew the truth, you'd reject me."

His head shook. "Surely, ye would think better of us, or at least, I hope ye would. We aren't angels, Abby. None of us are. We all have our demons, struggling through the worst life has to offer."

"Really? You all seem like you have your lives together. My life is a mess."

"Ahh," Thom said with a sigh, gesturing for her to sit. "Nothing is ever what it seems. Did you know Effemy and Brannan have another child, an older son, Randall?"

Abby shook her head. "She's never mentioned him."

"They don't these days. It's too hard to admit he's a drug addict who lives on the streets."

Abby gasped. "Oh, that's terrible!"

"They never imagined this for their oldest. But when the younger two came along, almost ten years separating them, he started hanging with a lairy crowd, getting into trouble—fights and run-ins with the polis. Lad stuff, they thought, something they thought he would outgrow. They didn't realize he was using. Over the years, they put him in rehab, bailed him out of jail, and nearly bankrupted themselves trying to set him straight. When nothing worked, they made the painful decision to let him go, cutting ties for the sake of the other boys. The town had their say—folks at Effemy's work blethered about her, calling her a bad mother, claiming she hadn't done enough. It wore her down, but she and Brannan had to learn that they only had to answer to themselves. They've made peace with it, or as much as anyone can. Sometimes they see him on the street, but they know there's nothing more they can do."

Abby couldn't help but think of Drew. How close they'd come; how thin the lines were. Her thoughts lingered there, caught between gratitude and what could have been.

"And then there's Mairi," Thom started, his tone softening, stepping carefully into another story.

"What about Mairi?"

Thom let out another sigh, this time it seemed more personal. "Her husband was a great man—kind, helpful, always the first to lend a hand. If ye needed a faucet fixed, a car repaired, or just a good chat over a pint, he was there."

"What happened?" Abby asked cautiously.

Thom's jaw tightened. "Mairi returned from school to find him hanging in the garage."

Abby's hand flew to her chest. "Oh, no ..."

"He struggled with depression," he shared. "In a note, he wrote that he wanted her to have a better life, one free of his burden. What he didn't understand, he was her life."

Abby felt tears sting her eyes.

"I wasn't trying to bring ye down, Abby. Just know, none of us are judging ye." He paused. "I don't know what you're going through, but life is going to bring ye challenges, good and bad. How ye face it, where ye take it, is yours alone—your journey." He tipped his head. "But it doesn't hurt to have people along the way to help ye. We're here, if you need us … I'm here, if ye need me."

Abby said nothing. She couldn't. The alcohol swirled in her system, leaving her exhausted and unsteady. Thom's stories clung to her, each one a reminder of the silent battles people fought behind closed doors. If Effemy, Brannan, and Mairi could find their way forward, surely, she could, too. But at what cost? No one seemed to walk out of this life unscathed.

That thought, that fear of what might wait on the other side, was the thing keeping her stuck.

As if sensing her turmoil, or catching the fear in her eyes, he took her hand. "Come on, it's time for bed," he coaxed gently. "Nothing will be solved tonight."

Abby crawled under the covers and sipped the glass of water Thom handed her. When she finished, he tucked the blanket around her and turned out the light. He lingered at the door, his presence steady, watching over her like a sentinel. In the dim glow of the moonlight, she traced the lines etched into his face, proof of his own heartache, loss, and survival. They were not just marks of time, they were wisdom and resilience, a life lived; they added to his quiet, rugged charm. More than anything, he seemed undeniably real, causing a yearning she hadn't realized she was missing, a sense of safety she hadn't dared to seek. In that moment, vulnerable in the dark, she felt seen and understood in a way she had rarely experienced.

If she asked him to stay, would he?

The thought floated through her mind, soft but cautious. Instead, she closed her eyes and let the remnants of alcohol lull her sense of longing. "You are a very good man, Thom Emerson," she whispered, her voice barely audible. "I am lucky to have met you."

"Aye, I'm not one to disagree with luck," he replied, his tone gentle. "But I'd like to think fate had a hand in it too." He lingered a moment, then added, "How about dinner at my daughter's house tomorrow night? I think she'd like to meet ye, and I'd like the same." He didn't wait for a reply. "I'll pick ye up at half past six." And with that, he slipped out, leaving Abby in the comforting stillness of the room.

27

FAMILY PROFILE

A knock sounded at Abby's door.

"Thom is waiting downstairs," Mrs. Landry said, presenting a tightly bunched bouquet of roses when the door opened.

Abby stared at the flowers. They were pale yellow, almost antiqued, reminding her of the fading light of a summer's day. She brought a flower to her nose, inhaling the mellow, sweet, herbaceous fragrance. It was light, with a crisp scent of citrus and green grass, unlike the heady, sweet floral boldness of a red rose. The butter color evoked a warmth of friendship, nothing more, she told herself, trying to dismiss the sentiment, if not silence the flutter of excitement that stirred inside her.

But she couldn't help herself; a smile spread across her face.

Mrs. Landry raised an eyebrow, her gaze lingering on Abby.

Abby tried to ignore it, taking the vase from Mrs. Landry and placing it on her bedside. "Did you know roses in the

Northern Hemisphere were mostly pink?" she said, filling the air with trivia to distract herself—and Mrs. Landry—from the questions that were surely begging to be asked. "Yellow roses weren't known until they were found growing wild in the Middle East in the eighteenth century."

When she turned, she found Mrs. Landry's brow still arched.

She pressed on. "My friend Jossi told me that. She told me lots of odd facts. Strange the things you remember ... and the things you forget."

Her voice trailed off, her life back home feeling distant, almost forgotten as if she had stepped into another reality. She was in Abby's body, but she felt like a stranger to herself, standing there, smiling at flowers from a man who wasn't her husband.

"Aye," Mrs. Landry replied, finally releasing her questioning gaze. "So many things my Willie used to tell me, fillin' my head with useless knowledge." She winked. "I'm partial to irises, myself. Willie always brought me a bunch, wrapped in paper, tied up in ribbon, on our wedding anniversary. Tomorrow, we would've been married sixty-three years. He was a good man ... a dear, good man." She smiled wistfully. "Well, there I am, ramblin' like an old lady. But then again, I *am* an old lady." She laughed. "I'll let ya finish gettin' ready." She closed the door, leaving Abby to her flowers.

Abby stood in the quiet room, thinking of Mrs. Landry's love that endured for decades, and wondered if she had truly known something like that with Marcus. Was it ever there? Or worse, did it disappear? Her eyes drifted back to the roses. She traced a petal with her fingertip, feeling the delicate softness beneath her skin. Her finger stuck on a note, tucked inside the tightly wound bouquet. She slipped the paper out, her hands trembling slightly. She unfolded the paper and read: *Sorry for your sadness. Hopefully, these will brighten your eyes again, Thom.*

She smiled, folded the note, and slipped it into her pocket, her heart feeling both lighter and heavier all at once. The room fell into a quiet stillness, but Abby sensed she wasn't alone. She turned to find Jossi across the room.

"You look good, Abby," Jossi said. "Better than I've seen you in ages."

Jossi's appearances had grown less frequent, making Abby startle when she did show up. Still, they were never entirely unexpected, especially when Abby was struggling. Hearing her voice sent prickles up Abby's spine, but she didn't jolt. Instead, she turned and met Jossi's gaze. Hands tucked in her pockets, Jossi leaned casually against the wall, her face as bright as ever, lips curling into a half smile. But Abby could see the intent in her eyes. Jossi wasn't going to let her sidestep the guilt simmering inside. Not today.

Abby crossed her arms, squaring herself for the inevitable. "You're trying to get at something, Jossi. What is it?"

Jossi's gaze grew more intent. "Have you contacted Marcus?" she asked, her voice cutting through the room.

Abby flinched. The reaction wasn't intentional, but a deeply seeded, undeniable anger flickered through her, causing her body to twitch. It caught her off guard, betraying her emotions to Jossi. She threw her arms in the air. "And there it is!"

"Well, have you?"

"No, not directly," Abby answered hesitantly, guilt tugging at her gut.

"Abby, look at me," Jossi insisted. "Marcus needs some assurance you're okay. He needs to hear from you."

The air thickened suddenly, the yellow walls seemingly

closing in on her as if to crush her. Opening the door, the chill of the old house brushed sharply against her face. Abby grabbed her scarf and swung it around her neck. "I've got to go ... Thom's waiting for me," she said, her eyes fixed on the staircase, her escape just a few steps away.

"So is Marcus," Jossi yelled after her.

Abby stopped in her tracks, the words hitting like a punch in the stomach. Her chest tightened, and her breath grew shallow. *Was it possible to suffocate in the open air?* She tugged at the scarf as if it was the culprit of the tightness in her chest.

Turning back, the light from the room spilled into the darkened hallway, casting a soft glow around Jossi. She stood in a presence that felt immovable, unshakable as if she were carved from the very fabric of reality. Her eyes, dark and deep, seemed to anchor Abby, drawing her in with a force she couldn't resist. Abby wanted to run to her, to embrace her, to feel the warmth of life that seemed so real, so close, and yet impossibly out of reach.

Taking a few steps toward her, Abby released a sigh. "What do you want from me, Jossi?"

"Abby," Jossi said. "You have to resolve these issues with Marcus. If you're leaving him, he should know."

"Leave ... leave him?" Abby stuttered. "I didn't say anything about that."

"No? In a way, you've already left him, Abby. You're here, and he's not."

Abby balked. She wanted to tell Jossi that she wasn't leaving—not really. Just taking a break. But the words caught in her throat. "What are you talking about?"

"Abby, the woman that left a few weeks ago is gone, and *she* isn't coming back. Marcus senses it, even if he doesn't understand why. And you owe it to him to explain why."

THOM'S DAUGHTER lived an hour out of town on a farm nestled amid sprawling green fields where sheep wandered in the distance. A group of shaggy, long-haired Highland *coos* gathered near a wooden fence, their breath visible in the crisp dusk, as Thom's car made its way up the drive. The scent of damp earth and hay filled the air. Abby wished it wasn't getting dark—she'd have loved to walk through the fields.

The old gate, worn from years of snowy winters and rainy days, creaked when they entered the front yard. A crushed stone pathway led to a red door set into the stone facade of the charming two-story house. Dormer windows peeked from the steeply pitched roof, while two chimneys rose at either end—one trailing a wisp of smoke into the night sky. Golden brown and black chickens pecked at the ground, circling Abby's and Thom's feet as they approached. At the doorstep, a sinewy black cat greeted them with a raspy meow, rubbing itself affectionately against Thom's legs.

"Hiya, Jinx," Thom said, bending down and rubbing the cat's head.

Abby smiled at the fairy-tale-like scene, so unlike home. *Home*, she thought, with a rush of emotions—longing, fear, sadness. A convoluted mess she was in no mood to filter through.

Thom touched her, bringing her back to the doorstep and red door. "Thank ye for joining me tonight," he said, giving the door a solid rap, followed by two more.

Abby gave him a smile, pushing away any regret she had for being there.

A tall, lanky man with dirty blond hair tied back in a ponytail and a scruffy beard answered the door. A broad smile crossed his face, and his blue eyes sparkled when they landed on Thom. Without hesitation, he stepped forward and wrapped Thom into a tight embrace, his joy expressed through laughter that echoed through the hallway.

"Aye, it's good to see ye," the young man said, slapping Thom's back.

Thom embraced the young man and then stepped back. "This is my son-in-law, Eamon," he said, nudging him toward Abby.

The young man didn't wait for permission and enveloped Abby in a hug. "Good to have ye here, Abby," he said, his head resting against hers.

"Da," a young woman's voice came down the corridor. When the woman reached her father, the two hugged. Still in her father's arms, her eyes met Abby's, and she smiled. "You must be Abby, I'm Marleigh," she said.

Abby nodded, shifting awkwardly. She hadn't realized she was already known to them.

Breaking free from her father's embrace, Marleigh turned to Abby and drew her into a gentle hug. "We've heard a lot about you lately."

Abby cringed, eyeing Thom. "What must you have told them?" She shook her head. "Please tell me you didn't mention last night?"

"Oh, we heard about that, too." Marleigh's hearty chuckle was reminiscent of her father's. She slipped her arm through Abby's and guided her into the house. "My da's escapades are notorious," she explained.

Thom chuckled, and Abby turned back, scolding him with a look.

"No need to be embarrassed, Abby." Marleigh patted her arm. "We've all been there with Da's motley crew of friends and a game of Pictionary. I'm surprised you're even standing here less than twenty-four hours later. My Eamon here didn't resurface for a whole weekend," she said, eyeing her husband, "missing his eldest daughter's recital."

Eamon tipped his head. "It happens to the best of us."

Abby tried to smile, but she wasn't as lighthearted as they were about an overindulgent night of drinking ... and everything else that followed. "Must have been quite a night," Abby murmured, a touch of humor in her voice, though she was still feeling the weight of the past night.

Marleigh led Abby through a warmly lit hallway filled with framed family photos. Abby paused briefly at one—a black-and-white picture of a young woman on a boat, laughing, with her hair tied back. She was wearing shorts, Wellies, and a windbreaker over a checked blouse, and holding a fishing rod in both hands. It was a candid moment in time, taken by loving eyes, not only capturing the woman's beauty, but her joyous spirit. She was beautiful.

"Your mother?" Abby asked, gesturing toward the photograph.

Marleigh nodded, offering a smile, before continuing down the corridor, leaving Abby only quick glances at the family she wanted to know more about.

In the kitchen, Marleigh pointed at a center island with chairs tucked under it. "Make yourself at home. How about a glass of wine?" she asked, reaching for an open bottle and pouring a glass preemptively.

Abby hesitated but took the half-filled glass Marleigh handed her. She barely had a moment to settle in before two young girls dashed into the room, their laughter echoing.

"Pop-Pa!" the girlish voices screamed in unison, diving into Thom's arms.

Thom patted the taller one's head. "This here is Caroline." He added, lifting the smaller one in his arms, "And this wee one is Jenny."

Abby couldn't help but smile. The girls' unguarded laughter reminded her of her own children when they were young. Her heart tugged, causing a pang of longing. She missed those simpler times. But the family she missed was no longer there. They were scattered and different.

And broken. She sighed.

"Awright?" Thom asked, catching the flicker of sadness in her eyes.

Abby forced a smile. "Of course," she replied, her gaze on the two girls clinging to him. "You have a sweet family," she uttered.

"Aye," Thom replied, catching her meaning.

Suddenly, Jenny looked at Abby, her eyes wide. "Are you Pop-Pa's girlfriend?" she asked.

Marleigh quickly stepped in. "All right, girls, time to wash up for dinner."

They both groaned.

"I'll take 'em," Thom volunteered, and the three of them disappeared down the hall.

"Sorry about that," Marleigh said once Thom and the girls were out of earshot. "Jenny didn't mean ..." She stumbled over her words. "It's just ... he's talked about you a lot lately. He's been happy since meeting you, more than I've seen in a while."

Abby didn't respond. She wasn't sure how to. She didn't want to suggest to Marleigh that there was more than a growing friendship. She glanced down at her hand, remembering that she had left her wedding ring on her dresser. She hadn't thought to put it back on that morning and wondered why she had been so careless.

Thom poked his head into the kitchen, stopping Marleigh

and Abby in mid-conversation. He sauntered to the stove, dipped his finger in the pasta sauce, slurped it, and nodded with satisfaction. "What are ye two gabbing about?" he said, eyeing them with a grin.

Marleigh slapped his hand away, half-smiling. "Nothin' you need to know, Da. Now shoo," she scolded.

He laughed and raised his hand in surrender. "Just washed up the girls, by the way," he said, sauntering to the next room.

Marleigh rolled her eyes. "He's a great da. Especially since my mum passed. He's always there for us. And he's amazing with the girls," she said, taking plates from a cabinet.

Abby grabbed the dishes from her, helping to set the table. "You all seem close."

Marleigh nodded. "Do you have grandkids too?"

Abby smirked. She didn't feel old enough to have grand-kids. "No, not yet. Maybe in a few years. My daughter's head over heels for a young man in college. She thinks it's serious."

"You don't approve of him?"

Abby shook her head. "I'm not sure yet. He seems nice enough. She believes he's *the one*. But maybe ... I'm afraid he's taking away my little girl. And I'm not ready for that."

"If it means anything from a daughter, ya never lose them," Marleigh winked. "My da and I are very close. Closer now since my mam passed away. However, I never stopped wanting him to be a part of my life. Well, maybe when I was shagging a bit here and there," she joked. "But never did he stop being the first man I'd run to. He's my da. I'll love him forever, no matter how old I get. Eamon too. He couldn't love my da more."

"It seems mutual."

"Fathers never think anyone is perfect for their little girl. Eamon is like a puppy, always trying to win his love. Little does he know, Da adores him. He shows it, but he's just too stubborn to say it directly to him. And I won't tell Eamon because it keeps him on his toes," she smiled, as if pleased with her deception.

Marleigh poured herself another glass of wine, emptying the bottle. She sank into a chair next to Abby, throwing off her shoes to the floor.

"Ahh," she sighed. "Nothing like the calm after a long day, the whole family safely home, knowing everyone is content."

"I remember those days," Abby recalled with a wistful smile. "There's nothing quite like the feeling after the chaos settles, taking a stolen moment, like now." She pointed to Marleigh's shoes tossed aside. "When the world feels right, because of what you did. Being the one they rely on is a fierce pride. You think to yourself, 'I did good today.' Those were the moments I knew my worth." Abby looked at Marleigh. "It's kind of our superpower, isn't it? The power to create, manage, and wield that sense of warmth and security of a family."

"Aye," Marleigh acknowledged. "Couldn't have explained it better myself."

"You'll miss those times, though." Abby sighed. "And then you'll wonder what it was all for."

Marleigh studied Abby's face. She was looking for something. "You remind me of her ... my mam. Oh, not that ya look like her. It's your quiet reverie, an intuitive truth you have, and an internal kindness. It's obvious. There's a light that shines around you—through you—lifting others out of darkness, someone to lean on. You're a lioness! I can see why my da brought you here."

Abby blushed with her kind sentiments, but then shook her head, questioning. "Why?"

A soft smile touched Marleigh's face.

"Because you feel like home," she said simply. "I never had the chance to tell my mam how much her love shaped me, saved me at times. It gave me the strength to become who I am. That's what I hope my girls feel from me—a love that stays with them, guiding them even when I'm not around." She gave Abby's hand a gentle squeeze. "Maybe through you, I can say it to her now. I miss her every day."

A timer buzzed, breaking the moment, and Marleigh rose with a small laugh. "My stolen moment is over." She downed the rest of her drink in a single sip, and reaching for another bottle, refilled both their glasses. "I'm glad my da brought you here to meet me. I can see why he's fond of you."

Abby sipped her wine, and warmth spread through her as Marleigh's words lingered. Her gaze turned toward the dimly lit doorway where Thom disappeared.

I'm fond of him, too.

28

GREEN-EYED MONSTER

A bby looked at her phone and blinked twice. She sighed, not wanting to read it.

Where are you? Marcus wrote. That was two days ago.

Drew is doing fine, but I think he misses you. Your friends are asking when you're coming home. What do I tell them?

He wrote that a day ago.

Abby?

The last text had come that morning.

Abby stared at her screen, a mix of emotions swirling in her head, pressing heavily on her heart. She felt burdened knowing she was neglecting her responsibilities, leaving the way she did. Yet, Marcus was pushing her to fix things on his terms, and she didn't like the pressure. This wasn't something he could fix. It was hers—all hers.

They were both struggling in their own way, the situation forced on him by her. And that wasn't fair. *She owned that!* Blame wasn't the problem, but the question lingered. Did he truly understand her struggles? Perhaps he did, though he was lousy at expressing it. It left her feeling conflicted, almost hollow. Empty. She couldn't just come home and pretend everything was fine. She had spent too long ignoring the issues that were ultimately driving them apart.

Her leaving wasn't completely about Marcus; it was about Abby figuring out who she was, and if she could truly embrace that woman without guilt or fear. She wasn't trying to hurt him—she loved him too much for that. The question was, would Marcus still love the version of herself she was trying to find?

Abby turned her phone off, tucked it in her purse, and drew a deep breath, pushing the turmoil aside. She wasn't trying to bury her problems—she had left on this journey to escape the pressure of solving them on everyone else's terms. If she hadn't known it then, she knew it now. This exploration, the metamorphosis, had a life of its own. She had tried to control it, keep it contained, manageable, something that wouldn't disrupt her life, or anyone else's. But life had other plans, and now she found herself at the edge, facing the fire whether she wished it or not.

This wasn't about breaking down, at least, not anymore. It was about breaking through. She had gotten this far, so far. For the first time, she felt a faint stirring of clarity. Of hope. Of happiness. Even if it was tangled with uncertainty ... and heartache.

With a deep breath, Abby pushed herself upright, the cool floor grounding her. The aroma of something cooking in the oven beckoned her downstairs.

"Good morning, Mrs. Landry," Abby said, inhaling the sweet scent of bread permeating the kitchen. "And happy anniversary."

Mrs. Landry smiled. "Oh my, aren't ya sweet," she replied, bending over to open the oven door.

"Mmm, those smell delicious," Abby said, eyeing the tray of golden scones.

"I have two couples arriving today. Nothing like fresh scones to keep 'em comin' back." She winked, placing the tray on the counter. "The reservations are fillin' up."

"Oh, do you need my room?" Abby offered, knowing she couldn't occupy the one and only bridal suite too much longer. It was time to start thinking of going home, or at least somewhere else, soon.

"No, no, of course not," Mrs. Landry said with a wave of her hand. "No newlyweds just yet. Ya stay as long as ya want. Besides, I'm growin' accustomed to ya," she said with a sparkle in her eye.

Abby hugged her spontaneously.

"Now don't ya be gettin' all sentimental," Mrs. Landry said, squirming out of Abby's embrace. "I'll be kickin' ya out soon enough."

Abby grinned, knowing she didn't mean it. "Join me for breakfast at Scran?"

Mrs. Landry balked. "Now don't you distract me from my duties ..." The bell jingled at the front door, indicating someone coming through. "Those are probably my new arrivals now. They're checkin' in early and droppin' off their bags." She handed her apron to Abby and went to meet her guests.

Abby eyed the hot scones but decided against thievery. She had too many other sins to atone for.

Heading toward the café, she noticed Thom's shop door was already open. It was early, but it didn't surprise her; she'd seen flower deliveries arrive even earlier. Curiosity tugging at her, Abby made her way over and stuck her head inside.

"Hello," she called into the empty store. A young man

lifted his head from behind the counter. "Oh," she said, startled.

"May I help you?" the young man asked.

"I ... I'm Abby, Thom's friend. Is he in?" she said, feeling the need to explain.

"He called in late today. Won't be in until later."

"Oh!" Abby's eyes widened. "Okay, thanks," she said with a small nod, pivoting toward the door to leave.

"Is he expecting you?" the young man asked, stopping her. "Because I can call him at Mairi's and let him know you're looking for him. He thought his calendar was open, so decided to come in late."

Mairi's? Abby's expression tightened, the name catching something inside her.

When Thom had driven her back to the inn last night, he gave no hint that he had further plans. The unusually warm night invited him to roll down the windows, letting in the gentle breeze that carried a faint scent of earth and greenery. "Sit back and enjoy," he had said, his voice easy, almost playful.

The night sky stretched above them, a rich, deep blue fading to indigo at the horizon, where the half-lit moon hung low, casting just enough light to outline the shapes of the trees and cottages dotting the countryside. Crickets chirped sporadically, gearing up for the mating season, and an owl screeched from somewhere above as if staking its claim to the darkness.

Thom filled the car with his voice—his superpower— sharing funny stories from his childhood. Abby mostly listened, finding a surprising comfort in the simplicity of sitting in a car on a warm night with no agenda. Somewhere in the rhythm of his words, they uncovered common interests: a love of books—though he leaned toward history while hers favored fiction—a shared fascination with old movies, and a mutual fondness for the quiet hours of the early morning when the world seemed to hold its breath and where one could almost hear the sun rise.

It wasn't until past one in the morning, Abby stifling a yawn, that Thom admitted he had an early morning and needed to get some rest.

Did he go to Mairi's after?

Abby felt a hollow ache in her stomach, like the first tug of a thread unraveling, an unsettling blend of longing and something close to resentment.

"Excuse me, Ma'am," the young man said, waiting for her answer.

"Hmm?" Abby looked up. "No, of course not—no need to bother him," she answered. "I'll talk to him another time."

Abby thanked the young man, dashed out, and jogged across the street to Scran. She waved to the ladies at the counter before settling in the back, avoiding any view of the flower shop. She didn't want to see Thom, coming or going.

"Mornin' Abby," Hazel said, as Abby took off her coat and dumped her purse on the table. "What can I get ya? Fresh cinnamon rolls or a ham quiche?"

"Coffee," Abby answered, falling into a chair.

"Just coffee?"

"Coffee," Abby confirmed, watching Hazel's expression change from cheerful to concern.

As Hazel walked away, Abby felt a wave of nausea come over her. She felt her forehead, looking for signs of a fever. Unfortunately, it was cool, like any normal, healthy individual.

What is wrong with me?

She knew she was being silly about Thom. About Thom and Mairi. There was no logical reason for her reaction, nor for the pit in her stomach. It wasn't jealousy, not exactly. *Was it?* She told herself it didn't matter. Thom wasn't hers; they were just friends. But she couldn't shake the small, but inconsistent ache. She cared. *There, she said it!* She cared more than she should, and it scared her.

After spending the evening with Thom, she went to bed with such a lightness that she almost didn't recognize what it was. But in those final moments before sleep, she had thought, *I'm happy.*

It wasn't one thing she could pinpoint. Maybe it was when he talked to her that first day at Scran, among a bustling café full of people, or how he acknowledged her when she was just standing outside his store. He noticed her. It was so unexpected that at first, Abby didn't recognize it. It wasn't lost on her that he was this way with everyone—Effemy, Brannan, Mairi, Hazel—treating them with the same attentiveness. She wasn't special, but she wasn't invisible either, which gave her the courage to be herself, to say more, react more, feel more. It was like she was unzipping a rubber suit of Abby and stepping out of it. Peeled away, she could now feel the chill of a breeze across her cheeks, and the warmth of the sun against her skin.

Mostly, she found Thom was easy to be with. It was easy to be herself when she was with him, causing her to feel liberated. And if she felt that way, she had no doubt Mairi felt the same. Who was she to act so possessive? She had no claims to him.

And yet, the thought of him at Mairi's house returned, vivid flashes of them together—touching, kissing, their bodies tangled—played in her mind, like a tune she couldn't quite shake. She curled over, hands pressed to her stomach, trying to force the thought of them making love out of her head.

"Ohhhh," she groaned, trying to steady the deep pangs twisting inside.

"Abby?" A deep voice jolted her out of her daze.

She looked up to find Thom standing before her, his eyes narrowed and concerned. He crouched down, bringing himself to eye level, his brow furrowed. "Are ye feeling ill?"

Abby flinched, heat spreading through her. Straightening, her eyes caught on the man in front of her—the cause of her unguarded moment.

God, he looks good! was all she could think.

He was freshly showered and groomed, his beard neatly trimmed. His shirt, a sapphire blue, making his eyes seem bluer, deeper, was untucked, loosely hanging over a pair of old jeans. He looked exactly like someone fresh from a morning of lovemaking.

Abby pressed her fingertips to her temples, trying to steady herself. "I'm fine," she said. "Really. Just a little queasy this morning. Probably due to a lack of sleep," she assured him.

"Ye sure you're all right?" he asked again, pulling out a chair next to her. "Brian said ye came by the shop."

"Oh," she murmured, the words barely audible.

Why did she go there?

"It was nothing," she said, waving the question away.

"Abby?" he said, his eyes steady on her. "It wasn't nothing," he insisted, a quiet certainty settling in his gaze.

She wanted to tell him how much she enjoyed their time together, but she chickened out. "It's Mrs. Landry's anniversary," she explained. "I want to get her a bouquet of irises. I wasn't sure you had any in stock. You didn't have to come and find me. It could have waited."

"Oh," he said, letting out a sigh, his shoulders slumping slightly.

A momentary silence fell between them. Abby turned away, noticing the café had filled up, every table now occupied. She'd been invisible in crowds before, but now all she wanted was to disappear. When she turned back, she found Thom still watching her, his eyes searching her face.

He leaned forward and took her hand in his. "I ... I was glad ye came looking for me."

Abby withdrew her hand, wishing she had a mug to grab. She looked toward the kitchen, relieved to see Hazel heading their way. However, she might as well have been a mile away, each step feeling like an eternity, as though the space between them grew wider.

"Here ya go," Hazel said, finally reaching their table, placing coffees in front of them.

Thom leaned back in his chair, letting his rejected hand find the coffee instead. He wrapped his fingers around the mug and indulged in a long, exaggerated slurp. "Perfect!" he said, giving Hazel a wink.

Hazel beamed. "Now don't waste all that charm on me when you've got a pretty lass here."

Thom side-glanced at Abby, who quickly looked away. "Aye, well, some are more smitten than others." He took another slurp from his mug.

Hazel eyed Abby, then looked back to Thom. "Looks like the spring weather is settlin' in. I'm sure you've a handful of weddings to prepare for."

"Almost every weekend until September. Not complaining, though. It beats the slow winters. I can start paying that tab of mine," he smirked.

"Oh, your money is no good here, Thom Emerson. Keeping those pretty flowers full by the register is payment enough," she said, indicating the freshly placed vase on the counter. "Oh, looky there, the line is almost out the door. I've got to run. See ya tomorrow?"

Thom nodded and Hazel scurried away.

Abby abruptly stood. "I should be going. You're probably busy. I won't keep you."

Thom reached for her arm. His touch sent a jolt through her, but she kept herself rigid. "Ye seem different this morning, Abby. Did I do something to upset ye?"

She felt the surge of heat creep up her neck, threatening to reach her cheeks. "I'll see you soon," she said, quickly brushing off the question.

"How about tonight?" he called after her, as she made a dash to the door. "The Garage? Mairi was going to call ... but since I saw ye first, why don't ye join us?"

The mention of Mairi only made Abby hesitate, her instinct urging her to refuse. But before she could answer, he added, "Invite Mrs. Landry. We'll celebrate her anniversary."

Why does he have to be so nice? Abby thought, feeling her resolve weaken.

"Great," she yelled from across the room, her voice sharper than she intended. "And don't forget the irises!" Without waiting for a reply, she dashed out the door.

29

FRIENDS AND LOVERS

T he smell of stale hobs and peaty whiskey hit Abby when she opened the door to the pub. Music pounded through the space, blending with the chatter and laughter of a lively crowd. On the far side, Abby spotted her friends gathering around a table by the wall. Effemy's laugh echoed through the room, catching Abby's attention despite the music. Clasping Mrs. Landry's hand, she tugged her through the crowd, leading her in between the tight spaces of the tables.

"I shouldn't be here," Mrs. Landry murmured, holding tightly onto Abby's hand, slowly shuffling her black responsible-looking shoes across the floor.

"Nonsense," Abby responded. "Being out, dancing, drinking are as much for the old as the young."

"Not at my age," Mrs. Landry said, looking around the room.

Abby spotted an elderly man sitting at a table, his hat and coat covering the chair beside him. His lips were flat, his eyes dark, unaffected by the lighthearted mood of the pub, as he cradled a lowball glass in his hand. He looked crotchety, so Abby didn't dare point him out to Mrs. Landry.

She preferred to show her an elderly couple who were holding hands on a velvet sofa sitting near the fireplace. The man's foot bounced, syncing in motion to the folk music being played by the trio on the makeshift stage at the far-end corner, while the gray-haired woman leaned against him with a glint in her eyes. Abby quickly changed her mind, thinking it would only sadden Mrs. Landry, knowing her dear husband was no longer there to share their anniversary.

Abby kept walking and spotted two white-haired ladies crouched in a bench seat near the windows, with two martinis sitting on the table in front of them. They were watching the people on the dance floor, when one exchanged a look with the other, and they both laughed, bringing their drinks to their lips, taking a sip.

Abby poked Mrs. Landry and pointed. "See?"

Mrs. Landry followed Abby's gaze. "Aye, well, not many my age," Mrs. Landry corrected herself.

Abby gripped Mrs. Landry's hand tighter, tugging her further along.

"Hiya!" the table cheered as the two approached.

Thom jumped up and seated Mrs. Landry at the head of the table, where a bouquet of irises wrapped in paper waited for her. Mrs. Landry looked at Thom, then at Abby, and mouthed a quiet thank-you.

Thom pointed to the seat on the cushioned bench for Abby, next to Mairi, and sat himself beside her after she scooted in. When their eyes met, he nonchalantly smiled. "I am glad ye came."

Mrs. Landry ordered a whiskey neat, while Abby chose red wine. She wanted to avoid joining the rest of the table, who were indulging in a concoction of cocktails. When they all had a drink in hand, they lifted them and saluted to Mrs. Landry, and to sixty-three years of loving one man.

"Here's to Willie!" Brannan shouted, and the clanking of glasses began.

After another round of drinks, Brannan grabbed his wife and dragged her to the dance floor, laughter bubbling between them. Thom, following their lead, rose and glanced between Mairi and Abby, inviting one of them to dance with him.

Abby nudged Mairi. "You go," she said.

Mairi nodded and slid into Thom's open arms, moving to the dance floor.

Abby watched as they swayed effortlessly together, their bodies close, and Mairi's head nicely tucked in his shoulder. She tried to look away but couldn't stop staring at Mairi, who leaned in and whispered something in Thom's ear. His laughter rang out, easy and genuine.

A sharpness tugged inside her chest.

Why do I feel this way? she thought, fighting the urge to turn away. The sight of them together, so close, left her feeling like a bystander in her own emotions. *It's nothing*, she told herself, but her stomach churned in protest.

A growling voice jolted Abby from her thoughts, drawing her gaze upward. "Would ye care to dance?"

"Who, me?" she questioned, looking at her empty table, except for Mrs. Landry, whose eyes were fixed on the dance floor, watching her friends enjoy themselves.

"Unless ye have a ghostly friend sittin' next to ye. Although, after a few rounds of whiskey, I've been known to dance wit'em, too." The man laughed.

Abby quickly thought of Jossi and laughed, accepting the man's invitation. He threw his muscular arms around her, caging her, and clumsily wobbled her around, trying to keep up with the beat. Abby couldn't recall a time when another man's hands were so predatory. Every time she lifted his hands, her dancing partner would dumbly smirk and try again. The moment the song ended, Abby slipped from his grasp, and stole herself away, beelining to the table.

Another man swiftly tapped her on the shoulder, stopping her. "May I?" He presented his hand.

Abby was going to refuse until she spotted Thom and Mairi still dancing—still wrapped in each other's arms.

"I would love to," she said, accepting his offer.

The man placed one hand on her shoulder, and the other in the center of her back, keeping an appropriate distance, before sweeping her into the middle of the dance floor.

"You are American," he said matter-of-factly. It wasn't a question.

"Yes, but you aren't Scottish," Abby said, noting his English accent.

"No." He brought her closer, pressing his lips to her ear, competing with the loud music. "I'm here for my goddaughter's wedding."

"That's a good reason to visit," Abby said, feeling his breath on her neck. "Is your whole family visiting?"

He laughed, pulling back to meet her eyes. "Are you asking if I am married, or how many people are attending the wedding?"

Abby smirked at being caught in her own curiosity. "Well, I guess I'm wondering why a handsome stranger is dancing with me and not his wife."

"Did you just refer to me as handsome?" he questioned, his lips broadening across his face.

A flicker of heat rose to her cheeks. "Did I?" she countered, an awkwardness slipping into her voice. "Maybe it's the wine, the music, the atmosphere ..."

He chuckled. "Convenient excuse."

Abby laughed. "Very," she said lightly.

"How about if we do this properly?" He put out his hand, his eyes twinkling with mischief. "I'm Peter Kelsey. And it is a pleasure to meet you."

"I'm Abby Kent," she replied, sliding her hand in his. He didn't let it go, drawing her back to him. Abby didn't resist. His brown eyes held just enough mystery, his cleft chin had a Cary Grant charm, and, well ... he wasn't a bad dancer.

"Now that we have that out of the way ... no, I'm not married. I am divorced, with three grown children. I am in advertising and live alone with a cat. Yes, a cat, and his name is Felix," he said with a hint of pride. "And I am dancing with a pretty lady whom I saw across the room."

Abby rolled her eyes, dismissing his flirtation. But if she were to admit it, it felt nice.

"And you, Abby Kent?" he asked.

Abby stopped mid-step. "I ... I'm married, Mr. Kelsey," she said, her tone firm, as if reminding herself as much as him.

"Oh," he said. "That does put a damper on things. So, which one of the gents is it? That one?" He nodded toward Thom. "He keeps looking over. Not the jealous type, is he?"

Abby followed his gaze, lingering on Thom for a heart-beat before turning back to Peter. "No," she said with an easy shrug. "He's just a friend."

Peter pointed to a few more prospects, with Abby turning them all down.

"Are any of the gents your husband? Or are you just being mysterious?"

Abby gave a soft, self-conscious smile. "My husband is back home, in the States," she admitted, lifting her chin a touch higher.

Peter smiled. "Now that is what I wanted to hear." He pulled Abby a little closer, his hand steady on her back.

They finished two more songs, during which Peter revealed that his ex-wife still hated him for agreeing to the divorce—though she was now married to a man half her age—and that after dating for five years, he had given up on love altogether.

"No one is willing to put up with me," he concluded.

Abby shook her head, "Or maybe they can see you're still in love with your ex-wife."

"Hmm." Peter touched his chin. "Why do you say that?"

"Because you're still talking about her," Abby concluded.

He paused, his expression tightening. "You may have a point." He laughed. "Or maybe she just ruined my idea of love—broke me a little," he admitted with a sigh.

Peter smiled, brushing off his words, but Abby could still see the dimness of light that only the loss of love can cause. She had seen it in her own eyes, and knew a little about being broken.

"May I buy you a drink? I could use a chat from a woman who calls it like it is. You'll keep me on my toes."

"You're very kind." Abby pointed to the table where everyone was now seated. "But I'm here with my friends."

"Maybe next time." He bowed before taking her hand and placing a kiss on it. "You were worth the try," he said with a smile.

Abby walked back to the table, her steps lighter, a soft, contented smile playing on her lips.

"You've still got it, Abby," Effemy cheered.

"Aye." Brannan lifted his glass to her. When Effemy slapped him on the arm, he added, "But not as much as my darlin' wife," prompting Effemy to throw her arms around him and plant a kiss on his cheek.

Mairi eyed Peter, making his way back to a table of well-dressed, well-groomed people amid a celebration, indicated by the open champagne bottles and clinking glasses raised in the air. "He's a looker, I agree ..." She winked at Abby, before turning to Thom. "You might have yourself some competition."

"Eh," Thom groaned, swigging a sip of his whiskey. "If ye like the soft, pretty type ..."

The band started up again, turning everyone's attention back to the dance floor.

"They're playin' 'Skye Boat,'" Mrs. Landry said, a tear coming to her eye. "It was the song that Willie and I danced to when we were married."

Thom stood and extended his hand. "I'm no William Lachlan Landry, but I would be honored if you'd dance with me."

Mrs. Landry swatted away the droplets filling the corner of her eyes and accepted Thom's hand. Effemy and Brannan followed, leaving Mairi and Abby to watch as the couples filled the floor.

"That's sweet," Mairi noted.

"I can't imagine being so in love ... even after all these years," Abby commented carelessly, watching the joy on Mrs. Landry's face as Thom swayed her, as if he were the embodiment of her beloved dead husband, if only for a dance.

"Abby ..." Mairi placed a hand gently on Abby's. There was a pause as if she were carefully choosing her words. "Is everything all right? I mean, you haven't really said anything about your husband. Feel like talking about it?"

Abby hesitated, her eyes dropping for a moment before meeting Mairi's again. She had never really admitted the truth to anyone. Because if she said it out loud, it meant it was real.

"I don't know," she said quietly. "I'm trying to figure that out."

"I only ask ..." Mairi started to say. "Well, because it's Thom."

Abby's gaze drifted across the dancers before landing on Thom. "What about him?"

Mairi followed her gaze. "He likes you—a lot," she blurted out. "What I'm trying to say is, don't hurt him. He deserves ... well, he deserves better than what you might be able to give him."

Abby stared at Mairi. Her eyes showed no malice, no hesitation—only love. Abby wondered what her own eyes might reveal.

"There's nothing between us," Abby assured her. "We're friends, that's all."

"Friends!" Mairi laughed, a deep, warm laugh. "Don't you see the way he looks at you? He talks about you all the time, Abby. We haven't seen him this happy in ages." She glanced at Thom. "Anyone would be a fool not to see that."

Abby blinked, shocked more by Mairi's bluntness than the revelation.

"Humph, you really can't see it, can you?" Mairi gave a bittersweet smile. "I'm not a jealous woman, Abby. I'm a sad one, and, yes, a lonely one. I love Thom more than you could know. But not in the way you think. I want to see him happy, and if you're the person who does it, then so be it." She leaned in, her voice lowering. "But if you can't give him what he deserves—and he deserves the stars and the moon—you need to set it straight. You know?"

Abby dipped her head and nodded. *Damn! What am I doing?*

The last thing she intended was to string Thom along.

She closed her eyes. If she had encouraged him—intended or not—she had to get control over that.

Mairi's voice softened. "I'm not sure why you're here, in the middle of our lives. But you landed here for a reason. Nothing's by chance. Destiny is a damned thing. Figure it out, Abby, before there's collateral damage."

Abby squeezed Mairi's hand. She knew there was more behind Mairi's message—she was living with collateral damage.

"I'm trying. I really am," Abby said, not sure if she was trying to convince Mairi or herself.

Mairi threw her arms around Abby. "We're here for you," she whispered in her ear. "You're not alone. Just be careful."

"Hate to break up your lovefest, ladies, but Effemy called a car. She thinks it's time for me to go," Brannan butted in, his words slurring, his grin loose and a bit broad. Throwing his wife's coat over his arm and snatching her purse, he turned to Mairi. "Are ya comin' along?"

Mairi nodded, reaching for her coat. "That's my ride," she said, giving Abby a hug. "We'll talk again ..."

Before he retreated, Brannan pointed toward the front. "Mrs. Landry is waitin' by the door. We've tired the poor old woman. Thom's gettin' a car to take ya both home. Do you mind grabbing' her things?"

Take her home. The notion sent a chill down her spine, mixed with anticipation and anxiety.

Abby collected her things, along with Mrs. Landry's coat, hat, and flowers, then made her way to where Thom was waiting.

"Ready to go?" he said, opening the pub's door.

No, Abby wanted to say, but instead, she nodded. Slipping her arm through Mrs. Landry's, she guided her toward the waiting car, acutely aware of Thom just a step behind.

30

WHO WE ARE

When Mrs. Landry said her goodbyes, Abby was going to follow her inside. But Thom gently tugged at her arm, stopping her.

"Want to walk? Or is it too cold?" Thom asked, his eyes bright with something just shy of hope.

Abby glanced at door, then at the moonlit streets, her breath visible in the cold air. Part of her wanted to say no, to avoid the intimacy of the quiet streets, but she nodded anyway. "A walk would be nice, but I might change my mind," she warned, tightening her coat around herself, the chill biting through her despite her best efforts.

Thom signaled her to take his arm, a silent invitation. Abby hesitated, her hand hovering in mid-air for a brief second before she finally accepted it.

As they made their way down the hill, they fell in step with a group of teens walking in the same direction. Cigarette smoke swirled in the cold air, and their conversation was peppered with cursing. Thom cleared his throat, loud enough to catch their attention. The boys glanced back, understanding his meaning. Their foul language stopped, but they puffed harder on their cigarettes, leaving a thick cloud of smoke in their wake.

Thom gave Abby a quick nod before guiding her down a narrow alley. It was dark and isolated, used for deliveries and quick getaways. A flickering light hung over a doorway, offering no reprieve to the shadows that lingered. Abby knew she was in good hands, but instinctually, she tightened her grip on Thom's arm.

He looked at her. "There's a late-night coffee shop about two blocks away. Are ye in a hurry to get back?"

Abby shook her head. She wasn't in a hurry for anything. She liked being with Thom, clinging to his arm, walking in the dark.

As if he could read her mind, he slipped his arm around her. "Are ye warm enough?"

She could see his breath rising from his lips, the cold cutting through the air. Abby nodded, not trusting her voice, as if speaking might shatter the moment—reminding her that the warmth enveloping her came from another man, a comfort she knew she shouldn't allow herself to indulge in.

The alleys eventually opened to a main road, where they turned. The stone street was well lit by lamps that hung over shops and businesses, now closed. People loitered about, some couples strolled hand in hand, while others made their way toward nearby pubs. An old woman paused to let her dog sniff a bush. The boys they had seen earlier were now seated on a bench, chatting with girls, their cigarettes extinguished. Thom gave them a nod as they passed.

"This way," Thom said, slipping his arm from around her and taking her hand instead.

His fingers curled around hers, warm and strong, chasing

the cold from her skin. She let him hold it, her frozen fingers melting into his grasp as he led her down the street.

They stopped at a red building with two large windows, and a glass door in between them. The sign above read THE SLEEPING ELEPHANT. Thom explained it was one of the few places that stayed open late, serving only coffee and desserts after eleven. It was apparent the crowd inside didn't mind the limited menu—it was packed. Thom spotted a couple leaving near the windows and grabbed the table, outmaneuvering a group of young men. He ordered two coffees and a piece of pie at the coffee bar before sitting down across from Abby.

"This is nice," he said, catching her eyes. "Being with ye."

Abby thought so, too, but avoided returning his sentiment —Mairi's words haunted her. "Mrs. Landry had a good time. You were sweet to dance with her."

"Aye, it's easy to be kind to her," he said. "She was incredibly good to Coira when she got ill. More so, to me, after ..." Thom looked away.

Abby put her hand on his. "Tell me about her, Thom."

"Coira?" He leaned back, took his mug in his hands, and gulped. "Do you really want to know about her?"

Abby nodded.

"Well, I can't say it was love at first sight. But I fell hard for her, all the same. We met at a pub. She was working the tables, flirting with all the college boys. She liked them and they liked her." He smiled. "They would do anything for her. It was her laugh, though. It was light and contagious and made you feel good. Why she picked me is still a mystery."

"If you were anything like you were with Mrs. Landry," Abby said with a soft smile, "I can see why."

Thom leaned in and continued. "I had more hair back then. Wasn't so bad looking, I guess. But who's bad looking at nineteen?" He rubbed the graying short stubble adorning his head. "She was beautiful ... and only got more beautiful over the years. Her hair was a dark auburn, with strands near her face that changed to a strawberry blond in the summer. She always clipped it up, but I liked it down. The day she died was the prettiest I had ever seen her. Oh, don't get me wrong, the cancer took away most of her, but her beauty shined through her frail, weightless body. But it was her eyes—green, bright, with these flecks of gold in the middle. In the last days, they still sparkled, letting us know she was still there, in that cancer-ridden body, not ready to leave. They held her essence until the very end." His grin faded.

"Oh, Thom ... I'm so sorry."

He looked up at Abby. "I'm not sad, Abby. Truly—not anymore. I love remembering her. She made me happy. We were good together. I'll admit, we argued like the best of them. Damn, that woman was stubborn! But I loved her fiercely, and that seemed to keep her in check." He winked.

Abby's cheeks flushed a deep pink, and she turned away, refusing to meet Thom's gaze.

Thom grinned, eyes crinkling. "Have ye not had someone make love to ye that fiercely?"

Fiercely? Abby parted her lips to speak but stopped. Memories surfaced—the first time she and Marcus made love, the night they conceived Emma, or the time they got a babysitter after Drew was born. She and Marcus had a *good* sex life until they didn't. She glanced at Thom, wondering if his, too, had grown perfunctory over time.

"Aye, well ..." Thom let the subject drop.

Abby shifted, her fingers fiddling with the hems of her sleeve. "And the flower shop? How did that begin?" she asked, her tone a little too bright, clearly eager to move on.

"Coira loved gardening. Flowers were her passion. So, I designed the structure, and she chose what to grow. Before long, people were asking for arrangements. We decided to make it our life's work and opened the shop. Everything I know about flowers, I learned from Coira. Oh, I had an eye for design—I studied art and architectural design at university—but it was she who made me see things out of the box, beyond the ordinary. She gave me a different lens to look at the world through," he explained. "I once wanted to create beautiful structures, but now I create beauty out of natural structures. She gave that gift to me."

"Wow." Abby sighed. "She sounds like someone I would have liked."

Thom nodded. "In fact, it was something ye did the first day in my shop that halted me. The way ye bent over and delicately cupped the flowers, gently brushing the petals with your fingertips, as if they had energy and ye were absorbing it through your skin. Almost like ye were making love to them." He looked up at Abby, "It was what Coira did."

"Oh," Abby said softly. She had never thought of it as so poetic.

His voice softened. "Ye reminded me of her."

Abby's eyes widened. Coira was an impressive woman—strong and determined, someone who embraced life with a clear sense of purpose. Abby wasn't like that. She hadn't taken charge of her life; instead, she drifted through it, unsure of what she wanted ... always just existing.

She fell quiet, lost in her thoughts.

Thom picked up a fork and took a bite of pie. "What are ye thinking, Abby?"

Abby hesitated. "The way you speak of you wife ..." She looked away. "I'm nothing like her, Thom. If anything, I'm a fraud."

"You're being hard on yourself. I remembered the moment I saw ye in the coffee shop. You sat at the table and observed the comings and goings, wide-eyed like a curious child. Ye engaged Hazel with friendliness, and not just as a customer. And you were attentive to me—a stranger—without reserve. You made me feel important. You cleaned your plate with abandon and made no apologies." He chuckled. "You're authentic, Abby," Thom noted. "Maybe it's just the lens you're looking through. You'd be amazed by what ye can see, by just changing your perspective."

Abby grabbed the fork out of his hand, cut through the crust, and shoved it in her mouth. "Be careful, I might finish this off with no apology," she teased.

"*That* is what you took from what I said?" he smirked, shaking his head. "How about that I noticed everything the moment I saw ye, wearing ridiculous yoga pants and snow-worn boots. That ye didn't have a bit of makeup on, and still, ye looked beautiful. That in a room full of people, I was drawn to talk to ye. And, of all the people in all the world, I want to be with ye, right here, right now."

Abby stopped chewing, swallowing the pie in a hard gulp. She put the fork down. "I'm married, Thom. Please don't forget that," she said. "I haven't."

Thom slid back into his chair, and stared at Abby, falling silent.

"It's late," Abby said, rising. "Will you take me home?"

Thom tipped his head and pushed out of his chair. "I'll call for a car."

Abby rode home in quiet numbness, alone. Thom opted to walk. He had pushed too far. When his intentions were unspoken, she could enjoy his company with a sort of plausible deniability. But now she knew his intentions—he wanted more. That forced her to hold herself accountable for her actions. It's one thing to enjoy a flirtation. It's entirely different to like it and purposely pursue more.

31

ALLIANCES

Abby rolled over in bed with no rush to get up. The conversation with Thom lingered, and she didn't want to deal with him or the feelings it stirred.

She wondered if it was time to go home.

"No." The word reached her ears, distinct, and not in her voice.

For a second, Abby wasn't sure if she imagined it. But then she turned over to see Jossi sitting by the window. "Errr," she groaned, before wiping away the sleep from her eyes. "What now?"

Abby didn't have to ask. She knew Jossi had heard every word last night and knew every thought—no matter how convoluted—that ran through her head.

"Sorry, but I need to make something clear." Jossi rose from her chair and stood by the bed. "You're not done here."

Abby squeezed her eyes shut, giving her head a small shake. "I know," she murmured. She didn't need Jossi to tell her that. It was something instinctual. She didn't feel finished.

"It's not just about Thom, although he's a good distraction."

"I know." Abby groaned again and threw a pillow over her head.

"Don't act like a child, Abby. It's time you face the actual stuff. Stop running. Stop avoiding."

"That's easy for you to say ... you avoided living," Abby replied, hoping her words were sharp enough to sting.

Jossi shrugged. "Fair enough. You got me on that one."

"Besides." Reasons to leave ticked through her mind. "Drew probably needs me ..."

"He's fine," Jossi said. "Trust me."

Abby sat up and looked at Jossi—beautiful, as always. Her heart ached with love. "You're watching over them, then?"

Jossi smiled. "Of course. I watch over all of you."

Abby's heart swelled with warmth, but the moment was fleeting. She pushed herself out of bed and grabbed her phone, where she was greeted by a bombardment of texts from Marcus.

Abby, seriously, where are you?

Graduation is coming at the end of next month. Lots to plan! Drew hasn't said much ... about you being gone, but I worry about him. Do you?

Talked to Emma. She says not to worry. I'm trying not to.

Rained all day. Your garden is beginning to bloom. It needs tending to. When are you coming home?

There were a few more messages from Emma, letting her know she had talked to her father. Effemy sent a text about having dinner on Friday. Mairi sent one to wish her a good day. There was nothing from Thom. She probably knew it was best, but it hurt a little. She looked up when there was a knock at the door.

"Come in," Abby called out.

"This just arrived," Mrs. Landry said, holding a vase of flowers—a cluster of English yellow roses bunched tightly together, surrounded with lemon leaves to offset the pale color.

She knew the rose well. Known for its tea fragrance with hints of violet, the Graham Thomas rose was one of her favorites. Her grandmother had grown them all over her front yard. She followed in her footsteps, planting them in a hedge along the side of her house—the sunny side—babying them to keep them from dying during the harsh winters. And, as if by magic, or maybe by the watchful eye of her grandmother, they came up every year. Reminding her of the power of renewal and rebirth.

Was this a message?

Abby grabbed the heavy glass container from Mrs. Landry's. "You shouldn't be carrying things up the stairs. This is too heavy." She placed the flowers on the dresser and pulled out the note that was attached, *I'm sorry. Friends? Thom.*

A surge of joy zapped through her, making her body tingle. She didn't want to feel so elated, but she did and couldn't stop it.

"Your room is becoming a little flower shop," Mrs. Landry noted.

Abby looked around at all the yellow flowers that filled her room. Her smile widened.

"He's a nice man," Mrs. Landry said. "Be careful."

"We're just friends," Abby assured her.

"I don't doubt that. So were Willie and me," she said, quietly. "So were we ..." Her voice trailed off as she walked away.

∼

With two coffees in hand, Abby ran across the street to Thom's flower shop. She passed a customer coming through the door as she reached for the handle, opening it for her.

"Thank you," Abby said, a little breathless.

The young man from the day before was standing at the counter. "Abby, right?"

"Yeah." Abby gave him a smile. "You remembered."

"I never forget a face. My mum says it is one of my gifts." He smiled. "Did you get the flowers?"

"Well, that's why I'm here. I wanted to thank Thom." Abby eyed the empty store. "Is he around?"

The young man cocked his head to a doorway. "He's working in there. You're welcome to go back."

Abby thanked him and, pushing aside the black curtain, made her way through the opening. She drew in a sharp breath as a wave of musk enveloped her, sparking her senses. *Lilies!* The fragrance was distinctive. She inhaled again, allowing the rich scent to penetrate her, when the smell of sweet roses and the green of mums followed. "Ahhhh," she said, releasing an exhale.

"Can I help ya?" a man's gruff voice said, popping up from a stool, with cutting shears in his hand.

"Oh." Abby's hands went to her chest. "I didn't see you there. I was looking for Thom."

"Aye," he said, and called into the dark corridors, "Thom? A pretty lady is lookin' for ya." When no one answered, he said, "He's probably outside signing for the delivery. Have a seat." He pointed to a chair. He leaned over a floral bucket filled with roses and continued to cut down the stems, the cracking of the wood echoing against the cement walls.

Abby sat and motioned to the workbench topped with an assortment of arrangements. "Those are beautiful. What's the occasion?"

"A wedding," the man grunted.

"I see," Abby said, eyeing the bucket of roses in front of him. "Are those for the bridal bouquet?"

"Aye," he confirmed without looking at her.

Abby could see why he was in the back and not at the front desk to greet customers.

"Oliver," Thom's voice came from the back, "they delivered the green spider mums for the maids of honor bouquets. We can start ... Abby, what are you doing here?"

"I brought you some coffee." She outstretched her hands, holding the two coffees. "As a thank you for the flowers this morning."

The grumpy man immediately snapped his head up, and one side of his mouth curled upward. "So, you're Abby. I should've guessed."

Thom shot him a look. "That's enough, Oliver," he warned, turning to Abby. "He's the beauty behind the brains and the creative genius."

Abby leaned forward and shook his hand. "Nice to meet you, Oliver."

"Thom hasn't stopped talkin' about you. It's nice to finally meet you."

Thom's eyebrow shot up, and he seared another look at Oliver.

"Says you're a flower lady yourself," Oliver continued, ignoring Thom.

"Only as a hobby, not a trade, like you," Abby confirmed. "It would have been a dream to do what you do."

"How'd you like to get your hands dirty for a while?" Oliver held up his shears. "I could use some help cuttin' those mums that just arrived."

"Really?" Abby jumped up. "I'd love to."

"Ye don't have to do this," Thom said.

"You're right, I don't. And it just so happens that I have nothing planned today." She looked at Oliver for direction. "So, where do I start?"

"Here." Thom took off his apron and handed it to Abby. "You'll want to cover your pretty outfit." He opened a couple of drawers and, when he finally found what he was looking for, handed her a pair of gloves. "You'll need these, or else you'll be pricked and bleeding in no time."

Abby tied the apron around her and slipped on the gloves. "I'm ready. Where shall I sit?"

Thom froze, staring at her. His smile disappeared, and his eyes turned dark.

"What's wrong?" Abby asked, looking down at herself.

"Nothing, ye look perfect," he said, then turned and abruptly walked away, heading down the aisle he came from.

Abby's eyes widened. "What's wrong, Oliver?"

"Nay," Oliver assured her. "I think it's just ... we haven't had a woman working in the back room since Coira."

"Oh," Abby sighed.

"Aw, it's nothin' you did. He's just havin' a moment. It happens," Oliver said. "Come, sit over here." He turned over an empty bucket and slapped it. Handing her a pair of shears, he said, "Finish cuttin' these"—he pointed to the white roses he was working on—"and I'll get the flowers that just arrived."

Abby sat down, adjusting to the hard surface of the bucket. She lifted a rose from the water and put it to her nose. It didn't have a fragrance, being grown for beauty, but it still had a scent of earth and water, like the petrichor smell after a rain. She snipped the end, letting the stem fall to the cement floor, before placing the rose back in the water. She finished the last dozen, waiting for the two men to resurface from the darkened aisles of the warehouse.

A large-paned window sat over the desk, giving the space the only natural light. Lamps hung from the open ceilings, encircling light every few feet along the aisles, where shelves held varying sizes of vases and floral supplies. She could see stacks of green floral tape and blocks of foam stored on the shelves. Abby heard a door open in the back, and light flooded the space. But it was quickly gone when the door shut.

Thom walked forward carrying two more buckets of flowers and placed them next to Abby.

Abby looked up at him. "You all right? I mean, if you prefer, I'll leave ..."

"No," Thom said, sitting himself down on Oliver's bucket and grabbing the shears on the ground. He grabbed a handful of flowers from the bucket and began cutting. "It wasn't ye," he finally said. "Sometimes we just need a break." He winked and continued with the next bunch of flowers.

Abby reached over and touched his shoulder. He laid his hand on top of hers, and for a moment, they held each other's eyes with understanding.

His eyes were dark pools, inviting her in. Abby could see he wanted to kiss her. If she had to admit, she wanted him to. But he didn't. She had made her stand last night. Thom was too honorable to push any further. She was safe from him. The thought should've brought her comfort, but it didn't. For she wasn't sure if she was safe from herself.

32

THE WEDDING

Thom, Oliver, and Abby had stayed up until midnight working in the flower shop, ordering terrible pizza and warm beer for dinner and munching on stale cookies to keep their energy going until the project was completed. After they finished the second beer, Oliver suggested that Abby help them set up the wedding in the morning. Thom shook his head, but Abby wouldn't let him say no.

Exhausted but satisfied, Abby fell into bed with thoughts of the wedding swirling in her mind. Even as she shivered under the covers, her thoughts were already racing ahead to the flower shop. She was no longer just helping Thom, she was a part of something bigger, and it felt exhilarating. Creating flowers for a wedding was her dream job, and now she was living it, if only for a day.

Just the night before, she'd stood in the middle of the flower shop surrounded by the intoxicating scent of lilies, roses, and freesia. Vases of flowers spilled onto the counter, waiting to be transported. Thom was organizing ribbons on the far side of the room, humming quietly to himself, and Oliver was whistling along to the tune.

Abby's eyes drifted to the sketch Oliver had pinned to the wall, a concept for the bridal arrangement they were preparing. It was lovely, but something about it felt too ... predictable. She hesitated, biting her lip as she studied the design. *A bridal bouquet should be unforgettable*, she thought. Yet his design felt safe.

"Thom?" Her voice called out. But when he didn't look up, she tried again, louder this time. "Thom?"

He turned, eyebrows raised, and his humming halted. "Aye?"

Abby glanced at Thom, then at Oliver. She'd never been one to challenge ideas, especially since they were the "experts." But her creativity was sparking, itching to try something different. "I was thinking ..." Abby walked over to a bucket of hellebores. "I noticed the design uses white hellebores, but if we mix in a few green ones ... it would add a layer of vibrancy, an earthy richness that compliments the ethereal white of the roses?"

Thom walked over, crossing his arms as he studied her suggestion with the drawing the bride had approved.

Oliver walked over, grabbing the green flowers and mixing them with the white. "She's right. It's subtle but adds just the right touch of drama."

For a moment, Thom said nothing, his expression unreadable. Then, to her surprise, he broke into a grin. "Aye, Abby. That's brilliant. Let's give it a go."

By the time they finished, the bouquet was stunning— vivid and unexpected, and exactly the boldness the bride would want. Abby couldn't stop staring at it, a small smile creeping onto her face.

"You've got an eye for this," Thom said, with a wink. "I don't know why you've been hiding it."

The thought thrilled her. *When was the last time she trusted her instincts like that? Expressed her creativity so freely?* It felt ... authentic, like herself.

Five hours later, her alarm was pushing her to get out of bed. The bouquet lingered in her mind, a reminder of what she could achieve when she trusted herself. She rose with a quiet determination to carry confidence into the wedding setup.

The streets were empty when she made it out of the inn. It was so early, even Hazel hadn't opened her shop yet, leaving Abby without her coffee. The temperature was still low in the mornings, but it had promised to warm up to a fair fourteen degrees Celsius later that day. Abby wrapped her scarf around her neck, slipped on her gloves, and headed for the flower shop, where Oliver was just driving off, the truck loaded with the arrangements and more boxes of flowers for decorating, and Thom and Abby followed in a car, equally loaded with supplies.

The wedding venue was an old chapel, a little over an hour out of town. As they arrived, Abby rolled down the window, breathing the crisp, fresh air. The scent of damp earth and pine drifted in from the nearby woods. Morning dew deepened the pale gray and creamy tones of the weathered stone. Outside the chapel, tents for the reception were being erected on the lawn, overlooking a glassy lake that shimmered with the morning sun, undisturbed by man, animal, or insect. Abby exhaled, taking in the majestic setting.

Yet there was nothing glamorous about the work they were doing. It was manual labor from start to finish, and Abby had never worked so hard physically. Thom had a small crew of college students to help with the heavy lifting, but that didn't lessen the loading, carrying, moving, and climbing the job required. Everything had to be picture-perfect, as Oliver's sharp eyes darted over every arrangement, the snip of his shears and the rustling of stems following him wherever he went. Still, no one had a better grasp on perfection than Thom, methodically directing each display with care. He was linear and precise, whereas Oliver was visual and creative. Together, they coordinated everyone's efforts like a well-choreographed ballet. Abby watched with amazement as it all came together in beautiful harmony. By the end, her back ached, her fingers were raw, and she was exhausted, yet she had never felt more satisfied.

Abby stood back, wiping her hands on her jeans, admiring the display of flowers before her. "Wow! You guys are amazing."

"It's not just us ..." Oliver shot a look at Thom. "*We're* amazing, Abby. I'd take you as a partner any time."

Abby sprang into Oliver's arms and hugged him tightly. "I'm so honored," she said. "Thank you for including me today."

"Well, there is no need for that," Oliver said, stepping back as his face turned red. "I can admire a woman's touch and hard work. You deserve the recognition. You're a natural with flowers—it's a rare gift."

Abby beamed. "I'm going to hug you again," she warned, and did.

This time, Oliver wrapped his arms around her. "You're okay with me, Abby," he whispered in her ear. "Just be careful with him."

Abby eased out of the embrace, and their eyes met. She could see Oliver wasn't warning her but inviting her to leap.

"You can take it from here," Oliver said, releasing Abby

before turning to Thom. "The smaller bouquets are in the chapel. Ya know the drill," he reminded him. "I'm goin' to leave with the kids. I've a date with a hot bath, a great book, and my dog, Bella." He winked at both of them before he walked away.

Abby felt a rush of gratitude for Oliver's encouragement, his playful spirit balancing Thom's steady, determined focus. Thom's concentration, his attention to every detail, every flower, was infused with thoughtful creativity and care. She admired the quiet strength brought to the delicate task of creating beauty for a memorable event. It was exactly the kind of dedication she'd imagined pouring into her own business, had she started one. She glanced over, catching Thom's gaze, and found an unspoken understanding in his eyes, making her feel unexpectedly giddy.

"Quite a morning so far, eh?" Thom said, closing the distance between them. "I hope we haven't burned the candle at both ends. We still have a wee bit more to do. Do ye mind?"

Abby shifted her weight to ease the pressure on her back. "I'm tired, but I'm having an amazing time. Bring it on!"

"Is working ye to the bone your idea of fun? Hmm, I think ye might need a holiday from your holiday." He laughed. "But seriously, Abby, ye did really good work. Coira would've been proud."

Abby's heart skipped a beat, and with impulse, she threw her arms around him.

Thom's arms easily wrapped around her, locking her into his embrace.

As if she had always belonged there, her head nuzzled into the crook of his neck, and his cheek pressed softly against her ear. She could feel his heartbeat against hers, as his warmth enveloped her entire body. She allowed herself to savor his warmth for a heartbeat longer, the world falling away in that perfect, private moment.

When she stepped back, she caught his gaze lingering on her, and an unmistakable warmth, both familiar and startlingly new, washed over her. She wondered if he felt the same quiet pull. Had they not been interrupted, she might have explored the question or at least lingered in the excitement of the possibility.

"Mr. Emerson," a young man's voice called out.

Thom looked up, but it was Abby who stepped away, now embarrassed.

"The groomsmen seem to be having problems with their boutonnieres. We were wondering ..." the young man explained.

"Abby, would ye mind dealing with the bride? Her bouquet is in the back seat of the car."

"Really? Me?"

Thom nodded, sending Abby scurrying off to the car.

With the box safely gripped between her hands, excitement fluttered in Abby's chest as she approached the medieval door of the church room. The bride was leaning into the mirror putting on lipstick, while the bridesmaids, all dressed in the same dress except in varying shades of green, were drinking champagne, excitedly chatting when Abby entered. The girls scurried over to see her unveil the bouquet.

Abby lifted the top, and all the girls gushed.

"Oh my!" the bride exhaled. "I never imagined it would be this pretty." She picked up the bouquet and cradled it in her arms, her fingers brushing over the flowers in loving affection.

Watching the bride's hand tremble, Abby felt a pang of nostalgia and longing, remembering the heady mix of excitement and nerves she experienced on her wedding day, a moment that felt both tender and full of possibilities.

The bride looked at Abby, her eyes brimming with tears, causing Abby to do the same.

Swiping away tears, Abby scanned the room for the mother of the bride, suddenly worried she might have intruded on a precious moment. "Where's your mother?"

The bride's face dimmed, and Abby knew immediately she had made a faux pas. Her eyes lowered. "I'm sorry."

The bride reached for Abby's arm and smiled sweetly. "It's fine. You couldn't have known. I know she is here in spirit. It was kind of you to think of her feelings. And you are right, she would have liked to see the unveiling."

The bride walked to the mirror and looked at the image before her. "I'm a bride," she whispered, her voice trembling slightly.

Abby rested her hands gently on the bride's shoulders. "And a beautiful one. Your mother would be proud, if not weeping with joy, to see her lovely daughter heading off to start her own life."

The bride embraced Abby. "Thank you," she murmured in Abby's ear. "I will never forget this moment. It is what I would have wanted my mother to say."

The wedding planner poked her head in the door and gave the girls their five-minute warning to line up outside the chapel. In a swoop of skirts, the girls rushed to the mirror, surrounding the bride, and made last-minute adjustments to their makeup and hair.

Abby picked up the empty box, hoping to slip out unnoticed. She took one last glance at the bride, fluffing her skirt, surrounded by the admiration of her bridesmaids. The day was all hers, a celebration of love a woman dreams about as a young girl. Cradling her bouquet, her fingers ran delicately over the white petals, and her smile softened. She looked back at Abby, catching her gaze. It was at that moment Abby could see the distant, aching loss of the girl's mother in her eyes, a void that nothing could quite fill.

"Miss," she called over the heads of the entourage. "I didn't get your name."

"Abby."

"Thank you, Abby." She blew a kiss in the air. "You were very significant to me today. Truly."

Abby bowed her head and left the small vestibule, feeling the bride's gratitude linger. She hadn't expected to feel so moved, her memories mingling with the joy of the day mixed with the sadness lingering in her heart about her own marriage hanging on by a thread. As she swiped back tears, a familiar voice stopped her in her tracks.

"Abby?" a man said, his accent unmistakable.

She looked up, surprised, with an unexpected flutter in her chest as she recognized him. "Peter?"

The man's lips spread in a broad smile.

She pointed to the door she had just left. "That's your goddaughter in there?"

"It is," he said, giving her a warm smile. "This is a nice surprise. Maybe destiny is on our side after all."

But when he saw her tears, his expression softened. He reached into his pocket and pulled out a handkerchief. The soft fabric brushed against her skin as he dabbed at the corners of her eyes.

"Everything all right?" he asked, his voice low and comforting.

Abby's lips curved into a faint smile, despite feeling exposed. "It's weddings ... they tug at the heart every time."

"Ah, yes, don't they?" Peter tucked the damp handkerchief

away into his pocket. "It must be fate we meet again. You needed a hanky, and I had one readily available."

Abby let out a laugh, conceding that Peter was charming. There was an ease of his presence—the melodic refinement of his voice, the debonair way he held himself—that settled her, even amid all the unexpected emotions stirred by the day.

"You are smiling. Does that mean you might dance with me later?" Peter said, his voice holding a spark of playfulness.

"Uncle Peter?" the bride cried out, glancing at Abby, then back to her uncle. "Wait, do you two know each other?"

"No," Abby quickly replied.

"Yes," Peter insisted. "She's an old friend. I insist she stay and celebrate with us."

The bride reached for Abby's arm. "That is a lovely idea. Oh, you must," she pleaded.

Peter threw up his arms. "Who are we to deny fate?"

The wedding planner tugged at the wedding party bottlenecking at the door. "Come, girls!" she insisted, dragging them all away.

Peter followed the entourage, but not before he mouthed, "See you later."

"What was that all about?" Thom asked, saddling up to Abby as the wedding party scurried off, leaving her alone at the door.

Abby watched as they disappeared from view before looking back at Thom. "Apparently we're staying for the wedding," she informed him, a mix of excitement and apprehension sparking within her at the thought of extending her perfect day, indulging in a beautiful wedding, and sharing it all with Thom.

33

TEARS

bby and Thom sat at the back of the church, nestled between an elderly couple and two young teenagers. She hadn't been to a wedding in a long time and had forgotten the emotional roller coaster they caused. The crucifix looming overhead, the candles burning on each side of the altar, and the haunting sound of the organ transported her back to her wedding day: her father's hand trembling as he let go of hers; Marcus whispering how pretty she looked when he lifted her veil; and the moment when he slipped the ring on her finger, his baby blue eyes locking with hers as his voice quivered, promising to love and cherish her, for better or for worse, till death do them part.

Watching the groom take the bride's hands in his, echoing out his words of devotion, Abby began to tear up. She had believed in devotion once, too, standing at the altar with Marcus, but somewhere between the vows and the life they built, it had slipped away, unnoticed until it was gone. For a moment, she wondered if she should halt the wedding and scream for the bride to run. Devotion, it seemed, was for the young to believe in, while giving the old something to hold on to. But what happens in between, no one ever warns you about that.

As she returned to the couple now present at the altar, tears fell down her cheeks. Abby swiped them off with the ends of her sweater, hoping Thom didn't notice. But before she could finish, Thom handed her some tissue stuffed in his pocket, keeping one for himself, drying the pools in the corners of his own eyes.

After waiting for the guests to exit the church, Thom and Abby followed the crowd to the tents outside. The bride was clever enough to add their names to the guest list, finding them two seats at a table in the back shared with two cousins, twice removed, the bride's dentist and his wife, and an old man who used to be the groom's high school math teacher. There, with the misfits, Abby and Thom indulged in a large quantity of champagne, a gourmet dinner of squab and rice, and two pieces of cake between them. When the music began, Thom didn't wait for approval, dragging Abby to the dance floor.

"It was a nice ceremony," Thom said in her ear, as they came together for a slow dance.

"Yes, a lovely wedding." Abby looked around the room, admiring the glow of the candles and the overflowing bouquets of imported green spider mums, white hydrangea, and white roses set in the middle of each table. "And whoever did the flowers should be commended. They're stunning."

Thom nodded. "Aye, well thank ye. But I have to give some credit to my talented protégé on the project."

"Talented protégé? Be careful. She'll get a large head and open a shop herself ... give you competition."

Thom caught her gaze, holding it. "You could, Abby."

"What?" Abby's eyes rolled. "Open up a shop? Don't be

silly." She looked away, quickly dismissing the intensity in his eyes. When she looked back, his gaze was darker, more intense.

"Stay," he said, dropping the sentiment flat in front of her.

Abby's heart pounded with hard, fast flutters against her chest. *Run!* she heard someone say. Was it Jossi? She looked around the room to see if she was leaning against a post or smiling from an empty seat at a table. However, she wasn't there. It was her own head shouting at her.

"I ..." Abby pushed out of Thom's arms, her eyes straining to see through the crowd, calculating an escape. The large tent now seemed to close her in, despite the open air. The press of bodies and music only heightened her need to escape. She wasn't ready to be swept into someone else's story, not again. She needed air, space, a moment to breathe. "I'm sorry, Thom, I just can't ..."

Abby began pushing her way through the dance floor, nudging the swaying couples aside, trying to make her escape. Suddenly, an arm grabbed her and yanked her back. She braced herself for Thom to draw her back into his fantasy, where, in that moment, she might say yes.

"Dance with me, pretty lady," an English man's voice said.

"Peter!" Abby stopped and turned to him. Her lip quivered as she tried to refuse him. "I really can't ..."

His eyes met hers. "Ah, I see why God put us together again." He reached into his pocket and retrieved his handkerchief once more for Abby.

Abby shook her head. "I don't need it." She was determined not to cry. "Really," she assured him, her voice steadier.

"A woman of resilience, I see," he said, stuffing the hanky away. "Now that we've got that settled, dance with me?" he asked again.

Abby gave a slight nod. "Just one," she said, wanting to repay his kindness.

He smiled with the win, bringing Abby closer. "So, three times, I am lucky enough to find you. What do you suppose it means?"

"Probably just a coincidence."

"Coincidence or fate?" Peter questioned.

Abby considered his words. "I don't believe in fate. It's not like our life is dictated by some grand design, or some fixed story waiting for you, or for me." She looked at the bride and groom dancing together, their faces beaming. "Maybe that's why we cry at weddings, because we want to believe in the fantasy. But life happens—bad things, good things. And every decision creates ripples, affecting everything, and everyone, that follows."

"Hmm." Peter gave her a thoughtful look. "How did one so pretty become so cynical?"

"I'm not cynical," Abby said with a wry smile, knowing she was. "I just see the world as it is. Life isn't a fairy tale, it has real consequences. Fate, if it exists at all, is just about choices. Some we control, and others we don't."

"And this man you are with? The one who seems to be watching us," Peter pointed to Thom. "He is not your husband, but twice I have seen you with him. Are you sure there is no fantasy in your life?"

Thom stood at the edge of the tent, cradling a glass of whiskey in his hand. He was watching them, and Abby knew he was waiting for the music to end.

Run, run, run, Abby's head screamed. *Stay, stay, stay*, her heart pleaded.

"Well?" Peter asked again, distracting Abby's thoughts. "Because if *he* isn't making a pass at you, I will."

Abby smiled at Peter for trying. "You're a charming man,

Peter, but you wouldn't want me." Abby lowered her eyes. "My own husband doesn't want me. And no one likes leftovers." She released her arms around his neck and kissed him on the cheek. "Thank you for offering, though."

With a nod to Peter, she excused herself, her emotions beginning to settle in as she made her way through the crowd toward the bar. She noticed Thom following her with a careful eye, and her heart pumped hard against her chest. Even from a distance, she could feel his presence—a kinetic energy moving between them. As the bartender handed her a bottle of champagne and a glass, she purposely turned away, slipping out of the tent in the opposite direction of Thom, praying he didn't follow her.

ABBY WAS SITTING at the bank of the lake, beyond the tents. The bottle of champagne lay discarded a few feet away, with an empty glass resting beside her. Her knees were drawn up, cradling her head. In the distance, the soft strains of big band music and the laughter of the wedding party drifted through the night air, blending with the quiet rustle of the lake's surface.

Thom sat down beside her. "How are ye feeling?"

"Tired," she answered without looking up. "Drunk, once again." She added, "My husband would be ashamed ..."

"Do ye want to talk about it?" he offered.

Abby turned her head to him. "Not really."

"Abby." Thom's voice was rough-hewn and wavering. "It pains me to see ye like this."

"Ooooh ..." Abby breathed a long, heavy sigh. She dragged her hand down her face, pressing against her cheeks, as though she could physically push the frustration away.

"I'm lonely. I'm sad. Am I allowed to admit that?" She glanced at Thom, searching his face for an answer. "It feels so wrong even saying it, like I'm letting everyone down. But I hurt, deep inside." She pressed her palm against her chest. "Like the blood inside me is thick and heavy, weighing me down. It's so overwhelming, sometimes I can't breathe."

Her voice got caught in her throat as she continued. "Everyone says you shouldn't care what other people think, that you should create a life of your own and surround yourself with love. But in my world, the life I've built is slowly disintegrating. I'm becoming obsolete, disappearing into insignificance ... and no one even notices. It makes me wonder if anything I've done in my life matters." She closed her eyes and took in a deep breath. "My marriage is empty, my kids don't need me anymore, my womanhood feels shattered, and I keep wondering who I am anymore?"

Abby opened her eyes, staring blankly ahead. "I ran away from my life, not even knowing what I wanted to find. I just couldn't stay in that place where I was lingering in obscurity, like a ghost lost between life and death. I'm on this journey with no direction. I keep searching for the answers from my best friend—who is dead—and all the while, I'm disappointing the people dearest to me. I'm failing miserably, watching my life fall apart." She swiped at the corner of her eyes and shook her head. "And I don't want to go—I can't go back—until I can find my way out of limbo. It's not where I'm meant to stay."

Thom shifted, watching Abby release her inner demons. He rubbed the back of his neck, his face showing no reaction to the heavy words she laid bare. After a long pause, he leaned forward slightly, his voice low and steady. "So," he said, with a half smile. "Ye don't want to talk about it, then?"

Abby turned to Thom. The moonlight was bright,

revealing the mature lines of his face. It was a manly face with a solid chin. She liked that about him—that he was reliable. In the night, his eyes turned gray, the blue fading into the dark sky, but they still sparkled as if they were part of the stars above them. She felt drawn to him, wanting to pull him close and kiss him. But she knew better.

"Why are you so nice?" Her voice came out raspy and tired.

"Because I like you," he said. "And I don't mean that in the way ye think." He shifted, searching for the right words. "I'm sorry if what I said on the dance floor was inappropriate."

Abby allowed him a faint smile. "It was sweet," she said. "And if I wasn't married, I might feel tempted. But I have so much to sort through. And it wouldn't be fair to bring you into the mess I've created."

"Abby, everyone has a right to sort things out. Why are ye so hard on yourself? When Coira and I got overwhelmed, she'd say, 'Let's take it one day at a time.' And that's how we got through it—doctor's appointments, chemo treatments, running the business—trying to fit in living the rest of your life in a few months. It could've gotten the best of us, but we wrestled with one thing at a time. And eventually, we found our way out." He paused and then corrected himself, "Well, I found *my* way out."

Abby reached over and brushed her hand across Thom's cheek, the bristles of his beard pricking her palm. "You're a good man, Thom Emerson." Scooting closer, she let the solid weight of his shoulder invite her in and leaned her head against him, feeling the steadiness of his breath against her cheek. A calmness settled over her, the tightness easing in her chest as they both fell silent, gazing upon the lake, listening to the distant music while watching the water ripple as the fish surfaced for the insects.

"I love my family," Abby finally said. "They've been my whole life." She paused, her thoughts reflecting back. "After battling cancer, I realized my life wasn't ending, it was just beginning, granting me the rest of my life. I guess it was God's way of forcing me to look closer at myself. To be present, and not take tomorrow for granted. Not assume I had all the time in the world to fix me ... to fix me and Marcus," she murmured, letting out a weary sigh. "When you see your life that way, everything shifts. Suddenly, happiness, purpose, and clarity can't wait. They become immediate. You reassess where you're going because you know you don't have forever to get there."

She looked down for a moment, reflecting. "I've wandered through life, watching it unfold, taking whatever comes. I thought that was what you were supposed to do—roll with the punches, adjust, reset, move on. But it never occurred to me I could take charge of life. Wield it." She glanced at Thom. "Like Coira did."

Thom's brow furrowed, the lines laying heavy in the shadows. "Abby, why have ye kept this all inside?"

"Because I'm terrified," she said bluntly. "Afraid if I look too closely, ask too many questions, I'll have to admit the truth." She began to cry. "About Marcus ... about who I am ... and I'm not sure of what I might be left with."

Thom tilted his head slightly, his voice low and soft. "Does he love ye, Abby?"

"I really don't know," Abby admitted. "I left without asking. I was too afraid to face the truth, because without him, I'm not sure what my life looks like."

"What do ye want?" Thom asked, his voice firmer, pushing her to confront the question head-on.

Abby opened her mouth, but her thoughts jumbled. "I want ..." she started, but didn't finish.

"What? Say it, Abby," Thom pushed. "Ye have to say it out loud and grab it, for ye may never know otherwise."

"I want it to be okay to be me, Abby, with my dreams, wants, and desires. When my best friend died, I lived. But I started living her life. I fell in love with her man, had her wedding, named my kids the names she wanted, and became the woman she would have become. I loved Marcus the way he deserved to be loved—*by her*. But if I am no longer *that* person, will he love *me*?"

"Damn it, Abby!" Jossi's voice ripped through the night air.

Abby jumped up, looking for her best friend. "Where are you?" she yelled into the dark.

Jossi approached slowly, stopping in front of her. With the moonlight highlighting her face, her dark eyes locked onto Abby's. "I never asked you to do that ... to become me."

Tears ran down Abby's cheeks. "I did it because I loved you."

"You chose to live, Abby. Now live!" Jossi stepped closer, her face softening, a quiet warmth replacing the intensity in her eyes. "I chose my fate. Choose yours."

"But I will lose you, forever ..."

"You won't need me then," Jossi said, her image slowly disappearing into the darkness that surrounded them.

"Jossi," Abby cried. "Please don't leave me ... not yet."

Abby didn't need to turn around to know Thom was still a few feet behind her, watching her as she spoke to the night, to the emptiness before her. His presence was calm, unintrusive, a quiet support she hadn't expected. He didn't say anything, didn't ask questions, but she felt his awareness, his quiet understanding of her struggles. He didn't need to see what she saw to know that she was wrestling with something larger than the present moment. Maybe that is why her heart ached so sharply—a longing she was trying, and failing, to resist.

When her sobs came in jagged gasps, he finally came to her, wrapping his arms around her. Her head dropped onto his shoulder as her trembling body shook against his chest.

"Cry away, my little bird. No one can hear ye," he said in a whisper.

Abby lifted her head to meet his gaze. "You must think I'm completely mad, yelling at ghosts in the night," she said, her voice hoarse and crackled. "But she was here. She's always with me."

"Who?" Thom questioned, looking into the darkness in front of them.

"My best friend, Jossi. We've shared our whole lives since we were in kindergarten, with a pact to grow old together. Then she died."

"And ye lived." Thom's voice was matter-of-fact. "Did ye make a pact to give up on your own life?"

Abby stared at him, cut by his words. "I was keeping my end of the deal."

"Maybe. Or maybe she is waiting for ye to let her go?"

"I don't know how to let her go," Abby admitted.

"Well, maybe that's what ye need to figure out, Abby. Sometimes ye need to let go so that someone else can be set free."

34

FINDING ABBY

Thom didn't say a word, but hummed an old Scottish folk song, his voice lifting in the air, as Abby lay her head on his shoulder and listened. His steady hum soothed her, gradually quieting her sobs. He never once complained about his stiff shoulder or his drenched sweater. As the last of her tears dried, the rawness of her confession left Abby exhausted. All she wanted was to escape into the serenity of the night.

"Can you take me home?" Abby asked, finally lifting her head from his shoulder.

Thom stopped humming. "Aye." He smiled down at her.

The wedding was still in full swing, the music and laughter carrying on into the night, when Thom stepped into the tent briefly to grab their things before heading to the car. Abby slumped into the seat like a rag doll and pressed her head against the window. She remained quiet as they meandered throughout the countryside, shadows of gray and green flashing by, the serenity offering a reprieve from the whirlwind of thoughts in her head. As they neared the inn, Thom grabbed tissues from his glove compartment, offering Abby a chance to clean her tearstained face before Mrs. Landry got a sight of her, but nothing would hide her red eyes and blotchy skin.

"Are ye sure ye don't want me to come in?" Thom offered.

Abby eyed the light still on in the front room, hoping Mrs. Landry had gone to bed. "No, thank you. I'll just make some tea and head up to bed."

"Ye know." Thom let a soft smile play on his lips. "I'm pretty good at putting ye to bed?"

Abby managed a faint smile in return, her expression saying all that needed to be said as she gently declined his offer.

Thom nodded with recognition. "Aye, goodnight then."

Abby never made that tea. When she saw Mrs. Landry's bedroom door shut, she turned out the lights and headed straight to her room, which was now her sanctuary. It was apparent she was becoming too comfortable with the inn and with the people. She wasn't sure if that was a good thing or a sign to move on. Either way, she was too tired to think, the hard labor of the day finally registering in her arms and legs. All she wanted to do was fall into the comfy bed. She threw down the sheets and stacked the pillows, awaiting her to climb in. She pulled out her phone to check messages, and seeing none, she shoved it in the drawer.

She stripped off her sweater, the scent of flower oils still clinging to the fibers—earthy and sweet tones filling her senses. Before tossing it aside, she brought it to her nose and inhaled deeply. The smell reminded her of the joy of working with flowers, of creating beauty with her own hands. Mostly, it reminded her of Thom, sending a warm, tingling feeling through her body. But when she glanced at the mirror, the giddy feeling drained away. The reflection showed her puffy-eyed and weary face, as well as the tattered woman she was.

She ran her fingers over her chest. New pink skin covered the red raised scars. They didn't shock her anymore. They were just another battle scar on her war-torn body, like her stretch marks from twice giving birth. Or like the raised skin on her right wrist from stitches when she cut herself by cleaning a vase that shattered in her hands. There she was, Abby in all her glory, standing before herself. She leaned in, took one more look, and for the first time in a long time, she didn't want to look away.

Abby put on her pajamas and crawled into bed, her aching body sinking into the pillow-topped mattress. Turning off the lights, her lids fell heavy. But as she lay in the dark, her mind wouldn't shut off, her thoughts rattling around in her head like balls in the lottery air chamber.

Abby's eyes opened wide. *He asked me to stay!*

The suggestion had made her legs go weak, a feeling of nausea washing over her. The notion that she could have another life—a changed life that didn't include Marcus— made her hit a wall. No, it brought her to a door. *Dare she open it?*

Instead, she had run away. Drunk, in a foreign country, on a grassy hill, in the dark, all by herself, Abby realized there was nowhere else to run. She had to face what she was doing there and why, and accept wherever it was taking her.

In the weeks that had passed, Abby was discovering herself, without distraction about who she had to be, being among people who had no expectations of her. It was freeing and scary at the same time. The woman who had come to Scotland was slowly disappearing, and somewhere in between, Abby had started to uncover the woman who was hidden inside her. The imperfect woman she saw in the mirror was recognizable, and she wasn't afraid to see her.

Was she afraid to be herself?

"You were never my replacement," Jossi whispered to her in the dark.

Abby turned toward the familiar voice. Seeing Jossi standing beside her bed, she opened her covers and invited Jossi to crawl next to her. They stared at each other, face-to-face, across the two pillows, like they did when they were little girls.

"I never wanted to be you, Jossi," Abby said, her voice quiet. "I just wasn't sure anyone wanted me ... after the accident ... in the shadow of you."

"I'm sorry for that," Jossi said. "But you were meant to be the survivor, Abby. Your life had a purpose, then and now."

"So did yours," Abby shot back, the pain of loss still a stab to her heart.

"And I fulfilled my purpose. I did what I needed to do in the time I was given," Jossi explained. "Don't you get that? My purpose wasn't to be on this earth for as long as you. Your life was meant for ..."

"Jossi!" Abby shouted, abruptly sitting up. "I lived! And the truth of the matter, I was happy to be the one walking out of the hospital." Her eyes grew wide. "I can't believe I just said that." She waited for Jossi to say something, but when she didn't, Abby continued, driven by her newfound courage. "If you want more truth, I was happy I survived cancer. I loved going to college, getting married, having kids, and every dull day of my life. I love living!" Abby cupped her mouth, not wanting to say anymore.

Jossi's eyes lit up, and a grin spread across her face. "Now, doesn't that feel good?" She sat up. "Gosh, I have been waiting a lifetime for you to admit that."

"What are you talking about? Don't you hear me?" Abby's breath hitched as her voice broke. "Jossi, I was happy it was you, and not me, who died." Her eyes lowered. "How horrible of a human being am I?"

Jossi burst out laughing, the sound full of genuine delight. "Oh, dear Lord, Abby, who wouldn't be glad to be alive?" Her laughter softened into something almost wistful. "What I wouldn't give to feel a warm breeze blow on my skin, to taste the sweetness of a peach, or feel the sensation of a kiss again. But, sweetie, I don't resent you for living. You were meant to have a longer life than me. But you've wasted it by living mine —a beautiful and full life that ended. Just as it was meant to."

Abby stared at Jossi, amazed by the love that Jossi had for her. Just when she didn't think she had any more in her, tears ran down her face.

Jossi reached out her hand but then withdrew it. "I wish I could wipe away those tears. The only reason I'd want my life back is to touch you, put my arms around you, and let you know I love you with all my heart."

"I know you do, Jossi. It's what has sustained me all these years."

Jossi sighed. "I know you think your life is messy, and you don't fit in anywhere. Unfortunately, people waste so much time hiding their feelings, hoarding love as if it is going to run out, or as if they have all the time in the world to express it. We know better, don't we? You're going to have to forgive them—your family, Marcus, and yourself—if you are going to find your way."

Abby lowered her eyes, Jossi's words echoing in her mind, urging her forward. When she lifted them again, she could see the gold flecks shimmering in Jossi's. She was so close, so real, it was difficult to delineate life from death. Her hand instinctively stretched forward, longing for the touch that would never come. "All these years, coming and going in my life, and you couldn't tell me this before? Don't you think it might have saved me from all this heartache and falling off the cliff?"

Jossi shook her head. "You don't need saving, Abby. It's time to figure it out on your own. There's no magic fix, no shortcuts." She paused, meeting Abby's eyes. "You've drifted through life, letting everything or everyone else steer you. But you have to be the one in control now."

Abby let out a heavy sigh. "But it seems like I've been doing it wrong this whole time."

Jossi leaned in closer, softening her tone. "Not wrong, it was just one of the many paths life offered. The key is to recognize that you have the power to choose. Choose you, Abby! The emptiness you feel is because you've been living someone else's story. You need to be yourself and live your own life. Not mine. Not Marcus's. Just yours. And when you do that, you'll know what real living feels like."

Abby inhaled the cold air of the room, breathing deeply, letting Jossi's words settle inside her.

Jossi slowly rose from the bed, her figure blending into the shadows, slipping away. "Trust yourself, Abby. It's time." She smiled, giving Abby one last look. "Now, get some rest. You've got a life to start in the morning."

Abby slid under her covers, tossing the comforter over her shoulders. "Jossi?" she called into the room.

"Yes, Abby?"

"You're not going to leave me yet, are you?"

Jossi lingered, her form softening into the shadows. "Not yet, Abby. My work here isn't quite done."

Abby wondered what she meant, but before she could question it, her eyes fell shut and she was asleep.

35

ROADS LESS TRAVELED

Abby's phone was buzzing. She turned over, opened the drawer, and pulled the phone out. Through blurry eyes, she saw a series of texts from Marcus. She ignored them, but before she could put the phone down, more texts started to come through.

Abby, when are you coming home? Now you're scaring me.

This is getting ridiculous, Abby! Why won't you talk to me?

I know you're fine ... Emma tells me. But why are you hiding?

I have to travel for a few days. Drew is staying with the Millers.

You are going to miss his banquets, the award ceremony ... do you even care?

Can you please call me? I need to hear your voice.

Abby sat up and pressed against the pillows, cradling the phone in her hands. She stared at the series of texts, reading them again. *Did Marcus miss her?* Because he never said it. She sent Drew a text telling him to be gracious to the Miller family and to make good decisions. She told him that she loved him and would be back soon. She didn't say when, for she didn't even know.

He sent one text immediately. *Ok.*

Next, Abby lifted her phone and pressed Marcus's number. Her thumb hovered over the call button, but before she could press her finger down, another call came in. She recognized the number.

"Hello?" Abby answered.

"Better today?" Thom asked.

"I'm ... yes, I'm better," she decided.

"That's good news," he said, his tone friendly and warm. "If you'll indulge me, I have a wee adventure. It's just for a few days."

Abby straightened, her curiosity piqued. "Okaaay," she said, cautiously, not wanting to seem too eager.

"I have a delivery up the coast. It's a few hours away ... with some stops. But there's somewhere I want to take ye. I think ... well, someplace special. I thought, if ye had the time, ye might like the drive. I have a cottage near the River Dee. We could stay."

When Abby didn't answer, he explained, "Abby, it's an escape. Barely a stone building with a fireplace, but it sits atop a small mountain and the countryside will take your breath away. Very peaceful and a place I go to rest my mind. I just thought, well, if it works for me, it might do ye some good, too." He paused for her answer, but before she did, he added, "And oh, it has two bedrooms, of course."

Abby smiled to herself. She thought he was being very honorable. "It sounds nice," she agreed. "When were you thinking?"

"Can ye be ready in an hour?"

～

Mrs. Landry handed Abby a tin of shortbread cookies before she walked out the door. "Have a good time, ya two. And be careful of those crazy tourists driving on the roads," she warned. "Oh, no offense, my dear," she apologized to Abby. "But our roads are narrow, and sometimes people don't realize that civilization is far and few between."

"No explanation needed," Abby said, leaning over the woman's elderly frame and hugging her.

"You're lookin' happy, my dear," she whispered in Abby's ear. "Be good, do what ya must, but be careful." She stepped away, shooing the two out the door. "Now, scoot, you'd better be off."

Thom grabbed Abby's bag and carried it to the car. A large dog's head stuck out the window as they approached, his eyes squinting and his mouth open as if smiling at Abby.

Abby looked at Thom. "Our driving companion?"

Thom walked up to the dog and patted him on the head. "I don't think ye two have formally met. This is Cronos," he said. "And don't be fooled by his fierce look. He's more a lover than a killer."

Abby walked up and rubbed the big face all over. "Cronos, god of agriculture?"

"Well, we found him in our garden, starving. Coira took him in and nursed him back to life. Now at one hundred and twenty-two pounds, and nearly nine years later, he is pampered like a god."

"Well, he's quite a creature. Aren't you?" Abby kissed him on the top of the head. "I guess you can't get any safer than traveling with a large German shepherd in the back of the car."

"Hey, what about a large strapping Scottish man?" Thom slapped his chest.

Abby rolled her eyes. "Yeah, that too. But just for the record, I'm sticking with the dog."

"Then ye don't mind?" Thom asked, opening the car door for Abby. "He loves the cottage. And I don't think I've been there without him since ..." He paused, the memory of his wife likely tugging at his heart. "Well, I've never been there alone, really."

Abby happily agreed and climbed in the front seat, whereupon Cronos tried to sit on her lap. "Oh, no you don't, buddy," she ordered and pushed him to his relegated spot in the back.

"Ready?" Thom asked as he climbed into the driver's seat. He looked at Abby, running his eyes over her, before turning on the car. "Ye look—*good*."

"Is that your way of saying I'm better than last night?" Abby covered her face. "God, I must have looked awful!"

"Aye, well, that's true," Thom said with a wry smile, though his eyes stayed fixed on her. "I don't know, just something about ye ... a sparkle in your eyes," he noted. "Maybe ye worked through some of those demons?"

Abby thought about it. She was happier, lighter.

Turning her gaze, she locked eyes with him. "How do you always do that?"

He titled his head, a flicker of curiosity crossing his face. "What?"

"Make people feel good."

Thom let out a low laugh. "Now, if Coira was in the car, she'd be the first one to tell ye that I'm just an arse like any other man. But I'm glad it makes you feel good." He reached for her hand and squeezed it before letting go and returning it to the steering wheel. "Ye seemed to have needed to get a lot out of ye last night."

"Maybe a lifetime of stuff," Abby admitted, with a

sheepish smile. "And if I didn't apologize a thousand times already, I'm sorry for crying all over your nice sweater."

"If that's a compliment, I'll be sure to wear it again," he said, giving her a wink.

Abby hit him on the arm. "I didn't say I liked it on you, just that it was a nice sweater ..."

They both laughed.

A warmth surged through her like a flow of lava from a volcano, spreading from her heart to the tips of her toes. She breathed in deeply, trying to subside the rush of joy she felt. Being with Thom, even in the simple moments, felt good. It was like a feeling of coming home from vacation—the familiar smells and sounds wrapping around her, reminding her that she belonged there.

Abby felt his eyes lingering on her, their openness a quiet promise tucked behind the simplicity of the moment. A look of caring more than he should. More than she wanted him to.

"I like being with ye, Abby," he admitted openly. "Please don't look away. Sometimes things need to be said before they can't be said. I've learned that lesson the hard way. I want us to be open and honest. Fair enough?"

Abby's cheeks flushed, and for a second, she wanted to look away. But the steadiness of Thom's gaze held her there, grounding her. She wasn't used to this kind of emotional honesty. Wasn't that partly why she was there? His sincerity left her both comforted and a bit on edge, not used to someone so openly admitting they liked being with her.

She glanced down for a moment, fidgeting with her hands.

Thom reached over, resting his hand gently on hers. "No need to worry. I didn't mean it the way ye think. There's no doubt how I feel ... I haven't concealed it very well," he admitted, a small smile playing on his lips. "But you've made your stand with me, and that's enough to be said about it. I'm no fiend. Well, Coira might argue otherwise." His eyes softened. "So, please don't pull away. I'm just happy to be with ye. Nothing more."

Thom didn't push for her to respond, but Abby knew he was waiting for something—anything. She shifted slightly, her fingers grazing the edge of her sleeve, keeping herself distracted from looking at him. He knew her face too well; she wouldn't be able to hide the fact that felt the same way. That she had the urge to move over and curl up next to him. That he felt really good to be with, too.

Instead, she managed a small, fleeting smile before letting her gaze fall on the passing scenery outside the car.

A beat of silence hung between them before Thom spoke again. "Coira and I would take this drive often," he said, changing the subject. "She loved road trips. She'd sit back, let the wind blow her hair, the music fill the car, and allow nature to keep her company. Toward the end, she begged me to take her on a drive. But I feared we'd be too far away from the hospital if something happened." His voice lowered, a slight tremor revealing the weight of the memory. "I still regret I didn't take her. If she had died on the road, what harm was in that? I won't make that mistake again."

Abby pictured Coira in the same seat, staring at the same trees, same hills, same sky. The sun was shining, and closing her eyes, she leaned her face toward the warmth penetrating through the window. "What mistake is that?" she asked, her voice quiet.

"Waste living life for fear of losing it."

She took in Thom's words, a tender honesty behind his voice drawing her back in. She found herself nodding, drawn in by the memories, understanding Coira's need. She angled her body just slightly and leaned toward him. "I like when you talk about your wife. The way the girls talk about her, and through Marleigh's stories, I feel as if I know her ... and maybe you a little better."

Thom's face softened, a knowing warmth taking over his focused expression. He glanced at Cronos in the back seat, giving the dog a fond pat before turning back to Abby. "She had this gift, Coira. She'd take in the ones who needed love the most, the lost and weary, like Cronos, and bring them back to life."

"Are you taking her place?"

Thom lifted his brow. "Huh?"

She gestured to herself. "Like me? Taking a lost soul and bringing me back to life?"

Thom didn't answer right away, his expression contemplative, as if weighing his own journey. Finally, he turned to Abby. "Maybe," he said quietly. "Or maybe I don't need to when you're finding your own way back."

Abby looked over at him, an unspoken understanding passing between them. She pressed the button on the stereo, letting Chet Baker's smooth tunes fill the car.

Thom drifted into a quiet reverie as he drove, and Abby felt herself easing into the moment with him. He had spoken his piece, and she got the message: He liked her—a lot. And she liked him—a lot. She just didn't know how that fit into her world. More importantly, she was trying to figure out how she fit into *her* world. Maybe this road trip would help her figure that out.

As they drove on, the uncertainty of her life seemed to fall away, one mile at a time, replaced by the promise of self-discovery.

36

THE FLOWERS OF MUIR

Their first detour was just north of Dundee. When Thom stopped the car, they had driven up a gravel drive in front of a small medieval castle amid generous lawns. A turret, leaded glass windows, and finely crafted stonework covered the exterior.

"Wow," Abby exclaimed. "You know the people who live here?"

"Aye. Roger Stewart and his wife, Glenna, clients from years ago and now good friends. Roger inherited the property, the bloodline goes back for hundreds of years."

"Or longer," a husky man's voice interceded. "A Stewart true and true."

A stocky man, with a gruff beard covering his face, walked up to Thom and gave him a bear hug. A woman of equal height as the man, only lankier, paler, and plainer, followed, planting a kiss on Thom's cheek.

"It is good to see you again, Thom," the woman said. "And may I add, more handsome than ever."

The stocky man bellowed. "How's that for loyalty? Me

wife flirtin' with the next man that comes along." He eyed Abby. "And who do we have here? Someone for me to set my eyes upon."

"Roger, Glenna ..." Thom stepped aside. "May I introduce Abby Kent?"

"Kent? That's English. The name originated in Berkshire, I believe, around the Norman Conquest around 1066 AD."

Abby smiled coyly. "Actually, my bloodline is Scottish, too, on my mother's side. My family's name is Prudence. We originated in South Lanarkshire," she said, proudly offering the little she knew of her heritage.

"Oh, but your accent is American," Roger noted.

"Guilty," Abby admitted.

"Well, welcome then, American Abby, with Scottish lineage. It's always nice to have fellow Scotsman or, in this case, a pretty lassie on the property."

"Always the historian," Glenna chimed in, and shook Abby's hand. "It's nice to meet you, Abby. Welcome to our home."

"Thank you. Had I known we were coming to such a grand home"—Abby gave Thom a side look—"I would have dressed better."

"Nonsense," Glenna insisted. "We aren't royalty." She motioned to the small castle. "We just live like we are."

They all laughed.

Glenna slipped her arm through Abby's. "May we show you around?"

Abby looked at Thom. "Do we have time?"

"Aye. Plenty. I'll unload while ye get the tour," Thom said, opening the door for Cronos. "Come on, lad," he called to his dog, who rushed off to a large patch of grass, Thom in tow.

Abby listened to the prideful history of the property as they wandered through the castle's many rooms. They passed through a sitting room bathed in light from the large windows overlooking the lawns, a library and a gallery of guns, a drawing room with a vaulted ceiling and an imposing stone hearth, a formal dining room with flagstone flooring and an oak-beamed ceiling, and three grand bedrooms. At last, they reached the Laird and Lady's room, where an open fireplace and barrel-vaulted ceilings held an almost regal charm, decorated in red velvet and heavily carved furniture. Roger then led her up the narrow steps of the turret—now a study—where Roger pointed out the far-reaching edges of the property, acres of trees filling the distant landscape.

After they strolled through the kitchen garden and a rose garden, both dating back to the Victorian era, Glenna playfully stole Abby away from Roger. She led her down a winding flight of stone stairs to the castle's former bakery, now transformed into a modern kitchen, where the stainless-steel stove contrasted with the castle's beige blocks of stone lining the walls. Glenna poured them each a cup of tea, the fragrant steam mingling with the faint aroma of herbs drying over the window.

Glenna's gaze drifted over the walls. "I may not have Roger's knack for history, but I have spent the last ten years becoming an expert on the Stewart home, determined to transform these old, cold walls into a place of comfort," she said, a soft pride in her voice. "Roger is very proud of his heritage. I only hope I can do him justice by keeping the history alive."

"It's a beautiful home, Glenna," Abby said, admiring how the warmth of the kitchen contrasted with the castle's drafty corridors. "I can only imagine the memories you have here, mixed with the history of the family."

Glenna's lips curled into a faint smile. "Oh, I didn't have a family heritage like he does. I was a spinster professor at

Pembroke College caring for my dying father when we met. My mother left when I was nine, and my father rarely spoke of relatives. I never thought I would marry or have a family to speak of, let alone a place to call my own. But then I met Roger, and here I am."

"Where did you two meet?" Abby asked, curious how a long-standing Scotsman married a lonely English spinster.

"We met, curiously, at a flea market. He bumped into me ... or did I bump into him?" She crunched her brow. "Either way, it was an instant attraction." Glenna's face brightened with the memory. "The moment I walked through the big wooden door of this castle, it was home to me. It was how I felt about Roger—he just felt like home. We have been together ever since."

"It sounds like a fairy tale, really," Abby said.

"Isn't love like that?" Glenna looked at Abby. "You must know, it beams from your soul." She put her arm through Abby's and led her out of the kitchen, pausing as they wandered down a quiet corridor. As they entered the library, they found the two men engrossed over a spread of old maps. Neither looked up as the two women joined them.

Guiding Abby to two chairs in front of the windows, Glenna continued in a low voice, "I haven't seen Thom so alive in years. You may be casting a spell on him."

Abby dashed a look at Thom, watching his excitement as Roger ran his finger down one of the maps, stopping and marking at a point.

Glenna followed her gaze. "It was like that with Roger. His wife had been gone for years, but a man never gets used to being alone. People used to say it was like he had risen from the dead when he met me. But truth be known, it was he who brought me to life." She paused, highlighting a few old relics on a shelf before continuing. "Thom is a good man, the kind that you can always count on, like my Roger. It thrills me to see him so happy. Indulge every minute, my dear, for men like them do not come around very often."

Abby blushed with her assumption that she and Thom were in love. It was silly, really, but she didn't have the heart to tell the woman otherwise. She could see Glenna was a true romantic, and the idea of love was as real as the stone blocks of the walls that surrounded them. She would feel the same way if she lived in a fairy-tale land with rolling green mountains that surrounded a small castle.

"Abby?" Thom's voice beckoned her back. "Are ye ready to leave?"

She frowned. "Do we have to?"

"Aye, we have a longer ride ahead of us, and there is one more place I want to take ye before it gets dark."

Glenna rose. "You are always welcome back, Abby."

Abby stepped forward and hugged her. "Thank you," she whispered in Glenna's ear.

Roger scurried over. "Nah, don't ye forget me." He wrapped his arms around her. "I'm holding you to it ... to return to us and stay."

"I'd like that very much," Abby agreed, not knowing if, or when, she might visit again.

"They're a sweet couple," Abby said, once they were in the car.

"Aye, like family to me," Thom explained. "I spent many nights with them after Coira passed. They brought me comfort and companionship when I couldn't stand the emptiness anymore. I'd show up on their doorstep at odd hours of the night. They took me in with no questions." He let out a heavy sigh. "They're good stock."

"So, you've stayed there? How exciting! I wonder if there are any ghosts," Abby said, more to herself than looking for an answer.

"I'd be lying if I didn't say I had an experience or two. It's Scotland for Christ's sake! We have lores of ghosts, fairies, and all that's magical. But we all have stories to tell, don't we?" Thom shot her a look. "Which brings me to where I'm taking ye."

Abby's eyes widened as he suddenly veered off the highway and drove onto a narrow dirt road, toward a forest of trees. "Should I be afraid? You aren't a serial killer who will leave my body to rot, hidden in an old clan burial site, are you?" She gave a soft, reluctant laugh.

"And what do ye take me for? I'd give ye a proper burial." His lips curled upward.

Abby slapped his arm. "Stop that!"

He chuckled, pretending to wince as he rubbed the spot.

They drove up to a dirt lot and parked the car. Cronos jumped out, nearly knocking Thom over in his excitement. The dog bounded a few paces ahead, looking back, waiting for them to catch up, his loyalty anchoring him close. Thom and Abby followed him along a narrow dirt path that wound through tall grasses that brushed against their legs as they walked. The path meandered, finally leading them to the edge of a forest, where the towering trees loomed with an almost ominous presence.

"Am I sure I want you to take me in there?" Abby asked, gesturing to the dense forest in front of her.

"Aye," Thom said, reaching for her hand. "Follow me," he ordered, tugging her through the trees.

Cronos followed in the rear as they hiked through the

trees, staying close along a flattened trail marked by years of footsteps on a soft, decaying earth. The whispering of the birds echoed from the tops, and the cloudy day layered a smoke-like fog surrounding them. The feeling among the tall, thick-bark trunks and mossy green that layered the floor of the forest was illusory.

Thom looked back. "Ye good?"

Abby nodded, her heart pumping from the slow grade of the terrain and the excitement of what was to come. She felt a sense of peace fill her body as Thom's hand wrapped tighter around hers, relishing in the comfort of being led by him. As they climbed, Thom's pace quickened. He tugged her arm to follow his stride, as if something magical was just ahead.

Suddenly, the trees opened to reveal a sweeping valley filled with thousands of flowers nestled within its embrace. An explosion of color spread across the expanse, with an exotic mix of flowers—daffodils, crocus, pansies—springing from the ground as if to greet them. It was as though someone had spilled a box of crayons, painting the field in every hue imaginable, a secret, hidden world of flourishing blooms.

Abby gasped, her eyes growing large. "Wow!"

"The first bursts of spring," Thom explains, dragging her along. "Come."

Abby stepped carefully into the field, avoiding the delicate plants beneath her feet. As the flowers brushed against her, she felt a tingling energy, like her body was being charged with life. A girl-like giddiness filled her, making her want to fall down and lose herself among the fragrant beauty. So many flowers bloomed here, varied and unique species from all over the world, all gathered in this hidden valley. The early-season blooms made perfect sense, as the valley's protective ring of trees created a warm microclimate where the sunlight poured in unimpeded, nurturing the plants into an abundance of life. Abby breathed in the mix of sweet blossoms and rich earth, savoring the fragrance surrounding her.

"It's your garden," Thom explained. "It's the Flowers of Muir."

"No!" Abby's eyes widened. "It's a real place?"

"Aye, or so they say," he quipped.

Abby let go of Thom's hand and walked to the center of the valley, turning around and around, taking in the incredible sight. "But how did all these flowers come to be?"

Thom chuckled. "Come," he beckoned, flattening a small section with his feet, and motioned for her to lie down next to him.

Abby meandered back to him, falling to the ground, and stared up at the sky. The sun had now disappeared completely, as clouds thickened above them. Rain was coming, but she didn't care. She felt like a little girl who had magically climbed into a storybook. Nothing was going to spoil the feeling of joy humming through her.

Thom took her hand, encircled it, and laid it on his chest to tell the story.

"A man lived on this land, long, long ago, Hamish Kerr. He owned these lands as far as the eye could see." Thom indicated with a glance at the expanse around them. "He had a daughter who grew ill and was slowly dying. Every night, he would tell her the story about a little girl whose heart had grown weak, no longer able to play outside like the other children. As her body grew frail, she found she could only escape in her dreams. There, she discovered a mystical place covered in flowers, where fairies hid and granted wishes. The little girl made a plea to the fairies to grow strong again, so she could be with her father, and play outside forever. But to grant her wish, the fairies said she must first learn the virtues of life: compassion, forgiveness, acceptance, and so on. Each spring a new fairy would emerge from a flower with a special virtue and send her off on an adventure to learn it."

Thom paused, glancing at Abby. Her eyes were closed and her breath steady. He squeezed her hand, making sure she was still listening before he continued.

"The sick girl's father traveled for a living, and each time he returned, he brought back a new flower he'd discovered. He planted each one in a field outside his daughter's window, promising that if she lived to see another spring, a new flower would boom. Then, when she was better, she could visit the field of flowers and discover the magic for herself, just like in the little girl's dreams. This hope sustained her, and she lived far longer than anyone expected. They called it a miracle. But eventually, her heart grew weaker, and she lay on her deathbed. Barely able to lift her head, she asked her father to carry her to the field, in hopes of finding the fairies and asking them to grant her a special wish. The father did as he was asked, carrying her as dawn broke. As the sun rose, the blooms opened to the warmth of its rays, sending a sweet fragrance across her face. The girl closed her eyes, whispering, 'I see them, Papa ...' and died in his arms."

Abby opened her eyes, her lashes wet from tears. "So, the story is true ... in a way."

"Aye, well, not about the evil king, but about the little girl. Over time, the flowers multiplied tenfold and spread their blooms across the land. They say the field continues to bloom every year because the fairies granted her wish—to continue to bloom for all little girls to have something to believe in."

"And they continue to bloom today?"

"No one can explain it ... nor do they want to. It is a guarded secret among the people here ... left for those who seek something beyond the trees."

"Thom," Abby hesitated to ask. "Did you and Coira come here? I mean, this must have been a special place for her ... and you."

"Nae, she never saw it for herself. As ye can see, it's not easily found. The locals keep it that way. Maybe they don't even believe it for themselves. Just a story that has been forgotten. I had only heard about it by shamefully listening to a couple in a pub. They stumbled upon it, not really knowing what it was. But I knew. The moment I cleared the trees, I knew. Coira brought me here as if she herself took my hand."

Abby began to cry. She was in the presence of something bigger than herself. This was not just a place to share a beloved fairy tale. This was a place of sanctity, a place eternal where souls connect. And Thom was sharing it with her.

Thom rolled over and gently wiped away the tears falling down her cheeks. "I was hoping the story would make ye happy," he said, brushing his fingertips across her cheeks. "And give ye hope, that beauty can come from tragedy."

Abby looked into the gray-blue eyes that stared at her. They were engaging, inviting her in to seek comfort. She wished desperately for his lips to meet hers. But they didn't. He stood and extended his hand to help her up. As she got her footing, Abby inhaled the fragrant air that surrounded them, as if to capture it and take it home. She gazed out to the field, almost hoping to spot the soul of the little girl who inspired such beauty. But it wasn't the little girl she saw. She let go of Thom's hand and walked forward to the young woman ahead.

"Please go away, Jossi," Abby said quietly.

"Do you really want me to leave?" Jossi said, moving closer.

Abby looked back to Thom. "Not here, not now."

"You may be right, more than you know," Jossi said, gesturing for Abby to follow her further into the field.

Abby followed hesitantly. "What do you mean?" she finally asked when they were far enough away from Thom.

"Abby ..." Jossi sighed, hesitating. "Careful of the road you travel." Her voice was soft but unmistakably serious, a weight in her gaze as she looked at Abby. "Crossroads are ahead, and choices will have to be made."

Abby felt a chill. The warning echoed in her mind, a flicker of unease stirred within her. "I'm being careful," Abby insisted, watching Jossi's face, searching for any hint of meaning. But Jossi only smiled faintly, a look of quiet knowing that Abby couldn't decipher. "I am," she said again, with feigned resignation.

"Abby!" Thom called, motioning her to come back. "We should be heading out." His eyes lifted toward the darkening sky.

Abby nodded, following his stare. The clouds had grown angry and dark, covering any last remnants of the blue sky that had greeted them earlier. A wind swept across the valley, sending a chill through her. When she looked back at Jossi, she was gone.

"Everything okay?" he questioned as Abby scurried through the field, back to him.

Abby tried a smile but was unsuccessful. Another chill ran up her and she shivered. "Brrr," she said, avoiding his question.

"Aye, we should've grabbed our coats," Thom said, and whistled for Cronos. "Let's hurry to the car."

As they headed for the trees, Abby stopped and took one last look. "Thank you, Thom," she said, grabbing his hand. "This is the most special gift anyone has ever given me." She stood on her toes and placed her lips upon his cheek, his warm skin leaving a tingling sensation as she pulled away.

Thom leaned in and locked eyes with her. "This isn't mine to give, Abby. It's a gift for anyone seeking sanctuary. It's yours, freely given, for the taking."

Staring into the depths of his eyes, she wondered, did she want to take it?

The rain started, not in a sprinkling, but in a thrashing downpour, forcing the two apart and sending them rushing under the canopy of the forest. But it was no use, the rain was too powerful, the trees offering little reprieve from the wetness. Thom and Abby covered their heads and made a run for it. They reached the car in a huff of breath, thoroughly soaked. Thom called out to Cronos, who had found shelter inside a hollowed tree fallen to the ground, and he came running to the car. The large beast rushed in the open door and coated the back seat in a spray of water as he shook out the dampness.

Abby ducked and laughed. "I wish it were that easy for us."

"I'll tell ye what," Thom said, turning on the heat of the car. "There's a pub in town before we get to the cottage. We'll stop, grab dinner, and get supplies for the house. They have a big hearth, and I'm sure a roaring fire. We will dry off soon enough."

Abby nodded and settled into her seat, welcoming the warmth that filled the car as Thom drove on. She shivered, not from the cold or the damp layers clinging to her, but from the unfamiliar feeling bubbling up inside her—a thrill of the unknown she could not shake from her bones.

She glanced over at Thom, his focus on the road as the rain pelted down. The strength in his profile, the quiet concern for their safety, calmed and excited her, adding to the underlying current running through her. She couldn't deny the unknown was drawing her in, coaxing her forward, a sense of possibility mingled with a quiet fear.

Where was she going?

The rain continued to blur the scenery outside, but it couldn't diminish the vast, unrestrained beauty of Scotland. It was a world of land and sky, so different from Chicago. Here, varied landscapes and endless spaces offered a freedom she was only beginning to grasp. She felt it in the air she breathed, activating her senses, and stirring a zeal for life that had long lain dormant. Savoring each moment, she hoped to etch every detail into memory, so that when she returned home, she wouldn't forget—or at least would know that this had existed, if only for a moment in time.

37

TAVERNS

s promised, Thom found a table by the large stone hearth. A fire was crackling, lighting the old tavern and warming up the space. Abby took in the flickering light dancing on the stone walls, the cozy warmth settling her. The rain continued to pour, and it seemed only a few people were brave enough to venture to the local eatery. Besides Thom and Abby, only two other tables were occupied. Three older men drank at the bar, entrenched in a discussion over local politics.

Thom shrugged off his sweater and draped it over the back of a chair near the fire. He prompted Abby to do the same. "They should dry quickly," he said.

Abby agreed, slipping off her sweater and laying it next to Thom's by the fire.

When the server came by the table, Thom ordered two bowls of Scotch Broth, insisting it was the only thing on the menu worth eating, a glass of wine for Abby, and whiskey for himself. "Having a good time?" he asked when Abby looked his way.

Abby nodded. "I am," she replied, with a lift in her voice. "However, it's one of those days that feels as if time is moving half as fast."

Thom ran his fingers thoughtfully over the short hairs of his beard. "Is that good?"

"Yes, very good, silly." She laughed. "I wish it could go on like this forever."

Thom leaned in. "Do ye?" he said, his stare direct, his tone low.

"Don't, Thom," Abby pleaded, the hum of his voice weakening the defenses she'd tried so hard to keep intact. "Please don't ask me that question when I can't answer it the way you want me to."

Thom leaned back, a silence falling between them. Abby could see he wanted to say more, his eyes shifting from the fire back to her.

Her phone buzzed. She reached into her purse and glanced at the lit-up screen. Emma was in a frenzy.

Dad keeps calling me. He's wanting to know where you are.

I'm not sure what else to tell him.

You need to call him!

Abby froze, her heart tightening, the ties to Marcus feeling both binding and suffocating. She urgently needed to break free.

Mom ...

Please talk to him. Dad isn't handling it well.

Whatever you think you need, I'm supporting you the best I can. But you need to call him.

Love you.

Abby shut off her phone. When she looked up, Thom's eyes met hers.

Detecting the color drained from her face, Thom ordered, "Call him, Abby."

"Yeah, I know," she said with a fragile voice, the earlier exuberance now faded and shallow.

Abby walked to the back of the restaurants where an alcove for the restrooms gave her a private space—a cave of protection. She propped herself against the brown paneled walls as if they could hold her up. Punching the numbers, she waited anxiously as the phone rang on the other end. Her heart started thumping with each ring. *Did she want Marcus to answer? What was she going to say?* Her thoughts raced. By the fifth ring, it jumped into voicemail. Rather than feeling relief, she noticed her heart pounded harder, wanting to break free from its boned cage. She leaned into the wall for more support and swallowed a gulp of air. The message beeped and waited for her to say something.

"Hey, Marcus. It's ... Abby," she said. Hesitant. Stalling. "I'm doing okay ... everything is fine." She paused, trying to find the right words. *Nothing was going to be right*, she quickly realized. "Wanted to check in with you. Will try again in a few days. Talk to you then."

She pressed the phone, turning it off.

A pain streaked across her chest, and she became light-headed. She grabbed onto the wall to stop the room from spinning. The brown paneled walls of the old pub seemed to close in, encasing her in an unyielding embrace. She looked for windows, anything that would take her out of the box she felt trapped in. The rain was still coming down, splashing against the glass, but it didn't obscure her view of the ancient stone buildings and the brick-lined streets. The Scottish accents of the three men arguing drifted from the bar to her ears, the words familiar, but rough-hewn and crude. The fire snapped, making her turn to the flicker of light, only to spot Thom sitting at the table, sipping his whiskey. She breathed in and exhaled, her feet still planted on the parquet floors of the pub.

She wasn't ready to go back!

With a few more breaths, she steadied herself. She returned to the table and tucked her phone back into her purse, not daring to meet Thom's gaze.

Thom put his drink down. "Did ye reach him?"

She shook her head, then met his eyes, finding a calm reassurance there. Yet, she hesitated, wondering how honest she could be with him.

Seeing her pale face, Thom slid the wine glass toward her. "Do you want to talk about it?"

Something in his steady gaze gave her the courage. "I ... I didn't want him to answer," Abby admitted. "I mean ... just his voicemail transported me back. Back to what, I'm not sure." She glanced at Thom. If he was judging her, he gave no indication. "It's as if the sound of his voice is the link, and once I hear it, I will be pulled back through an invisible curtain." Abby's eyes flashed downward. "I didn't want to talk to him."

Thom reached over and put his hand on hers. "I'm not telling you what to do, Abby, but if you spoke to him, you might come to terms with your feelings."

"What are those feelings?"

Did she tell him that her feelings were connecting with another man?

She jerked her hands away from his.

"I'm sorry," he said.

Was he sorry he was pushing her, or for seeing what she herself had been too afraid to admit?

"For what?" Abby questioned.

"For your husband," he said frankly.

Abby's mouth opened. "Am I that ruthless?"

"Nae, Abby," Thom said. "Quite the opposite, from where I'm sitting. You've a kind manner and gentle heart ... you've been nothing but good to me." He stopped and corrected himself. "To all of us. Maybe there's a demon inside that you haven't shown us. God knows we're not always what we seem. But I'm a good judge of character." He touched his chin. "I'm just wondering why he ever let ye go."

"Marcus didn't let me go. I ran away from him—"

"Didn't he?" Thom raised his brow. "Why are ye here? A woman doesn't run away from a man carelessly. Not unless she is being harmed or tormented."

"But Marcus isn't that kind of man." Her tone was sharp —defensive. She didn't like to hear someone talk about Marcus that way. It hurt a piece of her.

"Aye, I should hope not," he said more gently. "But he's a neglectful man. That's the most dangerous. Your husband's not bruised your skin, or broken a bone, but he has emptied your heart. Our bodies are meant to heal. We all have our scars to prove it. But our hearts? Nooo, they're not so easy to mend. And when a woman's heart has been bled dry, well, there's always collateral damage beyond the scars and fractures." Thom took a slow sip from his glass, seemingly collecting his thoughts. "Your heart is still in there, Abby. Beating as strong as ever. I've seen it. I can feel it. I'll not blame ye as a heartless woman. Not from what I have experienced in the time I've gotten to know ye. You've not a broken heart, Abby. Just an empty one. Maybe when you figure out how to fill it up, you'll find your way back."

Abby looked at him with darkened and wide eyes, unable to defend Marcus or herself.

"I won't apologize, Abby. I mean what I say. Ye know I only speak the truth. I'm not going to be ashamed of it. Nor am I a fool. I know a woman of substance when I meet her.

And I've met ye ... gotten to know ye. Maybe more than some? It's not every day I go putting strange women to bed or letting them cry all over my nice sweater." He smiled and waited for Abby to do the same.

She let her lips spread in a tentative smile, her shoulders softening.

"Are you flawed?" he continued. "Aren't we all? But I'll be damned, Abby, to let you sit here and tell me that your husband doesn't bear some responsibility. You wouldn't be here, with me, in the middle of rained-soaked Scotland otherwise."

Thom was right. Everything he said was true. The weight of his words sank deep, resonating with her, and she realized he was proclaiming his love in the only way he was allowed, with no expectations. However, he was also holding her accountable. She wasn't home with Marcus, she was far away ... and with Thom. And this man, sitting across from her, whose eyes searched her soul, saw exactly who she was —the good, the bad, and the ugly. Abby wasn't sure if she loved him for that or hated him.

Thom brought his whiskey slowly to his lips but halted, lifting his glass. "To us, and our timeless day. May you find what you seek, cherish what you have, and remember Scotland always."

Abby lifted her wine glass. "To us," she echoed softly, "and to the magic of Scotland."

And to you.

38

LANDING

It was dark when they drove off the narrow road and onto a dirt pathway leading to an isolated cottage. Abby was immediately charmed by the all-stone structure with a pitched roof and wood-paned windows. It sat on a cliff, outlined by a low rock wall, wildflowers emerging through tall grasses surrounding it. Cronos barked, knowing they had reached their final destination, and scratched at the door to get out. Abby hurriedly opened the door for him, and he ran to a patch of grass in the distance.

"Should we go get him?"

"Nae, he knows his way around the property." He reached for Abby's hand. "Let me show you around before it gets too dark."

They walked around the property and to the edge of the cliff where a river lay below.

Abby gasped. "This is spectacular! And it's yours?"

"Aye. It's been in my family for years. Not a castle, but a little piece of my Scottish heritage. The structure has been here for hundreds of years, but my family has only owned it since just after the First World War. Truth be known, my great grandad won it in a game of cards."

"Truth?" Abby questioned.

"On my mother's grave," he said, placing his hand over his heart.

They both laughed.

"Lucky for your grandfather."

"Aye, luck or cheating ... I'm not sure which it was."

"Can we eat out here tomorrow?" Abby asked, pointing to a picnic table.

Thom titled his head upward. "Absolutely, if the weather allows."

Abby followed Thom's glances at the darkening sky. The rain had stopped, and for a moment she thought the moon would come through. But the clouds rolled by, covering it up as soon as it appeared.

"I wouldn't care if it snowed."

Thom smiled. "Ah, kindred spirits, are we ... it's exactly how I feel. Now come, let me show you the cottage."

Abby followed him along a flattened path that wound up to the entry, where a weathered wood door with a metal knocker shaped like a boar's head awaited them. She gave it a playful knock, half expecting a decrepit old woman to answer, while Thom rummaged through his coat pocket for the key.

"Here it is," he said, dangling a vintage skeleton key in front of her.

When they cleared the threshold, Cronos suddenly appeared and pushed past them, finding his way through the dark. When Thom reached for a switch on the wall, Abby could see the dog already curled up in the bed that awaited him. Thom walked into the main room and threw down their bags next to the couch.

"I'll start a fire," he offered. "These thick walls keep this place icy year-round."

Abby stepped into the main room and glanced over the small space. It wasn't large by any means, but it was quaint. The rock-covered fireplace, a central feature of the room, contrasted with the stark white walls. A large picture window was directly across from it, which must have had an expansive view of the property, but due to the rain that now pelted the windows, Abby couldn't see anything other than a heavy mist. A knotted rug covered the wide-planked oak floors. She thought it was a shame to conceal so much of the rich color, but when she looked down at her muddy boots, she realized the purpose. She bent down, untied the now wet laces, and placed them by the front door.

"Make yourself comfortable," Thom said, inviting her in. "It gets cold in here, but the fire will warm ye up in no time."

Abby shivered, the icy chill wrapping around her. It was colder inside than outdoors. She moved to the fireplace, rubbing her hands together as the flames danced through dry logs, releasing much-needed heat.

"Getting warmer?" Thom asked, sitting beside her and extending his hands toward the fire.

Heat spread through Abby—not just from the flames but from Thom's nearness. Unsure of which to blame for the sudden warmth, she quickly stepped away and sank onto the couch, her eyes fixed on the flickering light.

"Mmm, I can already feel the warmth on my feet," Abby said, wriggling her toes in her thick, albeit wet, socks.

"It can be nice in front of the fire, but I warn you, the rooms are chilly."

"Don't worry, I brought my flannel pajamas."

Thom's lips drifted upward. "The ones with the Scotty dogs?"

Abby laughed. "Yes, the one and the same."

Thom walked over and turned on the lamp resting on the side table. A few books were stacked beneath it, crowned by a pair of reading glasses. Abby noted the reading choices. If they were Thom's, his interests lay in history and autobiographies of world leaders. Built-in bookcases lined an entire wall, and an overstuffed chair was positioned in the corner next to the picturesque window. With no television in sight, she understood Thom's purpose for the home—it was his escape.

"Do you like the house?"

Abby nodded. "I really do. It's an idyllic reprieve from the rest of the world."

"It's a no-clutter space," Thom said, settling beside her. "I told ye, it's where I come to think. My escape from the expectations of work, people ... life in general." He gestured at the windows. "As ye can see, there's no one around here to judge ye or hold you accountable for yourself. There's a freedom to that."

But how did you escape your fears, your failures? Abby looked at Thom. *Your desires?*

"You're still cold," he said, noticing Abby shiver. "How about a hot bath?" Thom offered, pointing to a door. "It might take away the deep chill that seems to be creeping inside ye."

"That might help," Abby said, lifting off the couch. She looked toward the dark hallway as if it was calling her in. "You don't mind me escaping for a bit?"

"Abby, this time is for you. Do what ye need. Pretend it's your own private getaway. Except, I'm here." He laughed. "I'll show ye to your room."

He grabbed Abby's bag, stopping at one of the two bedrooms. It was identical to the main room—white walls, wooden floors—and sparsely decorated with a black metal-framed king-sized bed, two mismatched dressers on each side, and an antique chest of drawers that sat beneath paneled windows with simple white drapes drawn to the sides. "This is the main bedroom," he said, before leading her to the second bedroom with similar furnishings, but with smaller windows. Thom nodded to a door along the wall, "You'll find a robe in there, and the bath is next door."

Abby eyed the sparse and rustic surroundings. "You do have hot running water, right?"

"Aye, we do now," Thom said with a playful smile. "I helped my grandad put it in when I was just a boy. Until then, we either bathed in the river or took a cold bath. Neither was ideal. Fortunately, we now have water. I'll go start the bath," he offered, then explained, "It takes a wee bit to get *hot* water."

Thom left, shutting the door behind him. Abby took in the room, with its bare walls and a green glen plaid duvet spread across the mattress. Black wall lamps flanked the bed, and a wooden rocking chair sat in a dark corner, a blanket hung over its back. With a backward glance at the door, she undressed, getting out of her damp things, and grabbed the robe hanging in the closet. As she hung up her wet clothes, she noted various seasonal coats—a quilted hunter's jacket and a suede brown overcoat—along with a pair of Wellies sitting on the floor. It didn't go unnoticed they were a woman's size. She wondered if Thom had brought other women to his place, particularly Mairi. She browsed through the dresser drawers, finding nothing left behind. If she had been there, there was no indication. Hearing the water running in the room next door, she cinched the robe's belt and hurried out the door.

"You look good in my robe," Thom said, meeting her at the bathroom door.

Abby looked at the oversized robe covering her. "This is yours?" She blushed, feeling as if he were wrapped around her himself. She pulled the robe tighter.

He nodded, moving aside for her to enter the bathroom. "Would you care for some tea? Or maybe a little whiskey to warm your blood?"

"Tea would be nice," she smiled slyly. "You know what whiskey does to me ..." She didn't need anything more to weaken her inhibitions. The rainy weather, the fire, the darkened space, the isolation, and her naked body standing next to Thom were all adding to her feeling of vulnerability.

"Aye, that I do. Tea it is." He chuckled, heading off to the kitchen.

Abby entered the bathroom, its generous space lending an air of serenity. The walls were stark white like the rest of the house, but the floors were covered in river stones in various browns, tans, and black, the irregular, soft-hewn rocks massaging her feet as she walked across them. Candles were scattered around, bathing her in a softened glow when she looked in the mirror.

"What are you doing?" Abby asked the woman who stared back. She didn't answer. She didn't want an answer. She just wanted to enjoy what the moment was offering. Sanctuary.

The window above the bathtub stood bare, with nothing to cover it, inviting the outside in. Abby couldn't see anything for miles—nothing but nature amid a thick mist, fortifying her privacy. She unrobed and climbed into the claw-footed tub filled with foamy bubbles. She sank into the water and let out a deep sigh as the bubbles covered her from neck to toes and warmth seeped into her, dissolving the chill that had settled in her bones. Her body melted into a delicious heaviness, turning her into mush within minutes, and all her thoughts drifted into emptiness. She closed her eyes in utter relaxation.

It was a knock at the door that broke her tranquility.

"I have your tea," Thom called from the hallway, the wooden barrier the only thing between them. "Are you covered enough?"

"Mmm," she purred. "You can enter, just as long as you don't look," she said, half teasing and half serious.

He poked his head in. "You realize I've seen ye almost naked already?"

Abby cringed. He had already undressed her, seen for himself her damaged body. He never mentioned it again after that morning, and the thought never occurred to her that he might have found her arousing. Especially after touching her. Hadn't Marcus proved her undesirable?

He carried in a small step stool and placed it by her tub, leaving a mug with a brewing tea bag inside. "Earl Grey ... I hope you don't mind. It was all I had in the cupboard," Thom commented. "I wasn't sure how ye drank it, so I left it still steeping. I, myself, prefer it plain."

"It's perfect," Abby replied, giving him a reassuring smile.

"More alike than we thought," Thom quipped. He grabbed the tea bag, bobbing it a few times before he threw it away in the trash, diverting his eyes from her in the tub.

"Well, I'll be letting ye continue your bath," he said, turning away.

Abby found herself reaching out for his arm. "Stay ... and talk to me," she asked, rather spontaneously, surprising herself.

Thom studied her, his expression curious. Abby felt the warmth rise in her cheeks but held his gaze, smiling softly.

Before the moment passed, Thom sat down on the floor

and leaned against the tub. "What would you like me to talk about?"

"Oh, I don't know, what you were like as a boy, your parents ... whatever comes to mind," Abby said, simply wanting him close, his deep voice—the superpower he possessed over her—drifting in her ears lulling her into a dreamlike state.

And so, he did.

Abby luxuriated in the hot water, while Thom shared stories of growing up with a single mom, his wild days of rebellion, and the time he was nearly arrested for stealing alcohol—the event that led to his being sent to live with his father in the States. Abby laughed and teared up as Thom wove his tales of mischief and memory—echoes of his life—shifting her thoughts from a playful curiosity to a place where sincerity and longing intertwined.

As his voice grew tired, his words began to slow, and the weight of the memories created a stillness neither of them rushed to fill.

"I've been talking a wee too much," Thom said, breaking the silence. "And there's not much more to tell ye."

"No, don't stop," Abby murmured, her voice warm and languid. "You soothe me," she confessed, loosening her restraint. "I like ... I like being with you."

Abby closed her eyes, leaning back against the edge of the tub.

Thom swallowed, his jaw tightening as he struggled to look away. "Don't, Abby," he said, his voice strained, pleading. "I'm only so strong."

Abby opened her eyes, meeting his gaze, seeing a depth of yearning in his eyes that she hadn't felt directed at her by any man in a very long time. She reached over and caressed his face, brushing the soft bristles of his chin.

"You don't want me, Thom." She looked down at her breasts that lay just under the surface of the water. "I'm not what any man wants anymore."

"God, Abby, who cares?" he shouted, shooting up from the floor. "So, you have scars over your chest. You survived breast cancer, for Christ's sake! Your breasts aren't you. You're a beautiful, sensual woman, don't you see that?"

Abby slouched into the tub, her eyes growing wide.

Thom suddenly swiped his sweater over his head and began unbuttoning the shirt underneath, exposing his bare chest for Abby to gaze upon. "See?" He pointed to the scar tissue covering his chest. "I've been cracked open and sewn back up just the same. Not pretty, is it?" he said to her. "My strength as man was put to question. No doubt, not the same as what you've gone through, but I do understand thinking yourself less than ... not recognizing yourself." He ran his hand through his hair, shaking his head, before turning back to Abby. "I failed as a man, Abby. I didn't save my wife. I didn't protect her. I wasn't strong enough, man enough. I thought I wanted to die. And I tried. But when on that cliff of choosing life or death, I chose life."

Abby blinked, absorbing his words, seeing the pained expression on his face.

His voice softened. "We aren't damaged, Abby ... we're people who've experienced good things, bad things, and have come through it changed. Aye, different, but no less worthy as human beings. All the more for it." He stood over Abby, locking onto her gaze with fierce intensity. "I'm alive, and plan on staying that way for a long time so that I can love my daughter, see my gran-lassies grow, and hopefully love someone like ye for the rest of my days, until my last breath."

Abby fought against the surge of emotions tightening her throat. A wave of uncontainable affection washed over her, drawing her toward him. She stood slowly, the water dripping from her body, shivering as vulnerability mingled with urgency. Reaching out, her fingertips trembled as they traced the rigid scars down his chest, feeling the raised lines of his skin. They felt the same as hers, only thicker, older, no longer tender pink like hers. His were healed, now remnants of his battle scars.

Thom pulled Abby into his embrace, his movements sure and tender before claiming her lips with an intensity that left no room for hesitation, only desire. "God, Abby, I want ye, so much," he whispered as his lips hovered over hers, ready to pounce again. "Tell me to go away or tell me to take ye, but please don't leave me here hanging."

Abby's legs went weak, anticipation swirling inside her, stealing her breath away. Thom's kiss anchored her in a way she hadn't felt in years, erasing all doubts and resistance to them. "Take me, Thom," she breathed. "I don't want to run away anymore."

Thom reached for the weighty terry robe, wrapping it around Abby's wet body, and took her willing hand, guiding her to his bedroom.

"Hold on," he said, rushing out of the room, leaving her to linger in the middle of the room.

Abby stood before the bed, her body soon to be entwined with his. Her heart pounded with anticipation and a touch of fear. She wanted Thom in the most intimate way, her body yearning to be close, her soul longing for connection.

Was she finally landing, or was she still falling off that cliff?

The aching in her heart to be close to him and the yearning inside were hardly recognizable to her. She had forgotten what it was like to want and be wanted, to desire and be desired. Long before her breasts were removed, she had forgotten what it was to be a sensual, desirable woman.

Her surgery was merely the final blow to a woman lost and forgotten, erased from all memory. But her sex, her sensuality, and the burning need for intimacy still lingered just behind the surface of her skin. Maybe the doctor's scalpel had tried to cut out the last remnants of that woman, but it only fueled something deep inside of her. Her soul—still female, still a woman, still significant—was pushed to the surface, not wanting to be left for dead.

Abby brushed her fingers against her lips where Thom's kisses lingered, recapturing the soft feeling they left behind. She wanted the sensation back, and turned toward the door, eager for his return. The house was now dark, everything shadowed in shades of gray. She heard the sound of logs dropped into the fire followed by timbers crackling, and a yellow glow broke through the dimness. Thom's low hum started to drift closer, the melodic tune filling her with warmth and comfort.

Abby glanced around Thom's bedroom with a sudden wave of panic. *What was the protocol of seduction?* His suitcase lay open with clothes spilling out of it; the socks he had worn earlier were kicked off and strewn on the floor. The pillows were propped against the headboard, and the duvet was folded back, revealing a plush sherpa blanket. His toiletry bag was open on top of the dresser, as well as his wallet and keys. Had he planned on sharing his bed with her that evening, there were no indications. Hearing his footsteps approaching, she felt a flutter of nervousness. Quickly shedding her robe, she slipped into his bed, nestling under the covers. The sheets were cool against her bare skin, sending a shiver through her as the realization sank in—*she was quite naked!*

Abby watched Thom as he stepped into the room, his gaze briefly falling on her robe where it lay crumpled on the floor. He moved to the light switch, dimming the room to a soft glow. "It'll get chilly tonight, and the fire is the only source of heat ... besides us," he explained, a mischievous smile tugging at his lips.

Abby's breath hitched, her pulse quickening as her heart warred with her sense of caution. His calm, unhurried movements seemed separate from the intimacy that was unfolding. He removed his watch, laying it carefully on the dresser before glancing back at her, as if reassuring himself she hadn't disappeared. He met her eyes and smiled, a silent question hanging in the air between them, precipitating his unhurried pace. She wondered if he was waiting for her to change her mind.

I want to be with him, her head screamed, the desire sharp and certain, bringing her back into her own skin.

He pushed down his jeans and boxer shorts with one motion, kicking them aside. Abby glanced away, giving him privacy to climb into bed without her stare, though she couldn't help but notice the well-toned, muscular physique that had been hidden from her until now.

He slipped under the covers, pressing his cold body against hers before wrapping his arms around her. "Aye, you're warm," he hummed, "and ye feel like a woman should."

Abby laughed nervously, tucking a stray strand of hair behind her ear as her cheeks warmed.

"What?" he questioned.

She tilted her head with a slight raise of her brow. "What else have you pressed against to compare a woman's body to?" she asked, knowing he had Mairi's for comparison.

Thom shook his head. "I didn't mean it like that. It's just ... ye feel good. Soft," he said as his hands caressed her back, down to her buttocks, and then back up to her neck, "and smooth." He brought his lips to hers.

His kisses were tender, and he was slow to taste her, indulging in the silkiness of her lips. But as his tongue enveloped hers, Abby's hunger grew, and she could no longer control her desire. She squirmed closer to him, wanting more, his heated touch igniting her.

His long legs entangled her, drawing her closer, cocooning her in his warmth. "God, this feels ..."

"Instinctive," she completed.

Thom's eyes met hers, trying hard to read what she wasn't saying.

"Are you scared of this, Abby?"

Abby ran her fingers down his solid chest, through the graying hairs. Neither one of them was young nor foolish. What was happening between them was more meaningful than she wanted to admit.

Abby kissed his neck, bringing her lips close to his ears. "I'm not afraid of you, Thom. I'm afraid of me," she breathed, her confession barely audible.

He caged her underneath him, looking deeply into her eyes. "Know this, Abby, I'm taking you with my body and into my soul. This isn't something fleeting ..." His gaze softened but held firm. "Let me in, Abby."

Abby brushed the sides of his cheeks, fondling his short beard with her touch. Finding her way to his lips, she kissed him, unable to capture in words the emotions surging within. Her hands traveled the long lines of his sinewy muscles from his arms to his thighs, her need intensifying with each brush against his skin. When she stroked between his legs, a low, guttural growl escaped him, deepening the intensity of his touch. She wrapped her legs around him, melting in the warmth of his nakedness, the thrill of a man's wanting touch awakening her desires she'd almost forgotten. She couldn't decide if she wished for time to hurry forward or linger here forever; her heart raced with unguarded excitement, eager for whatever came next. More kisses? More caresses? Thom drawing her even closer, binding her to the beat of his heart? If there were consequences, she felt herself surrendering to them, her mind and body now yielding entirely to Thom's love.

Abby's body was no longer hers, drawn and surrendered in sync with Thom's movements, guided by his desires. His breath brushed against her skin, and she sighed as he entered her. Her body was now awakened to its own needs and longings, moving in perfect rhythm with his. With each slow, pulsing movement, she surrendered to the deepening connection between them. Her breaths quickened, each one laced with pleasure, and she was unable to conceal the eruption he was creating. As he drew her nearer, his pace quickening, she cried out, her body melting within his embrace. His body tightened, releasing his own gratification, and she trembled beneath him, carried by the waves of pleasure that lingered between them.

They lay in silence, cradled in each other's arms, as their bodies surrendered, their breaths slowing and heartbeats gradually steadying, lingering in the warmth of their closeness. Abby guided Thom to rest his head on her chest, her fingertips tracing gentle strokes down his back.

"That feels good," he murmured, closing his eyes and letting the lilting of her touch wash over him. "I may never want to get out of this bed."

"Me neither," Abby said softly.

Thom opened one eye, catching her expression, then let his own eyes drift shut. "Tired?"

"Mmhmm," Abby purred, her voice a gentle murmur in

the dark. She nestled closer, savoring his warmth lingering between them. "You made love to me," she whispered, as if a secret.

Thom pressed himself against the pillows and drew Abby into his embrace. "Yes, Abby … and I meant it."

Abby rested her head against him, unable to hold back the quiet tears that began to fall.

He drew her nearer, pressing a kiss to the crown of her head. "Sleep," he murmured. "I've got ye now."

And she did.

39

DO NOT DISTURB

M rs. Landry had not expected anyone when the doorbell rang. Her next guests were not arriving until late morning the next day. The bell rang again, prompting her to rise slowly from her chair and shuffle her old feet across the wooden floor.

She peered out the peephole to see who was disturbing her quiet evening. A tall man stood on the stoop, looking out toward the street. His hands were wrapped around his body, bracing for the sudden turn of weather. *He should have a heavier coat*, she thought. She opened the door.

"Hello, may I help ya?" she asked.

The man turned his head at the sound of her voice. "Um, yeah, I hope. I'm looking for Abigail Kent." He blew on his hands.

He should be wearing gloves, she thought.

"Oh my, please come in. I'm afraid Scotland weather has done it again, foolin' us that spring is here, and then ..." She nodded up at the cloudy sky. "You're barely covered," she scolded.

He smirked, tugging at his lightweight jacket. "Well, I hadn't expected the weather to be so cold in May. It's warming at home."

"Aye," she said, and shut the door behind him. "With luck, it'll change again tomorrow." She showed him into the parlor where a fire was roaring. "Come, get warm."

"I know it's late," the man said, unzipping his coat. "I ..." He brushed his hand through his hair. "It's been a while since Abby and I have seen each other. I didn't want to wait until tomorrow, so I came straight from the airport."

Mrs. Landry eyed the man carefully. He didn't seem like a serial killer or a stalker. She had been around long enough to have an internal feel for people. He seemed safe enough. "And you might be?" she asked, knowing perfectly well who he might be.

"Oh!" He extended his hand. "I'm Marcus, Abby's husband."

"Mrs. Landry," she reciprocated, before suggesting he sit down. "May I get you something to drink? I can have some hot tea in a few minutes. Or maybe some whisky? It has a way of warming the insides a little faster." She winked.

"Whiskey, I think," he said, refusing her offer to sit.

She nodded and scurried to the kitchen, grateful for the reprieve. Abby's husband showing up uninvited had caught her off guard, especially since Abby wasn't here to greet him. She needed time to gather her thoughts before breaking the news that Abby wasn't there. But what did she tell him about where she was, and with whom?

She opened cupboards and banged glasses, letting him think she was busy in the kitchen. Grabbing the bottle of whiskey, she poured two fingers in each glass, and then poured a little more, hoping it would steady her thoughts and ease his. With a deep breath, she shuffled back to the parlor with two glasses in hand, her expression carefully composed. He accepted one of them and lifted it to her. They both took a sip, their gazes lingering, the silence stretched taut in the space between them.

Marcus let out an uneasy laugh and reminded her why he was there. "I was wondering about Abby," he said. "Can I see her?"

Mrs. Landry was cautious to not offer more than he needed to know. "She's expecting you?"

Marcus's eyes darted away from hers. "No, not exactly," he said hesitatingly. "I wanted to surprise her."

"Oh," she replied, and fixed her eyes on him.

He shuffled his feet, the old floorboards creaking under his weight. He glanced around the room, his gaze apparently catching on the clock on the wall. "She doesn't seem to have much reception out here. Otherwise, I would have let her ... you ... know I was coming." He cleared his throat. "I can see why. This little town is off the grid."

Mrs. Landry crossed her arms. "We have our share of tourists," she said, feeling defensive of her hometown. "It's more of a summer location. As you have experienced, it's a wee bit cold most of the year. But it's beautiful when the landscape starts to bloom."

"I'm sure it is," he agreed. "I got a glimpse of the quaintness as I drove in, although it was getting dark. I can't wait to see more of it—with Abby—in the days to come."

Mrs. Landry offered a subtle smile, with a slight nod. "That's what you should do. I'm sure our little town will not disappoint. This place has its own magic, a way of drawing out the good and helping folks cast off their demons."

"I have no doubt. Maybe the reason Abby chose it." He drained his whisky with one swift gulp. "Thank you," he murmured, returning the glass.

Mrs. Landry noted his hand clenched at his side. The whisky hadn't quite managed to ease him. "May I get you some more?"

His hand went up. "No. I'd really just like to see Abby."

Mrs. Landry cleared her throat, a faint effort to smooth the cragginess. "I'm sorry to inform you, Mr. Kent, that your wife isn't here this evening." She lifted her chin and met his gaze, ready for his rebuttal.

A muscle in his jaw tightened and his gaze sharpened. "Not here?"

"No, but she's still staying here," Mrs. Landry replied, easing herself into her chair and throwing a blanket over her legs. Her gaze returned to the man, whose brow was set in a stern line, his eyes fixed intently on her.

"Then where is she?" he demanded, moving closer.

"She's on a short holiday," she answered plainly, unfazed by his swift movement toward her.

"She is on a vacation from a vacation?" His voice lifted.

"Aye," she replied. "There is so much to see with a day's drive or so. 'Tis easier to make a base here and travel about." She hoped the explanation would suffice.

Marcus began to pace the room. He finally turned to Mrs. Landry. "Do you know where she is on this holiday?"

Mrs. Landry nodded. "I believe she went up the coast."

Marcus's eyes widened. "Was she planning on being gone long?"

"She's due back tomorrow, as a matter of fact," she said after a pause, offering him something without feeling like she was betraying Abby.

Marcus sighed. "That's good to hear. I thought maybe I might have missed her before moving on." He looked at his watch. "Um, it is very late, do you mind if I stay here tonight?"

"Course not," She threw aside her blanket and stood. "But

I cannot allow you in Abby's room without permission. I hope you understand. Rules and all. You'll have to take another room for tonight." She shuffled to her desk at the front of the house and took out the registry. "Abby is on the third floor, but I have something just below her."

He followed her, rolling his bag behind him. "Of course. I understand."

A sympathetic smile crossed Mrs. Landry's face. "Wasn't expecting anyone tonight, but the room is all ready." She gestured to the darkened stairwell. "If you don't mind, I'll just point you in the direction. My old legs and all." Marcus nodded as she handed him a vintage key adorned with a green ribbon, the room number dangling from it. "It's upstairs, the door on the left. It's the one with the green sign. The bathroom is across the way; fresh towels are on the dresser. I'll have coffee ready in the morning. Breakfast is ready by eight." She walked him to the stairs, gave him a comforting smile, and bid him a good night.

Marcus headed to his room, with his suitcase clunking up the wood steps until he reached the second-floor landing. She heard the door creak open and then shut and the rolling of his luggage across the floor. Eventually, it quieted, and she locked the front door, turning off the entry light. She wasn't expecting anyone else that evening.

Settling her aching body back into the comfy chair, she picked up the phone and dialed Abby's cell. No answer. She tried Thom, but he didn't answer, either. She knew phone reception was sparse where they were and decided not to leave a message. *Why spoil their retreat?* she thought. There was nothing they could do with the knowledge that Abby's husband had unexpectedly shown up at her door.

40

THE RING

Marcus settled his bag on the luggage rack near the armoire. Inside, he found only hangers and two white robes with slippers sticking out from the pockets. A television hung from the wall above the dresser, its remote nestled below it. He was too tired to turn it on, opting for the view outside the window. No one was on the street below, nor were there cars on the road. A streetlight flickered, eventually going out altogether. He closed the drapes and eyed his room. It was cozy, as Abby would say. A queen bed sat in the middle covered in all-white bedding, with a tufted down comforter folded at the end. Four pillows were fluffed against the headboard, and a series of mismatched vintage mirrors decorated the wall above.

Abby always insisted on down pillows. "It just wouldn't be a vacation without them!" she would declare. He squeezed one to make sure they passed her inspection. He fell onto the bed, knocking the air out of them, and thought as he sank into the fluffiness that she was right.

A pair of dressers flanked the bed, one topped with an

alarm clock flashing the time. Eleven seventeen. A chair with a decorative pillow filled the corner of the room. The walls were dark green, making the space seem smaller than it was.

Abby would hate that.

He sighed.

He thought he was exhausted, but the whisky pumped through his bloodstream, infusing him with a renewed energy. He kicked off his loafers and stretched out his feet. He was hungry but knew there was little he could do about it. He pulled out his phone and texted the kids he had made it safely. He collected his messages, finding a few from work that needed his immediate attention. The rest could wait.

He hadn't bothered to send Abby a text to let her know he was coming. He wanted it to be a surprise. Or maybe he didn't want to scare her away. She had been gone for almost two months, with little communication in between. She was fine. That was the most she had offered him. He lay in bed at night wondering what she was not saying. He understood everyone needed some time. God, he knew Abby had gone through a lot over the last year with her cancer. He'd thought she was doing well. She would say as much. How would he know otherwise? She'd never expressed that she was on the verge of cracking. But she did. She left. She really left! And she'd given no clue when she was coming back.

Was she coming back?

The unknown sent a fear through him he had never known. He did not know what to say to his kids. Emma seemed to think her mother was just going through a midlife crisis.

What does that entail? he wondered.

Drew had been oblivious for the first few weeks. But his graduation was coming, nudging him to question why his mother was gone. Marcus had lied at first. It wasn't actually a lie the way he understood it when he first told it. He told Drew his mother had gone on vacation to recoup from the last year. But when Abby didn't tell him where she was or when she was coming home, he realized it was more than that. As the weeks passed, with little communication, it just seemed too much work to keep up the lie. He finally told Drew the truth. His mother had left to figure things out.

Drew asked, "What things?"

Marcus had no clue, nor did he know when she was coming home. He wasn't sure Drew understood that. He was eighteen. What could he possibly know about the complexities of a woman? *God, even he didn't know the complexities of a woman!* The two of them wandered around the house, trying to ignore the elephant in the room. Abby wasn't there, and she might never return.

All those nights, sleep had eluded him. Marcus would wake up at three in the morning with his heart pounding. Panic pulsated through his veins. He would stare at the clock in a catatonic state, watching the numbers click by, until eventually, his eyelids would fall. By the time morning came, his eyes were red and heavy, leaving little energy for the day ahead. His work was suffering. His boss strongly suggested he take some time off, "to work on things."

Marcus had never thought about traveling across the world to go after her. He knew she would eventually come home. *Didn't he?*

The sleepless nights were more than he could bear. The waiting was torturous. He called Emma and cried. Something he was not proud of. She confessed that she knew where her mother was, where Abby had run away to. *Why there?* he asked himself a thousand times. Then he remembered. He thought of the Scottish story that Abby used to tell Emma when she was a little girl. About a little girl who escapes her empty life to find happiness.

Was that what Abby was doing?

The floors creaked below, distracting Marcus's thoughts. He heard shoes dragging across the wood and a door shutting. Pipes pounded throughout the walls as water rushed through them before all grew quiet. Mrs. Landry had finally gone to bed.

He decided to do the same and wandered across the hall to the bathroom. He leaned into the mirror, noticing the dark circles under his eyes. He rubbed his chin, thick with growth. *God, he looked like hell!* Abby wouldn't want to see him this way. He was almost grateful he hadn't seen her tonight.

Was she even thinking of him?

He splashed cold water on his face, hoping to dispel the anger rolling over him. He took out his razor and shaved before brushing his teeth and flossing. He wanted to look his best if by chance Abby returned in the morning.

As he crossed the hall and opened the door to his room, an eerie silence surrounded him. It was the kind of silence where ghosts hide—if he believed they existed. Abby did. How many times had he found her talking to the shadows? Looking into the corners of the room as if someone were standing there? He blew it off as crazy, an eccentric side of Abby he had learned to live with. He squinted, peering through the dark, and felt as if someone were there with him.

Light from his room spilled into the stairwell, tempting him to go up to the third floor. Extending his ear to the darkened corridor below, he listened for any movement from Mrs. Landry. Hearing none, he quietly padded up the stairs to Abby's room. At the top, he landed at a door labeled HONEY-MOON SUITE. He placed his hand on the handle, but he didn't think it would be unlocked. To his surprise, it opened.

As he entered the dark room, an overpowering sweet, earthy fragrance wafted across his nose. He felt his way to the light switch on the wall, and when the room brightened, he gasped. Bouquets of yellow flowers were everywhere.

Maybe Abby did find her field of flowers after all, he thought.

He quickly closed the door behind him and took a few more steps inside. The room was tidy—the bed was made, pillows were fluffed, and a large suitcase was tucked away in the corner. A coffee mug rested on top of a book by the bedside, the bookmark sticking out three-quarters through. He walked over to the armoire and opened it. Four shirts, two pairs of jeans, and a black dress were hanging, with a couple of sweaters folded neatly below them. He ran his hand over a bright pink one he had never seen before. High-heeled pumps and a pair of short boots rested on a top shelf. It was orderly, the way Abby kept her side of the closet at home. The way she liked it. He walked to the dresser. A bottle of perfume, a silver bracelet, and a pair of earrings sat on top. Marcus brought the perfume bottle to his nose and sniffed at the familiar scent of gardenias and citrus. It was Abby's smell —sweet, fresh, and intoxicating. Before he looked away, he caught a glimpse of something golden in a small crystal bowl nestled among her things. He hesitated as his hand hovered above the bowl, his heart pounding. Finally, he reached in and pulled out Abby's wedding ring. He cradled it in his hand, feeling the warmth of the metal against his palm, an ache spreading through him.

He sat on her bed, bringing a pillow close, wrapping his arms around it. Abby's scent lingered on it, stirring a tremor deep within him. He began to cry. For the first time in his life, he felt true fear that Abby might never come home.

41

AFTERGLOW

Abby was still nestled in bed when she reached for the man next to her, hoping to steal some warmth, but there was no one there. She sat up, encouraged by the smell of coffee mingling with the cool morning air. The drapes were open, exposing a gray rainy day outside. She heard the pitter-patter of the rain tapping the roofline and dripping to the ground below. The crackle of a fire came from the main room, and the couch gave a soft creak, followed by the quiet rhythm of footsteps crossing the floor. A moment later, Thom appeared in the doorway in gray sweats and a heavy cabled sweater, a soft smile playing on his lips. His familiar voice reached her ears, low and inviting, sending a tingling giddiness through her.

"I thought I heard someone rustling in the sheets," Thom said, cradling a mug between his hands.

She gave him a pouty look. "You make love to me and then leave me?"

"Never," he said, in a gravelly voice, still heavy with sleep.

He wielded his superpower once again, and her insides melted with contentment.

"Come, sit with me on the sofa. We will enjoy the warmth of the fire together." He gestured to the window. "It's going to be one of those days."

"But I'm naked!" Abby shot back.

"Well, I can resolve that problem!" Thom pulled off his sweater, exposing his broad chest, then his sweats, boldly presenting himself naked in all his glory. "Now will ye come and lie with me?" He wrapped his arms around himself. "But hurry. It's freezing and I can't stand here forever."

Abby didn't move to join him immediately. She just sat there, taking him in. It's one thing to make love to a man in the darkness of night, but it's another level of intimacy to look at the man in his full nakedness. She wanted to savor the moment.

Thom was not a youthful boy. His confidence in standing before her completely naked was not because he was in his prime. Abby knew that this was his way of saying, "This is me at my most vulnerable and I give it to you unadulterated." He was exposing himself, not for effect but for the submission of his soul.

He lingered in the doorway, letting her absorb his meaning, and then gestured for her to follow. "And bring the blanket!" he shouted as he walked away.

The sight of his firm and muscular backside was not lost on her.

Dragging the blanket off the chair, she wrapped herself inside it and followed his padding footsteps into the main room. He veered to the kitchen while she nestled herself in the corner of the sofa, curling her feet up, luxuriating in the heat of the fire now roaring, noting that Cronos was sprawled out nearby, half asleep.

Everything looked different in the light of day. The shadows were gone, exposing the true age of the building, with the cracks in the ceiling, worn baseboards, and faded patches on the wood floor. It didn't matter to Abby; the house was more charming that way. It had lived a full life until that point and was all the more beautiful for it. And now she was a part of its history, even if just for a stolen moment in time. The thought made her insides tickle.

From the kitchen, she heard a cabinet closing and the clanking of crockery. "What are you doing in there?"

"Taking care of ye," Thom said, stepping into the room with a cup of coffee in his hand. He held it slightly away from his body, careful not to spill any of the hot liquid onto his bare skin, visible above the throw blanket he had wrapped snugly around his waist. "I know how ye need your coffee in the morning," he said, placing the mug gently on the table.

Abby eyed the coffee and was tempted to reach for it first, but instead opened her blanket, inviting Thom into the cozy cocoon of warmth next to her. His eyes lit up and a slow smile spread across his face, seeing her expose her naked body in the light of day. She felt her cheeks flush and brought her hands to her face. "Now I'm truly embarrassed ..."

Thom secured the blanket around them, encapsulating the heat. "Why? Why should you be embarrassed to be naked next to the man you were completely intimate with just a few hours ago?"

The memory of making love to him the night before made her heart flutter. The sensation of his touch still lingered on the surface of her skin, causing her to blush even more.

Thom touched her face, meeting her eyes. "I touched ye in places that are sacred, kissed every part of ye, and now when I look at your beautiful body, it makes you blush?" He chuckled.

"Don't judge me, Thom." She slapped him playfully. "It's been a long time since I've been—"

"Desired?"

"Vulnerable," she corrected.

He gently placed a kiss on her cheek. "Sorry. I wasn't judging, just enjoying the sensual woman before me and feeling like a lucky man."

Abby shook her head. "How do you do that?"

"Do what?"

"Make me feel so loved," she said, before realizing what she was admitting.

Thom gazed into Abby's eyes. "Do I really need to tell ye?"

Abby looked away. She wished she could have taken back her words. The glimmer in his eyes made his feelings clear. But he did not confirm or deny the way he felt with words, likely aware that Abby was not in the same place. Her life was not as free as his.

Thom leaned back, inviting Abby to lie against his chest. It felt good and safe to be in his arms, skin on skin, their bodies naturally fitting together. His nose nuzzled behind her ear, but when his tongue tasted her skin, his desire got hungrier. His hands moved lower and slid between her legs. But he seemed in no rush to take her. He lingered with his exploration, allowing Abby to enjoy his warm hands brushing against her skin.

Abby, her long-dormant sensuality now awakened, found herself unable to control the wave of desire overtaking her. Her body yearned for his, the flames of passion engulfing any resistance she had. Shifting on top of him, she wrapped her legs around him, wanting him inside of her.

Thom's mouth came to hers, pressing hard, letting her

know his own desire to have her, but he slowed his rhythm, easing back from the edge of rapture.

"Please don't stop," Abby whispered, her voice edged with a mix of yearning and seduction.

"Dear God, Abby, nothing is going to stop this pleasure," he said, brushing a strand of her hair behind her ear with tenderness. "If my age has any advantage, it's the ability to indulge in the sensation rather than race to it." He winked. "I'm in no rush to take ye."

Abby met his eyes, drawn into the depths where passion and tenderness resided. In that moment, they shared a silent understanding, an unspoken desire between them. Her breath quickened as she held his gaze, the heat of passion rising in her cheeks. "But I am," she whispered, her voice laden with urgency.

His kisses came harder and deeper, sweeping Abby into a frenzy of wanting, his touch bringing about a new level of euphoria. His arms tightened around her, and their bodies came together in a heated dance of desire, the movement guided by an unknown force between them. Abby released a breathless moan. Thom soon followed, signaling his own pleasure created by their oneness. As Abby's breathing slowed, Thom held her trembling body, his breath rhythmic against her.

Thom's lids fell, and a grin spread across his face. "Ye happy?" His voice drifted into the air, lost to the sound of the embers crackling in the fire.

Abby nodded, placing her hand on his chest. "You make me feel good," she confessed. She felt something she had not experienced for a very long time—a soul-deep connection to a man. There seemed to be no boundaries with him; being with him was instinctual. He felt safe, as if her body had always belonged with his.

Thom took her hand and placed a kiss on her palm. He returned it to his chest, against the patter of his heart. "Dare I say, Abby, fate has given me a chance with ye ..."

Abby didn't turn away, like she had so many times, but allowed herself to feel what he was expressing, the steady thrum of his heartbeat against her hand grounding her in the moment. She knew what was transpiring between them. Goosebumps crept along her shoulders and down her back.

"Are you cold?" Thom asked, cradling her to him.

"Yes, a little," she replied in a half-truth, sinking deeper under the cover of the furry blanket.

"You should get some real clothes on. It'll warm ye up," he suggested. "And after breakfast, we'll take a drive up the coast. There's so much we have to fit in."

Abby knew what he was saying. They had so little time to share before she would return home.

Home. Her heart tugged and her stomach tightened.

She nuzzled closer to Thom, not wanting to let him go. Not yet.

He squeezed her tighter in his embrace, as if sensing her fear.

Both were aware that soon they would have to leave the enchantment of the cottage and face the world outside.

42

WAITING FOR ABBY

A barely there sweetness filled the air, a promise of something delicious, warm out of the oven. The smell dragged Marcus out of sleep. His stomach growled. He rubbed his face, his eyes still stinging and tired. He sat up, his body stiff from the cold surrounding him. With one eye open, he looked around and realized he had fallen asleep in Abby's room. His eyes darted from the door to the armoire to the long dresser, narrowing his sight on the glass bowl on top, now empty. Opening his hand, he saw the gold band cradled in the palm, the small weight pressing against his skin.

Marcus jumped from the bed and swiftly dropped the ring back into the bowl. Brushing his hands together, he tried to shake off the memories of the night before—thoughts he'd let creep in.

He wasn't ready to face losing Abby.

He took one last look at Abby's room before shutting the door and hurried back to his room. The clock flashed seven thirty-one. His stomach growled again, louder this time. He grabbed his Dopp kit and headed for the shower.

MRS. LANDRY WAS HOVERING over the sink, an apron tied around her waist, listening to the radio. It was local news, from what Marcus could tell. His footsteps were heavy against the floor, and she turned as he entered the kitchen.

"Ah, Mr. Kent ..."

"Marcus," he corrected her.

"Yes, of course." She smiled, quickly moving to turn down the volume of the radio. "How d'ya sleep?"

He hesitated, too embarrassed to admit he'd snuck into Abby's room, seeking comfort among her things. It had been weeks since he'd had a full night's rest, and being surrounded by her scent, he had finally let his mind settle. "Didn't wake up, so that's got to be a good sign." He gave her a sheepish grin, hoping she wouldn't ask him more.

"Awww, that's good," she said, wiping her hands against the apron. "Now, can I get ya some coffee?"

He nodded, pulling out a chair from the table and sitting.

"Take cream?" She tipped her head to the left, indicating it was in the refrigerator. "I hope you like scrambled eggs, they're from down the road. Nothin' like 'em fresh from the farm." She placed a plate in front of him, along with a thick slice of ham and a hot scone.

"Will you join me?" Marcus asked, looking at his full plate. "It seems a waste to eat this alone." He was thinking of Abby. He wondered if she was alone. Mrs. Landry didn't say.

"I don't mind if I do," she said, pouring herself the last of the coffee from the press. She shuffled to the cabinet and retrieved a sugar bowl, spooning in two teaspoons and stirring until the sugar dissolved. With a light clink of the spoon against the cup, she seated herself across from Marcus. "Not often we get unexpected guests out here," she said, her eyes sharp with curiosity. "Ya must have a good reason for the journey, eh?"

Marcus nodded, his mouth too stuffed to answer.

"Aye. If I had known ya were comin', I might have prepared a bit better," she added with a crooked smile. "Rather than banishin' ya to another room."

Marcus put down his fork and swallowed the remnants of food in his mouth. "Is she ...?" He paused. He wondered how much Mrs. Landry knew about Abby. About him. "How is she?"

"Well, I'll naught lie to ya. She was a handful the first few days. But she seems to have found her way," she said carefully.

Marcus smiled faintly, relief washing over him. It was good to hear. Good to talk about her, even in this roundabout way.

Mrs. Landry took a sip of her coffee, her eyes sharp as she studied him. She noticed the way his shoulders relaxed, the way his gaze drifted downward. Marcus's hand rested near his coffee cup, his thump absently brushing over the smooth surface of his wedding ring.

"I don't intend to intrude, for it's none of my business," Mrs. Landry said, her tone gentle but probing. "Abby hasn't spoken much about what's been bothering her. But I assume it's very personal, involving more than herself ... maybe a marriage?" She let the words settle before adding, "You'll not lie to me ... you're still married, then?"

Marcus's fingers tightened around the ring. A flicker of unease crossed his face as he raised his left hand, displaying his silver band. "Yes, we are," he replied, his voice steadier than he felt. He swallowed hard, remembering that Abby had taken off hers and, more painfully, wondering why.

"Aye. Just makin' sure." She offered him a reassuring smile. "Can't be too careful these days."

He pushed his plate aside, leaning closer to Mrs. Landry. Catching her eyes, he held them, wondering how much Abby had confided in her. Mrs. Landry's expression gave nothing away and he couldn't tell if she was being careful or elusive with her information. "Has Abby told you much?" He looked away, tapping his fingers on the table, before meeting her gaze. "I mean, did she tell you that she's been through a lot lately … the cancer and all? I guess she's trying to make sense of it," he explained, trying not to betray any judgment. "That is why she's here … staying so long."

"Well then, that would be between us two, wouldn't it?" She placed her crooked-fingered hand over his, giving it a squeeze, softening her tone. "I've not had you here for less than twelve hours, dear. You might give me some time to warm up to ya a bit." She winked, easing her reprimand.

Marcus rubbed his face. "Ugh, I'm sorry. I'm just anxious to see her and know she's all right," he confessed, lowering his eyes. "I miss her."

Mrs. Landry lifted his chin, studying his face, tracing the lines across his forehead and the dark circles lingering from many sleepless nights. "I can see that," she said. "Know that she's doing just fine. Got her color back, and smiles all the time. I think she has found some peace here."

Marcus's eyes lit up. "Thank you," he said. "That's all I wanted."

Mrs. Landry rose, tucking her chair under the table. "Now off with ya," she shooed him out of his chair. "I don't expect her back 'til the end of the day. If you're up to some hiking, I won't say you'll be disappointed if you find your way to

Kinnoull Hill. It'll reward ya with some sensational views across the River Tay, if not help ya pass the day. When you get back, ya might want to see the town up close, not shrouded in darkness. There's a pub down the way. The odd-lookin' man behind the counter is Dunbar. He owns the place. He's grumpier than most, but he can cook! Tell him I sent ya," she suggested. "Now, off with ya. She'll be home in no time and you'll see her soon enough."

Home? The word sent a chill through him. Did it still mean the same to Abby as it did to him, or had it changed like everything else?

43

EXPOSED

Thom packed the car and ran Cronos around the property, tiring him out, then brought in firewood to dry for the next visit, while Abby made sandwiches and cut up fruit for the long trip home. Neither said much as they hung fresh towels, changed the bedding, and swept the floors, keeping themselves distracted from the realization that their private little world was coming to an end. Occasionally, Abby looked up to find Thom watching her. She forced a smile, but she knew he understood. Her heart ached more with each passing minute, each chore bringing their time together closer to an end.

Abby stood next to Thom, a quiet reverie between them, as he retrieved the key to lock the door, their secrets sealed behind the wooden barrier ... where they would be safe forever. Thom kissed her forehead, then wrapped an arm around her shoulders, guiding her toward the car. Even Cronos walked slowly, begrudgingly climbing into the backseat, where he curled up and tucked his nose under his paw.

As Thom pulled away, the tires crunching pebbles along

the dirt drive, Abby looked over her shoulder to watch the cottage slowly disappear. Reaching into her bag, she retrieved her phone and noticed a missed call from Mrs. Landry. A flicker of worry passed through her. She dialed her back immediately, but the call went to voicemail.

On my way, she typed quickly in a message. *Call if it's important*, she added before tucking the phone back into her purse.

Thom glanced at her. "Anything important?"

Abby shook her head, though something still nagged at her.

Thom reached for her hand. "The day is beautiful. We won't waste it," he said. "We'll stop halfway for our picnic ... take our time, aye?"

Abby bestowed a kiss on his cheek, nodding softly, unable to speak. A lump in her throat, thick and heavy, made it hard to answer, and an ache settled in her heart. She bit down on her lips, willing the tears to stay behind her eyes.

The drive took them through small villages, passing a few pubs along the way. But Abby and Thom were not looking to be with people. They just wanted to be alone with each other. Thom eventually turned off the main road and found an isolated spot to park. He grabbed the picnic basket and Abby's hand, leading her along the meandering trails that were forged by earlier visitors, Cronos slowly lingering behind. They made their way through a valley of grasses and found a shady spot under some trees. Thom laid out a blanket and placed the picnic basket on it. Abby took out the cold beef sandwiches and handed one to Thom, but he turned it down, rising instead. He walked to the edge of the site and peered out to the valley. She saw his chest rise and fall several times, breathing in the crisp air, before he looked back at her. His shoulders slumped and his chin dipped as his brows drew together, a hint of sadness etched into his features. She understood. Had she not felt the same feeling creeping up inside of her?

She walked up behind him and wrapped her arms around him, resting her cheek against his back. "Make love to me again, Thom," she whispered in a fragile but certain plea.

He turned around, meeting her eyes. "Here?" His gaze swept over the vastness around them, the dotted tree lines and undulating landscape confirming their isolation.

Abby smiled, a surge of mischief flickering through her. She was never one to be so daring, but the urge to be with him one more time was overwhelming, as if the fairy tale was on the verge of ending.

Thom closed his eyes as he kissed her tenderly, his mouth rising and falling upon hers. There was nothing rushed in his touch, but only a desire to breathe her in with every brush of his lips, as if calling her soul to the surface to meet his.

Abby slipped her hands beneath his sweater, lifting it over his head along with his shirt, confirming her desire to make love to him right there and now. Thom met her urgency, unfastening his pants as he slipped off her coat, spreading it on the ground, before undressing and tossing her clothes aside. A chill crept over her skin, but Thom was soon beside her, his warmth pressing into her as he moved over her. When he entered her, Abby closed her eyes, surrendering to the feeling of him, wholly present and entwined with her.

"Abby," he breathed, as if taking ownership of her name as well as her body.

But Abby did not allow him to say more, placing her lips upon his, silencing his breathless reverie. Her eyes locked onto his, diving into the blue depths as if plunging into an ocean where no light, no sound could reach her—a place where only he could find her. His body cocooned hers, grounding her weightless soul. Pressing closer, harder, she ached to merge with him, to lose herself in the fierce comfort of his love, feeling his need pulse between them, demanding fulfillment. Thom's breath panted against her neck as his body writhed over her, sending shock waves through her.

A sudden rush of wings interrupted them, a cluster of birds lifting from the trees, sending a rhythmic feathery whoosh through the air. They peered up at the majestic sight as their bodies remained entangled, absorbing the kinetic energy surging through them, their hearts pulsing against each other.

They both laughed.

"Did you plan that?"

"If only I was that good." Thom winked. "It's us, Abby, as if nature commands us to be one. There's no denying it now." He brought his mouth to hers.

Abby felt it, too. There was no ignoring the richness of their lovemaking, the unspoken connection between them. She parted his lips to taste him, breathing in the essence of his soul—the soul now inseparably bound to hers. Falling into his embrace, Abby closed her eyes, giving in to her exhaustion.

A while later, a bird screeched across the sky as if warning them to wake up. The temperature had dropped, and they both shivered, their naked bodies pressed close against the chill. With a reluctant sigh, they rose, reaching for their clothes. When Abby put on her boots, she reached over to straighten Thom's shirt, pulling the collar out of the sweater.

"Do I look decent again?" he asked, their faces inches apart.

Abby nodded. "Terribly handsome as well," she said with a smile.

Thom kissed her gently. She could see he wanted to say more, but he didn't. *Did her eyes tell him not to?*

They found Cronos sleeping on the blanket, guarding the picnic lunch. Hunger had gotten the best of them, and they were grateful for Cronos's watchfulness. They sat down next to him and ate their sandwiches in quiet contentment, rewarding him with their leftovers. Abby was physically exhilarated, but emotionally exhausted, and knew from Thom's silence that he felt the same.

As if someone had to say it, Cronos barked twice, lifted his body, and headed toward the car. Thom and Abby looked at each other, knowing it was time to leave.

ABBY TURNED on the radio and leaned against Thom's shoulder as he drove. The windows were rolled down and the cool air was whipping her hair around her face. She tried to contain it behind her ears and finally gave up.

"Comfy?" Thom asked, his face beaming from pleasure.

Abby sighed with satisfaction and wrapped her arms around his bicep, nudging closer to him.

His eyes caught hers. "Ye make me very happy," he said unapologetically. "Happier than I thought possible."

Abby gave him a gentle kiss on the cheek without a reply. She wanted to say more. He deserved for her to express her feelings freely, the way he did. But she didn't have the freedom to be so carefree. She was married. She hoped Thom had no expectation beyond what had passed between them. They were both adults, entering the relationship with little to hide. But as she sat in the car, listening to Diana Krall croon out love songs in that unmistakable jazzy way, a sea of guilt surged through her, crashing against her newfound clarity. She'd made love to a man—a man who was cheerfully humming tunes in her ear and unapologetically accepting her into his life. This was not an affair, or a misstep. She had given herself, body and soul, to him. She didn't want to apologize, to feel guilty, or dismiss it as anything less. She loved him.

I love him! Her brain shouted.

Abby's body trembled, and she jerked away, releasing her hold on Thom.

Thom's brow furrowed. "Something the matter?"

"No," she murmured, her voice cracking slightly. "I'm just getting anxious to return home." She turned to fix her gaze on the passing scenery, hoping he wouldn't see what was written on her face.

"Home?" Thom questioned, wondering which place she was referring to.

Abby knew he was hinting at the truth. "Do we really want to talk about this now?" she said, unable to disguise her irritation.

"No. What I want is to turn around this car and drive back to the cottage, get ye naked, and make love over and over again," Thom quipped.

Abby's eyes narrowed as she pressed her lips into a thin line.

He grinned, a mischievous glint in his eye. "Okay, that may not be the most practical choice, but ye have to admit it's tempting?"

Abby folded her arms as her gaze lingered on him. "Thom ..."

"Seriously, though, Abby." He sighed. "We're avoiding the issue. It's going to explode in our faces if we don't address what we're both thinking."

Abby's mouth twitched. "I'm beginning to hate your honesty," she muttered, only half in jest.

Thom glanced at her, then turned his attention back to the road. He cleared his throat, pausing before speaking. "Abby ... you're going to have to go home," he said, his tone low and drained, as if the weight of his words was almost too much to carry.

Abby grabbed her stomach as if he'd punched her in the gut.

She had to go home.

Abby knew she could no longer keep running from her life. It wasn't fair to Marcus or to her children. For all the time she was away, she had a reason—to discover who she was, what she wanted, and where she was going. But that didn't mean they should be excluded. By distancing herself, she was cheating them out of a role in her journey. They were her family, a piece of her, and she had no right to leave them out. She couldn't keep going down this road alone.

Most of all, she wasn't being fair to Thom. They both had a lot to lose.

"Abby?" Thom whispered.

His voice hummed in her ear, bringing her back. "I know, I know. I have been avoiding it for far too long." She dropped her chin, refusing to meet his gaze. "I haven't been fair to you. How you ever fell for such a mixed-up woman like me is truly a wonder."

Thom lifted her chin, turning her to him. "I didn't fall for ye, Abby. We were just meant to be. Kindred spirits, eh?" He released his gaze. "You're far too hard on yourself. But if ye were my wife, I think I'd want to settle the score," he confided, his voice steady and warm. "He must be terribly lost without ye. I know I'd be."

Abby squeezed Thom's arm.

"Abby ..."

"Don't," Abby stopped him. "These last few days were ..." She shook her head, struggling for the words. "We've had a lovely adventure—"

Without warning, Thom hit the brakes, stopping the car in the middle of the road. "Is that what this was?" His voice was hard, intense.

Cronos jolted at the sudden halt, lifted his head, and looked around, then, sensing no real threat, resettled with a quiet huff.

Abby's eyes widened. "No, no, of course not. That came out wrong." She glanced behind them to check for cars, but they hadn't seen another vehicle in miles. Turning back, she saw the hurt on Thom's face. "I just meant ... we don't have to discuss it right now. Today hasn't ended yet. Let's not spoil a beautiful moment. Nothing is going to happen today," she begged.

Thom grimaced, but his voice softened. "I don't want to argue with ye. Not when I still have your warmth upon my flesh." He leaned over and kissed her softly on the lips. He began to hum the next tune on the playlist and motioned for Abby to lean against his shoulder.

That was enough for her, for now. She hoped it was enough for him.

Time passed quietly as they drove, the landscape shifting as they neared town. They arrived just as the sun set, the sky turning gray and the streets busy with people leaving stores or rushing into pubs as the evening fell upon them. The cabin of the car was filled with warmth and Abby dreaded entering the stark reality of the cold outside.

Abby pointed to the front of Thom's shop. "Drop me off here. I can walk back to the inn."

Thom looked at her but didn't say anything.

"I want to walk."

"Shall I carry your bag for you?" he asked when he turned off the engine.

Abby shook her head. If she spoke, she knew her tears would begin to fall.

Thom grabbed her bag from the back and walked her to the end of the busy street. "Be ready in an hour. We'll have dinner together," he shouted, leaving no room for her to decline.

Abby nodded, then turned away, making the steady climb to the inn. A chilly breeze forced her to pull up the collar of her coat and quickly button the front. With each step, a creeping cold sensation spread through her; all traces of Thom's warmth faded from her skin, as if they had never been there at all. As if they had never been, a fleeting moment now drifting into nothing. She turned back to look for Thom, hoping he had stayed to watch her, to keep her in his sights. But he was gone and the street now empty, except for a few straggler shoppers and merchants closing their shops.

What was she hoping for? She tightened her grip on her bag, swung it over her shoulder, and continued onward. Each step felt heavier than the last, the weight of the choices she would have to face settling deep inside her. As the inn came into view, she let out a sigh of relief, grateful for a little more time, telling herself that, for tonight at least, the answers could wait.

44

IT'S BEEN A WHILE

A bby entered through the side door of the inn and threw her bag on the kitchen table. She heard Mrs. Landry in the salon talking, probably to her latest arrivals. The town was finally booming with tourists, and the inn was expected to fill up by the end of the week. A newly married couple was coming on Friday, and Abby was going to have to move out of her luxurious accommodation. Mrs. Landry assured her that she could stay as long as she wanted, but Abby couldn't justify taking up the honeymoon suite. It was a sign from the universe. She needed to move on.

But to where?

Abby heard the crackle of a fire from the other room, inviting her to shed her coat and indulge in the warmth of the cozy house. She saw the French press filled with coffee and touched it to see if it was still hot. Tempted by an open bottle of wine nearby, she poured the coffee instead and took a much-needed sip.

Glancing out the window, she smiled. Weeks ago, Mrs. Landry had pushed her paralyzed soul out into the world.

She hadn't fractured. No lightning had struck her. Instead, the world cradled her as she walked out the door, stepping into the land of the living ... and into self-discovery.

Dare she explore what she has found?

Memories of making love to Thom resurfaced, and her smile grew wider. A surge of energy spread through her, her heart expanding with a lightness she could no longer suppress—nor did she want to. She felt truly happy to be alive.

Abby heard footsteps coming toward her. She downed the rest of her coffee, grabbed her things, and hurriedly climbed to the third floor, avoiding any new guests to the inn. As she turned the handle of her door, it flew open. Standing before her was Marcus.

Abby blinked twice. It was his voice that quickly solidified he was not a ghostly figure.

"Abby!" Marcus said, his voice raised an octave. He cleared his throat, trying to dispel the nervousness he felt. "Here, let me get those." He grabbed the bag out of her hand and moved aside for her to enter.

She took a few steps into her room and looked around, sensing if anything had changed, before she closed the door. *Had he gone through her things? And if he had, what might he have found?*

She hung her coat in the armoire and tossed her purse onto the bed. She ran her hands down the duvet, smoothing the dip where he must have been sitting, waiting for her. When she looked up, Marcus's eyes were transfixed on her. They followed her every movement, each step around the room, each bat of her eyes. Waiting for her to do something. Say something.

What are you doing here? she wanted to say. But she already knew the answer. He had come to take her home.

Say something! her head screamed, but her throat seemed to close on her. She brought her hands to her neck and rubbed it as if she could force it to move through the massage. She stepped toward him instead and, with one move, fell into his arms. He brushed his smooth cheek across hers, nuzzling into her neck. He had found *his* spot, and she allowed him to linger there, nestled close to her.

"Mmm, you smell good," he murmured, inhaling the familiar scents of her shampoo and body lotion. His hands smoothed down her back. "You feel good too."

His hands circled her waist, but she stepped back, meeting him face-to-face. His brows knit together, his mouth set in a flat line, yet he didn't press her to explain her sudden, cold response.

"Marcus." Her voice crackled. She tried again, this time offering a soft smile. "Darling, I didn't expect to find you here ..." She darted her eyes away.

He gave a tight, bitter smile, his tone deepening, his stare hardening. "So, this is how it's going to go down? I fly thousands of miles to be with you, and all you want to know is what I'm doing here?"

"Marcus, please don't take it that way," Abby pleaded. "I mean, you just surprised me, that's all. You should have let me know ..."

"Really?" He gave her an unimpressed look. "What kind of greeting is that? We haven't seen each other in almost two months, Abby." He threw up his arms and started to pace the room, eventually planting himself down on the bed. He looked at her from across the room, his gaze lingering on her red sweater. She brushed her hair behind her ears, a nervous habit she had never shaken. "God, you look good," he blurted out.

Abby slid her hand down her sweater, feeling the soft

cashmere fibers against her fingertips. She remembered it on the ground just hours ago, next to her naked body entwined with another man. A flush of red surfaced, and she quickly turned away.

"I shouldn't have said that ... it's too soon, I know." His eyes lowered and his voice softened. "I don't want to argue, Abby. I just wanted to see you," he confessed. "I miss you, babe."

Babe. He rarely called her that anymore. She walked over to the bed and sat down, taking his hand in hers. "Sorry, Marcus. It is good to see you. Truly."

Marcus drew her close, wrapping her in his arms. This time, Abby didn't resist, letting herself sink into his embrace.

A knock came at the door, and Marcus loosened his embrace. Abby found Mrs. Landry in the doorway, worry etched into her expression.

"I've brought some wine for ye," Mrs. Landry said, balancing two glasses in one hand and a bottle in the other. "I thought you could use a little refreshment. No need to mingle with the newcomers. They're a cute pair, but maybe a little overambitious in their enthusiasm." She winked. "Young love. They should enjoy it while it lasts."

Abby locked eyes with Mrs. Landry and shook her head slightly, indicating that she wasn't in any distress. "Thank you, Mrs. Landry," she said, her voice bouncing a little too high to be convincing.

Mrs. Landry shot up a brow. "Och," she said, nudging past Abby and placing the glasses and bottle on the dresser. "Mr. Kent ..."

"Marcus," he insisted again.

"Aw, you'll have to forgive me, Marcus. My brain gets the best of me." She shot a look at Abby. "It's cold out tonight, and I thought you might need a little refreshment after your long trip. I hope you enjoyed the Crathes Castle, Abby. I hear it's blooming nicely in spite of this cold snap," she said coyly.

"It was ... more than I expected."

"Good, good." Mrs. Landry leaned into Abby. "If ya need anything, ya let me know."

"I'm fine," Abby reassured her, showing her to the door. "We can catch up later." She squeezed the old woman's hand.

Mrs. Landry nodded to Marcus and closed the door behind her.

"Are you fine?" Marcus asked as he poured Abby a glass of wine.

"I am," Abby lifted her chin slightly, her voice carrying a confidence that surprised even her. "I really am, Marcus."

Marcus studied Abby's face. "You look better than *fine*, Abby," he murmured, then paused. "You look ... changed."

An unexpected excitement surged through her. *She was.*

"Abby"—Marcus shifted his stance, running his hand through his hair—"are you angry I came here?"

"No, Marcus," Abby said in a low voice, her heart tugging tighter in her chest. She kissed his lips softly. "I'm glad you came. It was time."

"That's good to hear. Because we've missed you." He cleared his throat before locking his eyes with her. "I mean, I've really missed you."

Abby brushed her hand across his face, his skin warm against her fingers. She wasn't sure what he needed from her, or what she wanted from him. It was too soon to say. She gave him a conciliatory smile, wanting to say so much more, but not having the words to express all she wanted to say. Their eyes held. Abby felt him weighing something, just as she was. How far could they push this?

Abby finally stood. "Let me freshen up, and we'll go and get a bite to eat?" she suggested.

"And talk?"

Abby agreed with a kiss on his forehead. "Relax. Let me shower and make myself pretty for you."

"You look beautiful now ..."

Abby smiled at his sincerity. She opened her luggage, grabbed her toiletry bag, and disappeared around the corner into the bathroom.

MARCUS LOOKED through the open bag on her bed. A pair of jeans, a T-shirt, a sweater, and some lace panties sat neatly folded, alongside a book. Just Abby's usual things—nothing unusual, nothing revealing.

He poured himself another drink, thankful for Mrs. Landry's attentiveness, and watched the passersby on the street below. He noted the expansive view of the main street. Like an owl on her perch, Abby must have lingered, mesmerized at the happenings below. Marcus followed a couple who came out of a pub and strode up the street, their hands interlinked, swaying in a back-and-forth rhythm. A man with a white beard sat down on a bench and threw breadcrumbs to some lingering birds. They pecked at the tiny crumbs, coming closer to the hands that were feeding them, until they were at his feet. He bent down to touch one, but the group of them flew away at the gesture. Marcus turned away from the spectating as he heard Abby humming a jazzy tune. The familiarity of her voice gave him the comfort he'd been seeking when he came, the contentment of knowing she was with him. Not knowing where she was and what she was doing had been eating away at him.

Marcus filled his glass once again and walked to the bathroom. Abby had left the door slightly ajar, allowing him to catch a glimpse of her. The shower door was steamed, but he could see the outlines of her naked body. Her head was tilted back as the water fell over her. He thought of stripping down and joining her, but he knew better, sensing she needed distance.

A knock came at the door. Marcus was expecting Mrs. Landry, but when he opened the door, a man stood before him, a vase of flowers in his arms.

"May I help you?" Marcus asked.

With some hesitancy, after giving Marcus a once-over, the man finally answered. "I have a delivery for Abby."

"Abby?" Marcus noted the familiarity in his tone, how her name poetically rolled off his tongue. He looked around the room, not sure Abby needed one more arrangement. "How often does she have flowers delivered?" he asked, his gaze steady.

"She's been in the store a few times," the man answered, offering little else.

Marcus took the vase in his hands, then placed them next to a bowl of roses that were drying up. He reached in his pocket for his money clip.

The delivery man stopped him. "You don't have to do that."

Marcus nodded, slipping it back into his pants. "I'll make sure she sees them. Thanks."

The man turned to leave but halted. "You're her husband, then?"

Marcus wasn't sure why the flower delivery guy needed to know that piece of information, but he nodded.

The man lifted his chin and left with no further questions.

ABBY HEARD THE DOOR SHUT. "Did Mrs. Landry come by again?"

"No. Your flowers arrived," Marcus said.

"My what?" Had she heard him right? With a towel wrapped around her, she walked out of the bathroom. "What did you say?"

He pointed to the newly arrived flowers. "Your regular delivery?"

Abby looked at the full bouquet of roses tightly woven together, submerged in a round bowl. They were not the usual assortment of yellow flowers, but red.

Her face flushed. "Thom was here?"

Marcus stared at her but didn't answer.

45

DATE NIGHT # 2

A fter exchanging pleasantries with Mrs. Landry, Abby walked out the door, Marcus by her side. With her arm looped through his, they fell into a familiar stride—a rhythmic pace that only intimate partners come to know—as they made their way down the street. Abby was grateful for muscle memory, because nothing inside her felt natural. *Fake it 'til you make it* rattled around in her head. She was glad to see people walking the streets and hoped to hide among them, especially from Thom. She could only imagine what he was thinking after discovering Marcus was in town, and in her bedroom. She wished she could talk to him, explain things to him, but that was no longer a possibility.

"Is that the flower shop?" Marcus asked, pointing to the store across the street.

"Huh?" Abby said, looking up.

"The flower delivery guy said you've been there a few times. Probably more, seeing your room and all the flowers. You must really like it?"

Abby looked at the apartments above the row of shops. Thom's was dark, his drapes closed. "Um, well ..." Abby pointed to the sign. "See the name?"

Marcus nodded. "Oh, the story you used to tell Emma."

"It was like kismet when I saw it," Abby explained, but knew there was no way to tell him the truth—what that place meant, or even more, the person who had come to mean so much to her. "It's the kind of shop I had always imagined having. I mean, if I had ever opened a floral design business," she said, her words spilling out in a rush.

Marcus halted, turning Abby to him. "You really wanted to do that?" His gaze searched her face. "You never really said anything after college. We both got those great jobs, and then after the kids"—he touched his chin—"we seemed to manage. I didn't know you wanted to go back to work or start a business. I mean, if you really wanted to, I guess we could've figured it out."

"I'm not looking back with regret." Meeting his gaze, Abby's expression softened, and she chose her words carefully. "But what if I want it now?"

"Abby." Marcus's tone deepened. "What's this really about?"

Abby shook her head. "I'm just thinking, Marcus. I've been doing a lot of that here."

"God, I hope so," Marcus snapped. He cleared his throat, shifting his stance.

Abby watched him, the tightness in his jaw and the sharp, deliberate movements of his hands betraying more than his words. He was angry. She could see he was trying to keep it in check, but any effort only made the tension more obvious. Things were not the same, and he knew it. The leverage he'd once had was gone. She wondered if he realized just how much had shifted between them. She had left, after all. And as far as she could tell, he wasn't certain she was coming back.

Suddenly, Marcus reached for her hand. "Want to show me what you like so much about it?" he asked, his voice gentler.

Abby jolted, pulling him back. "No!"

"Hey, what's with you?" Marcus's expression tightened.

"I ... I'm just hungry," Abby said, dropping her gaze to avoid his stare. "Maybe tomorrow we can go in. There are a lot of places I'd like to take you." She slipped her hand back into his, offering a faint smile that didn't quite reach her eyes.

Marcus searched her eyes for a moment before bringing her hand to his lips, placing a soft kiss on top. "Sure," he said. "I'm hungry, too."

As they turned to leave, Abby glanced back at the store. Through the window, shadows stirred, and a figure emerged in the dim light. Her breath caught as Thom stepped closer, his austere face illuminated by a streetlight. His hands were crossed and his eyes fixed on her and Marcus with an intensity that sent a jolt of shame through her. A moment later, Cronos leaped on him, drawing him back into the dark space.

Abby tore her gaze away and quickened her pace, her boots striking the cobblestones harder than she intended. She needed to get away—far away—from anything that reminded her of the life she was turning away from.

"This is a nice place," Marcus said, glancing around. "Have you eaten here before?"

Abby followed his gaze, equally admiring the restaurant. She hadn't been there before, intentionally choosing a place away from her usual spots. On Mrs. Landry's recommendations, she took Marcus outside the immediate area, where the uptick of tourists provided some welcome anonymity. She unfolded the large paper menu and slipped on her glasses, breathing a quiet sigh of relief.

"I thought we should try something new—*together*," she said, barely looking up as she scanned the farm-to-table specials. "They practically know me all over town. I keep going to the same places becoming a creature of habit." She brushed the menu aside and pointed to a listing. "You should try the Aberdeen Angus steak. Everyone has told me it's the best."

She caught Marcus staring at her. Her eyes widened. "What?"

"Abby?" He shook his head, letting out a low, smug laugh. "You've been here the whole time?"

Marcus's laugh made her stomach twist. She'd been caught.

"Why would you stay in one town for almost two months?" Marcus demanded, his voice rising, each word sharper than the last. "I thought you were traveling and exploring. What the hell have you been doing *here*?" His eyes narrowed. Abby felt pinned under his scrutiny as he waited for an explanation.

Abby peered over her shoulder, catching a few glances of patrons at nearby tables. She swallowed hard, willing herself to keep calm, gathering her wits and words. "Has it been that long?" she said lightly, trying to wave the question away like it was nothing. "Really Marcus, does it matter? Wait until you see all the sites to visit from here ..."

"Abby," he said, locking eyes with her. "There's something you're not telling me." He paused, his gaze intensifying. "I know you. God, I can feel it."

He did know her—the Abby she used to be. But she

wasn't the same woman anymore. His eyes studied her, as if trying to piece the person in front of him. *What did he see?*

A heaviness pressed against Abby's chest, and she was finding it difficult to breathe. *Get away!* her inner voice shouted. She glanced at the door. Someone was walking through, and she wondered if she was fast enough to dart out before the door closed. She shot up, jolting the table.

Marcus's gaze flickered between Abby and the door. "What are you doing?"

"I ... I ... need some air," Abby stuttered, her breathing getting heavier, as waves of heat rushed through her. It was like she was having an allergic reaction to Marcus.

"Look at me, Abby," Marcus begged. When Abby grabbed her coat, he tugged at her arm. "Why are you running away from me?"

Abby couldn't avoid his eyes. They were as blue as the sea, filled with confusion and, most of all, sadness. He probably just wanted his wife back, but Abby wasn't sure she could give him the woman he once knew. *Would he want me if I tried?*

Abby made her way across the restaurant, her breath quickening. Just as she pushed through the doorway, she collided with a solid chest, catching the familiar scent of a man.

"Thom!" she gasped, startled.

Before he could react, Marcus came up behind her, his presence casting a shadow she didn't need to see to recognize. He was a part of her, their connection lingering between them, even without explicit acknowledgment.

Marcus eyed the man standing in front of them. "Hey." His chin shot up. "You're the guy that delivered the flowers, right? I'm Abby's husband, Marcus." He stretched out his hand.

Thom eyed the hand in front of him before accepting it. "Aye. I'm Thom."

Abby froze. *Say something!* her head screamed. But no words came.

Thom cleared his throat and looked at Abby. "The crew is meeting here for dinner. I'd figured you'd be going to one of the usual spots, so I suggested this place," he explained.

"Usual spots?" Marcus questioned, glancing at Abby.

Abby's heart pounded, but relief washed over her as Effemy's voice broke through the tension.

"Well, aren't we the lucky ones? Look who's here," Effemy said, turning to her husband, close behind. "Thom said you might be leaving for good. I nearly cried. I thought, 'She can't leave without saying goodbye, right?'"

"Hiya, Abby," Brannan said, wrapping his arms around her and placing a kiss on her cheek.

Abby saw Marcus's forehead crease slightly as Brannan hugged her.

She tugged at Marcus's arm, dragging him into the circle. "Everyone, this is my husband, Marcus."

"Abby's husband?" Effemy shrieked.

Marcus laughed nervously. "She did tell you she had a husband?"

"Of course," Effemy replied, forcing an awkward chuckle before shooting a glance at Abby. "We didn't know you were joining her ... here ... in Scotland."

"Neither did she," he said, giving Abby a glance. "I thought I'd surprise her."

Brannan stepped forward and extended his hand to Marcus. "Well, it's nice to meet the other half of Abby. You have quite a lass there." He winked at Abby. "She told us all about ya and the kids."

Marcus gave an awkward smile, shifting his weight from

one foot to the other. "That's good to hear." He reached for Abby's hand.

"We were just going in for dinner. If you haven't eaten, would ya care to join us?" Effemy suggested, turning to Marcus for an answer.

"Oh." Abby side-glanced at the door behind her. "It was so crowded in there. We were going to try someplace else."

"Nonsense!" Effemy exclaimed. "I have a reservation. They'll find a table for all of us." She looped her arm around Marcus's and started for the door. "If you're Abby's husband, you're one of us now," she said with a smile, then dragged him away.

Brannan's eyes rolled as he watched his wife disappear on another man's arm, his expression suggesting he was too familiar with her flirtatious ways. "Effemy will keep him preoccupied for a while," he said, giving Abby a reassuring smile. He pointed at Thom. "It'll give you two some time to talk."

Abby squeezed Brannan's arm. "You didn't have to do that," she murmured. "I mean ... you didn't have to lie for me."

He leaned toward her. "We're friends, eh? Plus, I didn't really lie." He lifted his chin and brushed along his beard. "You told us about your family ... we just didn't hear much about a husband attached to that."

Abby lowered her eyes. "I don't know who's more shameful, me or you."

"Aye, well, there seems to be plenty of it goin' around." Brannan hit Thom on the shoulder. "See you inside."

As Brannan ducked through the door, Abby fixed Thom with a sharp stare. "They all know about us?"

"They heard we went away," he admitted. "They were only hoping ..."

Abby shook her head, cutting him off. She didn't want to

hear him say it—anything that tied them together. Besides, she should've known. They were a tight group.

"So, Marcus came," Thom said matter-of-factly. "To take you home?"

She shrugged. "I don't know." She really didn't. They hadn't discussed it yet. "I've been gone a long time. Probably too long."

Thom looked down at the ground, kicking a ghost pebble with the toe of his boot.

Abby touched his arm softly. "This isn't how I planned ... and I know you must feel awkward."

Thom recoiled from her touch. "For Christ's sake, Abby," he growled, his accent thick and rugged. "We aren't teenagers. I just spent the last few days making love to ye. How do ye think I should feel"—he gestured toward the restaurant—"with your husband here?" His jaw tightened as he turned sharply, taking a few steps away from her. Then he spun back around, his frustration spilling over. "Yes, damn it, this is bloody awkward!"

Abby cowered back, lowering her eyes. Shame and sorrow swallowed her voice, leaving her unable to fight with him, or for him.

Thom shook his head, frustration etched across his face. "Nothing to say? God, Abby, I'm standing here, holding myself back. It's taking everything I've got not to take ye in my arms." He stepped closer, making her meet his gaze. "We're talking about our lives here, Abby. Me and you."

Was there a Thom and Abby? Abby hadn't thought that far, hadn't dared let herself go there. It felt like an eternity since they had made love, though it had just been a few hours. When Marcus appeared, she hadn't been able to get in the shower fast enough, desperate to erase the evidence of

Thom's touches lingering on her skin; the taste of his kisses had long since washed away.

But now, with Thom standing before her, his eyes yearning to hold her, his words baring his love for her, all she wanted was to fall into his arms. Nothing could cleanse the essence of him that now settled within her. Her soul was bound to his now, the two of them forever connected.

"Abby?" Mairi's voice echoed in the evening air. Stepping out of a taxi, she sauntered up to them, turning her gaze from Thom to Abby, then back to Thom. "I don't understand, I thought you said her husband was here?"

"Dear Lord," Abby shrieked, throwing her arms in the air. "Is there nothing that you guys don't know about each other?" With a roll of her eyes, she turned sharply and started to walk away.

Thom called after her, "You're always running away, aren't you, Abby?"

She stomped back, narrowing her eyes at him. "That isn't fair," she shouted.

"Nooo ... it isn't," he growled through clenched teeth. "But it's true. You're a coward, Abby. You keep running, avoiding what's right in front of you—me and your heart."

Stepping in between the two, Mairi grabbed Thom's arm and nudged him toward the door of the restaurant. "Go inside, Thom," she ordered in the brisk tone of a teacher reprimanding a child. "Order a drink ... or two. Now is not the time for this. You know you'll just make an ass of yourself if you continue."

"Aye," he growled, shrugging off Mairi's firm grip, but he obeyed her orders.

As the door closed behind him, Abby shut her eyes, letting out a sigh. When she opened them, Mairi's face was planted in front of her.

"What? Are you going to scold me?" Abby said in an exasperated breath. "You didn't have to do that, Mairi. None of you have to save me. I made this mess, and it's mine to figure out."

"Aye? Maybe it's not you we're saving," Mairi replied. "Thom's full of passion, and while that's one of his finer qualities, it can also bring out the worst in him. If he'd stayed, he might have said things he'd regret. Thom's not a mean-spirited man. Nor do I think you purposely set out to hurt him. Yet harm is being done all the same, Abby."

Abby stepped back, crossing her arms. "I appreciate your help, Mairi." Her voice wobbled. "Truly, I do. But this isn't your concern."

"No, it's not," Mairi agreed. "However, Thom came to see me, after he ran into your husband ... in your room." Her brow arched. "Involving me whether I like it or not."

Abby's eyes flinched, her anger getting the best of her. "Isn't that where he always lands when he is seeking comfort?"

Mairi let out a knowing laugh, as if seeing straight through Abby's attempt at deflection. "Well played, Abby, but that isn't what we're talking about, is it?" She tilted her head, her smile fading as she studied her. "Thom is devastated. How could he not be? God, Abby, the man is in love with you!" Her face grew stern. "And he isn't the type of person who takes another man's wife."

Abby dropped her head. She wanted to defend herself, to say she never meant to hurt anyone, but the truth was overwhelming. Mairi's words burned through her, and she deserved every bit of it. Perhaps more.

Mairi touched Abby's arm softly, her tone easing. "Thom wasn't trying to hurt you when he came to me. He needed a release because he's hurting. He told me"—she met Abby's eyes—"that fate had given him another chance only for it to be taken away once again." She sighed. "You're breaking his heart, Abby."

Mairi might as well have kicked her in the stomach. Abby sucked in a breath, fighting to steady herself. Though she willed her tears away, they slid down her cheeks in defiance.

Mairi produced a tissue from her purse and dabbed at the wetness spilling onto Abby's face with a mother's gentle care. "And if your eyes don't lie, I can see that you're feeling the same way he feels about you."

Abby swallowed hard, wishing she could confirm or deny Mairi's observation, but it was more complicated than that. She couldn't face that much truth, not now with Marcus's arrival. The luxury of separation, the distance from reality, was gone. Looking away, she twisted her hands together, teetering between guilt and longing. "I don't know who I am anymore, let alone what I have to offer anyone," she finally said, followed by an exhausted sigh.

Mairi leaned closer, her gaze steady and kind. She took Abby's hand, holding it between her own. "When I first met you, there seemed a heaviness that hung about. I know that heaviness. It's a dark spirit. Call it Scotland or Thom, but whatever it was, it has caused you to change. It's like you have found yourself. And from my point of view, you and Thom seemed to have found each other. But what that means is for you to decide."

"I didn't set out to hurt him," Abby murmured, not sure if she meant Thom or Marcus.

"I know you didn't. But that bell has already rung." Mairi paused, her expression thoughtful, as if choosing her next few words. "I'm not going to fault you for what you did, or what you feel you must do. But there are two men in there with whom you're now entangled. Truth won't fix everything, but it gives everyone clarity. They deserve your honesty if they are going to make their own choices as well." Mairi's eyes lingered on Abby's face. "Thom is a good man. I want to see him happy. He deserves ..."

"You," Abby said, her voice trembling. "He deserves *you*."

Mairi smirked wryly. "We were never two souls fated to be connected."

Abby's thoughts spiraled. Was fate a fixed path shaped by circumstance, or something she could claim as her own? Isn't that why she was here, to figure it out?

In pursuit of answers, she had only tangled herself further, caught in complications that clouded the truth. She had been soaring so high that she had forgotten she would eventually have to land. *Where would she land, and with whom?* She stood at a crossroads. A decision loomed before her, yet she had no idea which path to take. Which one was truly hers? Which one was fate?

Abby covered her face and rattled her head, as if the answer just needed to be dislodged from her brain. "I don't know what to do," she confessed, her voice barely more than a whisper.

"The answers won't come until you're ready to face them," Mairi urged, her voice steady. She glanced at the door of the restaurant. "I'll go in first, distract the others while you pull yourself together. When you're ready, join us ... and finally face your husband, and Thom."

Abby nodded numbly, watching Mairi slip away, leaving her alone on the street. Her eyes drifted from the restaurant to the darkened streets, causing her to wonder what shadows lurked just out of sight. Her instinct was to run, to leave, but Thom's parting words echoed in her mind.

"You're a coward, Abby."

The words still stung. With a deep breath, she wiped her

eyes and pinched her cheeks before applying a fresh layer of lipstick in an attempt to mask her inner turmoil. Satisfied, or at least no longer a complete crying mess, Abby straightened her shoulders and pushed open the door, crossing the threshold to where her demons awaited.

A cacophony of voices rushed at her like a gust of wind on a brisk winter day. The mix of laughter, chatter, and clinking glasses hit her, making her flinch and pause momentarily in the doorway. Her eyes swept the room, finally landing on Marcus, who was surrounded by her friends. Effemy, of course, was keeping him entertained, her face glowing with animated gestures, likely tied to an intriguing story.

Laughter crinkled at the corner of Marcus's eyes, and for a fleeting moment, he seemed to belong with them. He looked content—happy, even. Abby wondered if it was a sign. Her chest tightened at the sight, her resolve wavering. She didn't have it in her to take away that momentary reprieve from heartache. Quietly, she thanked Effemy for providing the distraction, giving her the space to postpone what she needed to do.

Her gaze hovered over the table. Thom's absence from the group was glaring. She scanned the room again and found him sitting alone at a small table, cradling a half-empty glass. His eyes were brimming in sorrow, the blue that once warmed them dulled to a somber gray. His face was a blank canvas, betraying no emotion. Her heart tugged, a shard of pain ripping through her.

When he caught her glance, he hesitated before meeting her eyes. He tipped back his glass, draining it in one gulp, then set it down with deliberate care. Rising from his chair, he walked toward her, his steps measured and unhurried.

"Thom," she began, her voice trembling, but he stopped her with a soft shake of his head.

"Go to him, Abby," he said, his voice quiet but resolute. The bitterness was gone, leaving only the hollow echo of defeat. "He's been waiting for you."

His gaze lingered on her a moment longer, and she ached to reach for him. But before she could move, he turned and walked out of the restaurant, leaving her standing in the doorway, torn between the man she had once loved and the one she wasn't sure she deserved.

46

NUANCES

The first week that Abby was gone, Marcus did not question it. Her departure was a little unusual, but with all that she had gone through over the winter, a spontaneous vacation seemed reasonable, even if she hadn't told him about it. He was willing to oblige her, if time away was what she needed to heal her mind, as well as her body. He knew Abby was responsible and reasonable. She would never do anything drastic. However, after two weeks had gone by with no communication, worry set in.

At the end of the first month, Marcus got angry. Abby was in regular contact with Emma, and Drew had received regular texts, but she had not returned any of his communications. If she was mad, he had gotten the message.

He immersed himself in work to distract from his growing hostility, but a nagging feeling was starting to grow. *Was Abby coming back?* Two more weeks went by, and panic set in. He had to face the fact that his wife was gone.

Seeing her should have erased his fears, but her reaction to his arrival set off another panic button. Something wasn't right. He tried to brush it off, blaming two months of separation. They had never been apart for more than a week in all the years they had been married. He noticed her attempts to reestablish normalcy between them—a lean toward him, a casual brush of his arm as she walked by, a warm smile when he looked at her. But that was just the problem. It was all too deliberate, like an actor fumbling with lines in a poorly rehearsed play.

When he found out that she had not been traveling the whole time, but had stayed in one place, an alarm went off. He found it odd that she'd stayed in one small town instead of exploring the many places she'd dreamed of visiting. *Wasn't that the point?* If she'd just needed time away, why did she have to travel so far? And if she'd needed to travel so far, why hadn't she gone to more places?

He was going to address the issue at dinner, to ask her what was wrong and try to close the growing distance between them. It was the purpose he came, to see her face-to-face and try to make sense of the divide that had grown so vast it felt impossible to cross. She wasn't coming to him, so he needed to go to her. He wasn't going to let her keep drifting away.

But when he tried, she fled. Why? *What had he done to cause Abby to run away from him?* He felt helpless, lost as to what Abby needed or how to even try to fix what she felt was broken.

How could he make it right if she wouldn't let him in?

Later, as he sat among her new friends, he tried to piece together the puzzle of Abby's time here. With a few rounds of drinks, stories began to emerge, snapshots of a version of Abby he barely recognized. Abby got drunk on whiskey, arranged flowers for a wedding, danced with strangers who made passes at her, and was competitive at games—everyone laughing, as though sharing a secret they all were in on but him. They talked about a woman who let her emotions flow freely, who was silly and lighthearted.

He couldn't remember when the last time he'd heard Abby laugh—truly laugh.

Was it after the cancer? Or was it long before, and he'd simply failed to notice?

He listened, unsettled. Abby had always been reserved, practical, grounded. They relied on that as a family; he needed that for security. She'd never been one for whisky, let alone getting drunk. They hadn't danced together in years. Did she still like to dance? He wasn't even sure they were talking about Abby—*his Abby.*

And as he sat there, a thought hit him hard. Maybe Abby wasn't trying to leave him, but *she* wasn't coming back to him either. Abby wasn't vacationing, she was finding herself, changing into a version of herself he didn't recognize. Someone who might not fit into the life they'd built together.

"Tired?" Abby broke Marcus's silence as they walked toward the inn.

"Yeah," Marcus replied, his voice low and burdened with uncertainty.

Abby slipped her hand into his. Her hand fell like it was meant to be there. It was warm, comforting, familiar. So why didn't she look at him?

"Let's call it a night then," she suggested as they reached the front door.

Marcus nodded and followed Abby as she locked the inn door behind them and turned out the light.

She was very familiar. Too familiar.

Abby unlocked her bedroom and peered at her empty luggage stand, still folded and leaning against the wall. "It looks like Mrs. Landry hasn't brought your things to my room." She scanned the room to confirm her observation. "Do you want to stay here tonight?"

"Huh?" Marcus's eyes swept the room as well, searching for his things.

"Do you want to sleep with me tonight?"

Marcus's brows furrowed. *Of course he wanted to sleep with his wife!*

Meeting Abby's gaze, he finally asked what had been on his mind all evening. "Abby, why have you stayed here so long?"

Abby didn't answer him right away. Her eyes locked onto his, uncharacteristically steady, as though looking through him. Marcus noticed the pause, the way her expression shifted, measured and deliberate. She was never slow to respond, always knowing exactly how to react to him, almost as if she could read his thoughts. It had always been one of the reassuring things about her—she knew him, got him, understood him better than he probably knew himself.

What was she thinking now?

Abby looked away, breaking her stare, and walked to the window. She peered out before turning back to him. "I didn't plan on it. Honestly, Marcus. It was just a stopping-off point so I could get my bearings. But ... it was quiet here. Peaceful. Mrs. Landry was kind, motherly." A gentle smile crossed her face. "Ever since Mom passed, I guess I've been a little nostalgic for motherly advice, the comfort it brings. And, I don't know ..." She shrugged. "It just felt like it was where I needed to be."

"But two months?" Marcus groaned. "I mean, Abby, what could you possibly be doing *here* all this time?"

"I ... I ..." Abby stuttered. "I found the town ... the people charming. I liked them and they liked me."

Marcus wasn't convinced. "No doubt," he said, the words

clipped and flat, his jaw tightening. "Your new friends are fun. You seemed to have gotten close in such a short time." His gaze narrowed. "But what about us—your family? What about me, Abby? Am I supposed to be okay that you just left without any explanation?"

"No." Abby's voice wavered. "Well, yes, Marcus. I guess that's what I'm asking of you—to understand." She pressed lips together, and Marcus couldn't tell if she was hesitating or choosing her words carefully. "It might not make sense to you, and I'm not even sure if it makes sense to me, but I needed to do this."

She looked away, her gaze falling somewhere past his shoulder. Marcus felt that a wall had gone up between them. She wasn't acting like herself—something in her posture, her voice, the way her eyes wouldn't hold his. *God, how many times had she calmed him with just one look?* It wasn't just what she was saying, it was what she wasn't saying that was killing him inside.

Marcus crossed his arms, shifting his weight from one foot to the other. He held back the words pressing at the edge of his tongue, careful not to push Abby further away. The tug in his chest grew sharper, tightening around his heart.

Abby gently touched his arm, and he steadied. "Marcus, I was lost—truly lost," she said, her voice gentle. "I know that doesn't give you any comfort, but that's all I have to offer."

"Are you ready to come home?" he asked, hesitant about her answer.

Abby's eyes widened; her lips pressed tightly together.

"Abby?" Marcus said, his voice lower now, straining to remain calm. "You aren't answering me."

Abby reached for his hands, threading her fingers through his. She held them tightly, bringing them to her chest as she met his gaze. "I love you, Marcus. We have so much together. A family ... a lifetime of memories and history. That's not something one throws away. That hasn't been lost on me. Hurting you is the last thing I want. If there is one thing I'm asking, it's for you to be patient with me until I can figure things out."

"Figure out what?" Marcus asked, his voice wry, giving way to the pressure building inside. "Abby, you've got to give me something ... anything."

Marcus watched as Abby rubbed at her temples, the dark shadows under her eyes betraying her exhaustion. She sighed, a sign that expressed both weariness and impatience.

"We haven't seen each other in a long time and it's our first night together. Can we start with a new day tomorrow?" She offered him a soft smile. "I promise, we can talk then. We don't have to figure things out tonight, do we?"

Marcus nodded. He knew she was right. Nothing good could come from pushing. Their problems were bigger than what one conversation could to solve. He was just happy to be with her once again.

She kissed him one more time, this time lingering longer, before brushing the side of his face. "Why don't you get your bags? Come back and sleep with me." Nudging him toward the door, she disappeared into the bathroom.

Marcus reached for the handle of the door but halted. Something was still nagging at him, a faint unease he couldn't quite shake. Browsing the room, he noticed how carefully she'd surrounded herself with her favorite things, creating a private sanctuary for her escape. It seemed harmless enough. He could give her that ... time to heal, become better, or even become the best version of herself. Didn't everyone, at some point in their life need a little break?

But something caught his eye—the vase of flowers delivered earlier. The red blooms clashed sharply with the yellow ones, their vibrancy drawing his attention. He stepped back into the room and glanced at the bathroom door. Abby's humming drifted through the sound of running water, muffled by the closed door. Reaching for the card tucked inside, he slid it out of its envelope.

I gave you my body and soul, and I also gave you my heart. – Thom

47

REALITY SUCKS

A bby bumped into Marcus when she opened the bathroom door. He held Thom's card up like damning evidence. His heart pounded as he allowed her eyes to fall upon the words. When she looked at him, her face paled before crumbling into something unrecognizable. He threw the card to the floor, his jaw tightening. He searched her expression for something, anything, that would explain how they had come to this moment.

"What were you thinking, Abby?" Marcus's voice rumbled through the room.

Abby looked at him, like a deer caught in headlights. "I don't know ..."

"What do you mean, you don't know?" Marcus shouted, throwing his hands in the air. His face flushed red, his eyes narrowing, relentless in their pursuit of Abby's. "What kind of answer is that?"

"I mean," Abby stammered. "I wasn't thinking." She looked at him, her lips pressing into a thin line, her gaze unfocused, as if quickly calculating the situation and searching for the right response.

"God, Abby!" He turned on his heels and paced across the room, before spinning back to face there. "That's all you have to say? You weren't thinking?" He closed his eyes for a moment, catching himself, his words, his temper. "You sleep with some guy for what? Attention? Were you bored? Was it for a thrill?" His voice rose, unable to control his frustration and disbelief.

Abby shook her head. "It's not like that. It's more complicated, Marcus."

Complicated? What the hell did that even mean?

Marcus watched her closely as her words faltered. Her voice trembled, and her body recoiled, like an abused dog at a shelter. She seemed unsure and hesitant. His chest tightened, frustration bubbling up as he tried to wrap his head around her betrayal. *How does one explain infidelity?*

"Then try. Try to tell me why my wife would cheat on me!" Marcus's voice cut through the room, sharp and unforgiving. His chest puffed and deep creases carved into his forehead.

He waited and waited, but she didn't answer. Her silence was like a slap, and it gnawed at him. Was she refusing to explain herself? Or did she genuinely have no idea why she had done it? Nothing could have prepared him for this. Not from Abby. Never.

He wanted to demand more from her, to force her to say something that would make this betrayal make sense. But as she stood there, her eyes flickering with something he quite couldn't place, the world he thought he understood—the Abby he thought he knew—was becoming unrecognizable.

She was scaring him. With fear came anger, igniting his instinct to fight or flee. Choosing to fight, he hovered over

Abby, asserting his power, a primeval move, like an animal cornered by fear. "Damn it, Abby, say something!"

Abby pushed him away. "Stop it! Stop yelling at me," she cried, dropping to the bed, covering her face with her hands.

Marcus froze, growing silent, feeling a mixture of anger and something he didn't want to name—guilt, maybe. She was trembling, her shoulders shaking.

He didn't want to bully Abby. For God's sake, he loved her! He wanted to comfort her, to do something, but his feet stayed rooted. This woman, who now seemed so small and frail, wasn't the same woman he thought he knew.

He suddenly pictured her with *him*. His jaw tightened and his gut twisted. He leaned against the wall. Looking at Abby, her sobs filling the room, he couldn't shake the bitterness clawing at him. The sight of her tears didn't move him the way it once would have. Not today. Not after what he'd just discovered.

"Goddamn it," he said, his voice wavering. "You, of all people, Abby, were my rock. The one thing I thought was unshakable."

Marcus's fists curled at his sides, but he didn't raise them. He didn't need to. The words he'd just hurled at her hung heavy in the air, hitting her with more force than any blow could. She recoiled, her hands clutching her stomach as though the pain had become physical.

"Marcus," she pleaded, her voice strained. "Please don't ... It's not what you think."

A guttural laugh escaped him, hollow and bitter. "Not what I think? You screwed another man, Abby. How else am I supposed to take that?"

Abby's expression suddenly hardened, her tears halting. She dragged her arm across her face, erasing the evidence of her vulnerability. "You don't have to be that way, Marcus. I'm your wife, not some whore. I deserve a little more respect, even in the face of my infidelity. I didn't get *here* lightly. I'm owning what I did." She stood, firmly planting her feet on the ground, throwing her shoulders back as though bracing for a storm. "Get angry, yell at me, call me a horrible person. Do whatever you need to do. But when you're done, maybe we can finally talk. Isn't that why we're here? We don't talk, Marcus. We haven't talked in years. We've just been living our lives, going through the motions, avoiding our problems, hoping they'd go away. They didn't. So, I had to."

Abby's words hung in the air, her defiance unfamiliar and new to him. He couldn't decide if it angered him more or scared him. But if there was one thing he could always count on, it was Abby's steadiness. She had always been the solid one, cutting through the chaos and grounding him. Even now, in the middle of unraveling, she remained direct, unyielding, forcing him to confront truths he would rather avoid.

He knew he was being childish and defensive, beating down *the enemy*, clinging to the need to win the argument. But at what cost? This wasn't a war. This was Abby and him. If they couldn't figure this out, no one would win. And that was what terrified him the most: losing the one person who had always made sense of it all.

"Fair enough," he said, lowering his shoulders. "But I need to know, Abby. Why?"

The moment the words left his mouth he regretted the question. Wanting to know was one thing, but hearing her answer was something else entirely. He stepped back and braced himself for the gut punch.

A silence stretched between them, a lifetime of buried feelings building a wall that now separated them. Abby attempted to speak, but each time she opened her mouth, she'd snap it shut again, the words retreating before they could take form. Did he scare her? Or was she about to reveal something so devastating that she couldn't find the courage to begin?

Abby fiddled with the fabric of her sleeve, her eyes downcast, avoiding Marcus's gaze. He noticed the tremor in her hands and the deep breath she took, like someone standing on the edge, readying to leap. Then her words tumbled out, faster than he expected, piling on top of each other.

"Because I'm tired, Marcus. Tired of pouring myself out for everyone—being *your* wife, *their* mother, the volunteer lady who never says no—giving every part of myself away, piece by piece, until there's nothing left for me." She paused, drawing in another breath. "I'm tired of being everything to everyone but never being anyone to somebody."

Marcus scowled, leaning forward. "Come on, Abby, aren't you being extreme? You are my wife. Don't we all have roles? I'm a husband, a boss, a father. Isn't that just life? We all have roles—they give us purpose."

"But at the cost of being nobody?" Her voice cracked as she fought to keep her tears at bay.

Marcus huffed, rolling his eyes.

"You're dismissing me, Marcus. You always do, making me feel like I'm nothing. I'm not a person to you anymore, just something to count on, like an old chair you come home to. Reliable. Comfortable. Always there when you want it. But you don't really see *me*, Marcus." She pounded her chest. "Me, Abby. And God forbid that I change, grow older ... have cancer ... no longer a version of the Abby you expect. Always making me question if I'm enough." She paused, taking in a breath. "Did you ever think about how I saw myself? Did you not think I was already judging how I looked and who I was?"

Abby's words cut sharper than Marcus had expected. He

shifted, her accusations pressing against his heart. *Was that how she saw him?* He sounded cruel—selfish. His instinct was to fight back, tell her she was wrong. But was she?

Abby's voice wavered, but she pressed on, each word cutting deeper. "You never noticed how tattered and torn I've become. Not until I wasn't there, until I crumbled under the weight of it all and slipped away. Only then did you look up and see I was gone—out for repair. Only then did you care, hoping I'd come back as good as new, ready to be whatever, whoever, you need me to be." She looked at him, her eyes brimming with frustration and sorrow. "But what about me, Marcus? What about who I need to be for myself?"

Her fingers toyed with her earring, twisting it back and forth. "I didn't plan to leave, Marcus. I didn't plan ..." She paused. "I didn't plan for any of this. But my life, the path of obscurity, was killing me inside, and something just snapped."

Marcus rubbed his face. "God, Abby ... we've been married for twenty-six years." His voice faltered, low and uneven. "What did you expect to happen? We settled into each other ... isn't that a good thing? Isn't that what marriage becomes after all this time?" He paused, searching her face, but the silence between them felt like a verdict he didn't want to hear.

Abby drew a deep breath, her voice trembling. "Settled into each other? Marcus, do you hear yourself? I'm dependable, familiar, expected, but never more than that. And the sad part? I let it happen. I have spent my whole life fulfilling roles for you, the kids, and everyone else, until there was nothing left of me to notice." Her voice softened, but her words hit with a quiet force. "But no one bothered to look out for me. Not even me."

"How can you say that?" he questioned. "For God's sake, I chased you across the world. I'm here, aren't I?"

"That's your answer?" Abby's voice sharpened, her lips curling into a bitter smile. "Another man is in love with me, and your only defense is that you have ownership of me?" She threw up her arms in a sweeping motion, her expression a mix of disbelief and disdain.

"That isn't what I meant," Marcus protested, his voice rising as he took a step forward. "Don't twist my words, Abby. You know that's not what I'm saying. I'm just trying to understand what's happening ... how we got here."

He ran his hand through his hair, exhaling sharply, pacing the room. When he looked back at his wife, he tried to see the girl he'd fallen in love with all those years ago. She was not that girl anymore—how could she be? Gone was her youthful exuberance and carefree spontaneity; in their place was a woman shaped by years of sacrifice, love, and resilience. The lines around her eyes spoke of late nights and burdens she'd carried as though they were her own. She didn't need makeup anymore, her skin glowed with an inner radiance, a beauty born of strength and experience. She was ... a better version of the girl who stole his heart.

Abby caught his eyes, holding his stare. For a fleeting moment, he wanted to fall into them, to be drawn back into her heart. *Was she asking him to?*

His stance softened, as did his tone. "I don't get it. What are you asking?" His eyes narrowed slightly, confusion apparent on his face. "What ... what do you want from me?"

Abby walked to the window and stared out into the dark space. He saw her shoulders lift and fall in a rhythmic motion, her breathing steady and deep.

"Abby!" Marcus shouted, sharper than he intended, snapping her attention back.

Abby turned, meeting his gaze, but stayed quiet. Her eyes seemed darker, impenetrable. Was she figuring out her next move? Or did she see his fear? Fear that he didn't have the answers. Fear that he didn't know how to fix this. Fear that he wasn't enough to save them.

He felt like he'd jumped down the rabbit hole with her, with no clear way out. The only choice was to keep moving forward and hope they didn't end up somewhere worse.

"I need time," she finally replied, her expression unchanged.

Marcus's eyes grew wide. "You need more time?" He let out a sharp, bitter laugh, shaking his head. "That's your answer? Abby. I've given you space. I've made excuses for you to the kids, to everyone. And now you want more time?" His voice dropped to a pointed edge. "Do you know the pain you've caused? I would never think of hurting you like that."

Abby's eyes narrowed, a cold edge slicing through her exhaustion. "Oh really?" she said, her voice measured. "Not even with Adriana?"

Marcus froze, blindsided by her words. "What ... what are you talking about?"

"I knew," Abby said, her tone low and flat. "For years. And I said nothing."

Marcus blinked, his jaw tightening with her revelation. "If you knew, why didn't you call me out? Stop me?"

"What was I supposed to do, Marcus?" Abby said, her voice raw. "We had two young kids in school. My career was long gone, and my parents couldn't handle a family moving in with them. Where was I supposed to go? What options did I have?" She ran her fingers through her hair, letting out a long, exasperated sigh. "Time has a way of softening the pain, blurring the blame. I didn't like you very much then—our lives were so damn hectic. But I still loved you. I've always loved you," she said, meeting his eyes. "I wasn't being a good wife, Marcus. I wasn't loving, or kind, or attentive. I was so tired, so angry, so unhappy that I didn't have anything left to give to you—or us. *She* obviously could. And maybe, in some way, I was relieved you had someone to turn to when I couldn't be there."

"Nothing ever really happened. I swear, Abby."

"No, maybe not," Abby looked away, her voice distant. "But you had an affair all the same."

Marcus recalled those days, so long ago. They felt like someone else's memories, better left in the past. "We worked together, Abby," he said at last. "We spent a lot of time together ... probably more than we should have."

"Late-night business dinners, coming home tipsy. Tickets for two to sporting events. Extended business trips over the weekend." Abby shot him a pointed look. "I'm your wife, Marcus. How could I not notice the little things that used to be just for me? You looked forward to traveling. I heard you laughing on the phone with her. I saw you smile when you got her emails." She paused, flooding him with the ghosts of his past. "She made you happy. You wanted her. She wasn't invisible to you ..."

"I wasn't in love with her, Abby," he murmured.

"No? Does it matter now?"

Truth was a hard thing to face, but when it was Abby standing before him, it became almost unbearable. Her eyes were on him. They held no animosity in them, no anger. Not for his past. Not for Adriana. *So, what was it? What had driven her away?*

He stepped closer, instinctively wanting to reach for her. To feel her in his arms. To close the distance that had grown between them. But he stopped himself. "What's this really about? And what does it mean for us?"

She didn't answer right away, and the realization hit him like a sudden wave, cold and forceful, that she might not know. Or, worse, that she might not want *them* at all.

His thoughts darkened. *Thom.* He lingered like an unwanted guest. He thought of the card, now discarded on the floor. The name clawed at him, the words eating away his defenses. Suddenly, everything they were talking about—his past, his mistakes—felt inconsequential to what she had done. His chest tightened, any warmth or need for closeness evaporating with the rising heat of anger.

"You know what, Abby?" His jaw clenched. "I know that I didn't rip our marriage apart. I chose us!" His hands flew into the air. "What you've done ... God, it's not just a mistake, it was a choice. You chose to destroy everything we've had. For what?"

Abby covered her face, shaking her head. Marcus could see her retreating into herself, as if trying to block his words. "I don't know, Thom!"

The air hung heavy, unmoving, every sound swallowed by a suffocating silence.

"You mean Marcus," he corrected, his voice cutting through the stillness.

He shot her a look, abruptly turned, and headed out the door. The slam was hard and loud, reverberating through the quiet inn, a final punctuation to the words he hadn't spoken. Marcus didn't look back. He couldn't. If he did, he wasn't sure what he'd see—Abby begging him to stay or willing him to go. Either way, he wasn't ready to face the answer.

48

DRUNK

When Thom entered the pub, Dunbar tilted his head toward a dim corner. Marcus was slouched at a table, the overhead light casting a shadow around him that seemed to spotlight his solitude. Both hands gripped a glass with a clear liquid, his head wavering over it as if in silent prayer. He straightened slightly, brushing stray strands of hair from his face, then lifted the glass and took a swig. He grimaced, a harsh exhale escaping his lips before he slammed the glass back down.

Thom smirked. "Clear stuff ... explains everything," he muttered. He sauntered through the half-empty pub, stopping in front of Marcus and gesturing to the empty seat next to him. "Do you mind if I sit?"

Marcus looked up, his lids at half-mast. He tried to smile, but his mouth wouldn't cooperate. "I oughta punch you!" Marcus swayed as he stood, his hand curling into a loose fist before dropping back to the table.

Thom gave a quick nod. "Aye, probably," he said, then sat down next to him.

"Everything okay, Thom?" Dunbar called out from behind the bar.

"Aye," he replied, his voice steady and resolute. "And bring us two coffees."

Marcus straightened, his eyes narrowing in an attempt to focus. "Shouldn't we duel or something? Isn't there some Scottish code to fight over a woman?" He laughed half-heartedly, seeming to teeter between humor and discomfort.

Thom didn't answer, keeping his gaze steady on Marcus.

Dunbar's call echoed in his mind, a warning about a man at the pub making threats against him. Thom hadn't needed to ask who it was. It had to be Marcus. Abby's Marcus. He probably should've been more cautious about rushing over to confront the threat. Men had been shot for lesser reasons, and Thom certainly wasn't innocent of the crime Marcus was enraged about. A man can be driven to terrible things when he feels wronged, especially when it's about a woman.

Dunbar interrupted his thoughts, setting a cup down in front of him. "You're sure you can deal wi' this one, aye?" He eyed the drunkard, muttering a Gaelic curse under his breath.

Thom chuckled, giving a nod. "I've dealt with worse," he said, his tone light. "But keep yourself ready, just in case."

Dunbar nodded, placing the other cup in front of Marcus with a warning. "If ye've a mind to start a fight, a fight ye'll get. I'm no' too far awa' to step in, nor too auld to knock ye senseless."

"Leave him be," Thom ordered, sending Dunbar away.

Marcus barely spared Dunbar a glance. He likely found the smaller man no challenge. Marcus stood three inches taller and carried at least twenty pounds on him. But Thom knew Dunbar wasn't the threat to Marcus, nor whom he

ELIZABETH CONTE

wanted to fight. If he could steady himself, Marcus would've gladly swung across at Thom.

Marcus's glance fell back to Thom. "It wouldn't be a fair fight," he said, as if reading Thom's mind.

"No, it wouldn't be," Thom replied, unsure of what Marcus was capable of. He was drunk, angry, and in no position to fight, but Thom knew that never stopped a man from trying. He watched him warily, with his every move, ready for anything.

The two sat quietly, watching each other. There was no need for small talk. They knew why each was there, and Abby was at the center of it all.

Marcus reached for his coffee and took three long slurps. Thom could feel the weight of the man's stare as it lingered. Marcus put his coffee down and leaned in, his lips curling into a bitter smirk. His voice was raspy and dry when he finally spoke. "What's it like to fuck my wife?"

His expression wavered for a fraction of a second, as if testing the impact of his words. The provocation hung in the air, heavy and deliberate. Thom shifted in his chair, his jaw tightened, as the crude comment sank to the pits of his stomach. His instinct was to punch Marcus—he had been known to do worse to a man who crossed the line.

But this wasn't just any man. This was Abby's husband.

Thinking of Abby broke his restraint. Grabbing the collar of his shirt, Thom yanked Marcus forward, their faces inches apart. "Look, let's keep this polite, shall we? Or else I'll describe every fucking detail of how I made love to your wife so that every time ye touch her, you'll know I've been there!"

Thom wanted desperately to hurt him. He was silently begging Marcus to strike him ... fight for her. If only to release the fear swelling inside of him that this man could take away his happiness. Marcus would overcome a few punches. Thom wasn't sure he could overcome another broken heart.

Thoughts of Abby stopped him. He had to be patient, if only for her sake. Taking in a deep breath, Thom released him.

Marcus grunted, not taking the bait. He just brushed off the remnants of Thom's grip from his shirt, smoothing down the fabric, and sat back, the smug smile still lingering on his face.

Thom saw the damage the vodka had caused. Marcus's eyes were bloodshot, his face was red and blotchy. The alcohol was poisoning his body, as well as his brain. He was in no condition to react, let alone act. There was little chance Marcus could walk out of the pub without getting the crap beaten out of him.

Thom pushed a glass of water toward him. "Drink. You're pished as a fart. Abby doesn't need to deal with ye like this."

Marcus looked up at him with one eye closed, the other focusing on the man next to him. "You're a brazen fellow, I'll give you that," Marcus quipped, grabbing the water and downing it. "Not only did you sleep with my wife, but you also have the nerve to throw it in my face."

"I didn't come here to rub your face in it. I'm here for Abby." Thom's voice was firm, but his stance eased. He sat back in his chair and crossed his arm. "What were ye thinking, man? You're not gonna sort anything out while you're drunk and raging."

"Hell with her! She's the reason why I'm drunk," he shouted out, turning the heads of the few patrons lingering in the pub. "What do you care, anyway? You got what you wanted ..."

Thom let out a dry, humorless laugh. "What I wanted?" he echoed, brushing off Marcus's careless remark. *Did he even know her?* The man was too bitter, or too blind, to see what was in front of him. Abby wasn't something to win or lose, a conquest to claim. She was a force in his life, a fateful turn that forever shifted his course.

Thom felt a pang of pity for Marcus. He hadn't meant to lose Abby; Thom was sure of that. But intentions didn't matter when the damage was done. All he saw now were the remnants of Marcus's choices. As far as he was concerned, he'd gotten Abby fairly. There was no coercion, no manipulation. She'd come to him openly. Even so, there was no victory in stealing another man's wife.

Had he been straightforward, he might have told Marcus he wanted Abby entirely for himself. But he held his tongue. This wasn't his fight to win. Whatever was happening was between Abby and Marcus. For now, he stood on the outside, waiting.

Thom filled more water into Marcus's glass, handing it to him. "Drink up, man, and when you're ready, I'll take ye back to Abby."

Marcus grabbed the glass, swirling the water as if searching for answers, then took a long sip. Thom watched closely. The water wasn't going to sober him up, but it was a start. He cleared his throat, encouraging Marcus to drink more.

Marcus finally emptied the glass, then looked up, the effects of the alcohol no longer clouding his eyes. "Is that how it is, then? A handoff?"

Thom shook his head. "Don't be a fool. This isn't about ye, or me. It's about what's best for Abby. And if ye make her happy, I'm willing to lose her." He leaned in, ignoring the tightening in his chest, and locked eyes with Marcus. "But in the remote chance she chooses me, I'll spend every day, every breath I have, loving her."

"You're a son of a bitch." Marcus's voice dropped low, tinged with anger and something close to defeat. He shook his head, a hollow laugh escaping as he looked away.

"Aye, maybe so," Thom replied, feeling the hit of Marcus's resentment. He knew he deserved it. Expected it. Maybe worse. It had to be hard to know another man wanted the best for the woman he loved. "But I don't think it's up to us, now is it?"

Thom rose, reached for his wallet, and threw some money out on the table. He helped Marcus stand, steadying him on his feet. Nodding to Dunbar, he bid him a good night.

Marcus tore himself away and stumbled out into the night's air, his body seeming to stiffen from the stark contrast of the warmth inside the pub.

"That'll smack ye to your knees," Thom said as Marcus coughed. "Are ye going to be all right?" Thom asked, assessing how much help Marcus would need to get back to the inn. He wasn't sure how much of Marcus's weight he could support. He had dragged a few large men in his day after a night of drinking, but Marcus was close to Thom's own height and weight. The last thing he wanted to do was to carry the man up two flights of stairs, or run into Abby. He didn't want to see her. Not now. Not there. He wasn't sure if he could walk away and leave her with Marcus.

"I've got this," Marcus mumbled, pushing past Thom.

Thom stepped out of Marcus's way and watched as he pulled his coat tightly around himself, his shoulders squaring against the biting cold. The man's stride was determined as he headed up the hill. Thom could see it, Marcus wasn't bracing himself against the wind but gearing up for something bigger. Something final. Abby.

He just wasn't sure he knew which outcome he wanted for him.

THE INN WAS QUIET, and no one was around. Marcus was relieved as he hung up his coat near the door and took a few steps in. He could see the last of the burning wood still crackling in the fire in the salon, but the lights were out. A light had been left on over the kitchen sink for guests coming in. He poured himself a glass of water and, looking at his watch, turned off the light, concluding he was the last guest of the evening. His shoes clapped against the floors, creating an echo in the silent house as he walked to the stairs. He stood frozen, wondering whether he wanted to go up or turn around and leave, never facing Abby again.

He took off his shoes and climbed up to the second floor. He stared at his key before deciding to climb up one more flight. He put his ear to Abby's door. Everything was silent, except for his heart pounding heavily in his chest. He grabbed the handle and turned it. It gave way, and he slowly pushed the door open.

He found Abby curled up in a chair with a blanket surrounding her. The light on the table next to her was shining on a book in her hand, but she was oblivious to its contents. She was snoring softly.

Marcus couldn't decide what he wanted at that moment. She looked so peaceful and content, as if untouched by the chaos between them. But he wasn't fooled. Beneath the calm exterior, a storm brewed deep inside, one he had helped create.

His teeth clenched as raw emotions surged.

He knew Abby well enough to know she did not set out to hurt him, or to have an affair. That wasn't his Abby. His greatest fear, as he stood there, was the growing realization she had done it out of love. Love for another man. And he had no armor to fight that kind of battle.

For the first time in his life, Marcus felt truly lost. Without Abby, he didn't know what to do. He didn't know how to fix this and, worse, he wasn't sure he had the power to. This was Abby's journey now, and whether he liked it or not, he was just a bystander. That wasn't how he imagined a marriage to be—two separate people figuring out their problems on their own. They were supposed to be a team—partners—united as one. But wasn't that the problem? He had left Abby to fend for herself, left her alone when she needed him the most.

He bent over her and kissed her lightly on the forehead. She didn't budge. Marcus twisted the ring on his finger before tugging it. It easily slid off. He placed it in the glass bowl, on top of the dresser, leaving a note beside it.

This was a battle he intended to win, though not in the way he imagined.

Marcus had never truly relied on faith before, but now that was all he had. Leaving Abby behind felt like surrendering her to something beyond his control—a plea to God he wasn't even sure he trusted. Before closing the door, he took one last look at her, his heart aching. She had hurt him more deeply than if she had stabbed him with a knife. But his love for her was more real than his flesh and blood. She was a part of his soul, and he wasn't sure how to sever something so deeply woven into him. But he turned, knowing if he didn't leave now, he may never really have her again.

Abby wouldn't throw away their lifetime together. He believed that much. But she'd said she needed more time. As much as that hit him in the gut, she wasn't ready to come back, for whatever reason. If she didn't return of her own accord, then whatever they had left would never feel real. He couldn't force her to choose him; she had to want it on her own.

49

DESPERATE PLEA

Abby rubbed her neck, strained from sleeping in the chair. The bed was untouched, the light beside her still on. Marcus hadn't come back. She sighed, her heart tugging tight in her chest.

She had waited for him, texted him a dozen times. Each message felt heavier than the last, and when his phone went straight to voicemail, it only deepened her dread. At some point, her mind spinning with unanswered questions and regrets, she had taken a sleeping pill. She needed to escape— a few hours from the flood of thoughts haunting her. But it hadn't worked. Even in her dreams, she was waiting for Marcus.

Tossing the blanket aside, she jumped up and grabbed her phone. There was nothing from Marcus. Her heart sank deeper. Thom's name, however, glared back at her. One message asked her to meet for breakfast, the other asked if they could talk. She glanced at the clock. It was well past breakfast ... almost lunch. The thought of seeing Thom now, after all that happened last night, made her shiver. Facing him meant facing her sins.

As she looked around, her things scattered in every corner of the room were a silent reminder of her turmoil. *It was time to leave.* Nothing good could come of staying. But would leaving fix anything? She closed her eyes, praying Marcus would reach out and give her something. She needed to talk to him, to see him, to know whether there was anything left to salvage.

Her phone buzzed in her hand, jolting her.

Meet me?

Abby's thumb hovered over the letters; a nervous chill washed over her.

Yes, she answered. *Give me an hour. Meet me at Scran. See you soon.*

She tossed her phone on the table and hurried to the shower. The hot water rushed over her, the steam wrapping around her like a grandmother's comforting hug. The pounding in her head eased, and for a brief moment, the chaos outside felt distant, muted. All that had happened in the last few days now seemed a lifetime ago. *Was it even her life?* Abby wondered how she'd gotten here ... her world dramatically changed. She no longer had to choose where she was going. She had already turned left and now was on a new course. An unfamiliar road with no navigation. Her chest tightened at the prospect.

She leaned against the tile wall and closed her eyes. "Jossi, where are you?" she whispered.

The silence was deafening. Grabbing a towel, she tied it around her hair and slipped into a robe. At the sink, she wiped away the steam from the mirror. No Jossi. Just her own reflection, pale and uncertain.

Jossi had warned her of the crossroads ahead. Was her

absence a sign Abby was on the right path, or the wrong one? She shook her head, reaching for her lotion. As she rubbed it between her hands, her eyes caught sight of her bare ring finger. It felt empty.

Panic rising, the reality crashing down on her, she rushed to the dresser, where the glass bowl sat undisturbed. But as she reached for her ring, her breath hitched. Marcus's ring lay beside it, a note tucked under the bowl. Her hand trembled as she lifted the gold band. The metal felt warm between her fingers, familiar and foreign all at once.

Marcus had never taken it off. Not for basketball, not for golf, not even for Adriana. The simple domed band had been a constant, forever a part of him, a part of them. And now, here it was, sitting next to hers, both removed.

Her eyes fell upon the folded paper, but she couldn't bring herself to look at it. The symbolism was enough.

The room suddenly felt stifling, the walls pressing in. She needed to get out and get some air. Action. Movement. Anything to escape the stillness. She slid the ring into the pocket of her robe and hurried to get ready. Unfinished business awaited her down the street, mere steps from where it had all begun.

When she opened her door to leave, she hesitated, glancing back at the note still atop the dresser. She wavered, tempted to unfold it, but she stopped herself. Whatever the words held wouldn't change what needed to happen. She needed to hear Marcus's feelings from him, face-to-face. No more avoidance. No more overstepping the pain, the loss, and the sorrow they had both buried for too long. If there was any hope for them, it couldn't come from a note. It had to come from a decision they made together.

She threw her purse strap over her shoulder and set out to Hazel's. It seemed the perfect place to meet, bringing her full circle. The air there always felt lighter—a far cry from the suffocating stillness of her room. It was too public for tears, too neutral for heartbreak. There, she could remain stoic, do what needed to do—face the man whose heart she would most likely break.

As she entered the café, the bell rang. Hazel waved from the counter. Abby ordered coffee, foregoing the fresh scones she smelled, then slipped into a small table in the corner, her back to the room. She sipped her coffee, privately wishing it were a wine or whisky, anything that would calm her nerves. Every time the door opened her chest tightened. She finally put her head down, tired of reacting to the jingle, the minutes crawling, stretching her nerves thin.

She heard footsteps approaching.

"Abby?"

Abby closed her eyes, allowing the rich, resonant tone of his voice to wash over her. It calmed her, even now, as her nerves were frayed. She wanted to etch it into her memory, something she could always hold on to.

When she lifted her head, Thom was sitting beside her, staring intently, as if studying her. He furrowed his brow, his gaze softening as he took in her red-rimmed swollen eyes and blotchy patches along her cheeks. Abby covered her face. "Don't look at me ... I'm a mess."

He took her hand. "Dare I ask?"

Abby shook her head, scanning the restaurant. It was full, giving her more reasons to push back her tears.

Thom brushed her face with a gentle touch. "I wish I could help ye, Abby."

Abby pulled away, pressing her back against the chair, the motion deliberate. "But you can't. It's not of your making. I did this. I blew up my marriage. I hurt Marcus ... and all for what?"

Thom straightened, his jaw tightening as he leaned forward, his eyes locking onto hers. "For what? I love you, Abby," he said, placing the words at her feet. "This ... this thing between us is not just some misadventure."

Abby felt the weight of his declaration, the truth resonating through her. "No," she said softly, then more firmly. "It isn't. But I need more than this, more than someone caught between two lives, unsure of who she is." She hesitated, then grabbed Thom's hand, grounding herself in the connection she wasn't ready to let go of. "Don't think I'm not grateful for what you have shown me, reminding me what it means to be seen, to be alive. But now, I have to learn to stand on my own, to be the person I was meant to be, without leaning on anyone else to define me."

Thom pulled back his hand, the lines on his face easing as he studied her. "Ye already are that person, Abby. Ye just don't see it yet. But I do."

She met his eyes, her chest tightening. "You think you do," she said softly, almost to herself. But we barely know about each other, Thom. We had a few weeks of something special, but then what?" Her voice faltered, and she turned away, unable to bear the pain in his eyes. She didn't want to hurt him, but maybe she wanted him angry, to hate her like she hated herself.

When she looked back, his eyes had grown dark, but his voice carried a quiet intensity, conveying the depth of his emotion without breaking. "I may not know everything about ye, Abby, but I love ye all the same. Love isn't something measured in time, it's felt, deep and true." Thom's hands twisted, grasping for his thoughts. "I'm not a wee boy, Abby. I've lived long enough to know when it's real, and I'm not wasting my heart." He paused, catching her gaze. "If God's willing, I'd like to spend the rest of my days learning about ye. The rest of my life, Abby!"

Tears welled. All Abby wanted was to rush toward him—mind, body, and soul—to embrace the fragment of a life she had dared to imagine. But her heart ached, torn between two men who loved her, and the two men she truly loved. Each saw a different side of her: Marcus, who cherished the Abby she had always been, and Thom, who had fallen in love with the Abby she was becoming. How could she reconcile the woman she used to be with the woman she is now? She was caught between them, split in half, and the realization left her hollow. Loving them both felt like a betrayal. Hurting them both made her feel like she didn't deserve either.

Abby wiped away her tears. "I don't deserve you," she sniffled, wiping at her nose. "And I should have never asked you into my life ... not while I was figuring things out. It wasn't fair."

A gentle smile crossed his face, but there was a flicker of something deeper in his eyes, something that held both pain and solace. "I don't regret loving you, Abby," he said, his voice drifting as if seeing something far away. He exhaled, speaking almost to himself. "When my wife was dying, she reminded me that I was the lucky one—I had the rest of my life to love her."

His voice descended, softer now, as if the memory carried him to another time, another place, something etched into his soul.

THE HOSPITAL CALLED, waking him. They wanted him to come right away. He drove through dark thick clouds surrounding his car in the wee hours before the sun rose. The grief overwhelmed him, spilling out in silent sobs until there was none left. By the time he reached the hospital, he steeled himself. He didn't want his wife to see his tears in their last moments together.

As he entered her room, Coira's breaths were heavy and labored, death waiting for her. Hearing Thom's footsteps cross the threshold, she turned to him, beckoning him to her with her hand, her arm too weak to lift. He leaned in and kissed her softly on the lips. Her breath was cool, as if death was already there. He grabbed her hand with possessive force, unwilling to surrender her to the Reaper.

"Thom," she said, her voice loving, but frail. "I'm still here. Don't waste our time with fear."

"How are ye, my love?" Thom asked out of routine rather than wanting an answer.

"Mmm, not so good last night. But better now that you're here." She tried to smile but was too weak to turn up her lips. "Lay with me."

Thom climbed onto her bed, trying not to squish her fragile body. He threw his arm around her and nuzzled her ear. "I love you," he whispered.

"I know. I've always known," she said, brushing his cheek with hers.

"What am I to do without ye? What am I to do with all this love?" he pleaded, as his heart swelled with sorrow.

"Ahh, Thomas Michael," she chided gently, "you're a silly man. For someone so full of love, you're truly ignorant of its power. Be strong in your fortitude, grateful for your vulnerability. It's what I love best about you." She stopped to draw a short breath. Air was getting harder to take in, and she was struggling to continue. "The love I felt for you was multiplied a thousand-fold when united with yours. It is a constant ... and it's not going away." She gulped a breath again. "Continue its pulse as long as you live."

Thom wrapped her up in his arms and lay with her until her chest finally stopped exerting itself, and she took her last breath.

As he finished his story, Thom brushed his lips against Abby's. "I love you, Abby," he whispered. "I never thought that I could love someone in the same way. But I have. My love for you will always be constant. It won't go away. It is and will always be. Make no mistake, Abby, I will spend the rest of my life loving you."

Abby looked at him, her soul diving into the dark depths of his eyes. So strong was his love, she could no longer tell where she ended and he began. His gaze reached into her, dissolving her fear of the choice she had to make.

"Take me home, Thom," she said. Her voice was breathy and trembling with desire and desperation. "Make love to me again and again, so I never feel life without you."

Abby was not sure how her feet had carried her from the café to Thom's apartment. *Did they pass anyone along the way?* She couldn't say. But before the door was shut behind them, they were already tearing off their clothes. Thom's mouth consumed hers as she unbuckled his belt and unzipped his pants; his hands found her hips, pulling down her panties with desperate precision.

Thom pressed her against the wall, and she wrapped her legs around him as their bodies collided together in a fervent rhythm. His urgency drove him deep inside her, and she let out a guttural sound, the intensity of his pulsing motion unraveling her. With a sudden jerking motion, he nearly lost his grip as his body surrendered to pleasure.

Abby caught him, wrapping her arms around him, steadying them both. When he lifted his face to hers, their eyes locked, and laughter bubbled up between them, breaking the storm of emotion.

Still catching her breath, she asked, "What was that?"

"Passion," Thom said, his tone self-assured. Then more softly, he added, "Fear."

Abby nuzzled into the crook of Thom's neck as his arms wrapped around her, his chest lifting and falling against hers. An eerie quietness fell between them, broken only by the rhythmic pattering of rain against the rooftop. Thom stepped away and reached for his shirt on the floor. He handed it to Abby, and she slipped it over her head, breathing in the lingering scent of him woven in its fibers.

Taking her hand in his, Thom guided her toward the bedroom. "We aren't done yet," he murmured, his voice low and raspy.

"No," she replied. "We aren't."

As their bodies sank into the bed, they expressed a lifetime of love in one day. Desperation and longing intertwined, their stamina seemed endless, fueled by the fear of losing each other. They gave and gave until they had nothing left, their bodies finally succumbing to exhaustion.

Thom reached for Abby across the bed, pulling her to him. Her body, too weak to resist, melted into his arms, which wrapped tightly around her. The steady rhythm of his breathing lulled her, and together they drifted into a heavy, dreamless sleep.

50

THE QUIET AFTER

The sound of the bedroom door closing jolted Thom from his slumber. He did not try to get up. Instead, he lay still, listening to Abby's footsteps moving across the floor. He knew she was gathering her things.

He waited for the click of the front door lock. She must have paused at the threshold for a moment, for all he could hear was the rain. Then the door opened, letting in a rush of cool air before it was shut again, leaving the apartment in silence.

Thom stared at the ceiling, his chest tight with the ache of inevitability. The faint smell of Abby's perfume lingered in the air, a haunting reminder of her presence. He knew he would never see her again. She was leaving, returning to the life she couldn't abandon. She had no other choice but to go.

He remained in bed, the quiet pressing around him, acutely aware of love for the second time in his life. Love was constant—his love was constant—but sometimes, even that wasn't enough to make someone stay.

PART III: AFTER

51

HOME

The house didn't look changed, but everything felt different as Abby stepped out of the taxi and walked up the familiar path to the front door. The blue house stood steady among the magnolias she had planted years ago. Most of the white and pink blossoms were gone, but a few clung stubbornly to the branches, as if waiting to greet her. The sun hung low, casting a soft golden haze over the evening, reluctant to set. She glanced up at the evening sky, where an almost full moon was poised to glow.

Abby rummaged through her purse, searching for her house keys, a slight panic washing over her. Sifting through the gum wrappers, lipstick, pens, and sunglass case, she finally found the keys lodged in the corner of a side pocket, untouched since she had left all those weeks ago. Gripping the metal ring, she pulled it out and dangled the keys in front of her, searching for the right one to fit into the lock.

Was she stalling?

Her hand shook a bit, but the key fit. At the click of the lock, a wave of emotions—grief, longing, fear—washed over her, almost knocking her down. She turned, side-glancing at the street behind her, and the thought of running shot through her. This is when Jossi usually appeared to encourage her. She didn't.

Abby hadn't seen Jossi since Marcus left her in Scotland. The day since she left Thom's naked body lying listless in his bed. The day she decided to come home. The day she stared out the window of the inn, her tears dried up, and her bags packed.

"He's gone," Jossi had said, her voice coming first, familiar and certain, before her form materialized.

"Don't you think I can see that?" Abby replied, knowing perfectly well that Jossi was referring to Marcus and not Thom.

"I'm not trying to hurt you, Abby," Jossi said, her tone softening.

Abby blew her nose, salty tears staining her cheeks. "I know. I'm just numb right now."

"No, Abby, you're feeling ... really feeling. That's good. For the first time, your heart and head are syncing. It's like childbirth, every painful push is toward something miraculous."

Abby shook her head, desperately trying to shove away the ache pressing heavily on her heart. "Don't do that, Jossi. This isn't a game anymore. I screwed up ... really made a mess of my life."

Jossi shrugged. "It had to happen at some point, Abby. You couldn't have continued your life of being invisible ... being me." She offered a knowing smile. "Mistakes are inevitable. But without them, you never would have realized what you're capable of. Be proud of the woman you are becoming, Abby. You have so much more to give, to explore, to live, and to love."

Abby's gaze dropped to the floor. "I have hurt the man

who has loved me for most of my life. I have tangled with another man who wants to love me for the rest of my life. What is so noble in that?"

"Noble? Love isn't noble," Jossi said with a quiet certainty. "It's messy, complicated, hard, all rolled up in life and what it throws at you. But it's your ability to love despite all of that. That's what's noble."

Abby looked up, her eyes searching Jossi's face. "What do I do now?" she asked, her voice barely above a whisper.

"Conquer the world, Abby!" Jossi paused and leaned closer, softening her expression as her eyes locked onto Abby's. "Because I can't."

Jossi's words hit her hard—like she was standing frozen on the track, watching a train hurtle straight toward her. The meaning. The purpose of it all. Abby didn't need to mourn her death by living as though Jossi could only exist through her. She finally understood: Jossi's love hadn't disappeared; it was always there, inside her, still breathing through her, multiplying, expanding, growing. How had she gotten it so wrong?

Jossi smiled, perhaps knowing that Abby had found the answers she was looking for. "It's time for me to go," she said at last, her voice resolute.

Abby's breath caught. "No," she whimpered. "I'm not ready to be without."

"You've got this, Abby." Jossi reminded her. "Remember, they're *your* decisions now ... not mine. Not anymore." Her image began to fade, the outlines of her body blending into the walls behind her. "I love you ... always." Her words lingered in the air long after she disappeared.

"I love you too," Abby whispered into the emptiness, her voice breaking. She stared at the empty space where Jossi had been, her heart sinking like a stone into water, sending ripples of sadness through her.

How she wished Jossi were here now, standing behind her as she withdrew the key from the lock, crossed the threshold, and closed the door behind her.

The house was quiet. The pungent scent of cleaning supplies lingered in the air, a clear sign the housekeeper had been there. Abby put her bags to the side of the stairs and peered into the kitchen. It was spotless. Nothing looked neglected or out of place.

She set her purse down on the entry table, her keys clinking as she dropped them into the glass bowl. A stack of mail lay untouched—all addressed to her. She sifted through the top few envelopes, her fingers grazing over the edges. Nothing seemed urgent. Not anymore. She would go through them later.

The sudden grind of the garage door startled her, the sound reverberating through the stillness. She had forgotten the familiar creaks and groans of the house. Her heart stopped for a millisecond. Maybe longer. Her eyes fixed on the handle of the door leading in from the garage. It jostled. Her breath caught.

Then Drew stepped through.

Abby exhaled, a thrill shooting through her at the sight of her son. He looked taller, more handsome. *How much she had missed!*

"Mom!" Drew's voice filled the hallway, deeper than she remembered. Dropping his bag next to hers, he wrapped his arms around her neck, planting a wet kiss on her cheek.

Drew pulled back, his eyes scanning her face. "Gosh, you look different," he said, his brow furrowing slightly. He looked more and more like his father.

"Different?" she asked, tucking her hair behind her ear. "How?"

"I don't know. You look ... just different."

She was different. Better. Healed. Herself.

Drew grabbed his bag and slung it over his shoulder. Then, reaching for Abby's suitcase, started upstairs. "I'll come and get the rest. Be back in a minute," he said, glancing back at her.

Abby smiled. Things had changed.

Abby shot a look at the clock in the living room. The face loomed over the fireplace like an ever-present sentinel, the ticking a relentless white noise that echoed through her thoughts. For years, it dictated her days, a constant reminder for her to keep on schedule. It no longer had the same effect on her. She had no schedules to keep. Not anymore. She wondered if that was a blessing or a curse. The old structure kept her focused and on the path. Now, it felt like she was driving on a highway without lines or barriers to keep her from the edge.

She went to the kitchen and searched for wine—Marcus would be home soon. A bottle was open, and she poured the rest of its contents into a glass. But before she could drink the needed elixir, she heard the garage door open.

"Hey, Dad," Drew's voice called out. "Mom's home."

Abby heard Drew's sneakers squeak back up the stairs, but did not hear Marcus's footsteps move forward. She felt the cool air of the evening from the opened door and wondered if he was going to come in or retreat.

The door slammed shut, and she heard his heavy steps approach, followed by the scrape of something sliding across the floor, his briefcase, most likely, being tucked under the table. His keys clinked against the glass bowl, and then it was still. She set her wine down and walked to the entry, finding

Marcus with his head bowed, hovering over the bowl where her keys now rested beside his.

He didn't look up. "You came home," he murmured.

"Hello, Marcus," Abby said, her voice timid but sharper than expected, echoing off the walls.

Marcus didn't wait for more. With urgency, he took her into his arms and held her tightly. "Abby ..." His voice broke, raw and trembling, filled with an ache that seemed to reach into the very marrow of his being.

Abby succumbed to his embrace, sinking into his chest, resting her head on his shoulder. His heart pounded against hers, hard and fast, mirroring her own mix of fear and exhilaration. He felt thin under her touch, fragile in a way that broke her. She had caused that. She knew it. And she was sorry. Sorry for so many things she couldn't begin to name.

Drew came down the stairs, breaking the two of them apart. "I gotta run." He looked at his mom, then at his dad, their bodies inches apart, but their hands still lingering in a touch. "But if you want me to stay, I can cancel?"

Abby withdrew her hand away from Marcus's and walked to Drew, giving him a kiss on the cheek. "Go," she insisted with a reassuring smile. "We can catch up later."

"Okay," he said, and hugged her. "I'm glad you're home, Mom."

"Me too," Marcus murmured, averting his eyes as though looking at her might shatter the reality that she was home.

Drew opened the door but paused. "Oh, yeah, forgot to tell you, Dad. Emma texted me. She said she was coming home sooner than she thought. I think she said Friday." He shrugged. "Or something like that. See ya!"

"Emma is coming home early?" Abby tilted her head. "Doesn't she have finals to worry about?"

"She's arranged to take them early, so she could help with

Drew's graduation ..." he trailed off, as if unsure how to continue.

"In case I didn't come home," Abby finished. "Oh, Marcus ..." She reached for him. "I'm so sorry."

"But you came home, so ..." Marcus turned away, his attempt to avoid further conversation.

A silence fell between them, neither of them knowing where to begin, where to pick up from.

Abby finally broke the silence. "Is she bringing Theodore?"

"Teddy," Marcus corrected.

Abby smiled. She knew it must be serious if he was defending Emma's boyfriend. "Teddy."

Marcus started for the stairs when he suddenly halted, as if remembering she was still standing there. "I'm going to change. I'll be right down. We can catch up?"

Abby caught his gaze. "You want to talk about it?"

Marcus's face tightened; the lines along his forehead deepened.

She tried again, softening her tone, realizing how much harder this was for Marcus. She had left and decided to return. Now, it was up to him whether to let her back into his life. "I mean, I'm here when you are ready to ask me anything. Anything."

"Are you sure, Abby?" he said in a serious tone. "Because I've been waiting a long time for you."

"I came back. I came back because of you. I came back for us. I came back to our life."

Marcus gave a faint, bitter smile. "No, Abby, you came back to start over. You ran away from the life we had."

"Will that be good enough for you?" Abby's hands twisted. The question came out—it had been nagging at her all the way home—before she realized the consequence of it.

Marcus had never been verbal about his emotions. It was his eyes, always his eyes, that gave him away. The blue eyes she'd fallen into so many years ago. The same eyes that had been empty for so long. The eyes where she'd stopped seeing her reflection.

She saw herself now.

"You were always enough, Abby. And I just didn't show you. I won't make that mistake again."

52

FEAR

Marcus didn't invite Abby back into his life easily. He needed time. It was hard for him to let go, knowing another man had made love to his wife and almost taken her away from him.

He saw Abby was a transformed woman; she had come into herself. She was less reserved and more confident. When she smiled at him now, it felt real, more than just politeness. When she touched him, there was a tenderness. He knew the markings of a woman, content with herself. She had found her power. Thom was the one who had given that to her. Not him. *That* was hard to live with.

The night she came home was a prayer answered. He felt like he had been holding his breath for so long, not knowing if she was ever coming back. He braced himself for the worst, but his heart ached for her to return. He almost lost his balance when he saw her keys in the bowl. When she turned the corner, he wanted nothing more than to take her in his arms. All his anger and fear seemed to drift away when her eyes met his.

She picked me! his head screamed.

He had loved her for so long. When Jossi died, he thought he had lost his soul mate. They were so young, he later realized. Love at that age was probably always passionate like that. But with Abby, it was different. It wasn't passionate; it was deeper and more meaningful. He remembered the night they first made love. He never thought he could connect with another so intimately. She didn't just look at him, she looked into him and could see all that he was inside.

Why didn't he honor that?

He berated himself a thousand times over for his neglect when she was gone.

Was he angry at Abby? He felt so much hate, he thought it would consume him. Did he blame her? Yes. He cursed her name over and over again. *Abby is mine, not Thom's!* he would say to himself, justifying his anger. He didn't understand how she could be so careless with their marriage, herself, and with her love. But then it hit him late in the dark hours of soul-searching—those nights when he was lying in his bed alone, her side of the bed empty. Abby wasn't anybody's. Abby was hers. He had treated her like a possession and felt entitled to her. He wasn't entitled to her. He hadn't let Abby know what a gift she was to him.

Thom got it.

To lie next to the woman you love, knowing another man has shown her value, is humbling. She needed that. She deserved that.

It hadn't been easy since she came back. They acted more like new roommates finding their routine. It wasn't Abby's fault. She was trying hard to reestablish a relationship. He just didn't know what to say or how to touch her. He wanted to touch her, but he always ended up pulling away.

What if he wasn't enough for her anymore?

Months had since passed that night she came home. Drew had been packed up and sent off to college, leaving Abby and Marcus finally alone. Really alone, with no kids to take care of or distract them from each other. That's what had happened, why they grew apart. They got distracted from each other. He wondered if they could survive a life without the distractions. Abby must have believed it because she came back. She had faith in them.

Did he?

The moon cast its glow through the open windows, the cool night air breezing through the house. The stillness of the moment drew his attention to the woman lying beside him. Marcus turned to look at her. She looked like a little girl with her head sunken into the king-sized pillow, breathing softly. He watched as her chest rose and fell, and the strings of his heart twisted a little tighter.

God, I love her! he admitted in the quiet of the night. He hadn't told her yet. Every time he tried, something choked up in his throat. *Fear? Regret?* He knew she needed to hear the words, but she didn't push. Maybe it was her penance that gave her the patience. *Maybe she really did love me*, he would say to himself. Self-doubt was debilitating. It made him careful. Too careful to let himself feel again, want her again.

Things were good between them. They talked more than they ever had. Fights ensued. Bitterness came out. They talked some more. They seemed to move past it and move forward. They were finding a harmony. Not what they used to have. Something new. Something that scared both of them. But it also bonded them. And their life together was good. *No, it was better*, he realized.

He had spent months questioning, wondering if she truly wanted to stay. But now, lying beside her, he realized that she had chosen him. He reached over and softly brushed her cheek with his hand, sweeping her hair away from her face. He wanted to kiss her. Not just brush his lips against hers but really taste her. Unable to resist, he reached out and ran his hand from her shoulder to her elbow and back up again. He left a soft kiss on her neck.

"That's nice," she purred.

That was all he needed. He scooped her up, bringing his mouth to hers. Abby didn't resist. Her breath was warm, and her tongue was wet. *Oh, so wet!*

Although the room was shadowed in gray, her eyes were bright and inviting. He could see her desire ignited. Bringing his lips to her neck, he slid his hand underneath her nightgown. He had forgotten how smooth and warm her skin was to the touch. She shivered beneath his fingertips, sending a jolt through him, knowing he could still affect her.

"Oh, God, Abby, I need you," he heard himself say before his mouth consumed hers again.

Abby pulled her lips from his, signaling a retreat.

"What?" His expression tightened. "Do you not want me, Abby?"

She didn't say anything. Instead, she lifted her nightgown over her head, presenting her naked body to him. He didn't look away, not this time. He ran his gaze over her, taking in her beautiful form, appreciating the curves, the lines, and even the scars that made the woman he loved.

"This is me, Marcus." Her voice trembled, but her eyes held steady, searching for the truth. "Do you want all of me?"

Did he want her? *God! He wanted her.*

Her gaze locked on his, pushing him to answer.

Marcus stood and stripped away his shirt and pants, leaving nothing between them. Not his anger, fear, or regret. "Let's try this again, Abby. No barriers between us. Not anymore. Moving forward. Deal?"

Falling into his arms, she let her lips answer for her, demanding more of him.

Her warmth seeped into him, igniting a hunger he had tried for so long to contain. His eyes held hers. "I want you, Abby. I always have. Always will."

"I like you wanting me, Marcus," she purred, spurring him on.

He kissed her hard and long, wrapping his body around her, entangling her between his legs, sinking into her. They connected. Flesh upon flesh, soul within soul. Her body seemed new to him, her reactions unrestrained and urging. Yet, it was still Abby, familiar and effortless. Their motion became rhythmic ... and agonizingly blissful as their bodies reached their crescendo, rediscovering love and passion.

"I love you, Marcus," she whispered, softly brushing her lips to his, her voice gentle.

It was the last thing he heard before his body succumbed to exhaustion. He hadn't realized how much he needed to hear those words until now, her voice lingering in his thoughts as sleep claimed him.

53

ACCIDENTS HAPPEN

Abby got up with Marcus, scurrying downstairs to make a pot of coffee while he showered. He was leaving for a trip early that morning, and she wanted to say goodbye. The coffee would be a send-off and would take away the chill from climbing out of a warm bed.

As she turned on the light, the kitchen lay still, except for the hum of the refrigerator—the white noise of every household no matter how full or empty. Gone were the late-night dishes left in the sink, a cabinet half closed, the dog bowl needing water. With just the two of them now, the house remained tidy, everything in its place. Quiet. Abby still kept the house cleaner, though. It gave her time to concentrate on other things, like opening her flower shop.

She lifted the shade of the window, hoping to let the morning in. It was still too dark, though faint hints of the sun rising were appearing on the horizon. The birds were up, singing to one another from the trees, trash trucks rumbled down the street, crashing cans from one house to the next, and Mr. Halpin, the old man next door, was already walking his two terriers. She waved from her kitchen window as he passed by.

Abby closed her eyes and allowed the habitual sounds to wash over her like a warm embrace. There wasn't a day she didn't think about how she had almost given it all up. A year had gone by. A long year. A learning year. A growing year.

However, there also wasn't a day that she didn't think about Thom. That was her hidden secret, the last of her sins. He never left her.

But she was where she needed to be. She knew that.

Moving away from the window, she wrapped her arms around her body, shielding herself from the cold. Spring had arrived, heralded by the blooming magnolias, yet that morning, it felt as though Old Man Winter was reluctant to leave. The chill still lingered in the early hours, sneaking through the cracks of the window frame. She poured herself a cup of coffee and took a sip, letting the hot liquid warm her within. A soft sigh escaped her lips, her breath visible as a faint puff of white. She turned up the heater.

"Mmm, that smells good," Marcus said, as he entered the kitchen. He rolled his suitcase to the counter and placed a kiss on Abby's cheek.

Abby pulled a cup from the cupboard and poured him some coffee. "Want some breakfast?"

Marcus took a slurp before glancing at his watch. "I've gotta go. My flight is at nine. If I don't leave, I'll have to wait for the next one and that isn't until noon. I'll miss the first meeting." He grabbed a banana and threw it in his briefcase. "I'll be home tomorrow, late. Don't wait up for me."

Abby gave him a knowing smile, one that said she'd wait up for him, as she always did now. When he traveled, they made sure to talk before he went to bed. And when he came home, she stayed up to welcome him back. She wasn't the only one making an effort; Marcus reciprocated in small meaningful ways, like texting her updates on his schedule, coordinating his plans with hers, and including her in his decisions. These were their ways of recognizing each other, of showing the other that they mattered. They had both agreed to work to stay connected with the little things, daily habits that could otherwise leave them as mere roommates sharing space, rather than true partners. It was nice. They were finally nice together.

"What's all that?" He pointed to the pile of papers spread all over the table.

"Contracts for the retail space. I can't decide between the corner location with all the windows or the larger space in the middle," Abby shared. "So many decisions for one little flower shop."

Starting the flower shop was Abby's dream come true. With the kids out of the house and her degree in business lying dormant, it was now her time. Marcus had been more than supportive and hadn't thought twice about borrowing the 401K to help with the process. It was his way of saying he believed in their future. That Emma wanted to use her marketing degree to help run the business only solidified his enthusiasm.

Abby jumped at the chance to have her daughter move back home, clearing the storage out of her bedroom. But Teddy intervened and proposed to her before Emma could move her things back. She wasn't far, though. The couple lived in an up-and-coming community near the shop. Abby was confident that once they had kids, she would get Emma in the suburbs yet, close to home.

"It isn't just a little shop, it's your dream, Abby," Marcus said, kissing her on the forehead. "With your surgeries behind you, Drew settled in college, and Emma home, the timing couldn't be better. It's been a long year"—Marcus ran a hand through his hair, a habit she recognized as his way of processing emotions—"but I wouldn't have changed any of it. We're good, Abby, aren't we?" His blue eyes met hers, the depth of his gaze echoing the love he was feeling, even if he couldn't say the words.

Abby cozied up to him and tugged at his jacket, bringing him in closer and kissing him. A long, gentle kiss. "We are good, Marcus. Better than I had ever imagined."

His arms wrapped around her. "A later flight might not be such a bad option." His brow lifted with the innuendo.

Abby pushed him toward his suitcase. "Go on. I have a million things to do," she ordered, pointing to the door. "Call me when you land."

Marcus grabbed the handle of his suitcase and rolled it to the hallway, but then suddenly stopped. Letting go of the handle, he turned back and pulled Abby into his arms. "God, I love you," he whispered in her ear, his breath warm against her skin, before gently pressing his lips to hers. "Always will, Abby."

She met his gaze, finding something sad in his eyes. A loss still lingered in their depths. Her heart tugged, knowing she would always see that part of him—the fear of losing her—a pain she had caused. "Me too" was all she said. All she could say without losing the steadiness of her voice. She didn't want to leave him with that—her guilt, her sorrow, her shame.

He released her and they walked to the garage; their shared silence held something unspoken and tender. She waved until his car disappeared, the cold air biting at her skin as if to remind her of what she had reclaimed.

She got another cup of coffee and sat down at the table, poring over the flower shop plans. She looked out the window to see Mr. Halpin returning from his walk with his dogs in tow. She waved again as he passed, and this time he shot up an arm in reply. Before she looked away, Anderson's Volvo drove by.

Another baby on its way, she thought, and smiled.

Emptying her cup, Abby decided on a hot shower, wanting to shake the chill still lingering in her bones. When steam filled the small bathroom, she slipped under the showerhead and luxuriated in the hot water falling over her, hoping the heat would penetrate the layers of skin. She gazed down at her breasts as the water trickled over her new nipples. *They look good,* she thought. Her scars were still there, but they had become just another one of life's markers. A road map of her life thus far.

Her life. It felt good to finally claim it. After teetering on the precipice, she had leaped, but now she stood on solid ground. This life was hers, built with her own choices, her own courage, and by her own making.

Grabbing her towel, she quickly dried off and slipped into a terry robe with *Brynmoor* embroidered on the pocket. It was a parting gift from Mrs. Landry, as a reminder of her time in Scotland. *How would she ever forget?*

Wrapping a towel around her hair, she brushed away the condensation from the mirror, expecting to see her reflection. But as she cleared away the water, it was not her own face she laid eyes on. It was Jossi's.

"You look good, Abby."

"It's been a long time," Abby said, her voice trembling with the effort to steady the quick beats of her heart. A giddy smile tugged at her lips. "Too long," she added, her voice laced with playful reproach.

Jossi agreed with a nod. "It has been."

Abby cleared the rest of the mirror to see both of them together. Jossi looked beautiful. She always looked beautiful.

She never changed. Abby did. She had changed a lot. That is what life did to you.

Abby's stare softened. "I've missed you," she finally said. "I've missed us."

Jossi shrugged, looking away. "I haven't really been gone. Besides, you've been pretty good on your own. No need for me to show up anymore."

Jossi was avoiding engagement. An icy chill shot through Abby. Her presence had to be a sign of something difficult ahead.

"This can't be good … you being here," she said, bracing herself. "I thought I got rid of my demons."

Jossi's face was a mask. "I'm not here today to clear demons, Abby."

"Then why are you here? I'm happy. Truly happy with me, with Marcus, and the life we have," Abby explained. "My life seems full with the shop, Emma home, and Drew focused. I'm excited about what's coming."

"I'm glad," Jossi said, a faint smile finally breaking across her face. "You're going to need that outlook to go on."

"Go on to where?" Abby asked, her nerves prickling at Jossi's tone.

"Abby?" Jossi waited until Abby caught her gaze. "You're a survivor. You always have been. You have what it takes to live life to its fullest. You've proven that. However, you believe jumping off the cliff meant you had to eventually land. Well, it doesn't. You were meant to soar."

"Why are you telling me this?" Abby shivered, Jossi's tone casting a shadow over her encouraging words.

"Because you need to remember that you're strong and loved … always loved."

"Jossi, please." Abby's voice wobbled. "You're being cryptic. I hate when you do that."

"There are roads to travel and choices to make with their own set of consequences. All with the potential for happiness. Each with their own set of heartache. But that is life," she said, ignoring Abby's concerns. "Promise me you'll remember that." Jossi's gaze was unrelenting.

Abby put her hand on her chest. She nodded slowly, her voice caught in her throat.

"I've gotta go, Abby ... it's important," Jossi apologized. "Remember, soar!"

Abby blinked, and she was gone. The bathroom fell silent, save for the faint drip of water from the showerhead. A chill crept over her, seeping into her bones. Something was coming. Something that would change everything—again.

54

GRADUATION

Abby was alone. But she was in good company, sitting in a crowd of hundreds of parents, all beaming with pride for their child—young men and women now, ready to take on the world. Drew was among them, now a full-fledged man, graduating with honors in engineering. Marcus should have been by her side, enjoying this moment with her. He had always imagined this day, watching his son receive his college diploma. He would have been surprised that his not-so-good-at-math kid would be interning for the space industry and heading off to graduate school. When his father said shoot for the stars, Drew took his words literally. He wanted to make his father proud.

Abby looked around for him. She was almost sure Marcus would show up.

One can hope.

There were a lot of people to wade through before she could get to Drew. Abby stopped just short of reaching him, and stared, in awe at who he was, who he had become. Her heart fluttered, pride swirling through her veins. He looked just like his father had at that age, except Drew was taller. A fact Drew teased Marcus about. He didn't mind. Marcus couldn't have been prouder to watch his son become a man.

At least he got to see that.

"Hey, Mom," Drew came over and kissed his mother on the cheek.

"Hi, honey." Abby wrapped her arms around him, torturing him with two kisses on each cheek. "You looked very dignified up there in your cap and gown. But your family knows better," she said with a wink.

"Very funny, Mom," he smirked. "Hey, Teddy," he called out, looking over Abby's shoulder. Then added, "Hey, sis, you made it."

"I wouldn't miss my little brother's college graduation!" She rubbed her protruding belly. "I never thought I'd see the day you actually make something of yourself."

"He's right, Emma. Being out in this heat can't be good for you," Abby eyed the baby belly. "Go sit down before you faint."

"I'm pregnant, Mom, not ill," Emma whined.

"Isn't that the same thing?" Drew mocked.

Emma shot him an evil eye.

Abby slapped Drew's arm. "Will you two ever stop?"

"No!" they both shouted in unison.

Abby pulled them both to her. "I love you," she said. "Don't ever forget that."

Abby looked at her two children, their childhoods now gone, but their futures filled with endless possibilities ahead of them. Her heart felt like it would jump out of her with so much happiness as she stood in the middle of them, grateful to watch their lives unfold.

"He should have been here." Emma stated what Abby was thinking.

Drew's head fell; Abby's heart ached.

In spite of Marcus's doctor's appointments and diligence to stay healthy, fate took the lead. He died of a heart attack, like his father, on his way to the airport the morning that Abby had last seen Jossi. Abby didn't rush to the hospital when her neighbor Anderson called. He had just arrived at work when the ambulance drove up. He saw it was Marcus they were trying to revive in the hallway. When Anderson called Abby, he tried to give her hope. But Abby already knew —Marcus was in Jossi's hands.

Instead, she curled up on Marcus's side of the bed and cried a long time, until the tears dried up. Then she cried more. She couldn't remember when she stopped crying. But eventually, she did. And her life continued.

She hadn't seen Jossi since that fateful day. Not even at the funeral. It would have been too hard ... hard to see *them* together, and Abby not able to be with them—the threesome.

Do they roam the earth doing all the things we never could together? Are they living in eternity happily ever after? Do they miss me?

She often lay awake asking these questions, waiting for the answers. But Jossi had never come back, until today.

Jossi waved at Abby from across the lawn. She was leaning against the trunk of an oak tree that shaded the grassy quad of the college campus, a cluster of people separating them. Abby could still see that her friend hadn't changed over the years.

She still looks beautiful, Abby thought.

Abby raised her hand but quickly dropped her arm back down. She smiled instead. And without further ado, Marcus appeared. His blue eyes still took her breath away. As she had hoped ... Jossi had heard her prayers. Abby wanted to run as fast as her high heels would take her and fall into his arms.

To tell him how much his love was a part of the day, her life, for always. But she knew better. Marcus brought his hands to his lips and blew a kiss through the air. Watching it take flight, she reached out and grabbed it.

She blinked, and he was gone.

Her heart tugged with a bittersweet joy. "Thank you," Abby mouthed before Jossi disappeared.

"Mom?" Drew's voice brought her back.

"He's here," Abby whispered.

Drew looked around, then back at his mother. "Who?"

Abby smiled. "Your father," she said, her voice steady and sure. "Don't ever forget that his love surrounds you. Always."

"He is?" Emma asked. She rubbed her belly again and looked up at her mother with tears in her eyes. "I still miss him."

"God, Emma," Drew pushed his sister's shoulder. "Why'd you have to do that?" he said, swiping at his own tears.

Abby looked over at Theodore standing outside their intimate circle with his own eyes watering. Abby threw out her arms. "Come here, Teddy," she called to him. "No need to blubber all by yourself." She waited for him to wrap his arms around them. "Love is eternal. Know it lives in you, and through you."

55

MOVING ON

A bby heard something scraping across the floor. "I hope you aren't dragging the sign from outside," she yelled at her daughter.

"Not anymore," Emma answered, leaning the wooden chalkboard against the wall.

"Leave the buckets. I'll carry them in," Abby ordered, her voice echoing through the empty shop.

Emma walked into the back room. "Already done," she said, brushing off her mother's faint grimace. "Those look nice. Very English, simple—elegant. The bride made the right choice," she added, pointing to the finished bouquets.

Abby put her shears down and glanced at the roses and peonies tied up in pink satin that she had completed. "I think so, too."

"Where did you learn how to do that?" Emma asked, referring to the braided ribbon pattern tied around the ends of the bouquets.

Thom, she thought, but did not answer.

He often came to her mind in the darkened back room.

Working in her shop, smelling the floral abundance, surrounded by a garden of beauty, made her feel like she still had a little piece of him with her. Many nights, when it was quiet in the shop, she would wonder what he was doing.

Was he, too, sitting on a floral bucket ripping off leaves and snipping stems? Did he ever think about her?

"I only have a few more to do. I'll leave after that, and start again in the morning," Abby said, ignoring Emma's question.

"You've been here since six this morning! You need a break, Mom. More like a vacation, but that won't happen any time soon, will it?" Emma's tone was pointed.

Abby hadn't taken a vacation since Scotland, brushing off every suggestion with the same excuse. "I don't have time to waste."

"What does that mean?" Emma questioned.

"Time wasted not living," Abby replied simply.

"And are you living locked up here all day ... and night?" Emma countered, her voice tinged with exasperation.

Abby couldn't help but wonder who was the mother and who was the daughter.

After the business began, Abby worked harder than she ever had in her life. Lifting boxes and hauling water-filled buckets was more than she imagined doing at her age. But she loved it—every back-aching minute. *The Thistled Rose* was her creation, and business was booming. The work made her happy. It kept her busy—sometimes even distracted, she'd admit. But more importantly, it filled her heart—a heart broken after Marcus's passing. *Had he known she'd need this?* Whatever the reason, the shop gave her purpose and a direction forward. For that, she was grateful.

Grabbing her lower back and coaxing her muscles to cooperate, Abby winced at the stiffness caused by bending

ELIZABETH CONTE

over most of the day. She reached for her phone to check the time.

Emma touched her shoulder gently. "I'll lock up," she said, disappearing through the draped doorway.

Abby sat back down, grabbing her shears. "Okay, but leave the light on," she called after her.

"I know, Mother," Emma responded from the other room with a teasing lilt, feigning disrespect. Her tone a playful echo of the girl she used to be.

"I'm sorry," Abby said, when Emma reappeared. "It's an old habit. Once a child, always a child."

Emma smiled, grabbing her enlarged belly. "I guess I'll find out soon, won't I?"

"Yes. But you're still Emma." Abby caught her daughter's eyes. "Always Emma unto yourself. I need to respect that ... as do you."

It had taken Abby running away to figure that out for herself.

It took Thom.

Abby smiled, a slow lift of her lips, as the memory of him spread a warmth through her body. She couldn't help it. No matter how many years had passed, she would always think of Thom with unapologetic affection. She loved him. She loved Marcus. She couldn't explain it, but she held them both in her heart, for different reasons. Maybe that's why it didn't destroy her marriage. It was no secret between Marcus and herself. He had made peace with that in his own way. Abby never asked how or why. He had his own demons to fight. But Marcus was also conscious that Abby had chosen him, not Thom. And for that, he didn't seem to mind Abby loving them both.

"Are you ever going to tell me what *that* smile means?" Emma asked with a lifted brow, pointing to her mother's lips.

"No," Abby emphatically answered.

"It's not about Dad," Emma said, her words carrying an honesty that left no room for doubt.

Abby blushed from both embarrassment and shame, unable to hide her emotions. "How do you know?"

Emma dragged a chair from the desk and sank down to rest her bloated and tired feet. "Come on, Mom. We're both grown women. Give me some credit. Don't you think I have memories that make me smile when no one is looking? I call it the 'memory smile.'"

"Emma!"

"When I said Teddy was *the one*, I didn't say he was the only one." Emma laughed, causing Abby to do the same.

Abby was enjoying her adult relationship with her daughter. The time they spent working together helped them become more intimate, developing their relationship as mother and daughter. Emma shared openly and honestly with Abby, giving them both a friendship they had not expected, and maybe what Abby needed with Marcus gone.

As their laughter faded, a silence fell between them.

Emma caught her mother's gaze with intensity. "Hey, Mom ..." she broke off, hesitant to continue. "Dad told me ... what happened in Scotland."

Abby's eyes widened. Her voice caught. "Oh."

"He came to see me after he left you in Scotland ... showed up at my door, alone, Chinese takeout and a bottle of vodka in his hands. I knew it couldn't be good. I'd never seen Dad like that before—anxious, scared, sad. He told me then. Not everything, but enough." She looked at her mother for some recognition, but Abby didn't give her anything. "He cried. Really cried. It nearly broke my heart to see him that way. Maybe he needed that awakening," she murmured. "But he didn't give up on you. He knew you loved him, Mom, despite it all. I knew you loved him, too. He told me that night he would be the happiest man on the planet if you decided to come back. And you did. That's all I needed to know in the end. It worked out."

Abby's gut twisted. Shame was a hard emotion to bear. "Are you disappointed with me?"

"I was ... for a while. But after you returned, you were a different person. A better person. It was like you had been dormant and but then finally blossomed. Dad saw that. We all did." Emma gently touched Abby's hand. "Whoever that man was, the man that makes you secretly smile, he brought you back to us. And that's what is really important. I'll have to thank him one day."

Abby reached over and gave her daughter a hug. "I'm sorry for putting you in the middle of that. It wasn't fair."

"I don't know why you did what you did, and maybe you'll tell me some day. Or maybe it'll stay just between you and Dad. I can respect that. We're here now, on the other side, and I know you made Dad happy until ..." Her voice caught. "Anyway ..."

"Oh, Emma," Abby said, her voice fragile and distant. "He made me happy, too." Her words drifted into the dark shadows of the workroom, as if they might find him somehow.

Emma rose from her chair. "Well, time's up. This baby is pressing on my bladder, leaving me only short intervals when I don't have to pee." She laughed before leaning over and kissing Abby on the forehead. "I love you, Mom. We all love you very much."

"Love you too, honey."

A bell rang from the front of the shop, interrupting them.

"Oh, darn it!" Emma cursed under her breath. "I turned

the closed sign around but didn't lock the door. Sorry, pregnant brain—the memory goes. Want me to get rid of them?"

"No. Go. I'll finish locking up. See you in the morning." Abby hugged her daughter once again before pushing her toward the back door.

"Hello?" a deep voice called out.

Abby froze. There was no denying its familiarity, though she wasn't sure if it was real or just her mind playing tricks on her. Hesitantly, she walked through the doorway separating the workroom from the storefront—and there stood Thom.

"Abby," he said almost breathlessly, her name rolling off his tongue in a way that stirred something deep within her—*his superpower.*

Her first instinct was to run to him. Instead, she froze, her legs refusing to move. She never expected to see the ghost of her past. *Never!* Nor had she expected her heart to pound so hard, so fast, at the sight of him. She brought her hand to her chest as if to keep it from leaping out.

"I frightened you?"

She shook her head, but no words seemed to form.

"I should've called. I ... I just flew in. I didn't want to wait until tomorrow. I saw the light and took the chance," he explained.

He rattled off words, but Abby wasn't listening. She could only stare at him, lost in memories rushing back to her.

He looks good, she thought. His beard, now a little longer, was whiter than she remembered. Leaner than before, he still carried a healthy glow on his face. Time had only deepened his charmed looks, making him more handsome.

He shifted his stance and caught Abby's gaze. She quickly looked away, but it was too late. A smile crept across his face as he caught the faint flush rising in her cheeks—the same smile she had replayed in her mind so many times. The one that melted her heart.

Footsteps came from behind, and Emma was at Abby's back. She peered over her mother's shoulder to see a man standing by the door.

"Can we help you with something?" Emma asked.

Thom shifted his gaze to Emma and cocked his head, "Aye, well ... no, I don't think so. I just came to see ..." His eyes shifted back to Abby.

Emma followed his gaze to her mother's smile. "Oh," she murmured, her lips curling into a knowing grin. "I see. I think I need to thank you."

"Thank me?" Thom asked.

Emma chuckled. "My mom will explain."

"Abby's daughter?" Thom blinked, his gaze lingering on her face. "But yes, now I see it. You have her eyes. And your face lights up the same when you smile," Thom added.

"Yes, I'm Emma." She stepped toward him, extending her hand, while her mother still stood frozen. "It's a pleasure to meet you—"

"*Thom*," Abby interjected, her voice more a whisper than she wanted. More desperate than she intended. She cleared her throat and tried again, stepping forward, closer to him. "Emma, this is Thom Emerson."

Thom leaned forward, accepting Emma's hand. "It's nice to finally meet. I've heard a lot about ye ... and about your lad." He eyed Emma's rounded belly. "His, I hope?"

Emma smiled, lifting her hand to reveal her wedding ring. "For a couple of years now. Just in case you were wondering." She turned on her heels and waddled to the register, grabbing her purse she'd left on the counter. "Well, if you will excuse me, I have a husband waiting at home. Will I see you again, Thom—Thom Emerson from Scotland?" She side-glanced at her mother.

"Tomorrow, most likely."

"Tomorrow?" Abby's voice croaked, barely finding its way out as she stared at him, still trying to process him standing in front of her.

"It's the reason I'm here." Thom looked around the shop. "You're doing the flowers for a wedding tomorrow I'm attending. You remember Mairi?"

Abby nodded. She remembered everyone and everything. No one and nothing had been erased from her mind ... just tucked away for safekeeping. For the quiet nights when she allowed herself to revisit those memories before she drifted off to sleep.

Thom rubbed his chin, watching her as though he could see those moments of the past resurfacing, dragging her back without her permission. "It's her stepson's wedding," he explained. "The Cooper wedding."

"Oh. So Mairi married someone else?"

"Aye," Thom replied, not missing her meaning. "She met a nice American while he was traveling, and they were married about a year later. He has two sons who live here in the States. The oldest is getting married."

Abby couldn't help but think of the parallels between Thom and herself ... only she didn't stay, and they didn't get married. "I'm happy she found someone."

"Me too," Thom said, taking two steps forward, closing the distance between them. But when Abby instinctively stepped back, he stopped mid-stride and returned to his original spot.

Emma, watching the dance between them, cleared her throat as she moved to the center of the room. She glanced at

Thom before eyeing her mother. "Imagine that." She shook her head. "Of all the flower shops and they chose ours. What are the odds? It's like fate has a weird way of reconnecting people."

"Fate," Thom said, touching his beard. "Mairi sent me the link to your flower shop. I couldn't believe my eyes. You did it, Abby." He said her name, cradling it like it belonged solely to him. Catching himself, he looked up, steadying his voice. "She sends her regards, by the way. I think she was hoping ..." He paused before he completed his thought. "Well, anyway, I was driving by. I gave it a chance you'd still be here." He eyed the empty, quiet shop. "Am I keeping ye from anything?"

"Oh, trust me," Emma interrupted with a wave of her hand. "Not a thing." She offered him a conspiratorial smile.

"Emma! Don't you have a husband waiting?" Abby urged, her tone leaving no room for argument. She didn't want to be left alone with Thom—but she was certain she didn't want Emma to witness whatever was unfolding between them. Was it a weakness to run to him? Or a strength to stay away? She wasn't quite sure yet.

"Yes. Yes, I do." Emma gave her mother a kiss on the cheek before turning back to Thom. "It was indeed a pleasure to meet you, Thom."

"Aye, the same for me, Emma." Thom offered his hand again.

Emma glanced at his hand with a smile, then snatched a hug instead. "As my father used to say, 'Go get 'em, tiger.'" With that, she slipped out, closing the door behind her.

56

SOARING

A bby's heart was racing, her mouth dry. Every ounce of her was tingling, like someone had stripped her of her skin and the nerve endings were exposed. She now regretted allowing Emma to leave.

She watched as Thom browsed her store, wondering if he felt as nervous as she did. He sauntered across the floor, stopping every so often to lift a trinket, look at the price, and place it back on display. He appeared calm and confident in his stride, no rush of words to close the distance between them. He always had been an observer, carefully calculating his actions and reactions. She hadn't forgotten. But she had forgotten how he affected her, how she felt bathed in his warmth when she was in his presence.

"It's perfect, Abby," he said, finally looking at her. "The shop has an energy. It's all ye are—warm and inviting."

His words wrapped around her like a gentle embrace, coaxing out a smile she couldn't suppress. This is how she'd hoped someone would feel stepping into her shop.

"I'm glad you like it. I couldn't have done it without you."

She paused, catching herself. "I mean ... your shop was such a great inspiration."

When she looked up, his eyes were on her—warm and unguarded—reading right through her.

Who was she kidding? Not him.

"It was you, Thom," she admitted. "You made me believe I could do it ... could do anything, really."

He chuckled under his breath. "Ye would've figured it out on your own. I just may have nudged ye a wee bit?" He winked. "But I'd like to think maybe ... maybe it was me who gave that to ye."

His smile lit up his whole face.

Abby hadn't forgotten that either. Or the way it made her cheeks flush, betraying her, no matter how hard she tried to hide it. She quickly turned away. "I've got something ..." She pointed to the backroom. "Need to check the back door. Look around. I'll just be a minute."

In the bathroom, she leaned over the sink, gripping the edges as she tried to catch her breath. Her vision blurred, her head spun, as a voice screamed, *He's here!*

She stared at the reflection in the mirror, searching for strength. Was it fear or wonderment staring back at her? The dark pupils didn't distinguish. Neither did the wild thrum in her chest. "Breathe," she whispered.

Tucking her hair behind her ear, she pinched her cheeks, willing some color into her pale face. The pink faded almost instantly. "Damn!" she muttered. Grabbing the hand lotion, she rubbed it through her roughened hands, dashing a bit across her lips as an afterthought. It wasn't much, but it would have to do. As if heading into battle, she braced herself and stepped through the door.

Thom was sitting on a crate, waiting for her.

"You don't need to try with me, Abby," he said. "You look beautiful. Maybe more so than I remember."

She didn't know how he did it, but he always had a way of making her feel ... *loved*.

She shivered.

"Sorry," he said, breaking the silence. He glanced away, his eyes briefly tracing the darkened corridors before turning back. "I wasn't sure ..." His voice lowered. "Och! Too many thoughts, maybe."

How many times had she felt the same?

"No, Thom, I'm sorry," Abby finally blurted out, the words escaping before she could stop them. They had been on the tip of her tongue for too many years—too long stuck inside. "I tried to write ... explain," she said, her voice trembling as she shook her head. Her lids lowered. "I ... I wasn't brave enough to stay."

Thom held her gaze for a moment, unmoving. His jaw didn't tense, nor did his eyes darken. She must have broken his heart, but he showed no signs of it now. Maybe too many years had gone by. Instead, his eyes flickered, shifting as though he were measuring the sincerity of her words. *Did he believe her? Was it enough? Did she even deserve anything from him?*

"Or maybe"—Thom stood, turning, releasing his hold on her—"ye were brave enough to leave." He took a few steps away, disappearing into the dim light of the workroom, his footsteps echoing hard against the cement floors.

Abby stiffened, watching him retreat into the darkened aisles, maybe because he didn't want her to see his face. That could only mean one thing: Whatever he wanted to say would be difficult, something he couldn't conceal behind his usual composure.

"I'm sorry about Marcus," his voice reached her. "He

loved you. But you already knew that." He paused, and she could almost picture a tug at his beard or a faint curve of a smirk. "I would've been a fool not to see it."

A silence followed that seemed to stretch on forever.

"I'm glad ye went back to him—for his sake," he murmured.

Abby closed her eyes, letting the rush of emotions take hold. The love of Marcus. The loss of him. The years since his death and the life she had built ... all without Thom. Yet, somehow, he had lived through it, too. How could he have not? He was an extension of her soul.

His footsteps came nearer, slow and deliberate, until his shadow gave way to the light. She caught his eyes when he stepped forward, and this time, they did not hide his feelings. They held a lingering shadow, as if a storm had passed through, leaving behind a quiet, haunting stillness.

He spoke, his voice raw, sharing a vulnerability that felt both tender and angry at the same time, "I understood, Abby. Marcus was your life. Ye two weren't finished. Ye still needed each other. A man can handle the truth. But ..."

Abby looked away. She knew her sin.

Thom reached out, gently turning her face toward his, his touch gentle, yet unyielding, as if daring her to meet the truth. "All these years ... ye could've returned, reached out, something other than silence. But ye didn't." The furrows on his forehead deepened. "God, Abby, do ye know that can drive a man to insanity?" His head shook. "I'd hoped ..." He paused, his voice catching. "But ye didn't. I would've waited a lifetime for ye, Abby. Don't ye see?"

"Thom," Abby's voice crackled, her heartache now a lump in her throat. She stepped back, trying to distance herself from the feelings she had put away for so many years.

Thom caught her arm, his grip gentle but firm. "Don't, Abby. Don't turn away from me again."

Before she could stop him, he pulled her into his arms, his lips finding their home against hers. The world seemed to fall away as Abby closed her eyes, his breath stirring something deep, something long buried within her. Her body leaned into his, every fiber of her being drawn to the familiar warmth of his kiss. But then, alarms flared in her mind.

Reality slammed into her, sharp and unforgiving. It wasn't about wanting *this*, it was about surviving it. *She had survived so much!* She had made peace with her life—being alone—with its quiet safety, its predictability. Who was she to ask for more? To risk it all—again.

She jerked away, the pull between them severed as quickly as it had begun. Abby's hands flew to her cheeks, as if to steady herself, to contain the flush spreading through her.

Thom stared at her, his voice steady and unrepentant. "I'm not sorry for that, Abby."

Should I run toward him or away? She froze instead, her body caught between the two impulses, unable to move.

"Do you want me to go?" Thom's voice cut through the tension, low and raw. He lingered for a moment, but when she didn't answer, couldn't answer, he turned and walked away.

Abby watched him go, her heart pounding, her throat tightening with words she couldn't find in time. His footsteps were hard and heavy across the floor, echoing in the quiet spaces of her shop. She knew he had reached the door when the bells jingled.

"Thom?" she called, running after him. "Thom, stop."

She found him at the door, one foot in and one out, his hand gripping the handle. He didn't turn as she approached.

Hesitantly, she reached for him, gently placing her hand

on his shoulder. "I'm sorry," she whispered. "It's just ... you're a surprise. I wasn't prepared ..."

Thom shrugged off her touch, stepping back inside and closing the door behind him. His eyes narrowed, dark and intense. "Prepared for what, life?" His voice dropped, roughened and raw. "God, Abby, I didn't plan on you coming into my life on that fateful day. But ye did. I haven't regretted one moment. And when ye left me, stranded with all those feelings, I understood. Ye needed to leave. Ye had a life that couldn't include me. Our timing was off. But things have changed since then. So, what's holding ye back now?"

"Things *have* changed, Thom. We can't possibly be the same people."

"Oh really? I think our kiss would say otherwise." The faintest smirk curled his lips, and the glint in his eye told her he knew exactly what effect it had.

Abby's hand went to her hip. "Things can't be solved by a kiss, Thom."

"No?" His brow jutted up. "But it damn well works when words aren't enough."

"Thom ..." she started to protest.

"No, Abby, I don't want excuses. Time has moved on, too much time. But I haven't. We aren't finished. Heck, we haven't even begun. We have something between us. I felt it the moment I saw ye again. It's still there, Abby. Ye had to have felt it?"

Abby did feel it—had always felt it. She'd tried to let it go, but his love filled a part of her heart that seemed necessary for life. So, she kept it in a sacred place where it would always be. Safe. Safe from leaving. Safe from dying.

"Abby." Thom stepped closer, his gaze holding hers. "What are you afraid of?"

Abby shifted her stance, looking away, avoiding answering. It was safer that way. Being thousands of miles away kept her feelings forever buried. But Thom had a way of exposing her. He spoke in truths, raw and unfiltered. She couldn't hide from him then, nor could she now.

"Losing you!" Abby blurted out, swiping at the tears she could no longer hold back. "I have loved so many. I have lost too many. Somehow, it just seemed safer to keep loving you in memory. That way, I'd never really lose you. Your love would be forever. It could never hurt me that way."

"If your greatest fear is that ye love me too much, it seems rather silly to be wasting the rest of your life running from it," he quipped. "Abby, fear losing me if ye must. I can't promise ye forever. We both know that doesn't exist. But my love is forever—for ye to keep." He wrapped his arms around her, bringing her into him. "I need you, Abby. I want to live my life, loving ye with every breath I have left. We may have just today, or we may have until we are old and gray. Either way, it's ye I want to spend it with. That's the best I can offer."

Abby wondered why she'd been granted so many chances at life and love. Jossi called it fate. Marcus called it luck. Thom said it was mere will. *Did it matter?* Living was a gift—a journey to cherish. Some journeys were long, and some were short. However long the duration, there were blessings along the way. A fulfilling life was to behold those blessings as they came. Thom was one of those.

Abby knew there was no other choice. Bringing her lips to his, she kissed him, lingering long enough for him to understand she was jumping off the cliff once again—only not alone, but with Thom at her side.

"I thought you said things can't be solved by a kiss?"

"Sometimes words aren't enough," Abby replied. "Not this time."

"Aye, well then, enough said." He winked, reaching for her.

"Wait a minute, there," Abby stopped him. "Not so fast. You can't expect me to drop what I'm doing and succumb to you just like that?"

"Hmm." Thom scowled, crossing his arms in front of him. "It's not enough I travel thousands of miles to find ye, with my tail between my legs, begging for ye?"

Abby shook her head. "I have a business to run. And if I recall, you're pretty good with your hands."

"Aye, but I doubt you mean my knack for making ye weak in the knees?"

"No, not exactly." Abby laughed. "Why don't you roll up your sleeves and help me finish the bouquets in the back?"

"Abby, are ye asking me to share in your life?"

She smiled, the answer already in her eyes. "I believe I am."

His arms circled her, pulling her close. "I was hoping that was your meaning."

Abby rested her head against his chest, feeling the steady rise and fall of his breath—breath that would always ground her, no matter how high she flew. He would stand by her, love her—always. She closed her eyes and whispered, "Thank you."

"For what?"

"For helping me get here."

And so, Abby chose to soar.

ACKNOWLEDGMENTS

Therese Conte: Thank you for being the artist beside me, the quiet guide behind so much of what I create. You've been my editor, my eye for beauty, my sounding board—but more than that, you've been a steady hand and a soft place to land. You have mothered my spirit and mentored my heart. I cherish you more than words can hold.

Lee Ann Schertz: You are more than a friend—you are my daily companion in this creative life. We share the world together, one conversation at a time, and through it all, you've never stopped believing in me. You read every version, catch every detail, and lift me up when I need it most. Your loyalty, your presence, and your steadfast support are part of every word I write. I couldn't do this without you.

Billie Kelpin: You've been my cheerleader, my creative companion, and a bright light along this journey. My writing life—and my life in general—is fuller because you're in it.

Janet Simcic: Thank you for being a wise voice and a steady presence in my life. Your encouragement lifts me, your friendship grounds me, and our shared journeys—in writing and in travel—have brought light and laughter when I've needed them most.

Casey Dorman: Every writer needs a mentor—someone who offers clarity, encouragement, and honest insight. You've been that for me, and I'm deeply grateful for the time and thought you've invested in my work.

Beta Readers: Thank you for your sharp eyes, honest notes, and deep care. This book is stronger, cleaner, and richer because of your thoughtful contributions.

Sarah Tannas: The skilled genius behind the cover! Your patience and commitment humble me. Thank you for getting my cover to where it needed to be—beautiful!

Joy Hoppenot: Thank you for bringing such clarity, precision, and care to my manuscript. Your keen eye for detail and unwavering professionalism not only elevated the work but lifted my spirit. I feel truly fortunate to have found you and look forward to many future endeavors together.

and finally and most importantly...

To my husband: Thank you for your practical support in helping make space for my writing life, and supporting me quietly behind the scenes.

DISCUSSION QUESTIONS

1. **Abby makes the bold decision to leave her home and family.** What do you think ultimately pushed her to that moment? Was it a moment of recklessness or of bravery?

2. **Jossi, though deceased, remains a central figure in Abby's life.** What role does Jossi play in Abby's journey of self-discovery? How does their friendship transcend life and death?

3. **The novel explores the theme of invisibility, especially as women age.** In what ways does Abby feel unseen by those around her? Have you ever experienced or witnessed this kind of erasure?

4. **How is Abby's identity shaped by her roles as wife, mother, and daughter?** At what point do these roles begin to feel like cages rather than sources of connection?

5. **Discuss the symbolism of Abby's cancer diagnosis.** Abby's cancer diagnosis becomes a quiet but powerful shift in the novel. Do you think she would have had the strength to leave her life behind without it? Was the diagnosis a true

catalyst for change—or did it simply unearth what was already unraveling inside her?

6. The novel challenges traditional ideas of love, marriage, and fulfillment. What do you think the story is saying about what it means to truly love—and be loved—in a long-term relationship?

7. Abby's longing for sensuality and desire resurfaces as part of her healing. How does her reclaiming of her body and her sexuality reflect her broader personal growth?

8. Throughout the novel, nature (seasons, weather, animals) reflects Abby's inner world. Can you point to moments where the natural world mirrors or contrasts her emotional state?

9. The title, *Life of Her*, suggests an exploration of selfhood. By the end of the novel, how do you think Abby defines her life on her own terms?

10. What does this novel say about grief—not only the grief of losing loved ones, but of losing pieces of oneself? How do grief and growth coexist in Abby's story?

11. Thom and Marcus represent very different forms of love and partnership in Abby's life. What do each of these men reflect back to her about who she is—and who she wants to be? Who, in your opinion, is truly best for her, and why?

12. In *Life of Her*, Abby's story reflects the reality that many women experience their personal growth as something delayed—or even sacrificed—during the years of caregiving and family life, or a life interrupted. How does the novel explore the cost of this delay, and the quiet conflict women carry between duty and identity? Do you believe Abby's longing for more was an act of self-preservation, or something deeper?

ALSO BY ELIZABETH CONTE

FINDING JANE

When a heartbroken Jane Reynolds travels to England for a much-needed escape, she never expects to fall through time—and into the life of a 19th-century landowner. Swept into a world of propriety, passion, and fate, Jane and Henry must navigate their forbidden connection across centuries. A moving blend of *Pride and Prejudice* and *The Time Traveler's Wife*, this novel explores what it means to find love when destiny—and time itself—stand in the way.

CHOSEN MISTRESS

Set in early Victorian England, *Chosen Mistress* follows two women bound by loyalty, secrets, and a promise made long ago. When Charlotte returns to England after losing everything, she discovers her cousin Lydia's idyllic life is built on quiet desperation. What begins as an act of devotion soon draws Charlotte into an arrangement that tests the limits of love, loyalty, and desire—forcing both women to reconsider what it means to keep a promise.

ABOUT THE AUTHOR

Elizabeth Conte is an award-winning author devoted to "creating beauty for the mind." Known for her evocative storytelling, she has received acclaim for her historical novels, *Finding Jane* and *Chosen Mistress*. *Life of Her* is a contemporary novel where she continues to craft compelling stories that stimulate the mind and touch the heart.
Visit ElizabethConte.com

Cover Design: Tannas Creative
Art Direction & Cover Photography: Elizabeth Conte
Author Photograph: Izzy B Photography
Editing Services: Joy Hoppenot